# REX

### NINE: A DARK & DIRTY SINNERS' MC SERIES

### SERENA AKEROYD

# TRIGGER WARNINGS

Readers might find the following topics sensitive: assisted suicide, rape, references to sexual assault and domestic abuse, graphic scenes of violence, mass shooting.

## AUTHOR NOTE

Don't hate me. (That'll make sense by the end of the book.)
   Even if you do, you are loved. You are worthy. You are a survivor.
   We are strong.
   We are one.
   They will not beat us. Not forever.
   Much love,
   Serena
   xoxo

## PLAYLIST

If you'd like to hear a curated soundtrack, with songs that are featured in the book, as well as songs that inspired it, then here's the link:

https://open.spotify.com/playlist/6rSOgmKNhPs92ADFepkaI6?si=afd55831ob184526

# PART 1
## "WHEN WOMEN GO WRONG, MEN GO RIGHT AFTER THEM."

– MAE WEST

# ONE

## RACHEL: AGE 13
### REMEMBERING SUNDAY - ALL TIME LOW

"My mom said hers is a slut."

I tightened my arms around my knees, and though they couldn't see me, tried to burrow deeper into the corner.

While I was catching the tail end of a conversation, I knew who they were talking about. Knew who *everyone* was talking about today—my mom.

Not the tragic dead girl. Nope. Just the bitch who no one liked.

On the good days, Mom braided my hair and baked cookies with me despite the fact that I'd long since grown out of both phases.

On the bad days, she let her temper get the better of her.

On the worst ones, she let that temper explode...

That was what had happened earlier.

At a wake of all places.

Humiliated, I thought about how she'd slapped Rene, the only nice Old Lady in the MC, the Prez's woman, and I cringed.

But the floor hadn't opened and swallowed me up the last time Mom had gotten into a fight where she was punching above her weight, so why I held out any hope this time was beyond me.

"You're getting too big to hide out down here."

The intrusion wasn't an intrusion, but he was the last person I wanted to see.

King.

On anyone else, it'd be a weird name, but everyone knew that one day, he'd reign over this sinners' paradise—as Axel, Mom's boyfriend, called it—like an unofficial king.

I tilted my head to the side. "You outgrew it two years ago but you still come down."

He shrugged. "Knew this was where I'd find you, and if you're here, then I'm here."

'Here' was a crawl space beneath the building.

It was hard to get into, harder still to get out of. Sometimes, I wished I could live in this tiny space, live like the Hobbit, amass a hoard of books that'd protect me from the outside world. From vicious voices and mean looks. But even I wasn't weird enough to think this was a permanent solution.

I might be strange, but I wasn't Tolkien-strange yet.

Dust winnowed down as the girls overhead stomped off to another part of the clubhouse. I could have turned my flashlight away from the pages of my book and passed it over his features, but instead, I peered through the shadows and found him watching me.

He was only a few years older than me, having already turned sixteen, but he wore his years around him like a cloak. Life at the MC had made him older. More mature.

"You came to find me?" I asked unsteadily, nerves and anxiety coalescing in a way that was worse than when I'd seen my mother hit Rene—his mom.

I'd thought he'd hate me.

I'd thought, God, I didn't know what I'd thought.

Only, his words made it sound like nothing had changed, even though I knew this was the day *everything* changed. Mom wouldn't be allowed to get away with this, and I was glad for that.

Axel couldn't keep her under control, but that didn't mean Rene wouldn't.

"Wasn't your fault your mom's rabid."

"No, but—" I swallowed.

Association was everything in the clubhouse.

"No 'buts' about it." King shuffled nearer and his bony arm curved around my shoulder. He pressed an awkward kiss to my temple. "You're my girl, ain't you?"

A weird sensation fluttered through me.

He'd started calling me that recently.

I wasn't sure what being his girl meant, aside from the fact he hugged me when no one else did and that he'd sit with me and read.

I liked being his girl, even if I didn't understand why I was. I wasn't innocent, thanks to being raised by a woman who made the clubwhores look like nuns, but King didn't do anything men did with Mom.

If I was 'his girl,' I didn't know why he didn't shove his tongue into my mouth or why he didn't touch my breasts.

That wasn't a complaint, more an expression of my confusion.

Huddling into him, turning my knees into him, knowing he'd settle them on his lap, I whispered, "Some days, I wish she'd just go."

"Maybe she will."

"Then I'd miss her."

"Nah."

With a huff, I pulled back and asked, "How do you know that?"

"Because I know you. You read too many books. They fill your head with what a real mom should be, but there's nothing real about fiction."

I scowled at him. "You read too." I threw the words at him like they were an insult. "And you can't judge. You've got a real mom. She washes your clothes and feeds you. Heck, she feeds all your friends too."

"She'd feed you if you came around," he pointed out.

"They don't like me."

He snorted. "How would you know if my friends like you or not? You're too busy crawling around down here for them to even see you. I only know you because I came looking for that coin that day."

I bit my lip, knowing he was right.

I liked it here though.

I was a part of the world, while separate from it. I heard things, things I shouldn't hear, things I shouldn't know, but I filed it away. Kept it locked in my mind. Stored with all the other stuff I shouldn't have tucked up there. Plus, I could read without anyone judging me.

Carly had been my only confidante before King had come along. Now she was gone and I was feeling pretty lost. King had friends who he hung out with, now I just had my books.

He was so cool and I wasn't. I knew, one day, he'd realize that and would leave me to my Hobbit home and my misery.

But that wasn't today.

"It was fate you dropped that coin," I breathed, tucking my nose into his throat so I could suck in the scent of him.

He smelled like cake.

Always did.

I figured that was because he had a sweet tooth.

"It was fate I came and looked for it," he retorted with a soft laugh, "and found you living down here like something from *The Hobbit*."

Because I'd just made the comparison, I preened. "You know he's my favorite."

"I do. You gonna come up for something to eat?"

"No." I cleared my throat. "Everyone's still talking. I don't..." I wriggled my shoulders. "I'm not—"

"That bastard."

Both of us stilled at the sound of his dad's voice.

Bear was hard, he was mean, but he had kind eyes.

Even when Mom had slapped Rene, he hadn't had her beaten. He was letting Rene handle it.

King peered at me and raised a finger to his lips to tell me to be silent.

"How long?"

A voice sounded then. One that had my eyes rounding in surprise.

Young but throbbing with such hate that I felt it myself.

Nyx.

One of King's best friends, and the only one with a road name at his age.

"Years," Nyx rasped, sounding furious and miserable all at the same time. "H-He's the reason Carly killed herself."

King's brow furrowed as I mouthed, "What's going on?"

We stared up at the ceiling, *their* floor, and there was the muffled sound of boots thumping as someone clearly started pacing. With every step they took, the floorboards groaned and eddies of dust twisted and twirled around us.

Some must have gone up my nose because the urge to sneeze hit me.

My nostrils *itched* with the need, my eyes watered, and I sucked in a huge breath to stop it.

The tiniest noise escaped me as I contained the blast. My brain rattled with the aftereffects of trying to keep it quiet, and my lips ached where I'd accidentally bitten them as I slapped a hand over my nose and face—

"Did you hear something?" Nyx demanded.

Only, Bear, who was still stomping, clearly heard nothing as he ground out, "How do you know Carly was being abused by Kevin, Nyx?"

I swore that my heart stopped throbbing at those words.

Kevin Sisson.

I hated him.

He was a creep.

He had a way of looking at me and all the girls my age, sometimes younger, that reminded me of how Axel looked at my mom.

But there was a twenty-year age difference between Mom and me, and no one should be looking at young kids like *that*. Not even

King, who said I was his girl and whose chest puffed up whenever he called me that, looked at me like Kevin did.

I shuddered and King sent me a questioning look, even as he tightened his arm around me.

"I caught him," Nyx said miserably. "Them. I-I found them."

Nyx wasn't a bully. But he was mean. He was hard. So when I heard him start to cry, my whole being rejected the sound.

Nyx wasn't the kind of guy who cried. He was angry, so angry... Maybe this was why. God.

Maybe.

This.

Was.

Why.

I guessed I had an answer for the unthinkable thing Carly had done.

Shoving my hand against my still-aching mouth, I tried to contain the moan of pain that wanted to pop out and only succeeded when King turned my face into his throat once more.

"When?" Bear barked.

"Years ago." Nyx gulped. "I-I was too scared to come forward. Too scared to say anything. He threatened me, and Carly, she said..."

"What did she say?" Bear rasped softly when his words waned.

"That she'd deal with it. But Dad... he loves Kevin. That's why he's always at the house—"

There was silence then.

Deathly silence.

Bear's feet came to a halt. "You think she told your father and he didn't believe her?"

I heard a loud sniff, then a whispered, "Yeah. I think that's what happened."

More silence.

It thudded like it had its own heartbeat.

It pulsed through the room like the fallout from a nuclear bomb, only being broken by:

"Leave this to me, Nyx."

Five words.

I might have been thirteen years old but I knew what they meant.

"No!" Nyx snapped. "Carly killed herself because I was a pussy. Because I didn't put a stop to this—"

"This ain't your job, Nyx. Ain't your duty. This is above your pay grade. I'll see to it."

"She's—" His voice broke. "She *was* my fucking sister."

Bear sucked in a breath. "Leave this to me."

It was a command.

An order that the fifty-plus men in the MC would immediately obey.

But Nyx wasn't like those fifty-plus men.

Not just because he was a guy.

Not just because, as a part of his heritage, he was a man now.

But because he was Nyx.

Everyone knew a wildness flowed through his veins. Everyone knew that he was rabid and feral. Until it came to family.

Family was his weakness.

My throat tightened as I thought about poor Carly, and King squeezed me again in comfort.

Nyx didn't reply to the Prez, just stomped off, and as the door opened and smashed to a close, letting music from the bar trickle in, I heard the remnants of the wake the MC threw on Carly's behalf.

"Fuck," Bear rasped under his breath before he repeated, "Fuck."

There was silence again, then the tread of boots, and the soft snick of the door.

"I need you to tell me that Kevin didn't touch you like that."

It was the first time I'd ever heard King talk that way—*just like his daddy*.

Swallowing, I turned to him. "No. I didn't let him near me."

In the meager glow from my flashlight, I saw his eyes narrow. "Because you knew he was... a creep?"

I bowed my head. "He looked at me how the brothers look at the bunnies."

King's fingers went to my chin, and he urged my head higher. "Did you know about Carly? Did she tell you about this?"

"No," I whispered truthfully.

His shoulders slumped. "If she didn't tell you, then she wouldn't have told anyone else."

*He wasn't wrong.*

I might not have been here a long while, but Carly and I—

My eyes burned.

We were more than just friends; we were like sisters.

I'd lost my sister ten days ago.

Five years might have separated us, but she'd taken me under her wing the first day I showed up at the compound with Mom and Axel, and this was the first time I'd been without her for an extended period of time.

I'd been her shadow. She'd been a safe space for so long, so adjusting wasn't easy. Knowing that I'd let her down, that she'd thought I was too young to confide in hurt even more.

"Nyx won't listen to your dad," I told him after he held me for a good twenty minutes.

Twenty minutes of me crying, of me accepting his hug and of giving it back to him.

His voice was soft, sad. "No, I know he won't."

My throat bobbed at the admission.

That feralness, the wild streak in Nyx was about to be channeled somewhere.

The man who would find himself at the center of Nyx's crosshairs was about to have a brutal death at the hands of a teenager...

I didn't have any pity in me to waste on an animal like that.

A sick predator who'd taken my best friend from me.

I'd always believed the world was black and white, but it was the first time I recognized there was gray...

So much gray.

Sometimes, I realized as I nuzzled into King, letting him gently kiss my temple and pet my hair as he tried to soothe my tears and my grief away, gray wasn't a bad thing.

It was, in fact, the best thing in the world.

TWENTY-TWO YEARS, THIRTY-ONE DEAD PEDOPHILES, AND ONE CHILD LATER...

*From: Rach3lLadyLiberty@gmail.com*
*To: K1ngS1nn3r1@gmail.com*
*Subject: License*
You should thank whoever you bribed at the township. They came through with the licenses.
Rachel


*From: K1ngS1nn3r1@gmail.com*
*To: Rach3lLadyLiberty@gmail.com*
*Subject: Re. License*
Who says I bribed anyone?
Maybe they were just grateful for more investment in the town?
R


*From: Rach3lLadyLiberty@gmail.com*
*To: K1ngS1nn3r1@gmail.com*
*Subject: Re. License*
Do I look like I was born yesterday?
Rachel


*From: K1ngS1nn3r1@gmail.com*
*To: Rach3lLadyLiberty@gmail.com*
*Subject: Re. License*
Such lack of faith...
Maverick knows about the licenses?

R

***From:** Rach3lLadyLiberty@gmail.com*
***To:** K1ngS1nn3r1@gmail.com*
***Subject:** Re. License*
Of course. I notified him immediately.
I'll be meeting with the club soon to get things on track.
Will you be there?
Rachel

***From:** K1ngS1nn3r1@gmail.com*
***To:** Rach3lLadyLiberty@gmail.com*
***Subject:** Re. License*
I should be. But no. I'll be here. Thanks for keeping me in the loop.
R

***From:** Rach3lLadyLiberty@gmail.com*
***To:** K1ngS1nn3r1@gmail.com*
***Subject:** Re. License*
You're not at the clubhouse that much, are you? Is everything okay?
Rachel

*From: K1ngS1nn3r1@gmail.com*
*To: Rach3llLadyLiberty@gmail.com*
**Subject: Re. License**
*Has hell frozen over...? How hard was it for you to ask me that?*
*R*

*From: Rach3llLadyLiberty@gmail.com*
*To: K1ngS1nn3r1@gmail.com*
**Subject: Re. License**
*It wasn't hard. Don't act like I don't care. Don't make me ask again.*
*Rachel*

*From: K1ngS1nn3r1@gmail.com*
*To: Rach3llLadyLiberty@gmail.com*
**Subject: Re. License**
*My father's in pieces, Rachel. Literal pieces. They can tell me until they're blue in the face that he's getting better but he's not.*
*So while he's around, I'm not going to waste my time at the clubhouse when I should be with him. Even if he doesn't have a clue that I'm here.*
*R*

*From: Rach3llLadyLiberty@gmail.com*
*To: K1ngS1nn3r1@gmail.com*

***Subject: Re. License***
*I'll be in later.*
*Rachel*


***From: K1ngS1nn3r1@gmail.com***
***To: Rach3lLadyLiberty@gmail.com***
***Subject: Re. License***
*Bring the paperwork? I'll glance through it.*
*R*


***From: Rach3lLadyLiberty@gmail.com***
***To: K1ngS1nn3r1@gmail.com***
***Subject: Re. License***

*Will do.*
*Rachel*

# TWO

## RACHEL

"Pink."

I blinked, staring around the space with a mixture of bewilderment and distaste.

"Everything's... *pink*."

Link, clearly spying my aghast horror at the sight before me, snickered. "Thought you'd approve. Wasn't like you preferred the old clubhouse, birthday girl."

My brow furrowed at both his statement and endearment, the latter I ignored entirely. "I didn't think sperm residue and beer were anyone's idea of interior decoration but this... it's so..."

His lips twitched. "Pink?"

"Yeah," I breathed, twisting around as I stared at the pink accent wall, the pink sofa, the pink chairs. Everything was goddamn pink.

Even the white walls had a tinge of salmon to them like those opalescent nail varnishes I'd worn when I was a kid to try to discourage myself from biting my nails.

Nyx, ambling inside, arched a brow at me. "'Sup with her?" he asked Steel who was sitting his ass down on a pink cushion.

I felt like I'd wandered into some kind of Barbie version of an MC clubhouse.

"She's a little in awe at how much pink there is in here."

Nyx turned around and peered at the place. "Looks like a bar to me."

My eyes bugged—I understood how Bugs Bunny felt when they bugged out. "I think it's a good thing that I'm the one who defends you in court if you fail to realize your bar looks like Barbie puked all over it."

Link, his ever-cheerful self, grinned at me. "I like it."

"You would," I sniped, watching as he turned off the TV where President Davidson and his First Lady, Elizabeth, were shaking hands with some cops that had survived the recent Sparrow cull.

The PR stunt wasn't fooling anyone.

The cops were as corrupt as ever—with or without the secret organization that had infiltrated every aspect of American bureaucracy tainting them.

Steel snorted. "Link's never been scared of any threats to his masculinity."

"No, I've transcended that part of evolution," was his pious rejoinder. "I know where I like to stick my dick, and liking things shoved up my ass and having a preference for pink doesn't make me gay.

"Anyway, it's not like we had a say in it."

I frowned. "You didn't?"

"Nah. It's revenge—"

Before he could finish, Maverick walked into the room, albeit stiffly, grumbling, "What's wrong?"

"Rachel prefers our old bar," Sin mumbled from behind the bar. He was clearly stocking the shelves with liquor.

"Are you going to be serving still?" I asked, puzzled. "That's a Prospect's job, isn't it?"

He shrugged. "Prefer to keep my hands busy as we talk. Might as well unpack the bottles."

"Quin and Hawk should work here," Nyx rumbled as he propped himself against one of the pink stools.

I honestly wasn't sure if I'd seen a more discordant sight than black leather, denim, and flannel clashing with pink velour cushions on a rose gold-accented stool, but he apparently didn't seem to notice.

Men were often unaware of the minutiae, but *this*?

The Old Ladies had to be joking around...

Either that or the brothers were downplaying the vomit-inducing amount of pink in their supposedly ultra-masculine space.

"You're right; they should," Link agreed. "That'll get Hawk outta the strip joint. If I hear Amara bitching at Lily one more time about him coming home stinking of perfume, I'll shoot my brains out."

"He cheats on her?" I sputtered.

Steel turned to shoot me a look. "Are you okay?"

"What? Of course I'm okay."

Maverick sniffed. "He's right. Something's going on with you. Normally you make an iceberg look tropical. Your voice just shot into mezzo-soprano range. I didn't think you had it in you to squeak."

I glowered at him. "This is all very..."

"Pink?" Link added again, smirking at me this time.

"Discombobulating."

Nyx accepted the beer Sin handed him. "Try saying that when you're shitfaced."

"No, Rachel, Hawk doesn't cheat on Amara," Link finally answered me after I scowled at Nyx who, of course, just rolled his eyes.

"He'd have to be fucking crazy if he did," Sin muttered as, once he'd finished passing out beers, he began stacking some glasses on the shelves.

"He would," Steel agreed. "Almost as fucking crazy as Nyx if he cheated on Giulia."

The club's VP grinned. "Why would I cheat on my queen bitch?"

Steel hooted, "I'll pay you to say that in front of Giulia."

"What? And get her hot in front of you motherfuckers?" Nyx folded his arms across his chest. "I don't do public shows anymore. You should know that by now."

"Why does Hawk stink of perfume then?" I butted in.

I was well aware that Amara, a victim of sex trafficking, had shacked up with two MC brothers—Quin, Nyx's kid brother, and Hawk, Giulia's older brother.

Yeah, it was confusing.

And borderline incestuous.

But Amara's past meant she was on edge, and while I was currently in the process of making sure her visa applications were approved by the government, I didn't need to be defending her on charges of murder one because the headcase took a bottle to some stripper's throat.

Amara wanted to make the States her home, but I doubted that involved shacking up in a supermax.

Link shrugged. "The girls like him."

"He's taken," I said with a frown, knowing Hawk and Quin wore Amara's brand as much as she wore theirs.

"Since when did that stop whores from doing what whores do?" Sin asked rhetorically as Kendra, one of the clubwhores, wandered in wearing a white spandex dress that made her look like she was playing dress up as a sexy nurse for Halloween.

Except, it was a week before Christmas, *not* Halloween.

And Jesus, what had she sprayed herself in? Skunk?

The urge to puke hit me, and it had my tone darkening as I ground out, "Kendra, this is club business. Please leave."

Her brow puckered as she wandered over to Nyx, her hand sliding around his arm as she tugged on him. "Nyxy, I need—"

"I don't care what you need," I sniped. "This is church. Get. Out."

Steel mock-shivered. "The icy winds are making a reappearance."

I didn't bother glowering at him, just kept staring at Kendra. Her cheeks burned with heat as she whipped her ponytail over her shoulder. "You're not the boss of me."

"No, but I am." His upper lip curving in a sneer, Nyx picked up her hand as if it were dog shit and shoved it aside. "What have I told you about touching me?"

Kendra batted her lashes. "I'm sorry, Nyxy. I forgot."

Link snorted. "You've got the memory of an elephant, Kendra."

"And the gall of one," I muttered.

"Rachel's one of us, Kendra. She tells you to do something," Nyx intoned, the warning stark enough to have her eyes widening with nerves, "then you goddamn do it."

Gulping, Kendra backed off in those stocky heels of hers that clunked with every step.

I watched her go with a tangled web of emotions.

Relief that she took her stench with her, and a bitterness that surprised me.

Clubwhores served a purpose under this roof. Not just as walking holes either. This was a society within a society, a microcosm, as it were, of outlaws. But they weren't total asswipes.

If they were, I wouldn't be here.

Nyx wouldn't have just told Kendra that my word was as solid as his.

And this goddamn room wouldn't be bright pink.

"Does Rex know it's pink?"

"Jesus, are we still talking about the color scheme?" Maverick grated out, rubbing his temples where I had to assume a migraine was plaguing him.

His time overseas had led to his current woes, and because I loved him, was grateful for his service, and knew he meant no harm, I moved over to the bar and placed my briefcase on it.

"You'll be moving in this week?" I asked no one in particular.

"Yeah. We had an issue with the plumbing or we could have been back here ten days ago," Nyx rumbled.

I'd already known the answer, but for all that I was looking forward to the brothers finally having complete access to the clubhouse that had been destroyed in a bomb blast months ago, it came with repercussions I wasn't ready to handle yet.

"The licenses for the microbrewery have come in," I informed them all, well aware that Maverick was the only one, aside from Rex, for whom this wasn't news. "As have the new construction licenses for the hotel."

Nyx scratched his chin. "Good. About damn time."

"Rex's bribes are as good as ever," I sniped. "You bitching about how long it took when he sped up the bureaucratic wheels—"

"Yeah, yeah," Link grumbled, bored. "Don't get all high and mighty, Rach."

"It's what I do." I placed some more paperwork on the counter. "I looked into the guy who came around yesterday—"

The tension in the bar increased dramatically.

The paperwork was business, but *this* was one of two *real* reasons I was here.

It was also why I'd originally emailed Rex. I'd wanted to tell him about this guy, but when he'd explained why he was hardly ever at the clubhouse now, how was I supposed to dump this on his door?

"—and he *is* Harlow Dresden."

A whoosh of breath escaped Nyx. "Fuck."

I nodded. "I made discreet enquiries. The Chief of Police has written off Samuel Haune's death as a vigilante killing and, from what I've been able to discern, not a lot of effort was put into the case. But the FBI won't be so lax. They'll be profiling you, Nyx.

"If Harlow Dresden could figure it out, then as much as I even hate to say it, there *is* a trail back to the Sinners."

Maverick ground out, "That isn't possible. I made everything airtight."

"Apparently not or a kid wouldn't have knocked on your door yesterday, Maverick," I intoned grimly.

"He means no harm though," Link pointed out. "The kid was grateful, Nyx."

"He should be. That Haune bastard was too smart to get caught. Jessie Dresden suffered a fate worse than fucking death, and Haune didn't even get a slap on the wrist for it." Sin's bitterness resonated around the bar, triggering a wave of grim nods.

Before Nyx's Old Lady had gotten pregnant, one of the MC's many sidelines had been a dash of hunting pedophiles and slaughtering them.

I wholeheartedly supported their endeavor.

Jessie Dresden had died almost two years ago now. Kidnapped, raped, and butchered by Samuel Haune.

So Nyx had kidnapped him.

Lynched him.

Butchered him.

I dug my knuckles into the counter, appreciating the pinch of pain because the need to gnaw on one of my fingernails was suddenly strong.

So, *so* strong.

Lawyers with a four-hundred-thousand-dollar-a-year retainer didn't bite their nails.

Not in front of some of the payers of said four hundred K.

Even if they *had* all known me since I was a kid...

"He's said what he wants?" I inquired, trying to sound calm when I didn't feel it.

The need to puke, ever since Nyx had called me yesterday about this unknown entity, had made it hard to get any rest.

Link slung his arm around my shoulder, and controlling my immediate response, I groused, "Don't touch what you can't afford."

Link being Link cackled as the rest of the guys, like a bunch of high school girls, hissed.

"Feel the burn, Link," Sin said around a chuckle.

"I felt it. Worse than what Cruz uses to melt bodies," he joked, grinning at me, totally unoffended. Winking, he said, "The kid wants to join in the fun."

My brow furrowed. "But you're not in the business anymore."

Like pedophile-hunting *was* a business.

"Nope. Indy locked that up," was Nyx's bitter retort. He cracked his neck in a way that told me his demons hadn't gone any-damn-where, regardless of any promise he'd made to his baby sister.

"Speaking of, has the PI slunk back down to New Orleans?" I asked.

Link nodded. "He's gone."

I didn't want to know what had happened to Indy's ex-receptionist, but I imagined it meant he was a bag of soup or whatever it was Cruz did when he disposed of corpses for the MC.

Not that I was supposed to know about Cruz's proclivities.

"Good. That's something off our backs at least. David's family must be concerned at the lack of progress in the investigation into his whereabouts," I said, tone sober.

"He took off," was Nyx's retort. "What are we supposed to do about that? Not our fault if there ain't a trail."

Sin snickered, which confirmed it *was* the Sinners' fault there was no sight nor sound of David—and hadn't been for months.

I pursed my lips. "You all need to buck up because you've been reckless for too long and, now, when each of you are settled and finally happy, isn't the time for your asses to be hauled to jail."

"That's what you're for," Link charmed, batting his lashes at me.

Like that'd do anything.

"I'm damn good at what I do, Link, but I'm not a miracle worker." Huffing, knowing they'd do whatever the hell they wanted anyway, I murmured, "The PI might be back."

"Nah, he won't," Steel disagreed.

"That's wishful thinking," I retorted. "If he is—"

"No body, no crime," Nyx said smugly.

"That's a facile view of the law. It really *is* a good thing you pay me so much," I drawled. "Regarding the Dresden boy, what are you going to do about him?"

"How old is he?" Sin stopped stacking beer bottles in a fridge to ask. "*Legally.*"

"Said he was twenty-four," Link explained when I shot Sin a confused glance. "Looks about twelve."

I snorted. "He's twenty." And that wasn't the worst of what I'd uncovered about him.

At my answer, however, Nyx's mouth relaxed.

Just a fraction.

I didn't trust that.

Nothing about Nyx was relaxed.

Ever.

I blew out a breath, and decided to let it go.

They paid me a lot of money to keep their asses out of jail.

This wasn't my circus, and it wasn't my monkey—it was Rex's.

"You okay?" Link asked softly, almost in an aside as the others bitched about the Dresden kid.

I shot him a tight smile even as my stomach did the tango again. "I'm fine."

We both knew it was a lie.

I wasn't okay.

Nausea so bad that I felt like I was constantly on a turbocharged carousel, heartburn even if I ate a salad, and a hypersensitivity to smells...

No, I definitely wasn't okay.

I had a feeling it was an ulcer, but I was too chicken shit to go to the doctor about it.

"—you could be his Mr. Miyagi."

Well, that was one way to get my mind off a visit to the doctor's office.

I stared at Maverick. "Are you insane?"

His mouth quirked up in a sneer. "I'm many things according to the doctors, but nope, insane isn't one of them."

Scowling, I retorted, "You want Nyx to teach a kid how to kill pedophiles? This isn't *Cobra Kai*, Maverick."

Sin chuckled. "You watch *Cobra Kai*?"

My scowl darkened. "That's what you're taking away from this conversation?"

Link's grin lit his eyes up. "Rachel has a TV addiction. Mostly reality TV unless that's changed..."

"I don't have an addiction to anything," I said with a huff. "You know I don't have to take this shit. I could go into New York and deal with people who treat me with respect—"

"Who you can freeze out," Link inserted.

"Who I don't need to freeze out because they have boundaries," I said pointedly.

"Boundaries, schmoundaries," he scoffed. "You're one of us."

Despite myself, I couldn't deny that felt good to hear.

It really did.

"You are," Nyx said calmly.

He shot me a measured glance, one that speared me to the quick because Nyx didn't say shit like that. Nyx didn't make overtures. Even two-worded ones.

Coolly, I told him, "I stopped being that a long time ago."

Shuffling a deck of cards in his hands, Steel murmured, "You breaking up with Rex didn't change things with us, Rach."

Link nodded. "You froze him out and try to freeze us out, but you can't. Not entirely."

"You're only the Ice Princess when he's around," Nyx agreed. "Seeing as you broke up a lifetime ago, you'd think you'd be over it by now."

Hot and cold chills shot up and down my spine when a spike of nausea sliced through me. I could literally feel the beads of sweat forming on my top lip from the urge to puke.

I could have sniped at them. Could have roared at them, even. They'd take it. They took a lot worse from each other. But they were right—I *was* different when Rex was around.

"That's the problem with connections like that," Steel rumbled softly, his gaze fixed on mine as he broke into my thoughts. "Time and distance can separate them, but they don't die."

He'd know.

He and Stone had reconnected this year after almost two decades of infighting.

"This isn't about me. It isn't about Rex. It's about the Sinners, and about the fact that if a snot-nosed kid believes the MC had something to do with his sister's death, then what's to stop the FBI from doing the same?" I sucked in a breath. "Whatever the kid wants, give him, but in repayment, demand to know what evidence he found that led him down this path. When he tells you, find a way to destroy it before that destroys you."

And with that, I shoved all the paperwork I'd brought with me today onto the counter, closed my attaché case, then stepped back and away from the bar.

As I walked toward the door, however, Steel called out, "He's at the hospital if you wanted to know where Rex is."

Like I didn't know that already.

I didn't turn around, just bit off, "Didn't realize you'd turned into Cupid, Steel."

I heard them hooting at him as I left, but the tension didn't leave my bones until I walked down the driveway and was out of sight of the Prospect that was on gate duty.

That was when I puked.

And though the Sinners didn't see, Emile, my goddamn driver, did.

Fuck.

# THREE

## RACHEL
### WEST ORANGE GENERAL HOSPITAL

Ever since I'd heard the blast, ever since I'd run from my house to the compound with thoughts of Rex being no more, of us no longer sharing this earth, ever since I'd found Bear in pieces, ever since, ever fucking since *then*, I'd been less than my usual self.

I was still a control freak, but emotions had begun making an appearance.

A little like the cracks that global warming was making in the Thwaites Glacier, they'd begun to weave themselves into my personality.

I didn't like it.

Unfortunately, there wasn't much I could do to stop it from happening.

Grief and anxiety, anger and fear, need and love, they were coursing through my veins, lighting up parts of me that I'd purposely put in the deep freeze, destabilizing areas that *needed* to be stable for me to function.

Gnawing on my lip as I made my way to Bear's ward, the urge to see Rex was strong.

I'd been fighting that urge for days, but after church, after the mess the MC was trying to wade through with their main kingmaker out of action while he sat with his dad, I just needed to see him.

Pathetic.

"So fucking pathetic, Rachel," I groused in the hope that speaking to myself in the third person would wake me up.

No dice.

"Hi Kian," I greeted one of the staff once I'd walked into the ICU.

I knew him from school, and he'd been semi-decent to me back then so I saw no need to ignore him now.

"Hi Rachel. Happy holidays!"

I was sick of the goodwill already. When would this interminable season be over?

Pinning a false smile on my face, it was on the tip of my tongue to ask him what a loss of appetite, nausea, vomiting, stomach aches, and weight loss could mean, but I didn't want to know.

I really didn't.

It was there, a shadow at the back of my mind, but I had other fish to fry.

Those fishes were shaped like two Presidents of the Satan's Sinners.

"Any news?" I asked softly.

We both twisted so we could look at the window that exposed Rex and Bear to the corridor.

In all the months that Bear had been in here, little had changed apart from the number of bandages that covered his face.

It didn't inspire hope.

Rex looked depressed and exhausted—small wonder.

"Some good news, actually. He's slowly but surely making progress. The doctors want to start reducing the meds that keep him in a coma so they can begin the process of waking him up."

I cut Bear another look.

*That* was supposed to be progress?

"What's the prognosis?"

"There isn't one, Rachel," he said with a sigh as if I were being greedy in asking for a miracle. It made me wish Stone were here. I knew she'd have been liaising with Rex, but that was why I'd attended church so Rex could be at the hospital where he was needed. "It's time. That's all we need. Each day is a step forward."

Why did it look like he was stagnating then?

I bit my lip to stem the tide of thoughts that I shouldn't be thinking.

Memories kept flooding me lately.

Bear's booming laugh as he revved his engine and raced off the compound.

The cackles of glee as he and Rex worked on their hogs together, shooting the shit and drinking the grog he made at Christmastime that was sixty proof.

His intimidating presence in the bar where men gathered around him like he was the emperor of all he surveyed.

That was not even night and day to the sight of him now. It was enough to make me start grieving him while he was alive—how horrendous was that?

"His heart's a risk factor," Kian murmured, unaware of my thoughts. "Another cardiac arrest like the last one and that's..." He sighed. "We have to be positive, Rachel."

Did we though?

I hummed under my breath. "So, this *positive* news means he's going to be pulled out of the medically induced coma?"

"Yes. There could be periods of wakefulness, but they'll be few and far between to start with."

Limiting my expectations, I nodded. "Thanks, Kian. I appreciate you sharing that with me."

"No worries. I know he's like a father to you."

In the absence of Axel, my stepdad, Bear was all I had left so he was right on that front.

He shuffled over to me, Crocs squeaking against the linoleum.

I stared at him in surprise when he reached over and pressed a hand to my shoulder. "Yes?" I asked coldly.

Kian's smile was, in a word, winsome.

At least, I thought that was what he was going for.

Mostly, it looked like a man who wanted to get into a woman's panties.

He hadn't been too horrendous to me in high school, but that didn't mean I was interested.

"If you need someone to talk to, I'm here."

I arched a brow. "Why would I talk to you about anything?"

Something flickered in his eyes. "It can help to talk to someone with distance from the situation."

I made a show of glancing between the ward and Kian. "Yes, some distance. You're miles away from it."

He patted my shoulder this time, the gesture patronizing.

God, I hated men sometimes.

"Honestly, Rachel, it's good to talk."

"Does this work?"

"Does what work?"

"This? This act? Like you really give a damn." I snorted. "Try to play doctor and nurses with someone else, Kian. I'm not interested."

He scowled down at me. "There's no need to be a bitch, Rachel."

My lips twitched. "Wondered when the 'bitch' would come out. Men are so unimaginative," I said scornfully as I stepped into him, moving fast enough that he backed up against the nurse's desk. "I'm a bitch because I have no desire in 'talking' through my feelings and letting you pity fuck me to make me feel better? I'm a bitch because I can see straight through you?

"Consider yourself lucky that I don't report you for inappropriate behavior with the family of a patient."

"Jesus, you're crazy. Talk about reading me wrong—"

"I read you exactly right," I spat, sneering at him. "And unfortunately for you, Kian, my word means more in this town than yours does." I reached up when his head jerked back like he'd been slapped.

I pressed my finger to the tip of his nose. "I have to wonder how many other inappropriate liaisons you've instigated—"

He scurried away like the rat he was.

I pursed my lips even as success flushed through me, and spinning on my heels, I turned around and headed for Bear's room.

After his last heart attack, he was back in the ICU, so I re-dressed in some protective gear and made my way inside.

Rex, catching my eye, shot me a scowl the second I closed the door behind me.

God, he was gorgeous. Even with his hair shaggy and his jaw covered in thick stubble, beneath it all, in the stark light of the hospital room, he was beautiful.

Strong brow, blade-like nose, kissing lips...

My mouth had traced the hard lines of that jaw. My fingers had drifted through that onyx hair.

I knew his reflection as well as I did my own.

"Rex," I said calmly, belying the sudden surge in my pulse.

"Rach," was his greeting as his gaze glanced off mine.

My brow furrowed at the sight of his clenched jaw—was he mad?

"Heard the good news," I said brightly, *if* a little doubtfully.

Just a single glance at Bear would have any rational person reasoning that all was not well.

A part of me wondered if the doctors were concerned about Bear's relationship with the local MC and that had them fearing the repercussions of failing to save the old Prez from the inevitable...

But Stone wasn't like that.

She wouldn't spoon-feed us hope.

On the same track as I was, Rex rumbled, "Yeah. Not sure how it's good when he looks the same as ever just without the cuts and scrapes, but what do I know?"

"Bear... We're not used to thinking of him like this. He's larger than life. Never frail. This is an adjustment," I tried to reason.

He grunted, and I had to figure that said it all.

For a moment, we just stayed like that, our focus on the man who'd helped shape both our lives, who continued to do so even when he was unconscious.

Change was coming.

There was no doubting that.

But he wasn't wrong.

False hope was cruel—

"What did he want?"

I blinked. "What did who want?"

"The nurse."

My mind elsewhere, I was genuinely confused when I asked, "Which nurse?"

Rex's jaw clenched again, this time hard enough that I was sure he could crack nuts with his teeth. "The nurse at the station, Rachel. The one you were flirting with before you came in here."

My eyes flared wide at his accusation. "Flirting? Who was flirting? I sure as hell wasn't."

He mocked, "I saw you making a move on him."

"You didn't see me do anything," I growled. "And anyway, what right do you have to keep tabs on me?"

He growled back, "Think through that question, Rachel, and you tell me where you went wrong."

That statement, the tone of his voice, whispered through me.

Sinking into my bones.

My fucking marrow.

God.

Still, I was pissed. My ovaries were *not* in charge.

"Fuck you, Rex," I sniped.

"I wish you goddamn would," he sniped back.

A hiss escaped me and I shot Bear a pointed look. "Is this really the place for this conversation?"

"I don't know, Rachel. Where would be better seeing as you almost constantly ignore me and I'm nearly always in this goddamn room with my dad?"

He had a point.

Sort of.

"You should be coming back to my place more. You need the rest."

I knew Nyx visited nightly with news and updates on the club, but I also knew that Rex barely spent any time sleeping at my house. That meant he was in here far too much.

No wonder he was a grouch.

Trying to take that into consideration, I decided to do the diplomatic thing and ask, "What did Stone say?"

The storm was still in his eyes, making this the most fired up I'd seen him in months.

For a second, he seemed to be at war with himself, then he ground out, "That he's in bad shape. You don't need a medical degree to see that. Some of his wounds have opened on the amputation sites."

"Oh, no!" I cried, my distress real.

"Yeah." He rubbed his forehead. "You come to give me the lowdown on church?"

"That's Nyx's job."

He snorted. "Nyx can't delegate for shit."

"And you can?" I scoffed. "You're as bad as he is. He's settling in well as VP though, isn't he?"

"Knew it'd take an emergency to make him realize he was needed. You know what he's like," he said gruffly. "Always thinks he's disposable."

"There's an irony to that when you've made so many decisions around his proclivities over the years," was my careful retort.

"It's a sign of how messed-up he is. But we both know that better than anyone, don't we?"

"Yes. We do."

It wasn't difficult to figure out what he was referring to.

Nyx's admission to Bear that he knew why Carly had killed herself... His need to make his uncle pay.

Two decades might have passed, but it could still have been yesterday.

While his words were technically a compliment, the way he spat them out grated on me: "You're a prettier messenger than Nyx, that's for sure."

I locked up tighter than a convent during a Viking raid, remarking, "I said I'd visit, so here I am. Visiting. You need anything? I can stick around so you can catch some sleep."

"No. I'm good. Are you? You look tired."

"Don't start," I said angrily. I knew I looked like shit.

"You're allowed to care that I'm not getting enough rest but I'm not allowed to care about you?" was Rex's quizzical response.

"That sums it up."

"I don't think so." He got to his feet and pressed his arms to the guard on the bed. "What did Kian want if he didn't want in your panties?"

"Are we still talking about that?" I blandly countered.

"We are. You're the one who changed the subject."

"Because it's none of your business."

"And I repeat," was his calm, cool, *dangerous* response, "think again."

My jaw rocked from side to side as I attempted not to lose my shit. "*He* came onto me," I snarled. "I was not interested."

He studied me, and I waited, I just fucking waited for him not to believe me.

For him to say that it looked as if I'd been into Kian.

As if I'd craved his attention when that was the exact fucking opposite of what I wanted.

Men were superfluous to my lifestyle. I got my kicks from my work. Well, work and Rex. But not always. Certainly not goddamn now.

"Sorry." He scratched his jaw, drawing my attention to his stubble. "I didn't mean to jump down your throat."

My gaze flicked away from that stubble.

I liked the feel of it between my thighs, but hated it on him.

"I don't forgive you," I retorted.

"Didn't think you would," he said sheepishly.

My umbrage lessened at his admission but it didn't make me cut him any slack. "You have no right to question me."

"You know that's bullshit," he rumbled, his voice like a skein of silk unraveling over gravel.

"I don't."

"You do. I get that you're hands off, Rachel, and I play by your limits, but we both know the truth—I'm the only one who gets to touch you."

Fire flickered to life in my core. The sharp burn was enough to make me gasp, and I wanted to kick myself for that intense, visceral, and *obvious* response. Especially when his mouth kicked up in a grin.

I clenched my hands into fists, letting them settle at my sides because a part of me wanted to punch him, and the other part wanted to haul him into me.

He knew too.

Arrogant goddamn asshole.

When he smoothed his hair, straightening the tousled locks into some semblance of order, I peered at him out of the corner of my eye.

I loved when he looked neat.

He knew that as well.

A part of me wanted to ask him to shave, but I knew he wouldn't.

A fade and a shave and I'd probably let him touch me more often.

"Rach?"

I heard the amusement in his voice.

Shit.

He *knew* what was wrong with me.

He'd also moved.

I could have told him to fuck off, could have dissed him like I'd done with Link earlier, but instead, I was weak.

Fucking weak.

His hand edged and curved around my hip, and as his fingers slipped into the pocket on my navy pencil skirt, the weight dragged the fabric down. The heat was electric.

"Church must have been real bad if you're here for that," he drawled.

I crinkled my nose. "I'm not here for anything."

"I call BS."

"I'm not gonna hit you up for a booty call beside your dad's hospital bed," I grouched.

"Ohh, now I know you're riled. 'Gonna?' What's happened to those elocution lessons?" he mocked.

My temper faded when I saw the light in his eyes.

A light I'd brought to the darkness of this hospital room.

Sometimes, when I looked at him, I knew what we could have. Sometimes, that was too much, and sometimes, it was a relief.

It came as a surprise when his hand drifted to my hair, the fingers tangling with the ponytail as he tipped my head back and joined our mouths together.

He swallowed my soft exhalation and just sank into me.

It was a stunningly tender moment, but the way his hand held me fast, my hair tugging at the roots if I tried to move my head, had my heart pounding harder than the situation necessitated.

Most days, I was okay. Some days, I wasn't.

Rex was the only one I trusted to handle my broken soul, but even that trust didn't always register.

When he nipped at my bottom lip, mine parted. As his tongue thrust into my mouth, I slowly started to kiss him back.

Hand curling around my hair some more, he stunned me by demanding, "Do you want him like you want me?"

For a second, I stared up at him with dazed eyes, then his words registered. "Fuck you, Rex."

A cocky smirk graced his lips and his other hand came to band around my waist. I released a shocked breath because the move imprisoned me against him. I felt his erection, registered its presence, and had to tell myself that it was *his*.

No one else's.

"I'll fuck you if you ask nicely."

I saw red at that.

"You're a jackass. Kian came onto me," I snapped then, aware that the other guy could probably see us through the window, continued, "What is this? You pissing on me? Marking your territory?"

"Golden showers aren't my thing." A bitter anger unfurled across his expression. "Did he tell you that you could talk with him about anything? About your grief—"

"He did actually," I countered, and then, because I wanted him to shut the fuck up, I pushed against his chest and against his hold.

He'd prepared for that because his arm tightened around me, but I expected his predictability and pushed into him, leaning up onto tiptoe so I could snag a hold of his bottom lip with my teeth.

"You're not the only one who gets to stake a claim," I rumbled angrily as I jerked back.

The raging heat in his gaze would have burned another woman—but I wasn't another woman.

I was his.

He grabbed my arm and jerked me forward, not stopping until he was hauling me out of the room.

I should have been furious.

Outraged.

*News flash: I wasn't.*

A soft laugh escaped me.

Relief coated it, but there was also need.

So much need.

It was a wild burst of energy, almost adrenaline-like in its toxicity, that made me feel fucking alive.

That took me away from these moments where, for however long we were together, I could escape what was happening.

Bear's future, the shitstorm that was heading for the MC, whatever health issues I had, and this strange impasse between Rex and me.

Giddiness hit me as we stripped out of the protective gear then strode out of the room, followed by the ward itself.

Kian's brows were arched, and I knew he'd been watching us.

Sly bastard.

I ignored him, but Rex didn't—his hold on my arm tightened, and he spat at Kian, "Keep your hands to yourself or I'll let the administration know you approach visitors for hook-ups."

That need was back.

Crawling through me.

It was crazy—insane.

Wonderful.

I'd already told the nurse that, in this town, my word meant more than his, but now, I just felt like I was the Queen of West Orange with its king at my side.

Cockily, I smirked at Kian then, as we left the ICU, told Rex, "I'll give you a free pass for being a possessive asshole just this once."

He arched a brow at me. "Just this once? I don't think so."

Before I could utter another word, fifty or so feet from the entrance, there was a small side door. He glanced around the hall, quickly tried the handle to see if it would open and, when it did, he clicked his tongue in satisfaction.

As he drew me into the storage closet, that satisfied noise sent fire through my veins—I recognized it too well.

Craving him, all of him, I shoved him against the wall. Between a mop bucket and a cabinet of only fuck knew what, I pressed my mouth to his.

Escape—that's what this was.

A chance to escape the here and now, but more importantly, what was coming for us.

The second our lips collided, the welter of relief that flooded me was overwhelming.

It was like taking a Valium without wanting to nap.

The anxiety, my stress, the fear—it all faded.

My world was right when we were like this.

It was *after* that shit went to shit.

But that wasn't now.

I explored his mouth, his tongue caressing mine as we savored the taste of each other.

My fingers dove into his hair, but I didn't tug at the strands. I stroked them, calming the tangle but using the grip to tilt his head this way and that.

His hands went to my hips and he drew me into him, grinding his dick into my stomach.

The immediacy of his response sent another tsunami of relief through me, and I groaned at his hardness, needing that in me.

Now.

Memories of him being a jackass faded as I drew my skirt up, dragging it higher along my thighs.

He stopped me though, pulling back and twisting me around so my ass was against his dick. I groaned when his fingers slipped into my pockets.

"How do you always have these?" he growled into my ear.

"I get them sewn in," I whispered as he abused the pockets and twisted and stretched them to press into my pubic bone.

With a moan as he wiggled his fingers, I found that he was rubbing over the top of my pussy.

"Tell me you want me."

Grinding back into him, his cock hard and thick against my butt, I snapped, "You know I do."

His fingers dug into the pockets again, dragging the waist around some more. As the thick pad of fabric moved between my labia, I yelped at the solid presence.

"Tell me you want only me," he rumbled in my ear.

His arrogance pricked my lust-filled bubble, but because I *did* only want him, and even more, I wanted that cock of his inside me, I breathed, "Only you."

He soothed the area with gentle pressure. "I can get behind that."

"Why, thank you, oh, exalted ruler," I groused under my breath, arching onto tiptoe so he could get a better angle on my clit.

"You're welcome," he teased, his mouth settling in the crease between throat and neck, his mood experiencing an uptick now he'd heard what he wanted to hear. Now I'd admitted what I'd admitted.

As he fluttered his tongue there, trailing it along to my ear, I shuddered.

A shudder that merely deepened when he found my earlobe and tested its resilience with his teeth.

He licked it, then blew a breath on it. As a shiver rushed through me, he whispered, "You need my dick, baby girl?"

I groaned. "I do."

"Pull up your skirt," he ordered, removing his hands from my pockets.

I made sure to give him extra wriggle against his dick as I obeyed, and hissed when he asked, "Show me how wet you are."

Slipping my fingers between my legs, I dipped beneath my panties then raised them to his mouth.

When he sucked on them, tongue flickering around each digit until they were beyond clean, I released a breathless mewl.

"You're my personal crack, Rachel," he whispered. "Do you know that?"

I groaned. "I do."

"Give me some more."

Shuddering, I did as he asked, rubbing my clit to tease myself then inching down the slippery folds to the source of his personal addiction.

No matter who he fucked, no matter how often, I knew he'd always be mine first. That made me even hotter.

Thrusting two fingers inside me, I arched back against him, loving his whispery breaths that collided with the sensitive skin of my throat and that sent tingles fluttering down my nerve endings.

I reached up, hooked one arm behind his neck, and tormented

myself and him some more before he snarled, "Enough, Rach. Give me a taste."

Cheeks burning, I rubbed my clit on the way up then raised my fingers to his mouth again. He clasped me there, holding me in place, not letting me retreat.

As he sucked them in deep, slurping on them, my juices trickling down the digits and him chasing them, I moaned as his other hand went to my chest, dragging the blouse I wore down so that my bra sat on the neckline.

When he was done, he moved between us, and after I heard his zipper, I felt my panties being shoved aside and his dick was there, resting on the canopy they made as he tunneled against me.

"Do you know how fucking hot you are, Rach? My beautiful girl. So fucking beautiful," he crooned, his endless litany of praise something that I shouldn't need but did.

As his dick found my slit, he angled my hips just so until he could get the tip in. I groaned, the back of my head burrowing against his shoulder as I raised my other arm and hooked both around his nape.

His hands dragged down the cups of my bra and they squeezed and caressed my breasts as he encouraged me to find the angle we needed.

When he found his way inside me, his branding heat so thick that I almost choked on it, slowly, he started to thrust.

Muscles juddering, I started to rock back into him.

Staying still wasn't something I could do.

Not moving wasn't possible.

This itch in my skin, the nerves that were unabating, demanded I fight fire with fire.

When one hand dropped to my panties, I wasn't surprised when he slipped them down the front and found my clit.

As he teased me there, him slowly thrusting, me writhing and wriggling, he crooned, "Your cunt is perfect, baby girl. So fucking perfect. Made for my cock. All mine. Just mine. Always fucking mine. So tight and slick and always so goddamn wet for me."

I whimpered, the words and his tone guiding me through the darkness, not letting me forget *who* this was.

I shuddered as he tweaked my clit, and as my pussy clamped down, a chuckle escaped him, dark and hungry.

"Oh, baby girl, so fucking perfect. Why you gotta be so perfect? Miss this pussy so fucking much. So goddamn much."

I groaned as those drenched fingers tormented me the only way he could as he rasped, "Cover your mouth. Keep those moans in or we'll get caught."

The laughter in his voice told me he didn't care, but he knew I would.

Electricity shot down my spine as he started to pound into me, and I tumbled forward, grateful for the tight confines of the closet. Pressing one hand to my mouth, the other I placed on the wall to stabilize us both.

As he fucked me, harder and faster, the slapping noises worked against me and his voice, that sinner's voice, muttered, "Need to feel you come, baby. Want that cunt clamping down on me some more. Your pleasure's mine, always was, always will be. Give it to me, Rach. Give me that fucking O. Need it as much as you—"

The shriek was barely shielded by my hand as I finally hit the peak I'd been needing since the last time he'd gotten me off.

As the pleasure cascaded through me, he didn't stop. He continued, dragging me up again, higher, higher. Endlessly pounding into me, his fingers taunting my clit still, one hand pushing down against the front of my pubis.

Eyes clenching, I bowed my head, just wishing I could see him better in the murky light, but that worked against me too.

"One more, Rach, one more, baby girl. Gimme what I want. Gimme what I want," he growled, his breath hot and heavy against my nape.

I obeyed again—what choice did I have?

As I crested another wave of pleasure, his snarl came loud and clear, but his praise upped a notch.

"Mine, Rachel. Mine. This pussy is mine. *You* are mine. Always fucking mine."

I cried out as the words sank into my bones, but when he pulled out, I released a soft sob, and then, I felt him.

He jacked off, his cum drenching my pussy lips, the fingers that had been tweaking my clit were suddenly out of my panties and were pressing the fabric against me.

"So you'll remember later who this cunt belongs to."

He breathed the words into my ear, but there'd never been any doubt about that.

I'd always belonged to him.

Life just didn't work out sometimes, and we were but two casualties in the war that was existing.

*From: K1ngS1nn3r1@gmail.com*
*To: Rach3lLadyLiberty@gmail.com*
**Subject: Question**
Did you have a nightmare?
R


*From: Rach3lLadyLiberty@gmail.com*
*To: K1ngS1nn3r1@gmail.com*
**Subject: Re. Question**
Why would you ask me that?
Rachel


*From: K1ngS1nn3r1@gmail.com*
*To: Rach3lLadyLiberty@gmail.com*
**Subject: Re. Question**
Because we had sex.
R


*From: Rach3lLadyLiberty@gmail.com*
*To: K1ngS1nn3r1@gmail.com*
**Subject: Re. Question**
That doesn't give you the right to ask me that.
Rachel

*From: K1ngS1nn3r1@gmail.com*
*To: Rach3lLadyLiberty@gmail.com*
*Subject: Re. Question*
Doesn't it?
R


*From: Rach3lLadyLiberty@gmail.com*
*To: K1ngS1nn3r1@gmail.com*
*Subject: Re. Question*
Why do you always email me? Why not text?
Rachel


*From: K1ngS1nn3r1@gmail.com*
*To: Rach3lLadyLiberty@gmail.com*
*Subject: Re. Question*
Because Maverick can read our texts.
R


*From: Rach3lLadyLiberty@gmail.com*
*To: K1ngS1nn3r1@gmail.com*
*Subject: Re. Question*
And he can't read email? Ha.
I'll accept that you're too old school for text.
Did Nyx tell you about Harlow?
Rachel

**From: K1ngS1nn3r1@gmail.com**
**To: Rach3lLadyLiberty@gmail.com**
**Subject: Re. Question**
He did. I'm not interested.
R

**From: Rach3lLadyLiberty@gmail.com**
**To: K1ngS1nn3r1@gmail.com**
**Subject: Re. Question**
You're not interested in a potential FBI plant?
Rachel

**From: K1ngS1nn3r1@gmail.com**
**To: Rach3lLadyLiberty@gmail.com**
**Subject: Re. Question**
He isn't a plant. He's a kid who lost his sister in one of the worst ways imaginable. You know as well as I do that even the best of men wither away at that.
Back to your nightmares, did you have one?
R

**From: Rach3lLadyLiberty@gmail.com**
**To: K1ngS1nn3r1@gmail.com**
**Subject: Re. Question**
Whether I have nightmares or not isn't your concern.
Rachel

*From: K1ngS1nn3r1@gmail.com*
*To: Rach3lLadyLiberty@gmail.com*
*Subject: Re. Question*
That means you did, and that means you don't want to talk about it.
R


*From: Rach3lLadyLiberty@gmail.com*
*To: K1ngS1nn3r1@gmail.com*
*Subject: Re. Question*
Take the hint.
Rachel

# FOUR

## RACHEL

### WHY DO YOU ONLY EVER CALL ME WHEN YOU'RE HIGH? - ARCTIC MONKEYS

With distaste, I stared at the bowl of soup in front of me.

I loved cheese and broccoli soup. My grandmother had cooked it for me when I made her proud at school. It was my treat.

Right now, it felt like less of a treat and more of a punishment.

Why, when I should be salivating, was my mouth as dry as if I'd been gulping down ashes?

Swallowing, I picked up the spoon and dipped it beneath the creamy surface. The second I raised it to my nose, the nausea churned once again and that weird ache in my abdomen spiked.

Shoving the bowl away, gasping when it splashed on the table in globules that made my stomach rebel for the tenth time in as many minutes, I pressed my hand to my mouth and quickly sopped up the mess with a handkerchief.

The residue left behind had me grimacing, but as I pushed back from the table, my cell buzzed.

Thinking it was Parker, my executive assistant, I automatically went to answer, but seeing my high school best friend's name, I heaved a sigh.

I meant to be interested, but all Scott wanted to talk about was their surrogate and her pregnancy—that was always a subject at the bottom of a list of my conversational preferences.

For a second, I hesitated to answer, then, recognizing that that made me a shitty friend, I hit the connect button.

"Rachel!"

Surprise had me almost dropping the bowl the second after I picked it up when he started sobbing down the line. So he didn't deafen me, I put the call on speaker and placed my cell on the table.

"Scott? What is it?"

Scott was a very emotional guy. I'd known him since high school where the pair of us and his boyfriend, Craig, had been the trio of outsiders in our year.

I was a Sinners' brat—only, the Sinners' kids in my year disliked me so that set the tone for the rest of the student body.

After Carly had died, I'd been even more of an introvert, and I'd spent most of my time reading in the library. That meant I got straight As and the teachers actually liked me. Essentially, to my class, I was a weirdo.

Scott and Craig were the gay kids who'd been caught having sex in the locker room. They'd never talked to me before then, but after, they'd hung out in the library too and a friendship had been struck.

All these years later, a nation apart since their relocation to Oregon, I wasn't altogether sure how we'd remained friends when we were so different, but I loved them both regardless.

I was just grateful we were separated by thousands of miles so that I didn't have to deal with Scott's frequent bouts of crying.

"Rachel," he wept.

Frowning, I placed the bowl on the kitchen counter and demanded, "Scott, stop crying. Tell me what's going on."

He sniffled, but like he often did when I used that tone on him, he wailed, "She wants to steal Sarah!"

My brow furrowed. "Who wants to? Andrea?"

Andrea was their surrogate, and Sarah was the baby.

Well, they didn't want to know if they were having a boy or a girl yet, so by the end of it, the kid could be called Darren for all they knew.

"Y-Yes," he sobbed. "She isn't answering her phone, and the last time we spoke, she said how she loved being pregnant—"

His words made me shudder.

I'd *hated* being pregnant. Loathed it. Even before I'd been raped by a sicko who'd found my new curves sexy, I'd hated it.

Some women were maternal, then there was me—the alien in the room.

"Well, loving being pregnant doesn't mean she's stealing the baby. She can't keep it inside her after nine months," I pointed out dryly.

There was a sniff. "I knew you wouldn't understand."

I arched a brow. "I understand that you're overreacting. Scott, she didn't answer the phone—maybe she had it on silent. Maybe she was sleeping. You sleep a lot when you're pregnant, and when the baby's getting bigger and sits on your bladder all the damn time, you get the rest you can—"

"I knew I shouldn't have called you," he sniped, but I heard the quiver in his voice that spoke of an incoming barrage of tears that were heading my way.

"You should have called me," I said, rather gallantly I thought. Scott knew I found it hard to handle these emotional outbursts. "You knew I'd be the one to make you realize you were being—"

"What? Stupid?" he snarled.

My temper never surged—it turned frigid.

Coldly, I answered, "No. Not stupid. Over-emotional and quick to jump to the wrong conclusion. Let the damn woman get some rest. She's the one making a baby."

"It's not as if you'd understand what I'm going through. Why would you?" He sobbed. "We're fighting to have our child, and you threw yours away!"

For a moment, I couldn't believe he'd uttered those words.

My mind froze as I tried to process how this short telephone call had derailed.

I knew I wasn't the warmest of people, and that wasn't only to do with the things that had been done to me in my past.

A lifetime of being ostracized because of my mother's antics, being tarred with the same brush, certainly had helped matters.

Still, this was Scott.

*He'd* held *me* when Brady Jensen had grabbed my boob in the hall and the principle had put *me* in detention, not him, because I wore a camisole and Brady had told the faculty that 'I was asking for it.'

*I'd* held *him* when his stepdad had tried to kick him out of the family home for being gay.

I sucked in a breath, sharp words on my tongue, but I refused to let them fall.

This was Scott.

"Scott, I think you should apologize."

There was no intonation to the words, not an ounce of emotion in them.

Unlike his next ones:

"I don't think I should. You have no idea what we're going through. I don't even know why I thought you'd care that someone was trying to steal our baby. It's not like you even ask about Sarah or Andrea and how they're doing."

Mouth tightening, I demanded, "So why did you call? Free law advice? Is that it?"

A sharp gasp sounded in my ear. "I can't believe you said that."

"Well, that makes two of us," I replied coldly. "I can't believe you'd imply that I 'threw my baby away' when you, more than anyone, know what I went through.

"I don't ask about Sarah or Andrea for the same reason that you don't ask about my charities—lack of interest—"

"So you *don't* care about my baby?"

"I care, but I don't want to know when Andrea pukes or if her milk's come in. Why are you being so aggressive?" I snapped.

"Because Andrea is trying to steal my baby!"

"For God's sake, how many times did you call her?"

"I've been trying her since yesterday and she won't answer the phone or the door."

Okay, that didn't look good.

"Did you call the cops?"

"No. I don't want to get her into trouble."

"What if she fell or fainted and that's why she didn't answer the phone—"

A gasp sounded down the line, and a moment later, I heard the vacuum of nothing.

He'd cut the call.

I stared at the congealing soup on the counter, feeling like a blizzard had just torn down the front door and had blasted the place with three feet of snow.

"He had no right to say that."

A complex combination of shame and mortification curdled inside me, and my head whipped around to snap at whoever had intruded on my privacy.

When I saw Giulia watching me, her gaze calm, I clenched my teeth. "That was a private conversation."

"You shouldn't have had it on speaker then," she countered, her lack of embarrassment clear. What I noticed, however, was her curiosity. *Great.* "You were pregnant?"

Thoughts of Wynter always had me backpedaling—today was no different.

My throat felt thick with tears I couldn't shed, making it difficult to grind out, "When I was younger, yes."

Her head tipped to the side. "You had an abortion?"

"No."

I froze her out, grabbed a sponge so I could wipe down the

counter, but the process made the smell of cheese surge all around me and the need to puke was strong.

As a groan escaped me, Giulia stormed forward, demanding, "What is it? What's wrong?"

"Nothing. Just a cramp."

I wasn't about to tell her that I wanted to vomit.

"You work too hard," she chided softly, her hand coming to my elbow as she forcibly steered me toward the table. "Sit down. I'll get you some water."

"I should be getting you the water," I argued even as I plunked my ass down on the chair.

Rubbing my stomach, I watched her as she filled a glass with water from the refrigerator door, murmuring, "I'm not sick. I'm just creating hellspawn."

Blinking, I told her, "You shouldn't joke."

She sniffed. "Why not? I am. We're talking two sets of demon DNA percolating to create the original Damian."

"Hardly," I argued, but I accepted the glass with relief. "It's not like Nyx..." I broke off. "He had good reason to do what he did."

She hummed. "Maybe. Depends on who you ask. Thought you'd be on the side of the law."

"I'm on no one's side."

"Apart from the person who pays the most?"

The words shouldn't have hurt me. I could tell that she wasn't judging me; if anything, she sounded impressed.

But combined with Scott's judgmental sniping, it hit me hard.

"Sometimes," I rasped, my fingers sliding through the puddle of condensation on the table.

"Nyx once told me you and Carly were friends. Was that true?"

"Would Nyx dare lie to you?" I countered, gritting my teeth at the question as I wondered where the hell she was going with it.

Giulia laughed. "Yeah, he would. He's not as whipped as his brothers make out. It's a mutual whipping. It's the only way I work."

I didn't need to know that.

Frustrated, I grabbed the glass and pressed it to my forehead.

"You coming down with something?" Giulia asked, watching me with keen eyes. "I heard you puking earlier."

Cheeks flushing, I mumbled, "I'm sorry you had to hear that."

"With as much time as I've spent with my head in the toilet recently, I should be apologizing to you. I didn't realize the walls were so thin." She placed her hand on my arm. "Are you okay, Rachel?"

Very few people asked me that.

Rain and Rex mostly.

I always lied.

But as I looked at Giulia, I found that I couldn't.

Uneasily, I told her, "Scott... he said things that were..."

"Hurtful?" she prompted when I fell silent.

I nodded. "Very. He... I shouldn't have said what I did either though."

"I heard most of the conversation," she admitted.

I didn't bother cringing. "Is that why you asked if I had an abortion? Because he said I 'threw my baby away?'"

"Yeah. No judgment here if that's what actually happened." She squeezed my wrist. "Don't know you all that well, Rachel, but what I do know is that you're on the cold side. Me? I blow up. I get mad, set metaphorical fire to shit, punch the wall. You're the opposite. If I know that, I'm sure if you've been friends a long time, he knows that too—"

"Not sure that makes this better," I grumbled, rolling the glass against my forehead.

Maybe she was right to ask if I was okay.

I sure as hell felt feverish, and keeping any food down was next to impossible.

It didn't help that I hated doctors. Going to the hospital as often as I did for Bear was a fucking nightmare in and of itself. The last thing I wanted was to be back there with my own symptoms.

"Not sure I said it to make it better," Giulia replied with a soft laugh. "I was just saying that he must have come to you for logic."

"Or law advice," I muttered bitterly.

"That too. You'd have a problem with that?"

"Not ordinarily, no."

"What he said really *was* out of order if that helps any."

My mouth firmed. "I'm sure he thought I was invalidating his feelings."

She snorted. "So he invalidated yours? See, this is why I don't like people."

Despite myself, I found that my lips were twitching. "In general?"

"In general," she confirmed, planting herself on the seat beside me. Her nails, short and blunt but still long enough for the black lacquer on them, tapped the table. "They suck. Do you disagree?"

"How can I?" I countered on an exhalation. "You know most of my clients."

A choked laugh gusted from her. "True. But they're decent. Mostly, anyway. And for all that they'll kill a pedo, I mean, they wouldn't hurt us, would they?"

"No." I placed the glass back down on the table. "I'm okay, Giulia. You don't have to sit with me or anything."

"You still look pale," she said mutinously. "Do you want something to eat? Maybe get your blood sugar up?"

I shook my head, grimacing at the thought of food.

"Before I found out I was pregnant, I looked just like you. Turned my nose up at food, was puking all the time. I even lost weight, which is one of those ironic things, don't you think? Lose weight before you put on three times as much?" she complained but patted her stomach as if she were trying to soften the blow to her baby.

"I'm not pregnant though," I mumbled. "I think I'm coming down with the flu or something."

"Ugh, that's miserable. You should get some rest."

"I can't. I have things to do."

"Like what?"

"Like work?" I heaved a sigh. "Plus, I need to find out how to fight Scott's surrogate if she *is* thinking of absconding with their baby."

"Even after he talked down to you?"

"Even after that," I said grimly.

Her arched brow told me that she thought I was crazy.

Maybe I was.

She shrugged. "I'll leave you to it."

I watched her get up, wasn't going to say anything at all, then as she made it to the door, I said, "Thanks, Giulia."

She hitched a shoulder but her grin flashed as she turned back to look at me before she strode out of the kitchen. "I speak the truth and no bullshit."

No, her bullshit-o-meter was definitely low.

Most days, mine was too, but Scott had gone for the jugular, and he'd scored a solid hit.

A part of me wondered if I should contact Craig, see what else was going on. Scott had a habit of overreacting and blowing up at the smallest thing. Craig was a lot calmer. To be honest, I didn't know how Craig put up with Scott, and after today, after such a nasty sideswipe at me, I was left questioning that even more.

The rest of the afternoon, as a result of that one call, was unproductive as hell.

I couldn't get past how easy it had been for him to jump on everything I had to say and to cut close to the bone with each retort.

When I eventually gave in and tried to call Craig, he didn't pick up. Which told me he was taking Scott's side in this.

I guessed that made sense seeing as they were in a relationship and he had to live with the man, but that hurt too.

I hadn't done anything wrong aside from be myself.

Was it so bad that I wasn't maternal?

I'd never pretended to be. When they discussed their plans of using a surrogate, I'd listened because I loved them and wanted them to be happy—they'd been considering this for years by the time they'd contracted everything with Andrea—but I hadn't promised to be the best aunty in the US.

Nor had I said that I'd be their babysitter whenever they needed.

I'd figured that they knew how I was because upon realizing they were going to ask me to be Sarah's godmother, I'd told them that I wasn't a good fit. I didn't think they were offended—they hadn't said anything. After they'd offered the role to someone else, the topic had never been brought up again.

Maybe it was a point of contention, maybe they felt insulted, but I didn't see why. I wasn't the one who suddenly wanted a kid.

It felt as if they'd changed the parameters of our friendship and they hadn't told me.

Giulia, I realized, wasn't wrong—people sucked.

I just didn't think I'd ever lump Scott and Craig into that mix...

Fine. I was fine. Just, it was more F.I.N.E.

I'd never liked that acronym.

"What's with you?" Parker, my EA, demanded on our final call of the day. "You don't even have to go out again and you're grumpier than a sow's paw."

My brow furrowed. "Isn't it a bear's paw? Do sows even have paws?"

"My grandma used to say it."

I rolled my eyes, but I was used to Parker's grandma's *wrong* sayings. It didn't stop me from always correcting her though.

"I'm sure she did."

"She did!" Parker argued, but she was laughing at me, and my lips, I had to admit, *were* twitching. "Come on then, sourpuss. What's going on?"

"I'm just stressed."

"When aren't you?"

"Well, that was below the belt."

"The truth often is," she intoned, her fingers clacking away at her keyboard. "Just FYI, your groceries are arriving in two hours."

"Did they have the raspberry water kefir I like?"

"They did. That stuff's nasty. It tastes how farts smell."

"Lucky you're not the one drinking it then." My lips curved. "Thanks, Parker."

"No worries. Laundry service will be by before seven as well, and I managed to get a meeting with Francine Petronelli scheduled too—"

Parker managed both my personal and business life. Some days, I didn't know where I'd be without her, even if she did have bad taste in fermented drinks.

"Parker?" I asked when she was done telling me about the next couple days' schedule—most of which made me internally groan because I'd be spending more time in Manhattan than I'd like before Christmas.

"Yep?"

For a second, I contemplated blurting out the whole sorry mess with Scott to her. I'd long since learned that Parker had my back in all things, but...

It was humiliating.

Though I knew she'd make me feel better, I shoved those thoughts aside and turned it back to work.

When Rain came home an hour later and asked me how I was, even after speaking with Parker, F.I.N.E. was still my answer.

Frantic. Insecure. Nervous. Erratic.

He knew too.

Arching a brow at me, he asked, "Rach?"

Somehow, my baby brother had become a man who could discern that my throwaway answer was total bull.

As I stared at him, at his concern, I didn't answer, just blurted out, "When did you grow up?"

A grin creased his lips. "You were there for most of it."

Sometimes, even though I'd accomplished a lot while I was out of his life, I regretted those lost years.

Years where Axel had been the driving force in his childhood.

Years where my stepfather had managed to imbue a desire in Rain to become a goddamn soldier.

That was the last thing I wanted for him, especially knowing what Maverick had gone through during his service, but I knew that was his plan. He thought he could hide his dreams from me, but I could read him like a fucking book.

I huffed. "You've gone from an awkward teenager into this Captain America replica."

Something flickered in his eyes, something that made him backpedal. "Nah, not Captain America—" I almost scoffed but he spoke over me, "I'm just working out more."

More?

Ha.

He had muscles on top of muscles. I'd seen him working out in the yard the other day. He had actual pecs! My baby brother—pecs and abs. It was weird.

He was probably getting laid by all the clubwhores. We'd had the sex talk years ago, but I just hoped he didn't get one of those bitches pregnant. I thought I'd prefer for him to serve our country than become a dad at eighteen.

As judgmental as that sounded, I figured I was in the right place to judge. I'd been pregnant at eighteen, and it had been hell for me. Why would I wish that on him?

"No shit," I retorted. "Working out more? I've seen you training outside at all the hours God sends."

He shrugged. "I like it. Anyway, what's going on with you?"

Noting the quick shift in conversation, I didn't bother grumbling under my breath as I made us both a coffee from the machine.

This was one of our rituals.

He had school, a job, and he trained, but we always met up for a coffee after he returned home.

Dumping his bag on the kitchen floor, he perched on the stool as he waited for me to slide the mug in front of him.

"Nothing's going on with me."

He snorted. "You could probably get away with that with anyone else but me. I know you too well."

That wasn't a lie.

Jesus, he was eighteen.

He was going to leave home soon.

Worse, he'd be in basic training.

There'd be no more coffees after school or work.

A bewildering feeling settled inside me—it was hurt and grief and panic. An odd combination that made me breathless with dread.

Forcing myself to calm down, to act normal, to focus on the conversation with Scott so I could explain it to him, I muttered, "Scott was a prick to me earlier."

Rain arched a brow. "I don't like him."

"I know you don't." Rex didn't either. "That's not the point. I do."

"You spend most of your time arguing," he countered. "And he's usually the one who puts you in a shitty frame of mind."

I scowled. "That's not true."

Disbelief etched into his expression as he accepted the coffee. "What did he do this time?"

Rain didn't know about Wynter. I didn't want him to know. Not yet.

Someday.

But not today.

Clearing my throat, I answered, "He said that I didn't care about his surrogate."

Rain blinked. "Well, you don't, do you?"

I almost snickered. "Rain!"

"What? You don't!" he remarked guilelessly. "You're not the most maternal of women, Rach, and there's nothing wrong with that. I'd like to think you did a decent job with me but I don't see you signing up for babysitting duties—"

God, it was uncanny how well he knew me.

Grimacing, I agreed, "No. That's not me."

"And seeing how he's known you almost all your life, you'd think he'd have realized that by now." His sniff was dismissive. "Anyway, what was the emergency this time?"

"How do you know there was one?"

He rolled his eyes. "Because there always is with him. He's a pain. I like Craig. Craig's rational. Scott, not so much."

"I know what you mean." Even that made me feel cruel though. Scott was very emotional, and there was nothing wrong with that, but Craig and I were on the same wavelength. "His surrogate has gone missing."

"Missing?" Rain repeated blankly.

"Well, she hasn't answered her phone—"

He started to snicker. "He probably calls her ten times a day, wanting to know if the baby farted or something, and she got sick of it."

My lips twitched because I couldn't imagine Scott *wasn't* 'hands on' with the process. "That's mean," I chided.

"Mean but true," was all he said, a twinkle in his eye that probably had the girls in his class fluttering around him like a flight of butterflies. "So, what was the problem?"

"Well, he thinks she's gone missing, and I wasn't as understanding as he'd have liked."

"So?"

I swallowed and tried not to feel like I was back in grade school. "He called me names."

He tipped his head to the side. "What did he call you?"

"Even gay guys aren't imaginative," I mocked.

"Bitch?" he guessed.

"Yes."

He hummed as he took a sip of coffee. "I don't think it's a bad thing to be a bitch."

"Meaning I am one?"

Rain's grin was sheepish. "I mean you're you, Rach."

"Is that supposed to make me feel better?" I sniped.

"Not particularly. But if you had a dick, they wouldn't call you bitch. It's just that people expect you to be a certain way because you're a girl, but you're kinda masculine in how you respond to stuff—"

I gaped at him. "Rain, you need to shut up before you dig yourself a deeper grave."

He chuckled. "I'm always one foot in a grave with you anyway." He leaned over the counter and smacked a kiss to my cheek before he pulled back, drained his mug, and got to his feet. "You don't normally care what people think of you, Rach. I don't think you should let Scott get under your skin."

Because he thought I was a bitch too.

Wow.

Maybe I shouldn't have been hurt because I knew he didn't think it was a flaw in my character, but I was.

He was *accustomed* to me being a bitch and didn't know any other side of me.

And he perceived all that without knowing that I'd given up my baby for adoption, which would only lead to extra judgment.

Because, after all, what woman gave up her kid?

My teeth ached from how hard I ground down on them at the thought.

Like I'd had a say in things.

Like it was my fault I hadn't been fit to parent my daughter...

He bussed me on the cheek, telling me, "I love you whether you are or not, so that's all that matters, right?"

I didn't answer.

As he wandered off, muttering something about an essay he needed to complete before he headed for his shift at Crosskeys, the country club where he worked, I tried not to feel like he'd stabbed me.

Apparently, my baby brother wasn't as perceptive as I'd thought.

My throat was tight and thick with emotions that I didn't know what to do with. A part of me could have puked; the other part wanted to cry.

With how weird my body was behaving right now, I might have been able to do both at the same time.

Truth was, I didn't mind if the rest of the world thought I was a bitch. I lived up to the title in the courtroom and with my clients; it was, after all, one way of corralling the bunch of criminals that called me their attorney.

But first Scott, then Rain?

Ouch.

*Scott:* Andrea fell in the shower. She almost lost Sarah.

*Rachel:* I'm sorry to hear that. I'm glad she's safe now.

*Scott:* I shouldn't have said the things I did.

*Rachel:* No, you shouldn't have.

*Scott:* Forgive me?

*Scott:* Rachel?

*Scott:* Fine. I didn't even want to say sorry anyway. Craig just said that I should be the bigger person.

*Rachel:* You didn't say sorry, and I don't think you're capable of being the bigger person. It's okay if you lose my number.

# FIVE

## REX

"Do you think I'm a bitch?"

There was no part of me that was ready for this conversation.

Not even on a good day. Which today definitely wasn't.

I rubbed my bleary eyes and turned away from the fridge to find Rachel standing close by.

She was being serious.

Although that was probably proof that exhaustion was slowing me down because when *wasn't* Rachel serious?

"You're talking to me?" That wasn't wishful thinking, either.

She frowned. "Who else?"

Rach had a point—there was no one else in the kitchen.

But that wasn't what I meant.

"You don't talk to me after we have sex."

It had been nearly a week since we'd fucked at the hospital, and she'd been ignoring me as was her usual MO.

Normally, it took her a good month before she approached me again via anything other than email or text.

Her brow furrowed. "That's not true."

"It is."

I almost chuckled at her scowl and dipped my head into the refrigerator to grab a bottle of that water kefir stuff. Its promise to help with my gut health wasn't the reason I drank it though. It tasted damn good—and I didn't give a fuck if that wasn't very 'Satan's Sinners' of me either.

Twisting off the cap, I was on the brink of drinking it down with a gulp when she stormed over and snatched the bottle from me.

"That's mine."

I arched a brow at her. "Want me to give you a dollar for it?"

She huffed. "I want you to answer the question."

"Which one?"

"Am I a bitch?"

Yawning, I asked, "This is either a trap or some kind of joke, right?"

"No. I want to know what you think."

"You're a bitch for taking the drink when you don't want it," I grumbled.

Her mouth tightened as she stared down at the bottle, then she shoved it at me. "Never mind. And it's more like four dollars you owe me."

Four freakin' dollars?

Holy hell and there was me drinking a couple of these whenever I was in the house.

Before I could apologize, she marched over to the other side of the kitchen. I heaved a sigh as I watched her go and took a sip.

Not as good as JD, but I couldn't exactly ride to the hospital later if I was jacked up on whiskey.

Pulling out the makings of a sandwich, I grabbed some bread and shoved a few slices in the toaster, aware that she was hovering over by the window and staring out into the yard.

Her voice was small as she told me, "Scott said I threw Wynter away."

I stilled at that. "Scott's a jackass. I told you a long time ago to cut him out of your life. He's a toxic prick."

"I doubt we'll be keeping in touch anymore."

"Good."

When she gnawed on her bottom lip, I could have slammed my fist into Scott's head.

Rachel made an ice sculpture look effusive. Her face was about as expressive as a still lake on a fall day. Nervous gestures like biting her lip were the girl of old, not the woman of today.

I missed that girl something fucking fierce, but it didn't mean I liked the fact that her so-called best friend had hurt her feelings.

"Scott told me I could never understand what he was going through because I—" She swallowed. "—let Wynter go."

We never talked about Wynter.

Ever.

It just wasn't something we did.

For both our sanity's sake.

Mine because it killed me that we'd given up our kid. Hers because life had broken her before she'd given birth.

The woman I'd known would have made an excellent mother. The woman who'd given birth to Wynter had been a broken shell, a wreckage shaped like the Rach I loved.

Shoving those miserable thoughts aside, I settled my gaze on her. "Do you care what he thinks?"

"Obviously," she sniped, "or I wouldn't have asked you."

"You don't normally give a damn about other people's opinions." I arched a brow at her. "You're the one with a client list that would impress the Joker."

"That's work. This is personal." Her eyes tangled with mine before they dropped to the bag of bread in my hands. "This is Wynter."

"It's her birthday soon."

She tipped up her chin. "I know. Not like I could forget."

"I sometimes wonder if you have."

I didn't say that to be a jerk, just because I didn't know if she remembered or not.

Rachel's ability to compartmentalize was terrifying.

Her cheeks blanched, and her mouth turned pinched.

After her conversation with Scott, my comment clearly wasn't what she wanted to hear.

"Am I really so horrible that you'd think that? That Scott could?" She shook her head. "I don't know why I'm even bothering to ask. It's not like you lie to me."

"No," I agreed softly. "I don't lie to you."

"If I'm such a bitch, why did you fuck me last week?"

"Because I want more. I want you. You know that."

"Why? Why would you want more, want me if I'm so..." Her words waned. "I don't even know what I am."

"You're you."

"Is that supposed to make me feel better?"

Frustrated, I ran a hand over my hair. If she'd have shrieked the words at me, I'd probably have felt better. There was something in her expression, something lost. As if she were floundering.

If anyone could understand, it was me.

I was the fixer. I was the Prez. I made shit happen.

Right now, I was none of those things.

Right now, I was a son whose Dad had been in the hospital for months and who was only now being pulled out of a drug-induced coma when I was pretty sure his quality of life would be reduced even further.

And that was saying fucking something.

Right now, up was down and left was right.

Somehow, I had to keep it altogether.

Some-fucking-how.

While I was the only one who'd recognize something was wrong with her, I just wasn't firing on all cylinders like usual so, tiredly, I stared at her and asked, "What do you want me to say, Rachel?"

Her mouth worked, and her brow puckered.

It was clear she didn't know what she wanted me to say.

Much as I'd suspected.

"He had no right to use those words against you," I told her gently. "He had no right to draw a comparison."

She swallowed. "He was freaking out. He and Craig are having a baby through a surrogate, and he was crying about how he thought the birth mother was trying to steal the baby." A huff slipped out from between her parted lips. "It was ridiculous. Ludicrous. He was hysterical. Whatever I tried to say to fix it, he just cut me off, and then I guess I was mean too—"

"What did you say?"

"Accused him of wanting free law advice."

I snorted. "Didn't know you were an expert in family law too."

She shot me a glare. "I'm not. He hurt my feelings; I guess that I wanted to attack him right back."

"Makes sense."

"Does it? We're not children," was her bitter retort. "Yet, here I am, acting like I'm a teenager again, running to you for validation. Pathetic."

"Not pathetic." I reached over and cupped her chin. "He's your friend. He hurt you."

"He did."

My touch was firm enough that she couldn't turn her gaze from me or jerk her chin out of my hold like I knew she wanted to. "What did Craig have to say?"

"He wouldn't answer his phone when I called him." She bit out, "It's not my fault I don't like kids."

"No, it isn't," I confirmed.

"You don't like kids either," she pointed out.

"I don't."

"I think I'd have liked Wynter though."

"She's ours. That makes sense."

"Does it? My mom didn't like me." She pulled back, tugging her chin from my hold. "I'm being stupid."

"You're being human, Rachel," I said as she moved toward the door. "You can't always be a block of ice, no matter how hard you try to cut everyone out. Me included."

She stilled in the doorway. "Is that what you think I do? Cut everyone out?"

"What else could it be?" I drawled. "It's not like you have a hundred friends beating down your door. You live for your work. And Rain," I tacked on. "But that's it—"

It was only as I said the words, that I realized how bitter I'd sounded.

Rachel turned to stare at me. "You think that sums up my life?"

I just shrugged.

"And what about my charities? What about all the goddamn effort I put into those? They don't earn me a damn cent. If anything, they cost me a fortune. Where does that fit into my life, Rex?"

"That's guilt and shame talking."

Her eyes flashed. "Don't presume to understand my motivations—"

"I don't presume anything. You feel guilty about Wynter—"

"Actually, I don't feel guilty about that." She straightened up. "I would have been a terrible mother at nineteen. That's without everything else I had going on.

"Wynter deserved the best. She deserved to have a parent who didn't keep trying to take pills, and she deserved to have a mother who put her first instead of her own selfish needs. That isn't guilt talking. That's reality."

When she stormed off, I stared at her. The exhaustion was pulling at me, and mostly, I wanted to go and crash before I had to head out again. But this was Rachel...

She drove me crazy, but I loved her enough to deal with that.

Just thinking about seeing that bastard, Kian, with his hands on her made my temper surge.

Yeah, this was *my* fucking Rachel.

No one else could rupture my control like she could, and I knew it worked both ways.

I strode after her, my longer stride catching up to her as she made it down the hall to the part of the property that was her office. She had a waiting room here, an area where a paralegal could sit on the rare occasions Susanne didn't telecommute, then, just off her study, she had a den as well.

I caught her on her way to the living room. My hand snagged hers and I tugged her around to face me but she dragged her arm out of my hold.

"Let go of me," she bit off, her tone so cold she might as well have had goddamn icicles dripping off each word.

"No," I retorted. "You wanted to talk, so talk."

"I don't want to discuss your bullshit pseudo-psychology where you try to make me feel bad for what I've done in the past."

"That wasn't what I was doing, Rachel," I griped. "I was just saying that Scott tugged on your insecurities."

She narrowed her eyes at me. "Do you hate me for Wynter?"

I scowled at her. "Of course I don't. I wouldn't have gone through with the adoption if I didn't realize it was the wisest path."

"Then what's the problem? You agreed to it too. So why am I the bad guy?"

"You're putting goddamn words in my mouth," I snapped.

"I'm not. You're the one putting your fucking *foot* in it—"

"No, you asked me if you were a bitch because of what Scott said. I'm telling you that he was out of line, but you have to bear in goddamn mind, Rachel, that I might let you get away with murder but not everyone is as fucking forgiving as me—"

Fire flashed over her face.

A feat in and of itself.

Something only I was capable of.

To everyone else, she was like an ice queen.

Only I could make her defrost.

As much as her temper spun out of control, it lasted a bare second before it was immediately dampened down.

The usual ice made a reappearance, sliding over her like a screen that separated her emotions from her features.

Watching it was almost like magic.

I goddamn hated that magic.

I wanted that fire. I wanted to fucking burn in it. I was so goddamn tired of the ice. So sick of her defenses and her armor when she needed neither around me.

"Get. Out," she said on an exhalation.

Gritting my teeth, I told her, "We're only not together because of you, Rachel. You should be careful when you tell me to get out. One day, I might not come back."

With that, I started to turn on my heel and stride off, but she grabbed my arm and growled, "Don't you dare threaten me."

I was careful around Rachel. Always had been. Even before some fucker had hurt her, I'd always measured my strength, always been aware that I never wanted my temper to *ever* lash out on her. But at that moment, it was hard.

So fucking hard.

My temper, always latched, started to flicker.

I could feel the burn as I snarled, "I don't threaten, Rachel. I'm telling you the fucking truth."

Before I could leave, she grabbed a hold of my cut and shoved her way into my space. When her mouth tried to collide with mine, I jerked back and hissed, "Go and get a vibrator, Rachel. I'm not your sex toy or your fucking punching bag."

She jolted at my words, her eyes huge in her suddenly pale face.

I gave her a measured glance, my temper back under lock and key, and I left her to it.

I didn't bother returning to the kitchen for food, didn't even check my office for any mail Nyx might have left there. Nor did I head to my bedroom to crash—I just did as she'd originally asked.

I got the hell out of there.

*From:* Rach3lLadyLiberty@gmail.com
*To:* K1ngS1nn3r1@gmail.com
*Subject: Re. Investigation*
Did Nyx talk to you about Harlow?
Rachel


*From:* K1ngS1nn3r1@gmail.com
*To:* Rach3lLadyLiberty@gmail.com
*Subject: Re. Investigation*
He did.
R


*From:* Rach3lLadyLiberty@gmail.com
*To:* K1ngS1nn3r1@gmail.com
*Subject: Re. Investigation*
Is that all the answer you're going to give me?
Rachel


*From:* K1ngS1nn3r1@gmail.com
*To:* Rach3lLadyLiberty@gmail.com
*Subject: Re. Investigation*
What did you expect?
R

**From: Rach3lLadyLiberty@gmail.com
To: K1ngS1nn3r1@gmail.com
Subject: Re. Investigation**
More?
Rachel

**From: K1ngS1nn3r1@gmail.com
To: Rach3lLadyLiberty@gmail.com
Subject: Re. Investigation**
Here's all the 'more' I have to give you—that ice around you is getting thicker, Rachel. I wonder if you can see that or if you're blinkered and think it's armor.
But let's focus on business as usual because that's so much easier than facing how much is fucking wrong between us.
Nyx did tell me about Harlow. Why are you asking? Do you have an update?
R

**From: K1ngS1nn3r1@gmail.com
To: Rach3lLadyLiberty@gmail.com
Subject: Re. Investigation**
You're just going to ignore me now, Rachel? How very mature of you.
R

***From: K1ngS1nn3r1@gmail.com***
***To: Rach3lLadyLiberty@gmail.com***
***Subject: Re. Investigation***
*Fine, have it your way.*
*R*

## SIX

## REX

### CHRISTMAS EVE

"Rex?"

It took me a while to hear my name, my mind fixed firmly on whatever the hell was going on with Rach.

Replaying the scorching hot fuck from almost two weeks ago was better than thinking about the mess that was our last argument. I didn't think it was a crime to focus on something that had brought me pleasure over something that had given me nothing but a fucking headache.

Scrubbing a hand over my jaw when another 'Rex' was hissed at me again, I turned to the doorway and found Maverick standing there, leaning against the door.

He did that a lot.

Lean against shit.

I wasn't sure if that was because he could move around now and wasn't used to it or if it was because the CTE he'd been diagnosed with fucked up his equilibrium, but I just tipped my chin up and got to my feet.

Because Dad was still in the ICU and had yet to wake up, even for a scant second like the doctors predicted, I had to leave the room then shuck out of all kinds of sterile gear.

As I undressed, I tried to shove my mind away from mine and Rach's last email exchange and asked, "What is it?"

"You look rough, man."

"Like you can fucking talk."

His lips cocked up in a half-grin, but he turned to face the window that overlooked my dad's room. As he did, the half-grin died.

I stared at the man who'd always been larger than life, who'd existed like a giant in my mind, but who was on the brink of death.

It wasn't a new sight. This had been the status quo for far too long, but it was still impossible to compute.

It wasn't just that I was like any kid facing the prospect of being orphaned, it was that this was Bear.

Goddamn Bear.

The Prez of the Satan's Sinners' MC.

A dominant force in our society for the past thirty fucking years.

No other MC existed on this side of New Jersey because of him.

He was the reason we were millionaires.

But he was fading, and soon, whatever those fucking doctors on his case said, he'd be dead.

A hand clasped my shoulder, squeezed, and I twisted back to look at my brother, demanding, "Why can't Stone work on his case?"

He sighed. "You know they don't let doctors confer on patients who are close to them."

I just gritted my teeth before I asked tiredly, "What's up, Mav?"

"Came for an appointment but wanted to check in, see if you were around."

"Why?" It wasn't like Maverick to beat around the bush. On edge, I asked, "Sparrows?"

Those goddamn motherfucking secret society pussies who'd infested everything from law enforcement to the political stomping ground of this great nation.

His nose crinkled. "Nah. That's Lodestar's territory right now. She doesn't trust me." He tapped his temple. "Says that she'll have to shoot me in the head if I fuck this shit up with them, and I don't feel like adding to the brain damage."

"Never let it be said that you're not a smart man."

He shot me a dopey grin, and as he did, I saw something flicker in his eyes. Something I wasn't used to seeing.

Contentment.

He'd just found his Old Lady.

And no, that wasn't because she'd been in fucking hiding.

That was because Maverick lived with brain damage from his time served overseas. His awareness drifted in and out, with heavy duty shocks packing such a punch that he could be transported back in space and time to Afghanistan.

The blast at the compound my father had been caught in had destabilized the structure, and when dipshit here had gone onto the property to retrieve some files from our safes, the roof had caved in on him.

That, for his brain, was the final straw.

I scratched my chin where my beard was growing in. "Okay, so not Sparrows." A thought drifted into being. "It ain't the fucking Posse, is it? I told Nyx that if Giulia caused any more shit that was something he had to handle."

"No, for fuck's sake. It's nothing to do with the MC."

"Well? What is it? Jesus, man, spit it out."

He huffed and said, "Need to talk to you outside of the range of cameras."

I blinked but nodded and started walking with him down the corridor. We took it slow because he was still shaky, and as we made it into the foyer, I asked, "Where's Alessa?"

His Old Lady.

"She usually comes with me, but I needed to talk to you."

I cast him a look. "Bullshit."

He rolled his eyes. "Okay, so there *was* a meeting with the Posse."

"Fuck me, that's a disaster waiting to happen."

Only trouble was, I didn't have it in me to really be that upset.

The Posse were a bunch of Old Ladies who'd gotten together to give me migraines. For all that, maybe it was a sign I was getting fucking old, because I was tired of the clubwhores gushing pussy juice everywhere and missed having wives and kids running around the place—

The thought had me braking to a halt.

Jesus.

I really was getting fucking old.

Or, maybe, at this moment, I just missed the shit out of my mom.

Mom had been like Giulia. Not as fiery, but lethal in her own right.

"Rex? What is it?"

Shaking the melancholy off, I started walking again and muttered, "Nothing."

It was frigid outside as was the way in Jersey in late December, and as my breath frosted in front of me, I shoved my hands into my pockets and stared around the badly lit parking lot.

Maverick seemed to see what had me scowling too, because he told me, "I'll get Sin on improving the lighting around here."

"Nah. Get Steel in on that. His Old Lady's the one who works here. It'll make him feel like he has some control over her safety."

After Stone had been kidnapped by a serial killer in Manhattan, my brother was definitely struggling with the need to keep his woman safe.

"Pretty sure your job is nothing more than juggling egos," Maverick said, shaking his head at me.

"Eighty percent that, and twenty percent trying to make sure that my brothers don't end up in jail or dead." I grunted. "This far away enough from the doors?"

He peered around and said, "Yeah." Sucking in a breath, he rasped, "Been working on something for Nyx. You know, to deal with his little problem?"

My vice president's 'little problem' was the compelling need to torture and murder pedophiles.

It was a problem I backed fully, but one his family didn't. Nyx had made promises to the women in his life, promises that were jeopardizing his sanity.

"I still can't believe the fucker's gonna be a dad."

"You and me both," Maverick retorted. "Anyway, in between migraines, I've been working on a couple projects."

"Like what?" I asked, curious, because I knew those migraines were fucking killer and screen time exacerbated that shit.

Which meant he was sneaking around doing this work because his Old Lady was a mother hen, and she wouldn't have let him unless it was urgent.

"One's an app. I'm trying to make it open source."

Even more curious, I asked, "What kind of app?"

"Controlling kids' Internet use. They try to sext, it'll ping on their parents' phones. Gives the location of the device, so they always know where the child is. Porn-blocking. Shit like that." He shrugged. "It's easy coding for me, and I was looking out for parents who are below the poverty line. They can't afford the subscriptions for apps like that. I don't think you should have to pay to make your kids secure online—"

Seeing he was working himself up, I raised a hand. "I ain't arguing with you, Mav. Whatever you need, we'll get for you, okay? We'll make sure that it can stay open source because you're right. Shit like that *should* be free."

He blew out a breath. "It'll cost."

"What are we earning all this fucking money for if we can't put some of it to good use?"

"St. Rex," he half-teased.

"Doubt I'm getting canonized any time soon. Okay, was that the problem? You need cash flow?"

"No. That was... To build the app, I had to trawl the web. You know, to figure out the extent of what needed blocking? Came across some shit that made me want to bleach my eyes, but there's nothing new there." He shook his head. "We need more Nyxes, man. We don't need him taken out of action."

I grimaced because I knew where he was coming from.

"Doxxing those sick pieces of shit doesn't feel like it's enough, torturing them long distance ain't gonna pack the same punch, but—" His cheeks puffed out as he exhaled. "—I get it. Kid on the way, his priorities gotta change.

"Anyway, as I'm trawling, I came across this site. Like a private website. I shouldn't have been able to access it, but the kid had uploaded some porn on there."

"Child porn?"

"No. Regular spank bank shit. Kid's only sixteen. You don't need to know how my code slipped into his server, but what I found was... disturbing."

Maverick, with what he'd seen and done over the years, took a lot to disturb.

That wasn't to say shit didn't freak him out. Like he'd said, he wanted to bleach his eyes a lot of the time, but his tone had unease slithering through my system.

"What was it?"

"Blog posts about the best type of assault weapons for maximum damage, how fast they need to be reloaded, stuff like that. Journal notes about making kids in his class hurt like he's hurting. Making people suffer who've made him suffer."

I straightened. "Potential school shooter?"

"I'm thinking. All the signs are there."

"Do you know if he has access to weapons?"

"I know his father's got a concealed carry license."

We shared a look.

"Where is he?"

"Place called Chaparral. On the border between Mexico, New Mexico, and Texas."

I reached up and rubbed my eyes. "Christmas is tomorrow. Schools starts again early January."

"I know. He's slowed down with the messed-up content, but it amped up a couple weeks before the end of semester. His online diary is whacked. The shit they do to him... You'd burn in hell for doing it to an animal, never mind a kid." He shrugged. "He's a locked and loaded pistol just waiting to be fired once he's back in class.

"I don't know what to do, Rex. Shit's disturbing, but you know what it's like down there. Cops ain't gonna listen. Got their thumbs up their asses until it's too late and kids are dead.

"I can't have that on my conscience as well, man."

I reached over and grabbed his shoulder. "You don't have to. I'll figure something out."

He released a breath. "I'd go down myself, try to—fuck, I don't know. How do you reason with a kid like that? He's on the brink of mass fucking murder because of some bullies. He's the victim—"

"Until he becomes the perpetrator," I tacked on grimly. "You can't travel, anyway. You gotta stay here, continue with the treatment. Ain't about to lose you, Mav. Not again."

"I ain't going nowhere," he said gruffly. "But even if I wanted to flout my doctor's orders, I can't, man. Too shaky on a fucking hog. The pills they got me on are messing with me right now."

Nodding my understanding, I told him, "You ride here in a cage?"

"Yeah. Hawk's waiting for me in the parking lot."

"Good. Leave this with me. I'll figure something out."

"Sorry to bring this to your table, Rex. What with Bear and—" He made a gesture with his hands that I fucking felt in my soul.

Life right now was rough.

I squeezed his shoulder again. "Don't worry about it."

Guilt etched its way into his expression. "Bear—"

"He's dying. Won't be long now." I cast a look at the hospital. "Just a matter of time no matter what the fucking doctors say."

"Sorry, brother. Love the bastard. He's been a dad to all of us."

Mav wasn't wrong.

I clenched my jaw. "He has. You go home. Go and corral that Old Lady of yours."

"You gonna stay here?" he asked uneasily.

"Yeah."

"The clubhouse is ready to move into."

"I know."

We'd been working since the blast to construct a new clubhouse, and it was finally ready. Just in time for Christmas.

Ho, fucking ho.

"You moving out of Rachel's?"

I didn't want to talk about this now.

I stared at him until he pulled a face and raised his hands. "I'll leave it alone."

When he backed away, heading for wherever Hawk was waiting for him, I called out, "You did the right thing coming to me with this, Mav."

He twisted around and dipped his chin. "You're our Solomon, Rex. Wouldn't want the weight of the decisions you bear every day, but I'm fucking grateful you're man enough for the task."

As he strolled between cars, I stayed staring at the hospital window where I knew my dad was slowly dying.

Shoulders hunched against the cold, I knew I was shivering, but I didn't really care.

Solomon.

Funny how he called me that *now* when I wasn't feeling wise, wasn't even feeling like I had the capability of running the Sinners.

I was just a boy.

A son.

About to lose his dad.

"Maverick?"

He froze, and like he knew what I was about to ask without me saying a damn word, he turned again to face me. "Wynter's doing okay, Rex."

I gave him a shaky nod even as my hands curled into tight fists.

He didn't leave like I thought he would, instead he asked, "Rex?"

"Yeah?"

"Do you know what's wrong with Rachel?"

For a second, I just stared at him.

There were so many things wrong with my woman, after all—I didn't know where to start.

He angled his head to the side, reading into my expression and my silence without me having to utter a word. "You do. So why don't you fix things with her?"

"Because..."

It was on the tip of my tongue to say that she didn't want me to.

That wasn't a lie. But it wasn't the full truth either.

"I know why she's been grouchy as fuck this week."

"You know that wasn't what I meant."

With a sigh, I conceded, "I don't know what broke her. Not specifically."

"You didn't think to ask?"

"I don't need to ask to know. I—" Air gusted in my cheeks and the cold chill of the night bit into my flesh. But the ice in my soul that came from the separation Rachel insisted on between us was so much worse than anything nature could throw at me. "I know when things changed. I can guess what happened. She needs to tell me herself. I can't look into it. She's..." How the fuck did I verbalize this? "She's not like other women. She doesn't want me to fix things for her."

"She's not fixing it herself," he said, clearly unimpressed.

From his position, I got it.

I'd be unimpressed too.

I was her man.

I was supposed to slay her dragons and fix her crown.

Rachel, however, was capable of slaying her own damn dragons and fixing her own damn crown.

How did you make reparations for a woman who didn't need you to?

"I'm there for her. Always. When she's ready, she'll come to me."

It sounded like a weak as fuck excuse, and I half expected Maverick to snigger at me and call me a prick, but if anyone knew the lengths I'd gone to for Rachel, it was him.

Giving my daughter to another family to raise had been hell, but I'd done it. For Rachel. To keep her alive. That was just the tip of the Rachel Laker iceberg.

He blinked at me. "I think, if you're not careful, you'll be waiting the rest of your life for her to make things right. She's stuck. You both are. You need to cut the cord or bind it around you even tighter. Trust me, man, *I'd* know."

With that, he left, and I watched him wend his way through the cars.

He wasn't wrong.

I knew that.

Peering up at the sky, I released a breath that frosted in front of me and wondered if my girls were looking up at the stars too.

Rachel might be in the same town as me, but for all the distance between us, she could have been in Cali with our daughter.

"Fuck you, Maverick," I hissed under my breath as I heard a truck start up.

He knew this time of year was always rough on me because Wynter's birthday was on the fourth of January, so close to Rachel's. I'd forgotten Rach's this year, but I knew she'd have gotten my gift by now. Not that she'd thanked me for it.

That she was pissed at me was a given.

Hands clenching into fists at my sides, I stayed staring up at the night sky for a ridiculously sentimental amount of time, trying to figure out what to do.

Maverick wasn't wrong; that was something I couldn't escape from, so I didn't bother trying.

After a while, when the universe didn't right itself on the wish I settled on a shooting star, I trudged back to Dad's bedside, re-dressing in the protective gear I had to wear in the ICU, feeling the burden of my position as I sat my weary bones into the armchair I'd been sitting in for hours at a time.

For days and weeks and months since the blast.

I did most of my work here, only leaving for important club business, to rest, and to eat.

But tonight, I didn't want to work. Not even when Maverick sent me the school shooter's details.

I wanted to forget *this* and think about something else.

Swiping through the photos on my phone, I watched Rachel mature from a kid of about eleven to the woman she was today.

I had a Rachel album on my drive, and it was my go-to stress relief.

Each picture was a memory I wanted to hold dear. Each one was a trigger of something I didn't want to forget.

The time I broke my arm when I jumped in the lake in Verona because some fuckers had pushed her in when she couldn't swim. That was the first time she'd let me hug her.

The time when—

"Rex?"

My name was one syllable long.

Short. Abrupt. Just like me.

But Dad whispered it on an exhalation.

A rasp.

A death rattle.

My eyes watered as I jerked up onto my feet.

This was the first time he'd had a whisper of consciousness since the clubhouse bombing, and though the relief should have been raw, as I looked down at his ravaged face, his torn-apart body, it was guilt that drowned me.

"Dad?" I whispered back. "I'm here, Dad. I'm here."

His eyelids fluttered open, bright pink and patchy from burns. "Want—" He let loose a long breath. "Rene."

I swallowed. "She's not here anymore, Dad. She's dead."

"Need." A breath. "Her."

Eyes wet, I reached up and rubbed my thumbs against the lids. "I know, Dad. I know you miss her."

"No."

"No?"

The effort it took him to connect his gaze with mine almost blurred the staunch will behind that stare.

"Don't. Want." A breath. "To live. Without. Her." Another. "Anymore."

Each word was labored. The sounds tortured as he tried to verbalize the impossible.

"It's not your time to go yet, Dad," I rasped, wanting to touch him but not wanting to hurt him either. "The doctors want—"

"NO!" he growled, living up to his road name. "NO."

Then, he broke me, because there was no mistaking what he wanted, no mistaking the command of a man who'd led his own army of Sinners for decades:

"Help. Me."

## SEVEN

## RACHEL

"Motherfucker." The bathroom doorknob rattled and shook again. "Is someone in there?"

I pinched the bridge of my nose and tried to tell myself that my houseguests would be gone within the week to their newly pink abode.

"Giulia, that's why the door is locked," I said as calmly as I was able.

"Rachel?"

My brow furrowed at the hitch in her voice. "Yeah?"

"I'm really sorry, but are you almost finished?"

Awkward.

I heaved a sigh, then something hit me.

Giulia apologizing?

Giulia saying 'sorry'?

That was when I realized something had to be really wrong. Was it the Dresden boy? Nyx hadn't mentioned him during church today.

Seeing as I was only sitting on the toilet seat, not doing anything other than staring at my feet, my gaze trained on the test I'd thrown in the trash can, I unlocked the door. She reared back when she saw me sitting on the seat, clearly expecting my pants to be around my ankles, then frowned as she waddled in, belly first.

I stared at that belly.

Was transfixed by it.

I'd been there once before, and I'd vowed I'd never get pregnant again.

Fate was such a bastard.

She cleared her throat, drawing my attention to her face, so I straightened up, saying, "I'll leave you to it."

"No. You don't have to go."

I arched a brow. "I don't want to see you pee."

"I don't want to pee," she warbled before she closed the door, with me on this side of the bathroom, locked it, and then promptly burst into tears.

Holy hell.

Rattled, I stared at her a couple seconds. I'd known her when she was a kid, didn't exactly know her now that she was an adult and a Sinner's Old Lady even if she had been living with me the past couple months.

She was Nyx's woman. He was the VP of the Sinners, and his Old Lady was just as deadly as he was.

At least, that was what rumor said.

While gossip and hearsay could be useful in a court of law when used to manipulate a jury, around the Sinners, I didn't need to be wondering about what they did and didn't do.

The less I knew, the better.

*Fool me once, shame on you.*

*Fool me twice, shame on me.*

The old saying whispered through my mind as I cast another glance at Giulia's belly then at mine.

There was no sign of life there yet. No sign whatsoever. The pregnancy test had been a last-ditch effort of not having to go to the doctor's to see if there was something really wrong with me.

I guessed I should be happy I didn't have an ulcer.

Yay?

"What's wrong, Giulia?" I asked her wearily.

I didn't particularly want to know, but she was clearly distressed, and while my rep as an ice-cold bitch seemed to be set in stone in the tristate area, she was pregnant. If I could solve her problem in the here and now, I wouldn't have to hear Nyx and her arguing later on, followed by a three-hour-long session of angry sex.

Yes, *three* hours.

I wasn't sure if I'd had three hours' worth of sex in the past twelve months, never mind in one evening.

Of course, the hook up at the hospital ate into those one-hundred-eighty minutes for sure.

"I want to kill her."

Confusion laced my words as I asked, "Who?"

Giulia was the kind of person who wanted to 'kill' a lot of people, *verbally*. This was different. The tears, the bitter hatred in her voice, it felt off to me.

"Kendra," she hissed.

The memory of that white spandex dress had me grimacing.

"Why Rex lets her stick around, I'll never know," I muttered gruffly. "She's been trouble since she showed up."

Giulia blinked at me.

"What?" I asked awkwardly.

"I'm surprised you know who she is."

I watched as she knuckled her eyes, looking remarkably like the small child I'd once babysat many moons ago. She wouldn't recall that, I didn't think her brother Hawk did either, but *I* remembered.

My throat even tightened at the memory.

Babysitting her was what had led to my attack.

"I know everyone in the MC," I told her easily, my tone remarkably free from the horrors that had haunted me since I was seventeen.

I balled my hands into fists as she questioned, "You do? Why?"

"Because it's my business to know." I studied her. "What's the problem?"

"No problem. I'm just... I didn't think you liked working for the Sinners."

"I neither like it nor dislike it."

I worked for a lot of criminals. I was good at getting them off the hook, and it was far more challenging than siding with the prosecution. If I didn't like anything, it was working with Rex. *But,* I couldn't forget that I was only here because of him.

I'd gone to law school with enough money to pay for college and housing. I hadn't needed to work. He'd covered every single cost, all with the intention of tying me to the MC in a neat, pretty bow.

I didn't mind that, either.

I just minded that on the face of it, he wasn't simply tying me to the Sinners. Really, he was tying me to *him*.

Another tie I didn't need.

Giulia shook her head at my unruffled response. "How are you so calm and collected all the time, Rachel? Even when your friend talked down to you, you didn't react all that much. Don't you get mad? Don't you cry? I don't think I've ever seen you laugh. Are you happy? Are you sad? I know you have nightmares; I hear them sometimes, but you—" Taken aback, I straightened up and shot to my feet, but her hand was on my shoulder, pushing me down. "I'm sorry. I don't mean to intrude, but is there something I can do to help?"

Giulia... *help?*

God, there really was something wrong with her.

"I'm fine," I told her woodenly. "You're the one who came bursting in here in tears."

Her nostrils flared as she backed off, perching her butt against the vanity. "She said she fucked Nyx last night."

I couldn't help myself—I snorted out a laugh. Especially when I thought of how, the last time I saw her, Nyx had shoved Kendra's hand away as if it were coated in acid.

"You can't seriously believe her?"

She just bit her lip.

My eyes rounded. "Giulia, you know Nyx is nearly forty, don't you?"

"What does that have to do with anything?" she defended with a huff, a gleam of outrage bursting to life in her eyes.

The woman was malevolence personified.

Seemed fitting that only Nyx's hellspawn could be the chink in her armor—hormones, they were women's true enemy.

"It means that most men his age are starting to look for little blue pills to get them hard. You and Nyx fuck like there's an apocalypse the next morning. If he used it anymore, it'd fall off."

"You're right."

Her calm glance was somehow more disturbing than her tears.

"I know I am," I groused, just thinking about last night's three-hour marathon which had sounded like one or both of them were dying.

Only to myself would I admit that I was jealous.

Just a quarter inch.

"The question is," I plowed on when her look was more disturbing than any the Long Beach Butcher—a serial killer I'd defended last year—had given me during our interviews. "Giulia, why would you believe her?"

"I'm on edge," she argued.

"You're always on edge."

"More than usual."

"Why?"

Giulia huffed. "I'm pregnant."

"So? You've been pregnant for the last six months," I pointed out, then it hit me. "Oh."

"Oh, *what?*" she snapped.

"She called you fat, didn't she?"

Her mouth tightened. "That bitch."

"Yeah. That bitch," I repeated, even as I got to my feet and encouraged her to rest on the toilet seat. "Do you feel fat? You know Nyx looks at you like you can walk on water, Giulia, so I don't think—"

She sniffled. "I burst the seam on my favorite pair of jeans today, and none of my clothes fit."

"Do you want to go shopping for maternity clothes?"

I could think of nothing worse, but her misery hit me on the raw.

"I don't want to be one of those women."

I arched a brow. "One of those women whose clothes fit?"

Growling under her breath, she spat, "A *mom* woman."

"What kind of woman is that? You *are* a mom," I drawled, and though it was wrong of me to be amused, her disgust had my lips twitching.

"Yeah, but I can be a cool mom. A biker mom. I don't want..." She sucked in a shuddery breath. "The doctor said we can't have sex after I give birth for six weeks."

"That's normal." Christ, after I gave birth, I didn't have sex for years, never mind weeks.

"Might be for regular women, but Nyx is..."

Reading between the lines, I rasped, "If Nyx cheats on you because you're healing, I will defend you in court if you chop off his dick."

A snicker escaped her. "Thanks, Rachel. I needed that laugh."

Though I smiled, I told her, "I mean it."

"Yeah, I know you do." She patted my shoulder before she leaned forward and awkwardly rested her elbows on her knees because her belly got in the way. "Everything's changing, Rachel. Nyx isn't killing pedos anymore, so the sex is helping control things, you know?"

Of all the things I'd expected to happen today, this conversation was *not* on my to-do list.

Even if I liked to stay in the dark, I knew Nyx's days of killing pedophiles was on hiatus.

Gnawing on the inside of my cheek, I thought about the first one he'd ever slaughtered, and much as I'd done back then, I appreciated the gray.

That was why I defended the gray.

Because nothing was black and white.

Nothing.

"When you have the baby," I spoke the words carefully, "Nyx will be looking after it too."

Reaching for some toilet paper, she blew her nose. "*Him*. I'm having a boy."

Pain twisted inside me. Sharp, unexpected. "Nyx will be looking after *him* too," was all I said.

"I guess."

"He'll be exhausted as much as you are, and there'll be things he'll have to do that will take his mind off the hunt. He's going to be a dad, Giulia. That's going to affect him.

"He values children too much. He'll value you above all other women as well because you'll give him what no one else has—a child. A family."

She caught my gaze with hers. "It wasn't—I didn't—"

I reached up and squeezed her hand. "You can say whatever you want." I shot her a smile. "Client-attorney privilege."

Humor gleamed in her eyes again before it slowly died. "I'd let him sleep with her if it helped him control his demons."

"You would?" I sputtered.

Slowly, Giulia nodded. "I'm surprised too. I didn't think love would be like this." She rubbed a hand over her chest. "It hurts, but it makes you want what's best for them, you know? I need him to be..." She paused, blew out a breath. "Nyx isn't the kind of guy who wears happiness well. So it isn't that I need him to be happy. I just need him to have a baseline."

"You're his baseline."

"Sex is his baseline. Don't get me wrong, I'm horny as fuck right now. I'm on him more than he's on me—" Well, privacy just flew out of the window. "—but after I give birth, that's going to have to stop.

"I'm just worried, I guess. She hit me on a sore spot, and it blindsided me. Not just about the weight, but about Nyx needing more than I could give him."

Shaking my head, I told her, "Giulia, I've known Nyx a lot longer than you have. I've seen him fuck his way through a lot of women. Sex is a constant. It never stopped his demons from clawing at him. Sex isn't enough for that.

"You have more than sex. I don't know what you have, to be fair. You're both lunatics, but you seem to mellow him. Maybe you're crazier than him so it means he has to be the rational one; I don't know, and it's not my place to. You have your dynamic, it works for you, so now you have to have faith in that."

"We didn't plan this kid," she rasped.

"You didn't have to. The second Nyx put his dick inside you without a wrap, I know he'd have been prepared for this to happen."

Giulia stared at me. "You're right."

I patted her hand. "I usually am."

*Parker:* Well?

*Rachel:* I don't want to talk about it.

*Parker:* When do you ever? Remember that time you didn't want to tell me you had to go in for a Pap smear?

*Rachel:* That was our first year working together, wasn't it?

*Parker:* Yes.

*Rachel:* Those were the days. When you weren't insufferable.

*Parker:* You love me as I am.

*Rachel:* Sigh.

*Parker:* Well?!!!! Don't you dare leave me in suspense. Just because I'm in freakin' Pennsylvania does not mean I won't drive over and comb through your trash to find the pregnancy test.

*Rachel:* You know how creepy that sounds?

*Parker:* I know your menstrual cycle, Rachel. How's that for creepy?

*Rachel:* We need to work on boundaries. :P

*Parker:* My point is, if I know your cycle, I should know when that cycle stops.

*Rachel:* Isn't it starting?

*Parker:* No. It's stopping. If you're pregnant that is.

*Rachel:* I am.

*Parker:* Jesus, Mary, and Joseph.

*Rachel:* Reassuring.

*Parker:* Invoking them might get us through the next couple months of your first trimester. Honey, you're too busy to be pregnant.

*Rachel:* I know.

*Parker:* Damn.

*Rachel:* Yeah.
*Parker:* How are you feeling?
*Rachel:* Nauseated.
*Parker:* Saltines.
*Rachel:* I hate those.
*Parker:* I know. We all do, but they're a literal gift from God.
*Rachel:* Dramatic.
*Parker:* Eat them. I'm going to have to change your food order too. You don't eat enough.
*Rachel:* No, leave it as is. I'll be fine.
*Parker:* Shall I schedule you in with your OB/GYN?
*Rachel:* Leave it for now.
*Parker:* You need to make an appointment.
*Rachel:* Parker! I know you're trying to help, but I really just need to think about this.
*Parker:* Are you going to have an abortion?
*Rachel:* No.
*Parker:* Well, then.
*Rachel:* Just let me process it. Give me Christmas to figure things out.
*Parker:* Babies wait for no man. Or woman, I suppose.
*Rachel:* Trust me. I know.
*Parker:* Might just be what you and Rex need.
*Rachel:* How do you know he's the father?
*Parker:* Honey, that might be the funniest thing you've ever said to me.

# EIGHT

## REX

Rachel jumped when she flicked on the kitchen light and found me sitting there. Her brow puckered as she stepped over to the table.

"Jesus, Rex, you surprised me! What are you doing sitting in the dark?"

On any other night, I'd have logged the memory of her scent drifting toward me, her tired eyes, soft and warm if astonished, latching onto mine as she approached me in nothing more than a strappy cami and a pair of sleep shorts.

But this *was* tonight.

The night my father had asked me to help him rejoin my mother.

I wanted to scream that it wasn't fair, but I'd long since left my teen years behind. Naïveté was something that had drifted away before I hit eleven. I *knew* life wasn't fair. Had witnessed its inequalities with my own goddamn eyes, but this situation was somehow worse than all the shit I'd seen and done.

"Have you eaten?"

It took me a second to realize she'd spoken to me, and I just stared at her.

Did it make me fucking weak that the question filled me with despair? Hopelessness?

What was the point of *anything*?

My dad had taught me that a man cherished his woman, that he worshiped her. What was a man supposed to do when his woman didn't want that from him?

"Rex? What is it? What's wrong?"

Bitterly, I asked, "That's it, then? We're just going to act like we haven't been arguing?"

"We argue. It's what we do."

That wasn't much consolation.

Her frown deepened when I didn't answer as she rounded the table then stood at my side. I wanted, so fucking badly, to push my head into her stomach, to have her hands—

I closed my eyes.

That wasn't to be.

That wasn't how we worked.

The softest brush of her fingers drifted along my cheekbone, and when I felt them grazing a couple strands of hair away from my forehead, tucking them behind my ear, I turned my face into her hand.

That she touched me at all was a testament to how shitty I must have looked.

"You going to do a Storm?"

I didn't open my eyes. "Huh?"

"Your hair. You going to grow it out?"

"It needs cutting."

She hummed then surprised me by admitting, "It suits you." I didn't believe her. "But I always did like you with short hair." I didn't say anything, but after a good long while, she asked, "Bear?"

I nodded.

My whole body ached with incoming grief, but tears had no place here.

"Bad news?"

How the hell did I answer that?

Inside, words churned around in my head, but she wasn't my girl anymore.

Even if she'd always be that to me, now, she was the club's lawyer.

She was Rachel Laker.

DAs feared her, judges dreaded her appearing before their benches, and my ragtag bunch of outlaws actually fucking listened to her.

The reminder had me settling on what we did best: *business*.

"Plausible deniability."

Her fingers stopped their stroking at our code word.

Where she knew not to ask for more information less it mess with her ability to defend me in court.

I wanted her to be my Rach. To help me through this fuckfest, but we'd gone past that years ago.

So many fucking years ago.

The thought had me pulling away from her touch and shoving the chair back to give me some distance.

The ache for her hadn't gone anywhere. It never had. But I wasn't the one who'd broken us. I wasn't the one who'd pushed us apart.

So I sucked in a breath, logged my lungs down with air, then strode over to the fridge.

It was on the tip of my tongue to tell her that I'd be moving out and returning to the clubhouse over the next week, but I didn't.

Instead, I reached into the refrigerator and snagged a box of takeout and started to eat cold General Tso's chicken.

It tasted like shit.

"Rex?"

I didn't look up at her. "Yeah?" I snatched another sticky piece of chicken with my fingers then chowed it down.

"Look at me."

"Why?"

"What kind of question is that?"

"A valid one. What do you want me to look at? The sleep shorts that show your ass off or the way that camisole clings to your tits?"

They were things I'd never have said at any other time.

But this wasn't *any other* time.

This was the night my dad had asked me to assist his suicide.

My throat closed even as I registered the hissed intake of her breath.

"It doesn't..." Her words waned. "I didn't come down here to tease you."

"You breathe and you tease me, Rachel." I finally cast her a glance. "Ain't you figured that out yet, babe?"

Her nostrils flared, but there was no glee or smug satisfaction in her eyes. Just like I knew there wouldn't be. My girl was broken, had been for nearly two decades.

"When you look at me like that, you remind me of the first time I went into the basement and found you down there."

Her shoulders straightened. "What?"

Leaning back against the counter, I stuck my sticky finger into my mouth and cleaned some of the goo off it before I said, "You looked at me like I was going to attack you."

"I didn't," she scoffed.

"You did. I knew then someone had touched you."

"They hadn't."

I settled my gaze on hers, let her feel the weight of it. Let her feel the command.

I might not have been her Prez, but I *was* her King.

She knew what that look meant because her breath hitched. "Things had happened that I shouldn't have seen or experienced," she reasoned woodenly. "But no one had touched me."

"That supposed to make it better?"

If I could have killed her mom again, I would have.

"No," she said softly. "It isn't."

"Good, because it didn't work." I turned away from her and retreated into the fridge once more. Snagging a bottle of beer, settling on that instead of the JD I wished I could savor intravenously, I stated, "Not sure you came down here to reminisce about the bad times."

She flinched. "They weren't all bad."

My lips quirked up in a half smile. "Good to know."

"I wanted to make some tea. But... *is* it Bear?"

I took a deep sip of beer then dipped my chin in assent.

"Why do I need plausible deniability?"

"Me explaining would break the terms of that, now wouldn't it?"

She strode forward, her hand snagging the beer out of mine before she growled, "This is Bear, Rex. Bear. Plausible deniability, my ass. You tell me what the hell is going on."

"You were always scared of him when you were growing up. What changed?"

Her mouth tightened. "I was scared he'd throw me out. When Mom left, Axel needed me to look after Rain. I didn't have to worry about being thrown out, and I saw how he was with you. He was a great dad."

Whatever she might have said, I didn't think it'd be that.

I half-wheezed, "You can't seriously think he'd have thrown you out?"

Her gaze was steady. Measured. *She meant it.* She really fucking imagined that I'd have *let* him do that. "The word irrational exists for a reason."

"I guess it does." I reached out to tuck a strand of gleaming dark red hair behind her ear. "I'd never have let him kick you out."

Rach swallowed. "I think I knew that, but I still didn't want to make a bad impression."

Brain whirring with the repercussions of that, I told her, "Your place is with us." I wanted to say with me, but she didn't want to hear that. "Always with us. No matter where you fly off to for those charity cases—" I settled a tight smile on her, so she knew I knew her 'charity cases' were bullshit. "—this will always be your home."

"Your name's on the land registry," she rasped, showing no surprise at me calling her out.

"Your name's on the deed of this house." I snagged my Bud back from her. "Plus, you're my lawyer. Can I hire you to toss yourself off the lot?"

She didn't smile. "This is a moot point."

"Is it? Your place is here, Rachel," I intoned grimly, unsure why I wanted to ram this home, just needing to do it anyway. "Always here."

Neither of us broke the silence that fell, a surprising silence.

I should have known that she'd be the one who'd get my mind off this evening. She was the only one who could do that. Who could hold my whole focus.

With her eyes on mine, I swore the rest of the world stopped turning.

I didn't give a fuck about Nyx and his likelihood that he'd go off the rails, or the fact my dad had asked me to help him reunite with my mom. I didn't think about Mav's CTE or that there was a potential FBI plant floating around West Orange or that my mom had been murdered by the Sparrows.

She was all I saw.

All I felt.

She always had been.

"Tell me what's going on with Bear," she whispered after a while that could have lasted minutes or hours.

"You don't want to know," I said, and I meant it.

Rach watched me take another sip of beer. "I think we both know that I do."

Mouth tight, I bowed my head. "He woke up."

"He did?"

I felt her excitement and almost hated to squash it. "Not for long." I swallowed. "Just long enough to tell me he needed Mom."

A soft sigh escaped her. "He loved her so much."

"He did." She didn't get what I was saying, and who could blame her for missing the point? So I spelled it out, "He wants me to help him be with her again."

Her loose stance turned taut. Her back straightened like she'd been lashed, and the pain in her eyes matched it. But somehow, while it might have stunned the hell out of me, it hadn't shocked her.

It hurt her.

It didn't stun her.

"Nyx?"

Recognizing Hawk's voice coming from the hallway, I kept my glance fixated on Rachel's as I called out, "Hawk? I'm in the kitchen."

She shuffled away, heading to the kettle she had sitting on the stove. The tread of heavy steps sounded down the hall as I watched her fill it up and set it on the burner.

"It's okay, Rex. I wanted to speak with Nyx."

Knowing my VP had gone to hang out with Giulia in the den they camped out in here, I asked, "What is it? I'll deal with it."

"You sure?"

I grunted. "I'm the fucking Prez. Of course I'm sure."

"Nyx said to leave you alone." He shrugged. "But if you're okay with it—"

I knew I'd been out of it because of Dad, but his hesitation still pissed me off. "Get on with it, Hawk. What's wrong? Why are you here so late?"

"Think we have a problem down at the strip club."

Rachel frowned. "What kind of problem? Drugs?"

I saw Rach, *my goddamn girl*, drift away to be replaced with Rachel Laker. I could almost imagine a theme song starting up around her.

Rachel Laker, attorney-at-law, licensed to defend.

I almost smiled, but instead I asked quietly, "Inked?"

He nodded.

"Inked? The brother who works the bar?"

"He's on the take," I informed her.

She whistled under her breath. "The man's an idiot."

"He is."

My flat response had her mouth tightening. "I don't need to hear this conversation."

"You don't," I agreed, so I stepped toward Hawk and shuffled over to the dining room that Rachel was letting me work out of. As he moved inside, I turned back to look at her and rasped, "Rach?"

"Yeah?"

Her beautiful hair gleamed burgundy in the under-cabinet-lights, and the desire to stroke that silk made my hands curl into fists.

Her eyes were wide as she looked at me in question, and it drew my attention to the expressive arch of her brow, the high curve of her cheeks, and the soft pout of lips I wanted to taste.

Fuck, she was pretty.

Unable to utter the words I wanted to, I just said, "Happy belated birthday, Rach. I'm sorry for forgetting."

She swallowed. "Thank you for the gift. It came this morning."

*Better late than never.*

Shooting her a tight smile, silently, I headed into the office, seeing that Hawk had hit the lights.

I walked over to the table I was using as a desk, aware that Hawk was hovering, and I sat my ass down behind it.

"What news do you have for me?"

"It was Rachel's birthday?"

I blinked. "Yes."

"There wasn't a party—"

"There never is. Rachel doesn't celebrate."

He frowned. "Celebrate birthdays?"

I wished that were the only thing on her shit list. But it wasn't. Rachel didn't celebrate anything. Period. Case in point the lack of a turkey and all the trimmings in the refrigerator.

Ignoring him, I demanded, "Show me what you got."

Shrugging, Hawk shoved his hands in his pockets, left one there, but dragged out his cell phone from the other. A few swipes on the screen and he passed it over to me.

Staring at the video, I watched as Inked took an order, didn't ring it up, took the cash, then pocketed it.

Simple.

Without a word, I sent the video to my phone, then as it buzzed, let Hawk's slide back across the table to him and picked mine up. Within seconds, the video had been shared to the group chat I had with the council.

It wasn't just late, it was Christmas fucking Eve so I didn't expect much of a response at this hour, but I turned off the sound anyway.

"Thanks, Hawk. Good job."

He dismissed my praise with a shrug. "Should have gotten you proof sooner."

"No, I told you to be discreet. I was fine to wait."

His glance was confused, but that was okay. I preferred to be patient, preferred to understand what was going on behind the scenes before I acted rashly.

"Go home. Merry Christmas."

Hawk's grin was sheepish. "Thanks, Rex. Appreciate that and appreciate you getting me the time off tomorrow."

I shrugged. "There'll be more guards soon. You won't be spread so thin."

"That my Christmas gift?"

Snorting, I told him, "Yeah. Santa thinks you've been nice. Go on, get out of here."

As he departed, I stared at nothing in particular, trying to organize my thoughts, but in the face of Dad's request, this petty thievery was... nonsense.

Scratching a hand over my beard, I ignored the few texts that had trickled in from councilors who were awake and connected a call to Lodestar.

"'Sup?"

"Got a hypothetical for you."

"This about Inked?"

I grunted under my breath. "Whose phone have you hijacked?"

She sniffed. "Look, I retrieved my malware from your cell. You never said anything about the council text chat, and dude, you should be asking me to up the security on that, not bitching about me getting inside. Maverick's OS is tight, but it could do with some tweaks—"

"Lodestar, this isn't about Inked."

Silence.

"Oh. Shit. I gave that away."

I rolled my eyes at nothing then muttered, "Make the tweaks. Do whatever you have to do to make the lines of communication secure."

"And kick myself out of the chat afterward?"

Pondering that, I murmured, "You know we'd kill you if you turned us in."

"You'd have to catch me first," she pointed out, "but I'm loyal to the Sinners. You don't have to worry about me turning rat."

"I didn't think I had to, but I was just confirming it." More like ramming home her impending death if she betrayed us.

"So, don't kick myself out of the chat?"

"No." I sighed heavily. "I need... advice."

"I already looked into Inked's bank accounts. Whatever he's stealing, he must be snorting or injecting because it's not padding—"

"Star, dammit, it isn't about Inked," I snapped.

"Huh. Okay, Mr. Grouch. What is it?"

"How do you... kill someone and make it look like a natural cause?"

"I'm going to assume this isn't hypothetical, even if you said it was before?"

"No."

She fell quiet, but I heard the tapping of her fingers against the keys.

A part of me thought she wasn't concentrating, but I knew how her brain worked. The past six months had given me an insight into the fucked-up majesty that was the interior of her skull. I didn't try to understand its inner workings, was just grateful she was on my side and not an enemy.

After a good minute of silence though, I grumbled, "Star? Is this a busy time?"

"No. Coding helps me think." She hesitated. "For Bear, right? Or someone else?"

"Does it matter?"

"Location matters."

She had a point.

"Yeah, it's Dad."

"I thought the prognosis was hopeful," she said warily.

"He's dying. Slowly."

Star hummed. "Okay. Air embolism. Triggers cardiac arrests and strokes. I know that he suffered a massive heart attack after the blast. It should look like natural causes that way."

My throat tightened. "How do I do…?"

"Get a needle, withdraw it, then push the air bubble into—" She broke off, hummed again, then asked, "Does he have an injection site? Or only an IV?"

My brow furrowed. "This sounds very James Bond. I need this to work, Lodestar. I don't want him to suffer—"

She stunned the hell out of me by rasping, "To live is to suffer, to die is to be at peace."

For a minute, silence settled between us, then I murmured, "Help me help him. Please."

"Speed. Into his IV line. It'll work fast and will trigger heart failure. With the state he's in, even if he's showing signs of improvement, a heart attack will fly under the radar. There won't be an autopsy," she predicted before hesitantly asking, "Rex?"

"What?"

"I'm sorry for your loss."

She cut the call before I could thank her.

Without her tapping in my ears, a welter of exhaustion hit me. Compounded by grief, I heaved a sigh and, feeling ancient, staggered to my feet.

As I headed to the door, her advice whirled inside my head like

I'd taken a tab of LSD and it was sending me into a deep, dark, bad trip.

A part of me hoped that Rachel would have waited for me, that she'd be the light at the end of the tunnel, that she'd be sitting at the kitchen table with her usual glower, but when I left the dining room, the kitchen was just as dark as my thoughts.

Scrubbing a hand over my face, wishing shit were different for us, wishing things had been different for my folks, I made my way to my bedroom.

I didn't bother taking off my clothes, just shrugged out of my cut then flopped on top of the covers.

The second my head hit the pillow, I was graced with one blessing.

I slept.

# NINE

## NYX

**Unknown Sender:** *You should reconsider your decision.*
**Me:** *I don't deal with the 'unknown.'*
**Unknown Sender:** *My identity will be revealed upon our initial meeting.*
**Me:** *Yeah, I don't think so. This stinks of a setup by the pigs. Oink off, motherfucker.*

Irritated, I shoved my phone into my pocket and edged into the downstairs living room that we'd claimed early on after moving into Rachel's place.

The house was fucking massive, and she hadn't bitched about it, so I didn't feel guilty for stealing it.

I had to admit though—I was getting used to all this space and privacy. Enough that I'd fucking miss it when we moved back into the clubhouse.

Closing the door behind me and seeing her on the sofa, something inside me settled.

Giulia was a handful, a precocious pain in the ass who caused more trouble than a pixie on acid, but she lit my world up. Made me want more than to exist.

The moment I took a seat on the sofa, I hauled her onto my lap.

"Hey! I was comfortable," she groused.

I snorted at the lie. "Bullshit."

"How's that bullshit?"

"You're never comfortable now."

She blinked at me. "You have a point, and I'm not happy about it. You owe me."

"How do I owe you?"

"For stretch marks and backaches and constantly needing to use the bathroom."

"What stretch marks?" I scoffed.

Her eyes narrowed as she tilted her head back to glower at me. As suspected, she lifted her top up. "See?"

I peered over her admittedly big belly, grimacing when I realized I'd seen my mom's double in size. If she thought she was big now, she didn't have a clue what was coming.

Christ, she *was* uncomfortable all the time as well.

That was only going to get worse.

Guilt hitting me, I determined to make it as easy on her as possible. I slipped my hands higher and grabbed a firm hold of her tits. "That's all I can see." It was only half a lie.

Fuck, she was hot.

My dick ached from the sight of her alone.

She elbowed me in the abs. "Jerk." Then she squirmed against my lap.

Burying my face against her throat, I rumbled, "You like it when I'm a jerk."

"I like it when you *jerk* something," she agreed, wriggling some more as my dick became a more, shall we say, solid presence against her hip.

Nipping her throat, I licked the place I bit then told her, "You're gorgeous."

Squeezing her tits again, I let one drift down over the curve of her stomach. The skin was so taut that I knew it had to be discomforting.

Sometimes, when she thought no one was looking, she scratched the skin, but I noticed everything about her.

That's why, tonight, I'd come armed.

Letting go of her tit, I snagged the tube of cream I'd bought her. I had no idea why it cost fifty fucking dollars a fluid ounce, but with how the clerk had amped it up, I thought it had diamonds in it.

She stiffened when she saw what I had, then, the second I splatted some on her belly, she groaned as I rubbed it in.

"I really shouldn't let you do that," she panted.

"Why not? I did the crime; I should do the time."

That had her snorting. "You're so matter-of-fact about this stuff."

I shrugged as I smoothed the cream into her taut skin. It still fucked with my head that there was a kid inside her. This was Giulia. She already packed enough punch when there was just one of her, never mind two.

"Why shouldn't I be?"

"Oh, you know, because I'm gross?"

I sniffed. "Says who?"

"Me."

"You feel that boner?"

"Yeah."

"You can think you're gross, but me and it are in complete agreement."

"That I'm fuckable?"

I heard some amusement edging out the concern. "You're more than fuckable."

She groaned as I smoothed my hands along her side, flicking the edges of her tits.

"These sore today?"

"No. And you should have asked me that before you squeezed them earlier."

"True." I grinned. "I should have realized when you didn't knee me in the balls."

She sighed as I rubbed her tits too. It was less massage and more aftercare. Like I said—I'd done the crime. Not that my kid *was* a crime. But the havoc it was wreaking on the love of my life was crazy.

I pressed a kiss to the side of her cheek and mumbled, "You're fucking beautiful."

"I'm fat."

"Maybe, but you're beautiful."

She chuckled. "You're not supposed to say 'maybe.'"

"Damned if I do and damned if I don't," I joked as I teased her nipples which were bra-free for once. I figured that was because we usually ended up falling asleep on the sofa as we watched a movie.

This living-in-a-house shit was kinda cool.

We'd lived out of my room before the explosion, so we didn't have much personal space. Now, with the return to the compound imminent, I wasn't looking forward to it as much as I had been.

I'd lost all my shit in the blast.

Everything I fucking owned.

I had plenty of cash, so it wasn't the material crap I'd lost but the personal stuff that pissed me off.

Mostly photos, but I'd had a dreamcatcher my Native American grandmother had made me for my firstborn.

At the time, I'd never imagined having kids, but here this one was and the fucking dreamcatcher was in the wind.

"How do you feel about getting our own place?" I asked her softly.

She tilted her head back to look up at me. "That's what you're thinking about when you're manhandling my tits?"

"I'm capable of multitasking."

"Thinking and copping a feel? You're proof of the next evolutionary step."

My lips twitched. "I swear your snark upped a notch since you started baking this kid."

"I'll sit on your bladder for the next nine months and you tell me you're not snarky." She harrumphed. "Anyway, our own place? Won't you miss the clubhouse?"

The tension that throbbed through her might have been minute.

To anyone else, it might not have been noticeable.

To me, it was a massive red flag.

"I'll miss it, sure."

"Then why move out?"

"I'll miss this too."

"What? Teasing my tits on the sofa?"

I laughed. "Yeah. Personal space. It's nice."

"I know what you mean. Do you think we could have one of the bunkhouses? That'd be close enough for you to still feel like you were a part of things, wouldn't it?"

"We can live in town if you want to."

She shook her head. "You need to be there. I get it, Nyx."

My brow furrowed. "I think I just said the opposite." Or was I speaking Japanese and didn't realize it?

"I don't think it'd be wise for you to be away from the MC."

Even more confused than before, I told her, "I ain't glued to the fucking place, Giules. I can deal with a ten-minute ride to get there. When the kid comes, living out of one room won't be ideal anyway, and I wouldn't feel comfortable having sex when the baby was there."

"Is that why you want to move?"

"No," I retorted, but I grinned. "It's *one* of the reasons why."

"Uh huh, with that topping the list, I'll bet. Could we build on the compound?"

I shrugged. "Why the fuck would you want to? Bikes coming in at all times of the day or night sounds like a nightmare when you've got a baby it took four hours to get to sleep."

She'd never had baby brothers and sisters; well, *I* had.

"How about behind this place? That's still Sinner land, isn't it?"

"It is. Far away enough that you get some peace, close enough that I could walk if I wanted to."

"You really mean this?"

"Don't see why not. Look, if you want to live out of one room, we can until the kid needs his own space or whatever. I don't even remember how long that'll be. Six months?"

"Do you think they're ready to move out when they're toddlers? Parenthood's gonna be an eye-opener for you, my man."

I squeezed her tits. "Cut the snark, babe. I'm being serious."

"I know." She peeped up at me, looking, Christ, vulnerable.

I didn't get what the problem was.

Trying to understand Giulia, sometimes, was like attempting to maneuver around a labyrinth blindfolded.

"I'm talking about moving in with you. You did get that part, didn't you?" I clarified, wondering what was being lost in translation.

"Duh." Giulia huffed. "I'm just worried that it'll send you spiraling."

"The brothers don't keep me in line."

"They do," she derided.

"They *used* to." I gave her tits another squeeze. "You and the kid do that now."

"You gonna always call it 'the kid?'"

"Don't see why not."

She sniffled. "I know you miss the hunt."

"Sure I do."

A lot.

Some days, it was a fucking ache in my soul. The need to avenge the innocent was as solid a craving as the need to lose myself in Giulia's pussy. *But* I wasn't the man I used to be.

I had responsibilities.

I had a duty to Giulia and this kid and Indy, but also the MC.

She peered back at me again. "That's all you're going to say about it?"

"There's not much to say. We both know it's difficult for me not to..." I blew out a breath. "Planning helped," I said wistfully.

"I know, baby." She twisted to press her lips to my jaw. "I wish I could make it better for you."

"You do," was my soft retort. "More than you know." I rubbed my mouth against hers a couple times, but before things devolved and I ended up fucking her on my lap, I muttered, "You seen that kid hanging around the compound?"

Giulia tensed. "Kid?"

"He's in his twenties."

"You're gonna need a new noun. A kid can't be both our baby and a twenty-year-old dude."

She had a point.

Grinning, I informed her, "I hunted the pedophile who killed his sister."

Her eyes rounded. "Jesus! Talk about burying the lede, Nyx!"

"Nah. No lede to be buried."

"What's he doing here?"

"Wants to take part in the hunt."

She frowned. "He knows about you?"

"Apparently."

"That's bad, ain't it?"

"Very bad."

"Why don't you sound worried?"

"I'm not. Everyone else is, but not me."

"How come?"

"Because our sisters were both victims. Ain't no way in hell, no matter if you're a sinner or a saint, you're going to turn evidence over to the state against the man who took care of the bastard behind her death."

"You don't know that."

"I do."

She gulped and was clearly worried enough that she twisted around on my lap. Her thighs straddled me as her ass settled on my knees. Hands to my shoulders, she breathed, "This is a problem."

"It isn't." Staring down at her big belly, I rasped, "I'd tell you if it was. I'd want you to be prepared. But I'm really not worried.

"If I were, do you think I'd be talking to you about it? If I were, do you think he'd be hanging out around the compound?

"I made a promise to Indy that I wouldn't go to jail. That I'd be there for the kid. *But* killing any fucker who tried to stop that from happening wouldn't be reneging on that promise. It'd be protecting it."

She licked her lips. "Maybe you still should—"

"I'll monitor the situation. As of right now, I see a kid who's breaking. Who wants to make a difference but doesn't know how to. I do."

"You want to help him," she whispered, her eyes wide.

With her curls tossed around her shoulders, her beautiful face puckered in concern for me, her belly out, and her tits almost in view too, I already knew I was looking at my soul mate.

That night she'd come back to West Orange was my lucky fucking week.

If she thought I'd ever do *anything* to jeopardize my good fortune, she was insane.

Okay, well, she was already insane, but... I knew what I meant.

"I do want to help him," I confirmed.

"Do the others?"

I shrugged. "Not really. They're mostly concerned about him going to the Feds. That's what he's using as leverage. He ain't saying it, but it's clear he's trying to make that his bargaining chip."

"So why the fuck aren't you worried?"

I smirked. "He shouldn't play fucking poker."

"Can't bluff?"

"No. Not for shit." I patted her belly. "This is our future we're talking about though, and I'm not enough of a moron to make these decisions without your input."

Her throat bobbed. "You mean that?"

"I do."

She let out a cry and her arms flung around my neck. Her mouth glued itself to mine, and even though I wanted to finish this conversation, I didn't even try to.

Her tongue thrust into my mouth and she grabbed my hands and shoved them back to her tits as she started grinding into me.

Her own fingers delved between us, releasing my cock which—no matter the topic—was always hard as a pike when she was semi-naked around me.

The second she grabbed it, I hissed into her lips as she jacked me off.

Her hold was rougher than usual.

The piercings didn't hurt, but with a bad handjob, they *could*.

The way she jerked me off was enough to have me squirming as a dash of pain tainted my pleasure.

Red flashed behind my eyes as she pinched the tip, her thumb finding the divot where pre-cum was flooding from my cock.

Because all she wore was an oversized tee and a pair of panties, access was easy. I left one hand to tease her nipple, with the other slipping between her legs. I thrust a finger between her folds over the crotch, and she growled into my lips, spreading her thighs wider as she drifted further up my lap.

I tugged one side of the panties away, letting my thumb rub her clit, and wasn't surprised when she hurriedly arched up then sank down on my dick.

The moment her softness conceded defeat to my hardness, we both groaned into each other's mouths.

I felt every single piercing rub against her tender pussy, and she whimpered as she made tiny rocking motions that made sure she'd take every inch.

The Jacob's ladder wasn't much of a measuring system now, more like a competitive chart that Giulia always wanted to beat.

I wasn't about to complain about her 'die-trying' attitude.

When she bottomed out, she pulled back and nipped my lip. Her teeth clamped down on it, tugging it away from mine as she gnawed on it like a dog with a bone.

When she angled up again and started to ride me, she let go and laved it with her tongue, digging into the minute grooves she made.

I let my hands drop to her ass, and fingers digging into her cheeks, I encouraged her to ride me.

A growl escaped her as I started to pound into her from below, and she moaned, head falling back.

I could no more ignore that offering than I could hold back a grunt as pleasure bolted through my veins.

Reaching up, I started to kiss her neck. Finding all the spots I knew that got her hot, sucking and tasting and teasing as I nipped and did everything I fucking could to make her melt.

I knew before she did when she was about to come.

But I didn't just tease her—I gave her back what she'd given to me.

I bit down, hard.

Hard enough that she squealed.

Hard enough that she froze.

Hard enough that, when she detonated around my cock, it stunned the fuck out of both of us.

Quickly, I sped up too and groaned out my own release as her pussy went mad around me.

As she dragged every drop of cum from my balls, it was only then that I let go.

When I did, I saw…

Jesus.

I pulled back in shock, and her eyes were dazed as she took me in.

Her thumb moved to my lips, and she gently rimmed my mouth with her nail. Before I could even think to apologize, she leaned over and let her tongue take the same path as her thumb had.

"That's new," she whispered, licking her lips.

Staring at the smeared scarlet residue, I rasped, "I'm so fucking sor—"

She didn't let me finish. "Don't be."

"I made you bleed—"

"And you made me come harder than ever." She squeezed down on me. "That was fucking electric."

It was, but I'd made her bleed.

God help me—

"Shh," she chided. Her hand cupped my chin now. "I'd have stopped you if I wanted to. Instead…" She purred, repeating, "That was electric."

When she flopped to the side, I caught her, and I realized she was addled.

Whether it was endorphins or hormones, I didn't fucking know. But I urged her to rest against me. It was awkward because of her belly, but I made it work.

How long she lay there like that, I didn't fucking know, but I stared up at the ceiling, wondering what in the hell kind of animal I was that I could do that to her.

"Stop thinking. It's too noisy," she grumbled a while later.

"I'm sorry, baby."

"Don't be." Blinking at me as she pulled back, she muttered, "I want you to do that again when it's healed."

My mouth rounded. "Are you crazy?"

She smirked. "You know the answer to that already." Her hand came to my mouth again and she pressed a finger to my lips to quiet me. "You want to build a place, we'll build a place. You want to move onto the compound, we'll move onto the compound. You want to train this kid, you train him. Whatever makes you happy makes me happy. You got that?"

I swallowed, staring at the bruised, broken flesh. "I do."

"Good." She tapped my mouth. "Next time you bite, do that again. You got that too?"

Uneasily, I shook my head, but her finger moved with the motion.

"Nyx?" Her eyes flashed at me. "Do I look like I'm afraid of you?"

Nostrils flaring, I bit off, "No."

"Then listen to me. I was more scared of your dick the first time I saw it than I am of your love bite." Her lips twisted as she darted forward and kissed me again.

I had no idea what I'd done to deserve this woman. Whether it was the Catholic or Muslim God or the gods that Quin believed in, I knew that someone, somewhere, was watching over me the day they'd set her on my path.

I'd do anything to keep her safe.

Anything.

She thought she knew that—but she didn't.

She really fucking didn't.

"You gonna tell me what's had you crying these past couple of days?" I rumbled against her mouth.

Giulia heaved a sigh. "It doesn't matter."

That meant it did.

Fucking women.

"Need me to bite you again to get it out of you?"

She let loose a soft laugh. "I'd be a moron to say no to that type of persuasion, wouldn't I?"

# TEN

## RACHEL
### ISAAC - MADONNA

I tugged the blanket higher around my shoulders as I sank into the armchair in my bedroom.

Reaching for the tea I'd placed on the stand beside me, which I'd perched next to the leather box Rex had given me for my birthday, I took a sip as I flicked through the channels, finally settling on an episode of *90 Day Fiancé*, but I couldn't focus on it.

This morning, I'd woken up to the belated birthday gift outside my door.

Tucked in the card, there'd been an explanation that it was a memory box.

Memories... They were what goddamn plagued me.

Gaze drifting from the box, I peered out onto the pitch-black hill ahead of me. Spying the city lights in the distance, I watched a couple of cars moving here and there, and I tried to find comfort in the humdrum.

*It didn't work.*

Everything was changing.

This year, more than any other, I'd been feeling the passage of time, and that was before I'd learned I was pregnant and that Bear had asked Rex to help him die.

Rain was graduating, he'd be heading out into the big, bad world, and I'd be left here.

Alone.

Watching Rex from a distance.

Wishing things were different.

Knowing they couldn't be.

Until today, I'd thought about moving into the city.

My NGO work often had me heading into New York City, never mind the clients I had that were incapable of keeping themselves out of trouble.

But another baby…

Even if I knew I shouldn't be a mother, I was point blank incapable of giving up another child.

I tried to let the infusion of chamomile soothe me, but it wasn't a magical potion and couldn't wipe the slate clean—if only it could.

"Change isn't always a bad thing, Rachel," Axel, my stepdad, used to tell me when I was younger.

He wasn't wrong, but neither was he right.

These types of changes were *never* good.

Staring out onto West Orange, an urge hit me.

It wasn't an odd one. Since Rex had moved into my house, I often fought this particular desire, but tonight, it was harder to battle.

Harder to stay here.

Harder to ignore.

Making sure both my private and business cellphones were switched off—it was goddamn Christmas Eve; my clients and the few friends I had could wait until tomorrow if there was a problem—I drifted to my feet as that urge continued plaguing me. Like an itch I couldn't stop myself from scratching.

I headed downstairs, my destination the dining room. Only, it was in the dark—Rex wasn't there.

Checking out the other rooms on the first floor, I saw they were also empty apart from one of the dens where Nyx and Giulia were doing only God knew what. They were quiet though. The TV was on, its lights flickering beneath the door, but it wasn't blaring, so I left them to it.

On any other day, I'd have taken this as a sign. I'd have gone into my office and used work to push the thoughts away, to shove my need aside, but this *was* today.

I returned upstairs and headed for his room.

Knocking on the door heralded nothing, and while I could tell there were no lights on, I pushed it open anyway.

As quietly as a mouse, I closed the door with the faintest snick then padded into the room before I took in the lay of the land.

His breathing was heavy enough that I knew he was sleeping, so I shuffled over to the bed, knowing he'd be on the side nearest to the door, and I climbed on top of it with him.

He didn't stir, which spoke of his exhaustion, and I sighed as the scent of him hit me hard.

Every drop of air I inhaled smelled of him, and his warmth leached into me, filling me with him in a way that had me curling onto my side and snuggling close.

We'd not often slept together.

Not like this.

Not for years, either.

God, it felt good.

So good.

He stirred on the sheets when I pressed my face against his arm and breathed, "Rachel."

It wasn't a question.

Wasn't even a statement.

It was a soft sigh.

A sleepy one.

I closed my eyes, rubbed my nose against his flannel-covered bicep, and wished that things were different. Wished that I weren't me. Wished that I—

Clenching my teeth a second, I forced myself to relax and whispered, "I'm here, Rex. I'm here."

He didn't answer.

Why would he?

He was fast asleep.

He needed the rest too, so I didn't disturb him.

I just lay there.

For hours.

Thoughts crawled sluggishly through my mind, tumbling one after another, tiring me out but not letting me sleep.

Minutes or hours later, I heard Nyx and Giulia shushing each other as they climbed the stairs and returned to their bedroom.

When dawn began its approach, I heard Rain get up and the shower start in his bathroom. I even heard when he went downstairs and left for the job he had as a server at one of the local country clubs where he'd be waiting tables for the Christmas feast.

Once he'd left, the house was serene again.

When Rex finally awoke, I didn't bother moving. Not even when I felt him jolt in surprise at my presence here.

"Rachel?" he croaked tiredly.

I just hummed.

"What are you doing here?"

"Couldn't sleep."

He didn't answer, but moved his arm and I settled deeper into his warmth. Sighing as it leached into me, I whispered miserably, "I miss you."

"I miss you," he whispered back. But he didn't sound miserable. Just worn-out.

*So* worn-out.

Tears pricked my eyes, tears that only formed because I was exhausted too, and I nuzzled into him, seeking and giving comfort the only way I could.

"I miss 'my girl,'" he rasped. "I miss touching you without it being complicated. I miss the Rach who'd laugh and tell me I was an asshole instead of just looking at me like I'm crap on her shoes. I miss not being frozen out by you. I miss *you*."

I could have argued, but what was the point?

"I haven't been her for years," was all I said.

"No. You're in there. The real you is. She's just frozen. Encapsulated in ice. One day, I know you'll defrost. One day, I know you'll be back."

Something quickened inside me at his words, and it filled me with enough courage to ask, "Will you stick around for me?"

Breathless, I waited for his answer, but when he gave it to me, I cringed, deep inside.

"Always. I didn't leave, Rachel."

I gulped at his emphasis on the word 'I.'

Another time, another day, another week, I might have raged at him. Drowned him out with hissed words that left lacerations behind, but today, no. Not with Bear's impending death looming ahead of us. Not with the baby in my belly settling in for the duration.

"No," I admitted softly, "I know you didn't."

A sigh drifted from his lips as he pressed them to the crown of my head. It was only then that I realized he'd been braced for bitter words that would have burned like acid, and I sighed as, hesitantly, I placed my hand to his stomach and rested it there.

His was the only man's body I knew well. That I knew how to tease and how to taunt. How to torment and to tantalize. But approaching him was like approaching a lion and wondering if you'd get bitten. He might not maul me, but he could destroy me all the same.

My defenses, my walls, were barriers that protected me.

Not only from him, but from everyone.

The world.

"What's going on with you?" he asked as he tilted me into him so that I was leaning against him too and he could settle his chin on my head.

What the hell was I supposed to say to that?

How about the baby we'd given up for adoption years ago was turning seventeen in four days' time and, as a birthday present to myself, I found out I was pregnant again?

How about the fact his dad wanted to die?

How about Bear wanted Rex to do the job for him because he couldn't?

My tension levels were on the rise when he continued, "Jesus, something really is wrong. I expected you to jump off the bed and slap me, not start shivering in my arms, Rach."

I gritted my teeth. "I don't do violence."

"Liar," he taunted.

"That was one time."

He snorted. "Lies."

"I regretted it the second I did it."

"I didn't."

I blew out a breath. "I didn't—" I started again. "You shouldn't—"

"Stop stuttering."

Pissed, I jerked out of his arms and shoved him in the shoulder. "Don't be a dick."

"I'm just lying here," he retorted, his gaze calm. Much like it always was. "I'm not being a dick. And what was this about not being violent?" He rubbed his shoulder. "You pack a mean punch."

"Bullshit," I spat the word at him as I clambered off the bed and started pacing back and forth, well aware that his eyes were on every step I took.

My problem was that I liked being at the center of his attention.

My problem was that he was the only man who could ever get me mad, *and* who could calm me down.

"Why didn't you tell me about Kade Nunez?"

I jolted to a halt. "What?!"

Why in the hell was he asking me about the Long Beach Butcher now?

He folded his arms behind his head. "You heard me, Rach."

"I did, but I want to know why you're asking."

His focus was measured, but as I took him in, every inch of him, I wobbled.

Torn between the past and the future, stuck solidly in the present, I wasn't sure whether to stare at him or glare at him.

Mind reeling, I rubbed a hand over my face and muttered, "Why do you think?"

"Wouldn't be asking you if I knew, Rach."

I squinted at him. "It was an interesting case."

"And you take on every interesting case that comes your way?"

"Since we agreed, yes."

His mouth tightened at that, just a sliver. Enough that I knew he was still pissed at how I'd checkmated that agreement out of him.

He didn't like that I worked for anyone but the MC.

To be precise, *him*.

I refused to be controlled.

A compromise had been struck after I'd decided to be persuasive. Once I'd paid off my debt to the MC, I'd started making demands of my own, ones he'd eventually conceded to. That was when I'd started my charities and when I'd begun accepting clients who paid me partly in donations.

"Why are you asking about the Long Beach Butcher? That was last year."

He shrugged. "He's gotten himself a fiancée. It was in the *National Enquirer*."

Snorting, I countered, "Since when do you read the *National Enquirer*?"

"Something to do when I can't focus on work or a book. Those fucking beeps in the hospital ward are starting to get to me."

My throat tightened at that. "It's called alarm fatigue."

"I know." He yawned. "There's an interesting study about it. This ex-musician was in the ICU and she wanted to create a kind of —" Rex broke off to yawn again.

"You're tired," I pointed out unnecessarily.

"Not too tired to talk to you." He held out a hand. "No fighting. Not today."

Guilt speared me to the quick.

Arguing was my default. *Our* default. It made it easier to keep distance between us.

Bracing myself, I stepped over to him and slid my fingers into the clasp of his. The calluses on his palms should have been unattractive, but they weren't. I knew what they felt like against my body, knew what it felt like to have him brush the tips down my cheek.

I swallowed at the thought and swallowed again when he urged me onto the bed to lie by his side.

As he curled around me, I rolled back into him and let him take my weight.

God, that felt good.

I shuddered as his heat hit me once more and shivered when his hand moved over my stomach.

He had no way of knowing I was pregnant. No way whatsoever. But that he'd hold me *there*, that he'd unknowingly rest his hand against the place where his baby slept... God help me.

I closed my eyes as tears burned them.

"Will you ever tell me who hurt you?"

The words drifted into the silence of the room. Hell, not only the room, *the house*.

Much like everything that had happened in the last twelve or so hours, the answer I would ordinarily give him didn't match my response, "It'll serve no purpose."

His tension surged. "So, you finally admit that someone did?"

I let him take even more of my weight, let the flat of my feet press against his shins. I wished he weren't wearing jeans, so I could feel his body heat directly, but this was better than constantly feeling cold.

"A long time ago," I told him softly.

"You're my girl, Rachel," he rasped back. "Long time ago doesn't cut it. *Can't* cut it."

"You can't kill someone who's already dead," I pointed out blankly, careful with my phrasing.

His nostrils flared. "Was it brutal?"

I thought about the three men who'd hurt me and I smiled. "Yes."

He fell quiet again. "One day, when you're ready, I want answers."

"Maybe I don't want to give them to you." I didn't bother to tense up, not even when he growled under his breath.

For the first time, wrapped up like this, I was warm and comfortable enough to sleep.

For the first time, a gentle truth registered with me—I wouldn't need that gun under my pillow if he was in my bed.

It would be under his pillow.

And there'd be a knife somewhere too.

*He'd keep me safe.*

My eyelids blinked dazedly from exhaustion and I whispered, "Can we go to sleep now?"

"You'll have nightmares if we sleep like this."

"Won't," I mumbled, already half-asleep.

I didn't hear him say, softly, *sadly*, "Yes, baby, you will, and it'll fucking wreck me when you wake up."

## ELEVEN

## REX

It was heaven and hell having her in my bed, in my arms. Resting against me. Sleeping with me.

Heaven because skin to skin wasn't close enough for me with her.

Hell because on the rare occasions she allowed me to come this close, she always woke up in the throes of a nightmare that had her avoiding me for weeks afterward.

Sometimes, I was weak enough to deal with that. To try to sleep with her. Most times, I wasn't. I approached her in her office and we'd fuck, much like we'd done a while back.

A fast and fiery fuck didn't have her blanching whenever I approached. Didn't make her stilted with me. Didn't terrify the life out of her.

I'd never have said I was a selfless man, would have said I was the opposite, in fact. I believed that humans were selfish by their innate nature, and that it was normal to be self-serving, but Rachel proved otherwise.

Because of her, I was a different man. Not necessarily a better one, but a different one.

She was the only woman I wanted. The only woman I'd ever loved. *Would* ever love. But I stayed away because her mental health meant more to me than my happiness.

As she rested against me, sagging deeper and deeper into my hold as she relaxed, her body remembering me even if her mind flinched at my proximity, I knew I was too exhausted to cope with the ramifications of our talk.

It was the first time she'd ever admitted to me that somebody had hurt her.

When she said, 'a long time ago,' I didn't need to ask when.

I fucking knew.

Seventeen.

That was when she'd changed.

When my girl had morphed from an ethereal drifter into a brittle woman whose anger at the world was a mask for her fear, whose warmth had metamorphosed into ice.

I heard a buzz from the nightstand, and knowing from experience that she slept like the dead—one of the reasons her nightmares were so debilitating—I didn't worry about twisting back to reach for my cell.

My brows furrowed though when I read the text.

**Nyx:** *Lodestar's brought you a gift.*

**Rex:** *A gift?*

**Nyx:** *That's what I said. Or what she said to be precise.*

**Rex:** *What kind of gift?*

**Nyx:** *Don't think it's anthrax.*

**Rex:** *Reassuring.*

**Nyx:** *Thought we weren't doing Secret Santa this year?*

I grinned to myself. Nyx even knowing what Secret Santa was made me laugh every fucking time I thought about it.

**Rex:** *We aren't.*

**Nyx:** *Why's she giving you a gift then?*
**Rex:** *Dunno.*
**Nyx:** *Come down and see for yourself what it is.*
His nosiness had me fighting another grin.
**Rex:** *Can't.*
**Nyx:** *Why not?*
**Rex:** *Rachel's sleeping.*
**Nyx:** *She is?*
**Rex:** *Yes.*
**Nyx:** *With you?*
**Rex:** *Yeah.*
**Nyx:** *She sick?*

I'd have chuckled if he weren't fucking wrong. Rachel mostly came to me for work, but when she was sick, she tended to find her way to my office. I was pretty much the only person who could get her to go to the doctor's, *and* who could make her take basic OTC meds.

After her experiences, Rachel was not a fan of hospitals or doctors. Hell, even pharmacies didn't escape her ire.

**Nyx:** *She was okay yesterday when I saw her at church.*

I didn't want to go into any details, but I didn't want him thinking she was ill either.

**Rex:** *She's not sick.*
**Nyx:** *Good. BTW, Kendra's becoming a problem.*
**Rex:** *She's always a fucking problem.*
**Nyx:** *Worse than usual. She made Giulia cry last night. Took me a while to get it out of her, but Kendra's been spilling her poison for a while.*

My eyes bugged out at that.

**Rex:** *Giulia cried? I didn't even know she had tear ducts.*
**Nyx:** *She ain't a fucking robot.*

I mean, I didn't need to be told that. Nor did I think he'd appreciate me labeling his Old Lady as a fucking demon witch.

**Rex:** *She okay?*

Figured that was the safest question.

**Nyx:** *She cried, Rex. She fucking cried. My Old Lady cried because of a clubwhore cunt. I bite her and she doesn't cry, ffs.*

**Rex:** *Firstly, I don't need to know about your sex life. Secondly, you can't kill her.*

**Nyx:** *Didn't say I was going to kill her. Wanted it down in stone that if Kendra fucks with Giulia again, I'm throwing her out on her ass.*

**Rex:** *Affirmative.*

**Nyx:** *Good. You coming down to see what this gift Lodestar got you is?*

**Rex:** *No. I'm tired. Rach is too. We're going to get some rest.*

**Nyx:** *It's Christmas Day.*

**Rex:** *So? Merry Christmas?*

**Nyx:** *Fuck off.*

**Rex:** *Lol.*

**Nyx:** *It's Christmas Day, Rex. We're going to the clubhouse. Giulia has it all arranged.*

**Rex:** *Go ahead without me. I want to go to the hospital. Spend it with Dad.*

**Nyx:** *It won't be his last one, Rex. You know they said he's getting better.*

How could he be getting better when he was a shadow of his former self?

Maybe that was the bitterest of all the pills I'd have to swallow.

He'd live, but what kind of a life would it be?

Dad wasn't made to be tied down to a hospital bed.

That wasn't a life.

If he had to live without my mom, then I knew he'd spend it on the road. Much as he'd been doing since her death. Without his bike, stuck in a hospital room... I understood his request.

Understood it and would comply with it.

Even if it fucking hurt me.

**Rex:** *Nothing is certain. Didn't these past couple years teach us that?*

**Nyx:** *True.*

**Rex:** *What's happening with that Dresden kid?*

**Nyx:** *He's legit.*

**Rex:** *I know Harlow is Jessie's elder brother, but what's he want?*

**Nyx:** *To become my apprentice.*

Sighing, I nuzzled my chin against Rachel's shoulder. One-handed, I tapped out:

**Rex:** *You down for that?*

**Nyx:** *Rachel says I don't have a choice. If he figured out we had something to do with Haune's death, then we need to know how so we can plug the leak.*

**Rex:** *Before the Feds do?*

**Nyx:** *Exactly.*

**Nyx:** *Plus, he's me.*

**Rex:** *Worse for you.*

His uncle had gotten to both his kid and elder sisters, after all.

That sick fucking bastard.

A part of me worried that he'd hurt Rachel, but she'd changed at seventeen and Kevin had been long dead.

When he didn't reply, I continued:

**Rex:** *You okay with teaching him the ropes?*

**Nyx:** *He's gotta gain my trust first.*

**Rex:** *Makes sense.*

**Nyx:** *Need to make sure he's not a fucking rat.*

**Rex:** *You killed the man who abused his baby sister, Nyx. He ain't gonna turn you in.*

**Nyx:** *Could be one of those evangelical headcases.*

**Rex:** *Lol.*

I stared at the screen a second, and my cautious nature went to war with the solid truth that Nyx was *not* doing well without his hobby.

The promise his baby sister had extracted from him was slowly killing him.

Nyx needed to avenge his family. Indy didn't get it. I understood why she'd urged him to make the promise to stop with his pedo-hunting, but she didn't know that that was all that kept Nyx sane.

He had more responsibilities now, shit that kept him in line for most of the time, but he had to take out the trash.

It was a biological imperative at this point in his life.

**Rex:** *Think it'd be good for you.*

**Nyx:** *You do?*

**Rex:** *Yeah. It's an outlet, ain't it?*

**Nyx:** *Maybe.*

**Rex:** *Think about it.*

**Nyx:** *That's all I've been thinking about. I have to help him. We don't need the Feds looking over our shoulders.*

**Rex:** *Lodestar on it?*

**Nyx:** *Yeah. We're only on the ATF's radar right now.*

**Rex:** *Good to know. We have a run scheduled soon, don't we?*

**Nyx:** *Christ, you must be tired if you don't remember the schedule.*

**Rex:** *I am. I'm fucking exhausted. If we're on their radar, then maybe postpone it. Contact the O'Donnellys. Rearrange things, explain the situation.*

**Nyx:** *I'll set Sin on it. Tomorrow. Not sure if they'll appreciate us getting in touch today.*

**Rex:** *Why?*

**Nyx:** *It's Christmas, lol. Also, shit's exploded in Manhattan. There was an arson attack on the cathedral. It's been razed to the ground.*

**Rex:** *Jesus. I didn't know.*

**Nyx:** *All good. Lodestar said the Sparrows attacked the Five*

*Points too. They tried to invade Aidan O'Donnelly Sr.'s compound upstate.*

God, I hated those secret society headcases.

**Rex:** *Fuck, that was an insane move.*

**Nyx:** *Desperate measures. They know they're dying and are trying to cauterize the wound.*

**Rex:** *You're telling me.*

**Nyx:** *Either way, they failed.*

**Nyx:** *I'll let you know if Declan is willing to talk with Sin tomorrow.*

**Nyx:** *I'll be in later to visit with Bear.*

I stared at his message, wanting to tell him what was about to go down, but I knew he'd fight me on this.

Knew he'd try to talk me out of it.

I didn't need that right now. I didn't need Nyx's ghosts battling with my own. He'd have Carly back at any cost. He'd never understand my stance.

**Rex:** *All right.*

**Nyx:** *Rex?*

**Rex:** *Yeah?*

**Nyx:** *Merry fucking Christmas.*

I smirked.

**Rex:** *Merry Christmas, Nyx.*

## TWELVE

### REX

I'd drifted to sleep after my conversation with Nyx so her terror hit me on the raw, slapping me awake more than a fist to the face could've. I almost tightened my arms around her, but I knew from experience that made things worse.

Her scream was from the soul.

It was like poison infecting my blood.

Her fear ate into my skin, making me wish there were something I could do to help her. But she never allowed me to help. She didn't let me goddamn in.

I rolled away from her—giving her space on the mattress sometimes helped—but as I watched her, as the scream was torn from her again, I knew this was going to be a bad one.

Her hands clawed, the fingers dragging down her arms as if she were trying to get someone away from her, but the worst thing of all was when she dug her nails into her biceps as if she were trying to tear at her skin.

Then, she started sobbing. At least that meant she stopped scratching herself. Her palms swiped against her cheeks, like she was trying to get something off her.

Watching her broke my fucking heart.

Decimated me in ways that not even grief could match.

My girl, my goddamn woman, the only one I was supposed to protect, *hurting*.

And there was fuck all I could do aside from make it worse.

I started to clamber off the bed, praying that she wouldn't wake up before I managed to get off the mattress. If I did, then she wouldn't freeze me out. Wouldn't act like I was the one who'd attacked her...

Then she started sobbing and scratching at her arms again, and I couldn't help my fucking self.

Like a moron, I grabbed her hands and pinned them to the sheets so she couldn't hurt herself. The second I did, she locked up, her entire body freezing, and she released a scream so purely petrified that I jerked back in response. When her hands were free, she settled down, even curled onto her side, with heavy panting breaths that made me wonder if she was faking sleep.

I didn't push my luck—I'd already made shit worse. That last scream would haunt me for the rest of my fucking life.

As I staggered out of the bedroom, pausing only to grab my cellphone, I pressed my head back against the door. The nightmare still had her in its grip. Hearing her whimpers and sobs told me she hadn't been pretending to sleep. Each one broke me apart as if Nyx were slicing through me like he did one of his prey.

Hadn't I learned my lesson already?

In the early days, I'd tried to awaken her.

It did no good. Just made things worse. *I knew that.*

But leaving her to scream, leaving her to suffer made me feel like a piece of shit, like I was abandoning ship when she needed me the goddamn most.

It was selfishness that had me reaching out to make things better, but that wasn't what she needed from me.

She just needed me to leave her alone.

As I scrubbed a hand over my face, feeling the stubble on my jaw prickle against my palm, I knocked on the bedroom door, hoping that would wake her up before I loped down the stairs and headed into the kitchen to fix us some coffee when she was ready to face me.

She had one of those fancy-assed coffee makers that probably cost a couple of grand. I felt like a prissy fucker making myself a shot of espresso but it made the best coffee, so I set about creating a quadruple-shot because I needed the caffeine.

Once that was made, I slumped against the table and started sipping my drink.

That was when I saw the brown paper bag.

It had been sealed with packing tape so I knew Nyx and Giulia hadn't been able to sneak a glance at the contents.

Curious, I leaned over and snagged it, then tore it open from the side.

I'd have smiled if it didn't contain a baggy loaded with my father's death—a pre-loaded syringe.

Merry fucking Christmas to me.

Staring at it, I realized there was a note inside.

*It sucks when you have to be the one to make the hard choices.*

*I didn't know Bear, and he'd probably be glad he never had to meet me if he had to deal with me, but no one deserves for their body to be their jail cell. Not if they don't make that choice to stay alive themselves.*

*I know you'll do what needs to be done, but I figured I'd make it easier on you to fulfill his request.*

*The situation with the Sparrows had me taking my eye off the ball but I looked into Harlow Dresden. He's a good kid whose life Samuel Haune ruined. I'm making sure that the MC isn't implicated in his death.*

*Consider me Santa Claus.*

*L.*

Once I'd finished reading, I shook my head and reached for my cellphone.

**Rex:** *You couldn't have sent a text?*

But I didn't get a response.

**Rex:** *Thank you, Lodestar. I'm in your debt.*

After a couple minutes of staring at the pre-loaded syringe, flicking my gaze between that and the note, a soft tap sounded at the door.

A part of me expected it to be Rachel, although why the fuck she'd knock on her own goddamn door I didn't know.

Grunting under my breath at my stupidity, I shot a look at the ceiling as if that would tell me if she was still asleep. I didn't have to wonder for long—I heard the sound of the shower turning on. The pipes creaking in response.

Feeling ancient, my joints creaking as much as the pipes, I registered that the caffeine had yet to make that much of an effect on me as I headed for the door. Seeing the strange kid standing on the veranda through the window, assuming it was this Harlow I'd been hearing so much about, I opened it with narrowed eyes.

He was a couple inches shorter than me, weedy but wiry too. The kind of kid who lived on his nerves but who packed a mean punch. Mav had been like that back in the day. Whenever he'd had to stand still, he'd bobbed on his feet as if he had too much energy to expend.

Harlow didn't do that but he throbbed with intensity.

As our gazes collided, I asked, "What do you want?"

I didn't need this today. Not any day, to be frank, yet fuck, it never rained but it poured.

I knew our hands were tied where he was concerned. If we wanted to figure out how he knew we were involved in Haune's death, then we needed him to cooperate. But there were ways and means of making that happen.

Storing him in the Fridge was at the top of that list...

He had no idea that his words were what spared him. That tipped the balance.

"I want to make sure that no one's brother or sister goes through what Jessie did." He blinked as I leaned against the door jamb, lifting my arm so that it could take my weight. "I want to make sure that no one has to feel like I feel because they let their—" His voice choked.

"It's one thing to want vengeance; it's another to act on it."

"No, it isn't. I can't sleep. I can't eat without wanting to puke. I can't breathe without feeling like someone's standing on my throat. I let her down, man. I let my baby sister down." He sucked in a sharp breath. "I want to avenge her. I want to protect others like her. I want to do what the authorities won't—"

"Come in."

I stepped back to punctuate my statement, watching him jolt in surprise. But the relief that swarmed his expression had me tilting my gaze away because I knew he was going to cry, and the kid didn't need me to see that.

Respect filled me, but I wasn't the only one he'd have to convince.

I closed the door behind me then said, "Go straight ahead into the kitchen and take a seat at the table."

He peered back at me, more nervous now than before.

Smart kid.

But he did as I asked and sat down beside the head of the table where my coffee cup was resting.

I watched him all the while then asked, "Why are you here? Today of all days?"

He licked his lips. "I-I know that Nyx—" Harlow frowned down at the table. "I didn't expect to get through the gates when I first arrived at the compound. I figure it's because you want to know what I know that I'm even this far—"

I sat down. "What *do* you know?"

"I wouldn't tell the cops," he muttered. "Wouldn't help those fucking pigs—"

"What do you know, Harlow?"

He swallowed again but repeated, "I wouldn't tell the cops."

"Even if that's the only reason we'd let you tag along?"

"Whether you help or don't, I won't change my mind."

"You'll just end up in jail faster, huh?"

His jaw tightened. "I'm willing to do that. I'd prefer not to because those bastards don't deserve justice."

I studied him. "What were you doing before Jessie died?"

"I was a student."

"There's a big age gap between you and Jessie, isn't there?"

"Same dad, different moms. But I didn't care about that. I loved her," he said stubbornly, as if he'd had to justify the extent of his grief before.

"'Course you did," I said calmly, because if I was going to give him shit, it wouldn't be about *that*. "What did you study?"

Everything about him locked up, turned tense. An oddly mutinous expression drifted over his features before he ground out, "Theology."

I tilted my head to the side. "Theology?"

I was pretty sure with whatever Lodestar and Rachel had done to investigate him, they'd be able to tell me why he was being cagey, but his defiance keyed me in like nothing else could.

"At a seminary?"

He didn't look at me. "I was there that night. That's how I know who killed Haune."

Pursing my lips, I put two and two together. "We got to him before you did?"

"Yes. I hated you for that." He gulped. "Then I saw Haune when you lynched him, and I knew I would never have thought about doing any of that."

"Did you call the cops?"

"Only once I was sure he died."

"Did he speak with you?"

For the first time, a smile curled on his lips. "He did." His gaze finally drifted to mine. "He begged me to help him."

Mine narrowed as he maintained eye contact. "How did you know I'd be here today?"

He didn't flinch. "Eavesdropped."

"And what is it you think I can do for you?"

"Make your men accept me."

I almost laughed as I snagged a banana from the fruit bowl on the table. As I unpeeled it, I drawled, "I can't make them accept you." That was on him. Before he could respond, I asked, "You a sadist, Harlow?"

He didn't blink at the change of topic. "Once upon a time, I'd have said that I wasn't. Now I don't know. Now I just know that..." A breath shuddered from his lips. "These Sparrows—the headlines—I realized the cops are all dirty. If I want justice, if I want to give survivors peace, then I need to do it myself, but if I'm in a jail cell, then I can't do anything either. I need to not get caught."

His logic was sound.

Much as Nyx's was, when he'd come to me after he'd blown up Kevin's head with a shotgun he'd tampered with.

It was almost like twenty years hadn't passed.

Almost like I was sixteen again, wondering what the fuck to do, knowing that I needed my dad's help to make sure Nyx didn't go to prison for what he'd done.

How ironic when my safety net wasn't there anymore.

When, in fact, I was having to be my dad's safety net...

"Will you help me?" Harlow pleaded.

The last thing I wanted was to eat, but I chowed down a good quarter of the banana before I reasoned, "This isn't a charity." His shoulders slumped before I continued, "We're an MC. You're a guy who wanted to be a priest. We'll only help if you join us. Become a Prospect.

'I hate to be obvious but we're not exactly on the right side of the law—whichever philosophy of law you aspire to. Our ways of life are..."

"Discordant."

The word fired into the room like a bullet from a gun.

I cast Rachel a look, saw the shadows beneath her eyes and the exhaustion etched into her features, and I nodded. "Discordant."

Harlow had tensed at Rachel's presence, and it only amped up when she stepped inside. "So, you're the man who wants to avenge his sister."

He licked his lips. "I am."

"You were a year away from taking your vows, Harlow. Are you certain you want to step down this path?"

Her voice was soft, gentler than I was used to hearing from her. Rachel was more likely to bark directives at me than offer me hope couched in a dulcet tone.

He, not unsurprisingly, responded to it. "I-I made my decision when I left the seminary. This isn't about good vs. evil. This isn't about sinning. This is about *monsters*.

"If it means my eternal soul has to burn in hell to make sure those monsters can't torment another child, I'll do it. I've made my peace with that."

Rachel bit her lip as she shot me a glance. I half-expected for her to be cold with me, for there to be icicles in the connection between us, but instead, she looked... lost.

I got it.

I often felt like that around Nyx.

What was another burden to bear?

I heaved a sigh. "You become a Prospect. You patch in. You become a brother. Then we'll revisit this situation."

"How long will it take to patch in?" he rasped.

"Don't think about the duration. Think about it as a time to see if you can cope with what we're asking of you."

"Like the seminary," Rachel intoned. "Just with guns and drugs."

Harlow tensed.

My lips twitched at her comment, but his tension didn't escape my notice. "Harlow, once you become a Prospect, it's a turning point.

You can still leave, you can still back out, but if you report us to the cops, you will be dealt with. There's no way out of that."

His gaze was measured as it settled on mine. "I'd expect no less."

"Prospects get all the worst jobs," Rachel said softly as she drifted over to the table.

"She's right. They do. Disgusting jobs as well. Thankless jobs. No pay. You'll board at the clubhouse and we'll feed you and you'll have no bills but it's... grim. Until you become a brother."

"No grimmer than a jail cell. I know that's where I'll end up if I don't have help." He blinked. "I was a Stoic. Now, I'm a Pyrrhonist."

Rachel sighed. "You won't find *ataraxia* with this life choice, Harlow. You should really take a few days to think about your next steps."

*Ataraxia* was a philosophical state of being—it was mental tranquility.

Along the journey of achieving *ataraxia, epoche,* or suspension of judgment, was one of the steps toward finding happiness in this philosophy.

"It's better than the hell I'm living now but you're right. I'll think about my decision."

As he uttered those words, words that would be fateful for him, I stared at my girl.

Her life was hell.

She'd made the best of it, or she was trying to, but she was as trapped as Harlow was.

Did she know that I'd do anything to free her from that?

Did she know that there was no price I wouldn't pay to just give her a night's sleep free from her memories?

Rachel's eyes swept down as if she heard the questions I hadn't spoken aloud.

But much as I expected, she had no answer.

## THIRTEEN

## RACHEL

I'LL BE MISSING YOU (FEAT. 112) DIDDY, FAITH EVANS, 112

I went with him to the hospital.

I even rode bitch on the back of his bike.

The wind blasted me, smacking me flat in the face, cutting through my leather jacket and heavy-duty jeans, but I needed it.

I was still dopey.

Still fragile after that goddamn nightmare.

It was torture to find peace in Rex's arms, only to drift into a warzone once I slept...

I pressed my face against his back, feeling his tension, sensing his misery. He didn't want to have to do this, but he was a dutiful man.

For all that I disapproved of his life choices, well aware that he had the acuity to become so much more than the Prez of a bunch of outlaws, I knew he was selfless when it came to those he loved.

He'd do this today for Bear. It would eat away at him for the rest of his life, the guilt and the shame, but he'd do it because his father asked him to.

That was Rex.

My Rex.

I blew out a breath in an attempt to shift my train of thought, but it was either focus on what was about to happen or what had happened earlier. Letting myself remember the nightmare would only antagonize me, and as for Harlow, well, what was there to even say about him?

He was so fucking young. Had had so much potential. But since I was a kid, I'd known that the world wasn't black and white.

What he'd be doing would be worthwhile.

It'd make more of a difference than him taking vows of celibacy and poverty...

I wished the ride to the hospital took longer than it did, but too quickly, Rex was pulling up into the parking lot and I was climbing off the back.

I'd forgotten how intimate riding bitch was and knew that was why most of the brothers never allowed clubwhores on the back of their bikes—God forbid they move beyond their station.

As I unfastened my helmet and handed it to him, my phone vibrated in my jacket. While he rested it on the handlebars, I quickly replied to Parker's text and wished her a Merry Christmas, then gave him my hand.

He eyed it. "I must look like shit if you think I need my hand held."

My throat was tight. "Maybe I need mine held?"

He grunted but instantly tangled our fingers together.

"Do you think he'll wake up and talk to us?"

"Do you want to convince him against—"

"No." I shook my head to compound that. "I just want to say goodbye."

His smile was sad. "I don't know if he will. We'll find out, I guess."

He pulled me closer to him and, together, we walked through the parking lot toward the front entrance.

"I'm surprised you're not giving me crap about Harlow."

"Do I ever give you crap about Nyx?" I asked lightly.

"No. But... Harlow's different, isn't he?"

I hummed. "His family is wealthy. Did you know that?"

He shrugged. "Never really thought about it. Haune was their gardener, wasn't he?"

"He was. That's how he got Jessie."

"Bastard."

"Yes," I said, tone stark. "You know gray is my favorite color."

He snorted. "Good thing or you wouldn't be my lawyer anymore."

I'd paid my dues to him years ago, and we both knew that.

"I'm not here for the MC."

Rex paused. "No?" He turned to look at me. "I thought that was the only reason you stuck around."

"I was thinking, this year, of moving to Manhattan, but I wasn't going to dump the MC. I would never give up your account." When he tensed up at my admission, and wanting to change the subject, I muttered, "At least we know how Harlow learned who... you know."

He nodded. "Doesn't diminish his threat. He could still go to the authorities with an eyewitness confession."

"He could. Doubt it though. He wants to make a difference."

"Think he'll become a Prospect?"

"I do. Maybe it'll help Nyx. I spoke with Giulia... She indicated that he isn't doing well."

"No. He needs his hobbies."

"Passing on his wisdom... maybe that'll be good for his soul."

"If he has one left."

"That's gloomy."

"He's the first to admit that he's gone full Darth Vader."

I had to snort at that, but I didn't say another word as we wandered into the hospital and made our way to Bear's room.

The squeak and tap of our shoes against the floors, the noise of a busy hospital where the holiday didn't matter aside from the tinsel and the trees that had popped up around every corner, it all started to feel like a parallel universe.

Like we were distanced from reality.

We weren't here as visitors. We brought death with us.

"Thank you for coming with me, Rachel," he rasped, breaking into my thoughts just before we headed into Bear's ward.

"Nowhere else I'd rather be," I told him honestly as I waved to one of the nurses whom I knew from school, grateful that it wasn't Kian. Rex nodded at her too and we exchanged holiday greetings.

After, I continued like we hadn't been disturbed, "Better circumstances would be nicer, but—" I squeezed his hand. Silently telling him that we were in this together.

"When I... you should step outside."

"I don't think so," I told him brightly before I pushed open the door and started to dress up in the protective gear that wouldn't be necessary for much longer.

The grief hit me then. Like a strike to the throat. It almost choked me, made it harder to suck in a gulp of air, but I forced myself to remain calm because Rex didn't need to see me like this.

He needed me to be strong.

Later, I could collapse into a puddle on my bed.

Later.

Sucking in a breath, I forced my expression to appear blank then turned to look at him.

His face was gray.

The torment in his eyes hurt something in me that would never heal.

He'd looked like this when Rene had died.

His pain gave me strength because I needed to be that for him. I needed to be his backbone so that he could go through with this.

I grabbed his hand this time, not giving him a moment to reply, and together, we walked into the room.

The smell, the beeps—I knew why Rex was getting fatigued of this place. It was exhausting. The lighting didn't help; it exposed exactly why Bear wanted to let go.

He was a wreckage. A living, breathing pile of flesh-covered bones with organs that functioned only because of chemicals and machines.

I sucked in a breath as I took one of the seats to the side of his bed, and Rex slumped into the remaining chair, the one closer to his dad.

For a second, neither of us said anything, but when Rex just stared at Bear, I murmured, "Do you remember that time when you stole his bike?"

It made sense why that memory came to me.

I wanted to think of Bear like that, not like *this*.

Able to ride a bike, free to live his passion. Not capable of only withering away in a hospital bed.

Rex surprised me—he let out a soft chuckle. One that sounded relieved. Like he too wanted to think about then and not now. "Which time?"

I grinned because there'd definitely been a couple of 'hog heists' over the years. "When he got that new ride. The black one."

Rex shot me a look. "The black one? After all these years, that's the only way you can identify a bike? By color?"

"It had horsepower and ccs."

"Very informative. Did it also have two wheels?"

My lips quirked up again. "Maybe. It could have had a handlebar as well."

"Surprise surprise."

"Rachel... never— did... like— bikes."

Bear's agonized response had my breath catching. I hadn't expected him to speak, but that he was awake and aware enough— God, I couldn't imagine the agony he was in.

"Hey Bear," I whispered, unable to speak louder than that.

"Hey darlin'." It took a good minute for him to get the two words out.

Jesus.

His head didn't even move.

He was imprisoned on the mattress. A feeling of claustrophobia surged inside me on his behalf.

My mouth worked, but all I could think to say was, "I love you."

"Love." He exhaled. "You."

Tears pricked my eyes, but I didn't stop them from flowing.

Bear had earned my tears.

He deserved to be grieved.

"Son?"

Rex swallowed. The sound was thick, like his emotions were choking him. "Yes, Dad?"

"Hap-py." Inhale. "Hol-i-days."

Rex reached over but he stopped himself from touching Bear. His hand hovered like he was unsure where to place it. I couldn't blame him. The bed alone was a battlefield of wires. As for Bear's body... it was a wreckage.

Pure and simple.

Unable to reconnect physically, he rasped, "I got you a gift."

"Did?"

"Yeah. I figure Mom's waited long enough for you to come home, don't you?"

A single tear appeared at the corner of Bear's eye. As it drifted down his cheek, I gulped back a sob.

"Tell her I love her, and that I miss her, and that no one makes biscuits and gravy like she does." Rex's tears were clear, and he let them flow just as I did. "Tell her that whenever it rains, I always check the fuse box because she hated when it went dark in the middle of a storm.

"Tell her that I think about her every fucking morning when I force myself to eat breakfast because she told me it was the best meal of the day."

Rex's fingers tightened more and more around mine, not to the point of pain, but to the point where I knew he was leaning on me for support.

I squeezed back as he whispered, "And I'll think of you, Dad.

When the gates open and they squeak, I'll always wonder if you've come back home to us.

"When I'm in the shit, I'll always want to call you. When I get ribs from the diner, I'll always wonder if you'd want some too. I'll always think of you, Dad. Always."

With a final squeeze to my fingers, he let go. His hand went into his pocket and he pulled out a syringe that he rested on his lap.

I wasn't sure I needed to know where he got that from, didn't even want to know what it was, I just watched as Bear breathed, "Best. Son in." Exhale. "World. Love. You."

Raw with grief, I got to my feet, moving around Bear's other side so that nothing could be seen through the window into the room.

Rex placed the injection to the IV line, and after he squeezed the drug into it, the syringe disappearing into his pocket a moment later, I leaned down and pressed a kiss to Bear's grizzled cheek.

"Be at peace, Bear. Thank you for everything. I promise I'll look after him—"

And that was when he flatlined.

## FOURTEEN

## REX

I was shaking as I got off the back of the bike, so fucking hard that Rachel had to help prop me up.

Feeling like an old, old man, I wobbled up the stairs, just in time to drop to my knees.

The roar of pain that escaped me didn't do anything to expel the agony deep inside.

I'd known this was coming, this day where I lost him, but I hadn't thought I'd be the one behind his death.

I heard Rachel's soft sob, but I didn't listen. I just roared again, my face crumpling, my agony unreal as I tried to expel my grief.

It didn't work.

The feelings inside me were like I had a hurricane tearing me to pieces. Destroying me and leaving devastation in its wake.

Hands on the floor, sorrow and guilt taking a chokehold on me, I finally heard Rach's sobs as she tried to help me up when one of her tears splashed onto my hand.

That was my wake-up call. That was when I realized where I was and what I was doing.

Everything felt both crystal clear and hazy all at the same time. Like the pain clarified things but the desolation blurred it.

I'd been here before.

Too many times to fucking count.

But that didn't make it easier.

Nothing about this was easy.

Still in a daze, I let her help me to my feet because I knew she'd hurt herself if I didn't—I weighed over two-fifty. She was one-thirty max, soaking wet.

When I was standing, I curved an arm over her shoulder and hauled her into me. My face burrowed into her throat as I tried to hide from what was happening. I felt her hands on my back, fingers clenching down on my coat. A sharp breath soughed from her lungs, whistling past my jaw, but in my state, I didn't realize she was struggling.

Maybe I should have.

Maybe I should've recognized these things by now without any conscious thought, but I didn't.

When she finally squeezed me back, it didn't register how long it had taken her to hug me, and I didn't care. I just needed her.

I fucking needed her.

Did she know how much?

"Rex? Come on, baby. Let's get you inside."

"Nothing's ever going to be the same again."

"No," she agreed rawly. "But that doesn't mean we can't make things... *better*. Let's get inside. It's starting to snow."

She turned in my arms, hiking one of mine over her shoulders and sliding a hand around my waist to prop me up.

Together, we staggered like I was drunk into the house. I stared up at the staircase like it was Everest, knowing I couldn't make it that far.

She must have known because she didn't guide me that way. Instead, she took me down the hall that led to her workspace.

Over the years, I'd grown fond of her offices. Sometimes, that was the only place she'd see me without putting a wall up. It was where we fucked. Only, she didn't take me inside her office—she took me to the den off of it.

I was surprised enough by the sight of the fancy living room to blurt out, "What is this place?"

She shrugged. "It's where I unwind. Rain knows not to disturb me here."

The house was large, with several living rooms. Too large for a pair of siblings to rattle around together in. Why she needed this private one, I had no clue, but when she drew me over to the sofa, I let her.

The second I slumped on it, I stared blindly ahead, uncertain of what to do or say. My eyes burned with emotion, and when I swiped at them with my fingers, I brought tears forth, but they didn't express how I was feeling. They were inadequate for the task.

I wanted to scream.

I needed to rage.

My dad was gone.

The Sparrows had taken him from me.

The hurt was raw; the bitterness was real.

The desire for vengeance was paramount but even that was futile. Justice was being served to the Sparrows. Lodestar-style. That knowledge didn't, however, take away the ache in my soul.

As I stared at nothing, waiting for my new reality to settle in, Rachel surprised me again by carefully propping herself on my knee.

I shot her a blank look, which she ignored and settled herself deeper on my lap. Her arms went around my shoulders, and she nestled into me.

The heat of her, the comfort, it rolled off her and into me, making me slouch against the sofa.

It was clearly stuffed with feathers, because the cushions conformed to my shape and weight, so, cosseted on all sides by the scent of her, by the heat of her, I tipped my head back and whispered, "I don't know how to—"

"—be in a world without him. I know." She pressed a soft kiss to my jaw. "I'm here, Rex. I'm here."

"You're here now," I said bitterly, my voice thick as I closed my eyes.

"I'm always—"

"You're not. Don't lie, Rach. You're here until I freak you out and then you back off." Hell, she'd even admitted that she was thinking about moving to fucking Manhattan. "And that's okay. It's how we roll. But don't make out like I can depend on you—"

"Hush," she whispered, and I heard the tears in her voice. "You can always depend on me. Always. It might not be how you'd like, but I am *always* here for you."

Before I could speak, she pressed her lips to mine to stem my denial. I knew it was crazy, knew it was inappropriate but I didn't fight her off.

I didn't stop her.

I let her kiss me, let her gentle pecks dot around my mouth, let her trace her lips over the hard line of my jaw. I felt the butterfly soft caress as she pressed them to my eyelids and then settled one on my forehead.

"I'm here, Rex. I'm here," she repeated, and like the fool I was for her and her alone, I fell for it.

This year had been impossible. Not just Dad, but so many of my friends lost to the blast. So much change and so much grief and misery.

She was, and always would be, my home.

So I *went* home.

My mouth opened around the tender flesh that was the arch of her throat and I sucked down, enough to make her moan. I let my lips travel down to the curve of her shoulder, and I nipped the part where it met with her neck. Her whimper had me groaning and encouraged me enough that I reached up to shape the curve of her with my hands.

The feel of her was so rare, that it was like a treat. Like a kid who wasn't allowed sugar from a helicopter mom who deep dived into a bag of gummi bears come Halloween.

The sugar hit went straight to my brain.

And my dick.

I burrowed beneath the layers, the very un-Rachel-like plaid shirt she wore that had a fleece lining for warmth. My fingers found bare flesh, and when she moaned as I started to tug on the buttons, her chin tipped forward, her forehead colliding with mine. I pressed my lips to hers at that point, needing to taste her. Needing to rediscover her.

Hers parted to let me in, and as I stroked my tongue along the length of hers, I unfastened her shirt and started to explore her by touch alone.

Her bra gave way under my demanding caresses, and my hands found her and shaped her, savoring the feel of her. She was chronically underweight, to the point where her ribs usually bumped my palms, but her tits were heavier.

Her ribs less pronounced.

If I'd been in my regular headspace, I'd have asked what was going on, but I didn't. I just took what she offered.

Accepted what she gifted me.

I groaned, savoring the taste of her, the feel of her.

God, she was like fucking fire in my hands. It was like I'd been swallowed up by a blizzard and she'd been sent to thaw me out. *This was my Rach. Not the ice queen. The firestarter.*

Her tongue had been hesitant at first, but now, her confidence regrowing, she started to taste me back.

Rachel wasn't shy. Not with me. But it took her a while to remember that.

I knew her body as well as she knew mine, and she knew what drove me wild as well as I did with her.

As she became more aggressive, her nails digging into my shoulders, her grip on me tightening, I dragged off her shirt, exposing more silken flesh to my hungry hands.

Exploring the length of her back, I felt the vertebra of her spine, but they weren't as pronounced either. I savored the small curves of her hips and reached around to flick at the fly of her jeans.

When I slipped my fingers between the tines of her zipper, and I rubbed over her panties, I found her hot and wet.

She shuddered against me, her mouth tearing away from mine as she pushed her forehead into me too.

"Oh, God," she mewled as I teased her with my hand.

When our lips collided again, as she whimpered into my mouth, I finally dragged her panties away and brushed up against slick, silken flesh.

She was so goddamn wet that I hissed under my breath and, as I found her slit, I thrust two fingers in, knowing how ready she was for me.

Scissoring them had her squealing, and her back arched against my hold even as I snagged her mouth in a kiss that I knew stole her breath away.

It was mine.

All fucking mine.

As I fingered her pussy, she rocked into me, her knees spreading as she moved to straddle me. With her knees digging into the sofa, I expected her to rock against me, to finally get some fucking friction, but she didn't.

She launched off it.

She started to strip out of her clothes and, once bare, her hand went between her legs.

When she rubbed her clit, her eyes closing, she might as well have put a gun to my head and pulled the trigger—she raised her fingers to her mouth and tasted them.

I growled, and it was deeper than before, outraged and hungry and fucking desperate for this woman.

My mate.

I darted forward and dragged her against me as she let loose a choked laugh and straddled my legs again, rubbing against me like I'd hoped she would before.

Then her fingers were shaping my dick, and her hands were delving into my fly, and her palm was suddenly holding my cock in her fist.

As she stroked me a couple times, I tipped my head back, watching as she arched upward on her knees, legs parting wider to straddle higher up mine, and she rubbed the tip of my cock against her slit.

She nudged her clit a couple of times, until she gasped with the sensation, before she tucked it against her gate and let me slide home.

The pressure, the sensation, the fucking delirium that triggered had me closing my eyes a second as I let the sofa take all of my weight. Then, I realized what I was missing, and I quickly opened them again and watched the flush on her chest slowly start to spread.

Her tits were tinging pink, her cheeks too. Her eyes grew misty, and her breath started to sough from her lips.

Before my eyes, Rach became the woman I knew. The woman I recognized. Not the icicle who'd taken my girl's place. She returned to me.

Somehow, that was more painful than anything today.

She was there—within touching distance.

But she was only here for a short amount of time.

She was on loan to me.

Partially thawed.

But fuck, what she could do to me half-frozen was decimating by comparison to another woman.

I'd learned a long time ago that Rachel was it for me.

It.

She groaned as she started to ride me, finally drawing higher on her knees, rocking into me, grinding down hard as she twisted her hips to take every inch.

Her hands drifted to my shoulders, and she leaned on me for strength as she started to move faster.

I watched her nostrils flare as our eyes clashed and held, and I twisted us around so she was flat on her back and I was looming over her. Her nails dug into my shoulders and this time, she ordered, "Rub my clit."

The second I did, letting the tips of my fingers slip and slide through her juices, she immediately clenched down around me and her hands slid around to the back of my neck, her heels digging into my ass to urge me on.

We both groaned at the change in angle, and her pussy started fluttering around my cock like it was panicking, choking on me like it needed the orgasm to survive.

She screamed, her hands finally moving, dragging through my hair, nails scraping over my skull as she ground into me, chasing release, finding it and rewarding me in return.

The second her cunt clamped down around me, clutching at me, milking me, I let go.

Of the present, the past, the future, and everything else.

As my orgasm hit me, I felt the whack of it like a punch to the solar plexus.

It stole my breath, melted my bones, and made me feel like the world beneath my feet was shaking.

That was Rachel.

Always Rachel.

My girl.

Mine.

I gripped her hips, urging her to ride me a couple more times, and as the ecstasy slowly started to fade, the comfort of our proximity, of our rejoining hit me.

Pivoting us to the side, I flopped down, encouraged her to keep one leg straight so I could stay inside her for as long as possible, and burrowing my face into her throat, my goddamn *home*, I fell asleep.

## FIFTEEN

## REX

For the second time that day, it was the scream that woke me.

The terrorized call of someone who needed help but who was no longer in danger.

Whatever dragons Rachel needed slaying, they'd died years back. At least, according to her.

I couldn't fight the demons in her mind, couldn't stop them from attacking her.

But that wasn't what broke me.

That happened when she started slapping me. When her nails dug down and she clawed at me like *I* was her attacker.

Like I was the one who'd hurt her when I'd hurt my-fucking-self before I ever did anything to bring her pain.

She kicked at me and shoved at me, slapping and pinching and scratching and aiming to do anything to maim me.

She'd broken me years ago, but this?

The chasm ruptured.

Splintered.

I twisted us around so that I was no longer with my back to the sofa, but as I tried to get away from her, she took it as another sign of attack.

"NO!" she screamed, the word hoarse like she'd been saying it over and over again.

"NO! King—he'll... NO!"

My name on her lips tore at my insides.

"NO!" It came again as I finally managed to clamber off her, my knees colliding with the rug beneath the coffee table. It was a tight fit so I wasn't surprised by the shard of pain that hit me when I collided with the edge of the glass table, but it was nothing, *absolutely fucking nothing*, to the agony that came when she whimpered, "He'll kill you, Grizzly. When he finds out, he'll kill you."

Grizzly.

My uncle.

If she'd kicked me in the balls, I'd have been able to catch my breath sooner.

Instead, I just sat there. There were too many punches to field. Too fucking many.

If I'd been in my right mind, I'd have known to get the hell out of there.

Jackass behavior or not—I knew how Rachel worked.

And I wasn't wrong.

The second her eyes opened and they clashed with my stunned ones, it began.

"Grizzly?" she asked rawly, with that one terrified word clawing her fingers into my chest so she could pluck my heart out.

Then, she blinked dazedly and started freezing me out.

I could see the ice forming between us, creeping into being like it was a tangible thing. Stacking higher and higher as she created those fucking walls that kept me out and that locked her in.

Walls that protected her from what my uncle had done to her.

"Grizzly did this to you?" I demanded.

She stiffened, her tension soaring. I thought she'd answer but all she managed to rattle off, in a voice hoarse from her screams, was, "Get. Out."

## SIXTEEN

## RACHEL

When I told him to get out, I half expected him not to.

I thought he'd ram through my walls, force me to talk, to finally share my sordid secrets with him.

Maybe a part of me wanted him to do that?

Maybe I wanted to finally be liberated from my past?

Only, he *didn't* do that.

He jolted as if he'd been shot, then he staggered to his feet, turned his back on me, and walked out of my living room.

Shock went to war with the ghostly hands of his uncle as they collided with my hair, as they touched my body against my will, as he took what I *didn't* give.

"Just like your whore mother," he'd said as he pinched my nose until I opened my mouth to suck in a quick breath.

The second I did, he snapped a hold of my chin, forced it open then he spat in there.

Later, he'd come on my face, and I'd been left, wiping the fluid away as it mingled with my tears.

I shuddered and leaped to my feet.

At that moment, my thoughts weren't with Bear, the *good* brother, but with Grizzly.

One of the men who'd ruined me.

Dragging on my shirt and panties, I scampered toward the nearest bathroom, and dropping to my knees, I puked.

Those ghostly goddamn hands trailed along my body where he'd touched, and I retched some more. The only trouble was that I'd barely eaten today, so there wasn't much to vomit.

Sagging against the toilet, my face against the seat, I didn't even care that it was gross. I just sobbed.

The sobs and the retches seemed to go in turn as my body urged me to expel the poison once more, but the poison had gone too far.

It had hit my bloodstream.

It was everywhere.

I'd die with this inside me.

With *him* inside me.

Shivers wracked my spine as I wiped a tired hand over my face, and that was when I heard it—his engine revving.

As exhausted as I was, as twisted by the past, I jerked to my feet and rushed toward the front door.

Rex was in no fit state to ride!

Goddammit.

I moaned as I made it to the door, but it was too late.

Hauling on a pair of flats and a coat that didn't belong to me, I shrieked, "REX!"

Either he didn't hear me over the engine or he was purposely ignoring me as he headed out of the driveway.

Praying that he was just going to the clubhouse, I ran across the graveled path toward the road, but he was riding past the gates to the compound and onward to West Orange.

The guilt hit then.

God, if anything happened to him—I'd die.

I knew I would.

My balance hinged on him.

As unfair to him as that was, I couldn't help it.

I couldn't stop it.

That had happened years before I'd been attacked, and it wasn't something I could unlearn—even if I wanted to.

As the lights from his hog faded into the distance, I leaned over as a memory struck me.

'You should be careful when you tell me to get out. One day, I might not come back.'

The words pierced my skin and organs like a bullet would, and I puked again.

This time, bile came. It burned and it hurt, but that was good. I knew from experience that meant it'd stop soon.

I pressed a hand to the stone gatepost, and I leaned over to get it all out, so lost to my misery that I didn't even register Rain's car driving past me or his clambering out to help me.

"Oh, sis," Rain hissed. "What the hell happened while I was at work?"

I stared at him with tortured eyes, unable to hide what I'd sheltered him from forever. The only thing I could do was lie.

"Bear died."

His mouth gaped and he jerked, straightening up as my news hit him. "Bear's... He can't be! They said he was getting better."

"What kind of better would that have been, Rain?" I rasped. "He'd have moved out of the ICU but still been stuck in there for another couple years?" I shook my head as I swiped my fingers over my burning lips. "A h-heart attack took him." My face crumpled as the tears hit. Not just for Bear, but for Rex. For Rex and, selfishly, for me. "H-He... Rex and me... We were with him at the end."

"I thought I saw Rex's hog, but I didn't imagine—" His brow puckered with confusion even as he swiped a hand over his eyes. "Where's he going? Why didn't he stay?"

I wished the answer I had was palatable, but it wasn't.

"I-I'm ... I don't know."

He blinked at me then slipped his arm around my waist so he could haul me against him. "Let's get you inside," he said gruffly, sniffing as he dealt with his own grief.

God, the next couple days were going to be hell...

# SEVENTEEN

## REX

### WALKING AWAY - CRAIG DAVID

I felt drunk.

Like my faculties weren't firing on all cylinders.

As if I'd been blasted in the chest with a shotgun but there was no blood.

So much shit made sense now. So many fucking things, and for the first time, I didn't want there to be sense. Couldn't handle there being reason.

When Rachel woke up after a nightmare, the reason she screamed when she saw me was because she thought I was my uncle.

I'd literally gone to hell.

Not for helping to end my dad's misery, not for murder, but *this* was hell.

Actual fucking hell.

As I rode out of town, I went past the strip joint.

That blurry mind of mine worked against me because instead of riding on, instead of doing the smart fucking thing and maybe heading high into the hills where Lily and Link or Sin and Tiff lived and bedding down at one of theirs for the night, I parked.

I fucking parked.

Like a moron.

I was *not* a moron.

Rachel, however, had turned me into one.

It was Christmas Day but the place was open. It never fucking closed because there were always dumbfuck rich pricks who wanted to have some stranger's pussy and ass waggled in their faces.

I knew Inked was on the roster because Sin had sent me the schedules a couple days ago, and as much as my mind was blurry, that memory was as clear as glass.

Of course it was.

With my control fluctuating, I knew this was the last place I should be.

My temper was already wavering under the restraints I usually tackled it into, and the need to let go, to let it fly free, to feel anything other than how I was currently feeling was imperative.

I needed oblivion.

Climbing off my bike, I stared up at the mini mall that had earned the club a fortune since its inauguration. There was no denying that. It had also caused its share of misery too.

I still couldn't go into Daytona without thinking about what Giulia had gone through in there.

That fateful night had triggered so much, had brought us to this point. To this moment in time.

Fate.

I was too logical to believe in it, but everything was feeling pretty fucking fated right now.

This level of fuckfest had to be at some greater being's behest, didn't it?

Sucking in a breath, not even feeling the cold through my leather gear, I strode toward the strip joint.

Hawk was off work today because I knew Sin—not that he'd

admit it—was terrified Amara would stab him in his sleep and making him work on Christmas Day was one such way to earn a stabbing.

As a result, Hungry John was the one doing a double take at the sight of me.

"Prez?"

Hungry John was one of the men whom I didn't hear much from. He kept his head down, ear to the ground, heart loyal to the Sinners, and didn't cause me shit.

On a night like tonight, I recognized that I didn't fucking appreciate that enough. Hadn't shown him that appreciation either.

Clapping him on the back, I said, "Merry Christmas, Hungry John."

He blinked at me, but I could see that the rumor mill about Dad hadn't started yet because he shot me a sheepish grin. "Merry Christmas, Prez. What the fuck are you doing here?"

I shrugged. "Got to take out some trash."

His brow furrowed, but his gaze was resolute on mine. "Hawk showed you the footage?"

"That surprises you?"

"No. I told him to wait until after Christmas though."

"Why?"

"Things are hard enough on you right now. It could be the last Christmas with your dad, things are crazy with the MC... It didn't seem important, especially since Inked ain't even on staff tomorrow or the 27th. Not like he could have stolen much else."

"I appreciate that, Hungry."

"Wouldn't normally have told him to keep it back. Know you like to be involved. But it's Christmas, you know. After a tough year, waiting didn't do no harm."

"You're not wrong." Hawk was trying to impress me though. He wanted off bouncer duty at the strip club. Amara was insanely possessive so it wasn't like I could blame him. "Is Inked behind the bar?"

He peered at his watch. "Should be on a break."

Fate, again.

"Around the back?"

"Probably."

"I need your cage."

"Need me to give you a hand?"

"Nah."

Hungry passed me his keys. "See, cages come in handy."

I shot him a glance. "You just hate the fucking cold."

He smirked at me, but when a couple of drunken assholes wandered over to the door, his attention split, and I clapped him on the back to let him get on with his work.

Before I could head down the walkway at the side which separated the bar from the club that was for security and deliveries only, he snagged my arm and asked, "You doing okay, Prez?"

I locked up. "I'm doing fine," I lied.

He shook his head. "You've got murder in your eyes."

How right he was.

"I'm fine," I repeated.

He shrugged, but there was a knowing look on his face that I'd have smacked off if we didn't have an audience.

As he let me go, I walked down the passageway and, irony of ironies, that was where I found him.

One leg cocked back against the wall, smoke in hand, head tipped so he was looking up at the covered roof of the path.

At the sound of my booted footsteps, he didn't bother shooting me a glance, just drawled, "Fuck off, Two Knives. I got five minutes."

I didn't answer until I was a few steps away. "You ain't got five minutes, Inked."

He straightened up in surprise because I never came down here, but didn't move away fast enough to stop me from grabbing him by the stubby ponytail, twisting him around, and slamming his head into the wall.

He groaned as he staggered back, and when his hands came up to defend himself, the quick one-two jab had him turning in a drunken pirouette before he face-planted on the ground.

Picking him up by his jacket, I started to drag him down the pathway.

Once the door was a few steps away, and aware there'd be CCTV on the streets, I hefted him over my shoulder with a grunt seeing as I could hear that Hungry was alone now.

I called out, "Inked's pissed, Hungry John. Better get him home. Think the bar staff will manage without him?"

"Yeah. Don't see why not," Hungry replied, opening the door for me.

I nodded at him then walked over to his cage. "I'll have it back to you in an hour."

"Thanks, Prez," he said cheerfully.

Slamming Inked into the truck bed, the only place I could go was the motel...

Or the Fridge.

I could access that around the back of the clubhouse.

That seemed like a smart thing to do. The motel was closer and there were fewer chances of me seeing one of my brothers, but even in the haze of grief and misery, I had some good sense remaining.

Like a man possessed, I drove back up the road to the compound, and when one of the new Prospects saw me, a guy called Jensen who I knew would make a great addition to our security team, he nodded as he opened the gates.

"Merry Christmas, Prez," he called out, and I returned the greeting even though nothing was fucking merry about this Christmas.

Goddammit, if I heard that again today, I'd lose my fucking shit.

It took an extra five minutes to get to the clearing between the compound and the Fridge, but I wasn't disrupted on the way.

I heard Inked start groaning and slammed on the accelerator to make it there in time.

Again, fate was on my side.

Only after I'd dragged him out onto the ground, only after I'd hauled him up the few steps to the Fridge and when he was spreadeagled on the floor, did he start to stir in earnest.

The second his eyes opened, though they were dazed, I grabbed one of my knives and slammed it right between his fucking legs. The floor was concrete, so the tip glanced off the surface, sending a shockwave of pain down my forearm, but that was nothing to the grief suffocating me.

As Inked yowled in surprise at how near the blade was to his family jewels, I rasped, "Since when did you think I was running a charity?"

Dazedly, he stared at me before he slurred, "What the fuck are you talking about?"

"I'm talking about you not putting every dollar in the cash register and pocketing whatever you fucking feel like taking."

His eyes widened and his flight-or-fight responses kicked in because he cried, "I ain't done nothing wrong."

He tried to kick me but I tilted the knife backward so the edge of the blade was digging into his dick.

It wouldn't slice him, but the pressure could fucking hurt.

He made a move to snatch the knife, but he was still dazed, and his movements were slow and sluggish. Taking advantage of that, I grabbed that hand, slipped another blade out, and slammed it right through the meat of his palm.

The scream that escaped him made my heart pound. The rush of adrenaline was like no other, and it was both terrifying and haunting.

This was not something I did for fun.

I wasn't like Nyx.

But this motherfucker was stealing from us.

That came at a price.

A message needed to be rammed home, and while some of the OGs, my father's crowd who'd retired and who had nothing better to do than talk smack about me behind my back, might think I was a pussy, I figured it was time I showed them I wasn't.

Inked was going to be made an example out of.

***Rex:*** Clean up needed in the Fridge.
***Cruz:*** I'll deal with it.
***Rex:*** Appreciate that.
***Cruz:*** This my Christmas gift?
***Rex:*** Tell me after you've cleaned the place up.
***Cruz:*** Will do. Heard about Bear, Rex. I'm sorry, man.
***Cruz:*** Want me to tell the council about Inked?
***Cruz:*** I'll tell them you need some space. Be safe, man.

## PART 2

# "HOPE IS BEING ABLE TO SEE THAT THERE IS LIGHT DESPITE ALL OF THE DARKNESS."

- DESMOND TUTU

# EIGHTEEN

## RAIN

"Who the fuck are you?"

The guy froze like I'd shot him then twisted around to stare at me. There was a strange stillness about his expression that had me wanting to run off, but he raised his hands and murmured, "I'm Harlow."

I blinked. "Harlow? The guy I've heard Rachel talking about?"

"I assume I'm one and the same. I wouldn't like to make assumptions though."

Oddly soft spoken, I questioned, "What are you doing out here? It's fucking freezing."

"The same could be said for you," was his retort.

My brow furrowed. "I'm in training."

"What for?"

"I'm going to enlist after graduation."

Wow.

That felt good to say out loud.

I'd never admitted it to anyone before, but the way he stared at me... it made me want to tell him the truth. It was like he'd know I was lying if I gave him some BS.

What the hell?

His head tipped to the side. "Which branch?"

"Army."

"You want to fight wars?"

"I want to fight for people's freedom."

"Freedom's relative."

"No, it isn't."

"It shouldn't be, but it's definitely relative. What you and I consider a breach of our civil rights is so far from a woman who's not allowed to drive anymore because Afghanistan has changed governments."

"I want to fight for women like her."

"By killing people?"

I scowled. "What is this? A philosophical debate? I wanna know why the fuck you're sleeping in a tent in my backyard?"

"This is your backyard?" He exhaled. "I didn't realize. I thought it was just state land."

"Well, it isn't. Why aren't you staying at the clubhouse?"

"Because I haven't been invited to stay there yet. When Rex left... I don't think he told anyone I was thinking about becoming a Prospect."

My scowl darkened. "It was below freezing last night."

"Of this I'm aware," Harlow muttered before he popped a squat and started rearranging some logs on the ground.

It was only then that I saw he'd made a proper hearth for a campfire. It had stones around it and everything. I was an Eagle Scout, so I recognized someone who'd had the safety shit drilled into them.

And I wasn't just talking about Smokey Bear either.

"You were a scout?" I asked carefully as I stepped over to him, watching as he built a fire then set it to blazing.

All without us uttering a word.

Like I hadn't told him he was trespassing, and like he didn't know he was camping in my backyard.

"I was a scout, yeah," he rumbled, shadows flickering on his face thanks to the flames.

I crouched down in front of it, feeling the heat seep into my frozen limbs.

I'd researched SEAL training, knew it went down in subzero temperatures, and had decided I could start preparing myself for that day.

Didn't matter it was years in the future, preparation was everything.

Rach had taught me that.

"How are you staying warm? This fire won't do dick."

"Paper."

"Paper?"

He nodded. "Shoved into my coat then down around my legs into my sleeping bag. It works well."

I huffed. "It's going to be colder tonight."

"Maybe. It's all good."

Was it?

"If the brothers knew you didn't have anywhere to go, they'd let you stay at the clubhouse."

"I'm not forcing myself on them."

Hesitantly, I said, "My sister, Rachel, mentioned there was going to be a new Prospect."

"She mentioned that? To you?"

I grunted as the desire to stay quiet morphed and I admitted, "No. I heard her talking on the phone to someone in the Sinners. Are you the new Prospect?"

"Potentially."

Getting pissed at the non-answers, I grumbled, "Is that a yes or a no?"

"It's a 'Rex told me that was the only way I could get what I want.'" He cast me a look, and something in his eyes...

He didn't need the fire in front of him to look like he was burning in the flames.

There was something reminiscent about those eyes of his. Not the color, not even the Arctic frigidity in them that didn't invite conversation.

Nyx.

That was it.

Nyx.

He looked the same kind of tormented.

Like he'd been damned and sent to hell, but this was earth. Not the devil's playground. This was reality.

People shouldn't look like that. They wore masks that got them through daily strife and locked shit down with red wine after work. Rach did that. She didn't think I saw her pain, the anguish she endured, but I knew.

I'd caught her on Christmas Day, puking beyond the gates as Rex rode off. She'd looked like she was dying. I knew she grieved Bear, I did too, but there was no way that look was for Bear.

Sometimes, I thought she believed I was an idiot.

I knew how she looked at him; I just didn't understand what held her back.

"There are worse things than being a Sinner."

"There are?" He laughed. "Like what? If they're so great, why don't you want to be one?"

"I'll Prospect eventually with them. Rach won't like it, but I'll do it."

"She's your sister?"

I hummed. "I think she wants me to be a cop, but I'm not going to be one of those corrupt bastards."

I knew for a fact Rex wanted me to go into law enforcement. We'd had a couple conversations about how 'good men' like me were what 'the country' needed.

I didn't disagree—that was why I was enlisting and not becoming a pig.

Harlow rubbed his hands together, letting the flames heat them. "Can you fight for people's freedoms as a soldier then inhibit other people's on your home turf?"

"What do you mean?"

Harlow cast me a look. "They run guns and drugs, don't they?"

Pretty much. Not that I said that.

"People's freedoms involve being able to bear arms and to smoke whatever they want..." My lips twitched. "Nothing freer than being on the road."

"Why not just go straight into the MC?"

I shrugged. "Got things I want to do first."

"Like what?"

"Prove shit to myself. What about you? What were you before you came here?"

"Broken?"

I thought about that. "Lots of broken folk in the MC. Seems to be what puts people back together again."

"I don't think anything can put me back together again."

Nyx sprang to mind, but I didn't say that. I wasn't supposed to know that he hunted pedophiles in his spare time. It was one of the major reasons I wanted to be a Sinner.

Theirs was a righteous cause.

"Then why are you here?"

"Because at least I'd be around like-minded men."

"Not sure any of the brothers would be camping outside at the beginning of January. They're not fucking crazy."

Harlow's lips quirked up. "I'm one of a kind."

Jumping to my feet, I muttered, "I gotta get going."

"I'm not stopping you."

No, he wasn't.

But... there was something magnetic about him.

I fully admitted that I wasn't a leader. Neither was I a follower. I was a team player; I guessed that was the best way to describe me.

Harlow gave off a weird vibe, but it didn't seem right, leaving him here.

"Want me to intro you to the brothers? Get you set up on the compound?"

"They already know who I am."

"Then what's the problem?"

"I want what I want and, to get it, I need to Prospect. I guess my principles are the problem."

Confused, I asked, "What about them?"

"Carry on with your training, soldier boy. My problems and my freedoms aren't something you can solve."

While that annoyed the living fuck out of me, I couldn't let the dick stay out here. Not when he could end up dead.

And it wasn't *just* because the last thing we needed up on the hill was more cops roaming around, sniffing over the compound.

I couldn't think of a worse way to goddamn die than being slowly frozen to death.

Shuddering at the thought, I asked, "Are you a cop?"

He barked out a laugh. "No."

"You wouldn't tell me if you were undercover though, would you?"

"No, I wouldn't," he agreed with a smirk. "The MC helped my little sister out. That's why I'm here."

Our eyes clashed and held, and his phrasing rammed its way home.

"I'm sorry for your loss," I whispered.

"Thanks." His gaze darted back to the flames.

"You want..." Jesus, how did I say this without getting the Sinners into trouble? "They're good people, Harlow. Might do shit that's technically not approved of by certain members of society, but they're good people. They save lives. They just do it in their own way." I hesitated. "My conscience won't let me leave you out here. There's a spare bed at home. Tonight, you can sleep—"

"What makes you say they're good people? Don't they live up to their names?"

"Sure they do. Not saying they're not sinners, but isn't to be human to invite sin?"

"You go to church?" he asked flatly.

I scoffed. "No. Rach isn't the type. The Sinners aren't the type either. More likely to sleep in on a Sunday than go to church. That doesn't mean you can't though. So long as you do your shit, I'm sure if you wanted, they wouldn't stop you."

"Are you trying to sell them to me? This sounds like a sales pitch."

"Mostly I'm just trying to get you inside and out of this cold," I admitted. "But I'm not lying. I don't do lies." Especially with him and those weird eyes of his that seemed to see everything.

"Why not? Everyone lies."

"Because lies can be caught out. Rachel, she's a lawyer, she taught me that. Better to say nothing at all than to lie."

"Good philosophy."

"She's smart."

Harlow hummed as he got to his feet. "It really bothers you that I'll be sleeping out here?"

"Yeah. It really does."

"You've never slept on the streets before?"

"No. I couldn't imagine anything worse—"

"Oh, I could," Harlow rasped, his voice breaking.

*Shit.*

"I'm sorry, man. I didn't think—"

"It's all good." He raised a hand. "I'll put the fire out and head to the compound."

"You will?"

He rocked his head back to look at me, and in the firelight, his eyes burned even hotter than before. "I will."

I felt like a kid, but I asked, "You swear?"

"I swear."

I didn't realize that would be the first of many promises I'd ask of this man.

And I sure as hell didn't realize it would be the first he'd live and die by.

***Unknown Sender:*** Tell me you don't think those fuckers should die.

***Nyx:*** Plenty of people should die. Just don't feel like serving a murder one.

***Unknown Sender:*** What if I could guarantee you wouldn't get arrested?

## NINETEEN

### SIN

"Fancy place for a fancy outfit," I mocked, watching as Declan O'Donnelly shoved his sleeves further up his arms and ran his middle finger along the length of his nose so he could flip me the bird. "That's what I have to say to that, Padraig."

I sniffed to hide a smirk. "Sin."

"Sin. *Padraig*. Dual personalities—that a problem for you?"

"Not really," I drawled as I took a deep sip from the bottle of beer in front of me. "Schizophrenia's never really been in my bloodline. Just anger problems."

"Why am I here, Sin?" he groused as the waiter made an appearance. "And how the fuck did you get in looking like that?"

"I charmed the hostess."

"I'll bet."

"I'm here for the personal touch," I answered honestly.

"I'm taken."

I snorted. "Yeah, so am I now."

"The female population of Hell's Kitchen is in mourning, I'm sure."

"Yeah, it probably fucking is." I arched a brow at him. "How's the family?"

"You mean after our compound was raided and we lost a bunch of men... then after the red alert on the city thanks to the arson attack on the cathedral and the—"

I raised a hand. "After all that. Yeah."

Declan smirked. "It's been crazy. You heard from Mary Catherine?"

"She's in Ohio."

"I know. Is she happy?"

My voice was deceptively calm as I mused, "Told me some shit about your da trying to take her kid from her?"

"Fucking head case," Declan muttered under his breath as he smiled at the server and grabbed his drink as soon as it was on the table. "This year was supposed to be better than last year."

"Never works out that way. But we live in hope."

"That we fucking do." He rubbed his temple. "Conor would never have let Da take Mary Catherine's kid away from him."

I thought about my baby sister, the woman I'd known for too few years, who'd fallen for one of my MC brothers, and who'd fled to Ohio to escape her parents...

She'd had it too hard, and I knew Digger was intent on making shit better for her.

There was a reason I wasn't pissed about him making my baby sis his Old Lady—he was one of the fucking best.

No matter what Aidan O'Donnelly Sr. and MaryCat's goddamn family had to say on the subject.

"She's got postpartum depression," I informed him.

"I know. Conor gave me the lowdown. Said it was your mom who went to Da, tried to get the kid taken away from her."

I grunted. "Sounds about right. Bitch."

"She ain't changed," he agreed.

"Shame, but I'm not surprised. Fucking cunt could die tomorrow and I wouldn't hurry to her funeral."

His lips twitched. "Never was much love lost there."

I took a deep sip of my beer. "No. I definitely made my own family."

He clapped a hand to my back. "Glad to hear it. We okay?"

"You and me?"

"No. The Sinners and the Five Points," he demurred. "I know *we* are. You'd have greeted me with a gun under the table, not a fucking smile if we weren't. Shit like that would be a declaration of war to a lot of people."

"You're lucky I understand how your father works. Otherwise I'd be the one starting shit with you." I scratched my chin. "I know Aidan Jr.'s woman helped get her out of there, so that's made things better on my end. She wasn't alone."

"No. That hacker of yours helped as well."

"That she did." I shot him a look. "I'm okay with drawing a line under this so long as your da leaves MaryCat the fuck alone and lets her live her life in Ohio in peace."

He clucked his tongue. "Of course. Da's got bigger fish to fry at the moment anyway. No offense intended to Mary Catherine."

I tipped my bottle at him. "I get it."

And I did.

"Fucking Ohio? Shit must have been bad in Manhattan for her to go there," Declan said with a shake of his head.

"Trust me, I've visited," I drawled. "It's not the prettiest place in the world."

"I'll bet." He took another draw on his whiskey.

"What's going on with the Sparrows?"

Declan peered around the five-star restaurant and murmured, "How *did* you get in here?"

"My woman's got contacts."

Tiff might not be a real estate mogul's daughter anymore, but that didn't mean she didn't know her shit about the best places to wine and dine someone in the city.

Not that I was doing that—but I liked putting people on edge.

Especially shady fuckers like the Five Points. Even if I *did* like Declan. In another fucking life, I figured we'd be good friends.

"Why here?"

"Wanted privacy."

"Why?"

"Because I wanted to know if you had any high-ranking Sparrows in the Five Points."

He arched a brow. "You thought I'd be more likely to tell you here than in a dive bar near one of my warehouses?"

I grinned. "I'll buy you the porterhouse steak if that'll smooth things over."

"Yeah, just consider that lube." Declan snorted, shaking his head as he eyed the swanky lunch crowd.

It was all bankers and trust fund fuckers who didn't have shit better to do with their time than sit around places like this. Neither of us fit in here. Even if his suit was as fancy as what the bankers were wearing.

"You gonna tell me?" I prompted.

"Why are you asking?" he queried carefully. "You got Sinners who are Sparrows?"

I derided, "You kidding me? Nah. Rex might not be the head case your father is but no one would dare cross him."

That had Declan frowning. "He's that bad?"

"Got a temper on him," I confirmed, cracking my knuckles. "Bad one."

Declan pursed his lips. "How bad?"

"That bad he rarely loses it."

Declan's frown deepened. "What's that supposed to mean?"

"It means that he has himself on a self-imposed lockdown."

"Like you?"

"Like me," I confirmed.

"You who beat your father to death," he mused.

I shot him a smug smile. "Exactly."

He rolled his eyes at my smugness then, carefully, answered, "We're having a small problem with Sparrows in our nest."

"How many?"

"Depends on who you ask."

"I'm asking you."

He rubbed his chin. "Unofficial figures are two."

"Official figures?"

"Twenty-four."

"That's a fucking big leap. And why the fuck is that official?"

"Junior's got a plan." He rolled his eyes again. "I just think he prefers existing in misery."

Curious, I tipped my head to the side. "Why?"

"Dipshit's engaged—"

"I know. To Savannah Daniels. She's the one who helped Mary Catherine get out of New York."

He nodded. "You know she's a journalist, don't you?"

"She eased my morning wood a few times over the years—"

Declan snickered. "Don't tell Junior that."

"If he hasn't realized that already then there really is no fucking hope for him."

Grinning, he continued, "Asswipe told her there are twenty-four."

The fuck?

"Why?"

He shrugged. "Testing her."

My eyes flared wide. "You shitting me?"

"No, almost wish I were."

"Why the fuck is he doing that?"

"She's a reporter," he repeated.

I read between the lines. "So he wants to see if she spills a story to the press?"

"Or posts it on her blog."

"This is a disaster waiting to happen."

"Tell me about it," Declan rumbled, scraping a hand over his jaw. "She's reckless so I guess it makes sense. Anyway, it's not a total lie."

"No?" I retorted wryly. "Just a semi?"

"Just a semi," he agreed with a laugh. "We've probably had that many in the ranks, but there were just two in the higher-ups."

I nodded my understanding. "So, there's no real change to how we'll be working together—"

"Wait, let me guess, you're asking because you want to know if Mary Catherine's dad is a Sparrow?"

"This is about business."

He grunted. "Bullshit."

"It's semi-business," I conceded. "Nyx wanted me to reschedule the next run. Got a problem with the ATF sniffing around."

"Shit. Okay, I'll email over a new plan." He rubbed his eyes. "What's with the in-person meeting? Couldn't you just have called?"

I shrugged. "Wanted to be face to face when I asked you about the Sparrows. I don't like Mary Catherine's father."

"Well, unluckily for you, he's loyal to Da."

We shared a glance.

"That really is unlucky," I grumbled.

"Damn straight." He raised his glass, and I knocked my bottle against it. "I don't like him either."

## TWENTY

## RACHEL

"Where the fuck is he?"

Tiredly, I rubbed my temple where the headache from hell was attacking my brain.

The guys had cut Rex some slack until New Year's had come and gone without any updates from him.

Not even a phone call.

They were growing concerned, but I'd been worried since Christmas Day.

"You've spoken with Storm?" I rasped. "Checked he isn't in Coshocton?"

Nyx grunted. "What the fuck do you think, Rachel?"

"Watch it," Link grumbled. "This ain't Rachel's fault. Rex just... He needed to get away. Fuck, I can't blame him. I want to get away too."

"You can't escape grief," was Steel's somber retort as he shuffled the deck of cards in his hands.

I wished he were wrong, but he wasn't.

I also wished he'd stop with the damn cards.

With a sigh, I murmured, "If he doesn't check in soon, do we file a missing persons report?"

Nyx snorted. "It's almost like you don't know us at all, Rach."

"Fuck off, Nyx," I snapped. "We have to do something."

"No, we don't. He's just lost his dad." Nyx scrubbed a hand over his face. "He just needs a fucking break. He's not gonna get himself killed. This is Rex we're talking about, not me. We should be talking about the deal the Irish just struck with the Russians and the Italians, not a grown-assed man who can do whatever the fuck he wants with his time while he's grieving."

Silence fell in Rex's new office.

An office I didn't think he'd even sat in yet.

So far, we'd only been using the bar, but when discussing Rex's absence, we'd moved in here for privacy.

It didn't feel right.

Not at all.

My phone buzzed.

**Parker:** *The Valentini sales contract has come through.*

**Rachel:** *I'll check it later.*

**Parker:** *Still with the hotties?*

**Rachel:** *I won't tell them you said that. It'll make them more impossible than they already are.*

"He *is* a grown-assed man," Link concurred, breaking into my conversation with Parker. "But... this is Rex. The MC is his life. His lifeline. He wouldn't just go without leaving orders, Nyx."

"He didn't have to. I've been running point with him since the compound blast. He's not been as on hand since then anyway. He deserves some fucking time to himself without us calling in the pigs to make sure he's not MIA."

Ignoring that, Sin's knuckles cracked as he pressed down on them, rumbling, "You know what he's like..."

"He's got a better handle on his temper than before."

"He still snaps," Link pointed out. "His control ain't gone off the rails for a while, but it *does* happen. You can't deny that, Nyx."

Sin, unperturbed, tacked on, "It's in our blood, Nyx. There's no getting away from that."

Steel eyed him. "You can't say shit like that. Not with me around."

"Steel, there's a massive difference between being a goddamn child-abusing piece of fucking shit and having anger issues."

Maverick, being Maverick, didn't get distracted by the argument that snapped to life between the two of them, and he focused on me. "You sure he didn't say anything?"

Uncertainly, I licked my lips.

What could I say to that?

Their attention felt more threatening than a grand jury's.

In regular circumstances, I wouldn't have been affected, but this *was* my fault.

My anxiety soared as I felt their concern for Rex surge around the room. Trying to hide from it, I stared down at the wooden grain on the expansive table that was more befitting a boardroom than an office in an MC compound.

This room was a lot swankier than the last one.

I was pretty sure that Bear's council would have taken the piss out of Rex's decor choices, never mind all the goddamn pink in the bar. But this was a different generation.

This was *my* generation.

Not Bear's, not Grizzly's.

Mine.

I clenched my hands into fists as I pressed them into the table, but before I could say a word, Steel rubbed my shoulder. I hadn't expected it, so I flinched so hard that there was no way the assholes wouldn't notice it.

God, I hadn't done that in months.

Closing my eyes, I waited for them to comment, but instead, silence fell.

Silence that had more nuances than an orchestra.

"When I was seventeen, I babysat Giulia."

I felt their confusion, but they didn't question the start of my confession. Link's voice was soft, however, as he said, "I remember. You used to sit for most of the Old Ladies."

"Yeah. Quin and Indy too, right?" Nyx tacked on.

Swallowing, I finally opened my eyes, and this time, I looked at Link.

I knew he'd keep me going.

Knew he'd be my... *link*.

That was how he'd gotten his name, after all. He kept us together.

"What is it, Rach? You can tell us anything," he coaxed.

"I'm only telling you this now because I pushed Rex away. I'm the reason he left."

I didn't need to peer around the table to know that the brothers were all looking at each other. To know that they were shooting questioning glances back and forth.

Except for Link.

He kept his gaze locked on mine like he understood that he was the only thing keeping me from bolting out of the room.

"Do you remember Dog and Grizzly used to hang out?"

"How could I forget? Two dipshits together," he mocked, but his smile faded as he reached out and slipped his hand into mine. I clenched down around his fingers.

"One night, they came back stoned. They saw me... They raped me."

Link didn't react, but I heard Sin hiss, just as Nyx let out a snarl.

Steel grated out, "Those bastards."

I jumped when a fist smacked into the table, the noise overly loud as I blurted out, "You believe me?"

I didn't look away from Link.

"Why wouldn't we?" Nyx demanded. "Those fucking pieces of

shit." Both hands slammed against the table this time before he picked up his coffee cup and hurled it against the wall.

Steel snapped, "Back off, Nyx. Calm the fuck down."

But his anger helped me. It was cathartic. I needed that. I needed anger. Not disbelief.

"Grizzly said no one would believe me." With my free hand, I swiped at my eyes. "He said I was just like my mom—"

"We would always have believed you," Link chided softly, leaning over so that he was closer to me. "Just the once or more...?"

I bit my lip hard enough to feel the pinch. "Just the once," I choked out. "By them. I-I stopped babysitting."

Link froze as he read between the lines. "It happened again?"

"In college." I sniffed, wiped my eyes some more. "But that isn't related to this conversation—"

Before I could finish the sentence, the table, the heavy walnut expanse that was cut from one tree, went flying.

Nyx upended it.

Papers, glasses, pens, computers all went soaring through the air.

Link knew his brother too well because he'd dragged my seat quickly away, his own too so that we weren't in the danger zone.

Nyx tossed over the table like it weighed nothing, and he let out a roar that reminded me of Rex's on Christmas Day.

It was pain-filled.

Hurting.

For me.

That was when I sobbed.

"You believe me," I whispered, sitting amidst the chaos that Nyx had created; a chaos I didn't even know I needed.

Nyx dropped to his knees in front of me, papers crunching, glass smashing as he did so. His hands went to either side of my seat cushion and he stared into my eyes, his face moving uncomfortably close as he rasped, "I'd kill Grizzly and Dog for you if they weren't already dead."

I could feel my face crumple at his words, but I shook my head and pressed my hand to his shoulder. Squeezing down, I rasped back, "You made a promise that I intend for you to keep."

"The only people I care about... Why?" His mouth worked and his fingers tightened to the point where the chair groaned under the pressure of his hold. "Any brother who touches a woman against their will, I'm going to saw off their cocks in the future. I'm the VP now. This is *our* motherfucking MC."

He said it like he was telling me he was going to punish Prospects by sending them to clean the gutters.

Like it was an everyday point of conversation.

Instead, it was candid. *Raw.*

He meant it.

"Then, I'm going to make them watch as Cruz melts it in his chemicals."

I gulped. "Y-You can't do that."

"I sure as fuck can and I sure as fuck will!"

A tissue appeared in front of me, and I shot Steel a grateful look as I snagged it and blew my nose. Gingerly, he patted my shoulder.

It was such an unlikely move that I whispered, "You don't have to treat me like I'm a delicate flower. I'm the same Rachel. I-I just—"

"Is this why you're such a bitch?"

"Fuck's sake, Mav," Link ground out.

I was almost grateful for the question. I didn't want them to behave differently around me. "You had guns to protect you. I had ice."

My flat response had Mav nodding. "Makes sense. Wish you'd told us. Nyx wouldn't have been the only one lynching those bastards."

"I'm glad Lodestar got to Dog now," Steel muttered.

Mouth tightening, I nodded. "That was a very nice gift."

"She didn't make him suffer enough," Nyx snarled. "I'd—"

"You don't own torture," Link grumbled. "I'm sure he didn't want to die. I'm sure she made it nice and painful."

I blinked. "I shouldn't be hearing any of this."

"If you think Lodestar's ever going to get caught, you're crazy," Mav said flatly. "You don't need plausible deniability for her."

"Stop being a prick, Maverick," Sin snapped. "This is Rach. We're not talking statistics—"

Maverick narrowed his eyes at Sin. "Fuck you. Do you have any idea what I do for this club? The shit I've trawled through to get Nyx his evidence? His righteous kills? The things I've seen would get that temper of yours really fucking firing."

"This isn't a competition," Steel tried to placate. "We've all been through the wringer."

I swallowed. "I didn't mean to start an argument. I just wanted to explain—"

Nyx peered up at me. "Giulia said you're pregnant."

A shocked breath gusted from me. "She wasn't supposed... How the hell did she know?"

"Saw the pregnancy test." In his gaze, I saw that feral side of him that he was struggling to contain soar to the surface. "Is the kid Rex's?"

"Yes."

Link crouched down next to me. "I know you've got a weird dynamic. It's why he spent most of his time playing fucking chess with Peach than—"

*He'd been faithful to me?*

My eyes widened as I grabbed his arm. "They used to play chess?"

Link shrugged. "Most of the time. Figured you were..." He paused. "Well, to be honest, I don't fucking know what was going on with you two. I just knew that you had his cock in a vise."

Brow puckering, I asked softly, "I didn't mean to."

"Women never do," Sin drawled. "Doesn't stop it from happening."

Nyx cracked his knuckles. "What happened on Christmas Day? Did you tell him he was going to be a dad?"

"No!" I scowled at him and shoved his shoulder. "Nyx, you seriously think Rex would run out from his responsibilities? Shame on you!"

Link chuckled. "There's our Rach."

I didn't stop scowling at Nyx who finally raised his hands in apology. "I'm just trying to figure out what's going on here."

Pissed on his behalf, I grumbled, "Not *that*. Rex would never, ever—"

"Yeah, yeah, Saint Rex," Nyx sniped. "What did happen then?"

"We had sex." My cheeks blossomed with heat as their faces turned expressionless. Which, of course, meant I'd be the topic of conversation the second I left the room. Men were such terrible gossips. "I-I have issues."

"Understandable," Link attempted to soothe.

"Is it?" I asked bitterly. "I'm already a walking trigger. It wasn't even his fault. Christ, it never really is." I rubbed my brow again. "It was... It happened on a sofa. I didn't think it through. He was on me." My mouth worked. "He wasn't... He was asleep. I was asleep too. But if I share a bed with him, and we—" God, how did I explain?

"His weight makes you think it's Grizzly. Or Dog," Nyx said flatly.

"Yes. And after, if his hair is messy and—"

Sin seemed to understand what I struggled to verbalize. "He does look like his dad."

"Who looks like Grizzly," Link groaned.

It was tough to swallow when your throat felt sealed shut, but I managed it and whispered, "I screamed and froze him out. I do that a lot," I finished miserably. "I never thought he'd take off. Not like this."

"That's why you're so worried?" Steel questioned.

"What with Bear and everything, yes."

"We don't want to get the cops involved," Nyx muttered. "That's just asking for trouble."

Maverick's expressionless voice caught all our attention. "He could be heading down to New Mexico."

"New fucking Mexico? What the hell's down there?" Sin rubbed the back of his neck. "It's not like he's on the lam because of Inked."

My ears pricked at that, but then, as I so often had to, I shut off my curiosity.

It got me nowhere and meant that, down the line, I wouldn't be able to defend him from whatever he'd done to the thief in the Sinners' midsts.

"Maybe there or California?" Maverick mused.

"New Mexico or California?" Determined not to think of Inked and whatever might have happened to him at Rex's hands when he definitely wasn't my priority, I frowned and remarked, "Big difference."

"Not really," Maverick said grimly. "Two reasons for him to visit those states."

"What are they?" Steel demanded.

"Cali's where their kid is."

I could feel the color drain from my face as everyone froze.

"Their kid?" Link questioned, his gaze tripping between Mav and me.

Maverick nodded. "Their kid."

As one, the brothers turned their attention to me.

"Your kid?" Nyx rasped, and there was hell in his eyes.

"*Our* kid," I whispered. "Not Grizzly's or Dog's."

A breath stuttered from his lips. "Why the hell is that kid in California?"

"Because we gave her up for adoption."

"And Rex let that happen?" Steel sputtered.

Link raised a hand. "When the fuck was this?"

"First year of college."

He winced. "The kid... The second time you were assaulted?"

"No. She's Rex's. I was pregnant when that happened," I managed to get out. I reached up and covered my face. "I can't believe I'm talking to you all about this."

"You should have come to us the minute you could. We'd have lynched Grizzly and Dog and made them pay," Steel growled.

"Fuck yeah we would've," Nyx grated out. "We're your family, Rach."

"You weren't then. You were Rex's. Are we even friends now? I just keep your asses out of jail."

"I'm gonna forgive you for thinking that because we're having a tough conversation," Steel sniped. "But you question our friendship again, and I'll get Rex to spank your ass, and if he won't do that then he can make you stand in the goddamn corner.

"I don't give a fuck what he does so long as you realize you're one of us. You think we let any bitch into church? You think we trust just anyone? You're one of us, Rachel. Whether you like it or not."

My eyes pricked with tears again when I received a bunch of nods in agreement, even Mav gave me a grunt of assent, and I sniffled in response.

A week ago, I'd have coldly told them that I *did not* goddamn want to be their friend, and I'd have walked out.

Right now, I just felt the love and was embraced by it.

God, I hated being pregnant.

Last time, I'd been a crybaby. This time looked set to be just as bad.

"Rex is a possessive bastard," Link said softly. "He'd never let you put a kid of his up for adoption."

"After the second time, I wasn't in a good place. I tried to kill myself twice." I didn't feel like telling them I'd been hospitalized. "Rex knew. He arranged things."

"Rex has had me keep an eye on her since the day she was born," Maverick inserted.

The idea that he had was both comforting and distressing.

*I was her mother.*

I should have been interested, should have cared, but all I'd done was lock up that part of my life so I could forget about it. Thinking about her made me think about *it*.

I was such a shitty person.

Blowing out a breath, I asked, "Has he met her?"

"Not since she was a baby."

"Does he know who her parents are?"

"He got her placed with them. To this day, he still pays her way."

Nyx twisted back to gape at him. "Who the fuck are they, Mav?"

"You remember Ally and Jeremy Kinnock?"

Steel groaned. "Prom King and Queen?"

His lips twisted in a half smile. "You always did get a boner for her."

"Fuck off," Steel grumbled.

"Jez fires blanks, so they were looking to adopt. Rex arranged it with them. He has a direct influence on her life—picked her school, shit like that. They even kept the name Rach gave her." He cast me a look. "Wynter."

I swallowed.

"I'm surprised they agreed to that," Nyx murmured, "Jeremy was the QB, wasn't he?"

"He was."

"Arrogant asswipe," Nyx said with a sniff.

"Jeremy's business was going bankrupt, so Rex handled that and put them in his debt." Mav shrugged. "I'm not sure how deep his involvement is aside from what I do for him."

Link frowned. "Which is?"

"Monitor her."

I shivered. "That sounds creepy."

"Keeps her safe," he disregarded.

Despite myself, I liked the idea of that. "That's all that matters, I guess." I sighed. "She'll be seventeen in a couple days."

"Rex asked about her on Christmas Eve."

"If she's in California and her birthday is soon, why do you think he could be going to New Mexico?" Sin questioned

"I'm making an app. It's an open source means for parents to be able to monitor their kids' Internet usage. Rex has given me the go ahead to make it happen.

"But, along the way, I found this kid. He's a school shooter just waiting to happen. I told Rex about it. Second I heard he was missing, I figured he'd gone on a long run to clear his head."

"And to stop a school shooting at the same time?" Sin rolled his eyes as he leaned down and hauled the table back into a standing position. "It's a wonder he can get to sleep at night with that halo."

The wreckage crunched beneath the heavy table, but no one said a word as they hauled their chairs toward it.

Everyone but me.

Nyx was still in front of me.

Still on his knees.

Still watching me.

I sucked in a breath. "It's okay, Nyx."

"Nothing about this is okay. I've killed strangers to protect kids I haven't met. But the people I love were hurting all along, and I didn't do anything to make it better."

"You dealt with Kevin," I pointed out.

"That wasn't enough. Grizzly and Dog... I should have those kills inked into my skin." His hand hovered a second, until he settled it on my arm. "You can say what you want, Rachel, but you flinch like it happened yesterday. You're still as fucked up by the past as I am."

I couldn't deny that he was right. I wanted to, but I couldn't.

"Killing them wouldn't have helped me," was all I could think to say.

"Why not?" he growled.

"Because my second attacker was murdered right in front of my eyes." I tipped up my chin. "If anything, that just makes the nightmares worse."

***Unknown Sender:*** So many perverts out there...
***Unknown Sender:*** You're running out of time.
***Nyx:*** They're for the cops to hunt.
***Unknown Sender:*** That's why there are so many still free. No one cares. Kids don't have a voice. You gave them that.
***Nyx:*** I didn't do anything. I'm just a regular citizen.
***Unknown Sender:*** You keep on telling yourself that.
***Nyx:*** Got nothing to prove to anyone.
***Unknown Sender:*** You don't want to make a difference?
***Nyx:*** Why the fuck is this on me? If you're so all-fired 'special,' then why the hell aren't you the one going out and getting rid of these bastards?
***Unknown Sender:*** This is a young man's game. No jail time, son. Just think about it... the freedom to do what the cops aren't doing.
***Nyx:*** This is entrapment.
***Unknown Sender:*** Do I sound like a cop to you?
***Nyx:*** No, but I'm not in the business of listening to shit that sounds too good to be true either. Fuck off.

## TWENTY-ONE

## REX

PUMPED UP KICKS - FOSTER THE PEOPLE

"Shut the door behind you." I cocked my gun. The click was loud in the silent room. A sharp gasp escaped the kid in front of me. "Don't say a word. Turn around. In that order."

The door closed, the boy twisted around, and in his eyes, there was stark, stark fear.

What I was doing was wrong.

Very wrong.

But it was also fucking right.

His eyes were massive, big doe-like almonds that gawped at me, taking me in, taking in the weapon in my arms.

His weapon.

A weapon he was going to use against other kids.

He swallowed at the sight.

For the first hundred miles after I left Rachel and dealt with Inked, I just rode. I wasn't going anywhere, was getting away. Doing as she'd requested—getting the fuck out of there.

Then, when my tank hovered close to empty, I filled up at a gas station. It could have been fucking fate for all I knew but the news came on the TV—a shooting. In New Mexico. And all of a sudden, I'd remembered.

The kid. The potential shooter.

Maverick had emailed me the little bastard's details on Christmas Eve, and suddenly, I'd known where I was going. What I was going to do. And here I was, about to deliver a judgment worthy of Solomon himself.

"You want to piss yourself, don't you?" I rasped.

His gaze locked on mine, and he nodded.

"You should think about how you feel right now and think about how the kids in your school will feel when you go in there like you're in a first-person shooter game." I patted the body and resettled the butt against my lap. "You ever shot anything, kid?"

He shook his head.

"Not even some innocent deer in a forest with your dad?"

"No," he whispered.

"I have," I told him calmly. "The second you press the trigger, it's like the clock slows and speeds up all at once. I've never known anything like it. It's the only time it ever happens. You don't see where the bullet goes until it hits someone, and by that point, any regrets are in the wind.

"There's no taking shit back. No making shit right. That's it. Someone's hit. All GSWs are reported to the cops, so there's no fixing things. No escaping it." I narrowed my eyes on him. "What makes you think you can drag this out and hurt innocent people, huh?"

He squeaked, "Can I answer?"

"I ask you a question, you can answer. You call out, I won't shoot you with this." I grabbed the knife from the table beside me where I'd rested it as I waited for him to eat his dinner. "I'll just slit your throat instead."

Those big doe eyes got even bigger.

"I never miss."

He gulped.

"Go on," I quipped. "Answer me."

"I want them to die."

"Who's they?"

"Bullies," he breathed.

It was more than bullying. It was torture. I'd seen that in his journal notes. "You've talked about being bullied with your family?"

"Yes."

"What do they say?"

"That I'm a pussy."

Well, of all the motherfucking things to say to a kid.

I reached up and scratched my chin. "Are you a pussy?"

"Maybe."

My brow furrowed. "Ever had sex?"

He shook his head quickly. "No."

"This path is one helluva way to never get laid. Just saying. Well, with a pussy." I thought about that a second. "You'd get your ass reamed in jail if they ever let you out of solitary. Maybe you're gay. Maybe you'd like that. Is that why you've never had sex?"

"I'm sixteen," he squeaked.

"So? I had sex when I was twelve."

He gaped at me. "Twelve?"

"Yeah. Twelve. Anyway. You don't know this *yet*, but pussies can take a pounding. They bleed every month and they don't die. Babies come out of them. Seven-pound monsters. You think a pussy is weak if it can do all that?"

"N-No."

"That's right. So, are you a pussy?"

"Is this a trick question?" he whispered confusedly.

"Naw." I leaned forward and set the gun on the ground then placed my booted foot over it. "Just trying to make right what your fool parents told you. You ain't a pussy, but if you were, there's no shame in that. Older you get, the more you'll realize a pussy is the only place you *want* to be."

"Now, killing all these folks… How will that help?"

"They'll know how I feel."

"How do you feel?"

"Like I don't matter."

I scoffed. "No one matters, kid. Not really. We're all ants in this massive universe. You want to matter to someone, you can achieve that by not going into your school, not firing a submachine gun, and expecting to be heard.

"You want to matter to anyone other than a judge and a jury, and maybe an executioner—" I started flipping my knife in my hand.

"New Mexico isn't a death penalty state," he whispered, his back flattening to the door.

I shot him a smile. "Plenty of ways to get sentenced to death that don't involve a lethal injection."

"I'd be in solitary."

"Guards kill prisoners all the time. Anyway, you really want that to be how you live and die?"

"I want them to know how I feel," he repeated, like that'd make the shit he was spewing be more reasonable.

"You thinking about jail or shooting yourself afterward?"

He licked his lips. "I want to die."

I hummed. "I can kill you now if you want?"

I wasn't surprised when a puddle of piss made an appearance.

"I think we got our answer, don't we?" I mocked, staring down at the proof he was all BS.

"Y-You... I can't, won't... I'll scream!"

I smirked. "Scream away. Won't change shit. I'll still do it. Today can be the last day you're on this planet if you want."

"B-But—"

"But what?" I arched a brow at him. "Why do they bully you?"

He ducked his head. "I'm not popular."

"Do you want to be?"

"No." He snapped a scowl at me. "I don't care about popularity."

"Good thing seeing as shooting up your fucking school is how you lose it."

His glare darkened, anger starting to replace fear. His hands balled into fists as he stormed forward. "You think I deserve to be bullied?"

"Nope. Bullies are pieces of shit who deserve to rot in hell." I shot him a smile. "Wouldn't that be nice? You being fucked up the ass by hot pokers by the devil himself right next to the bastard who bullied you. You can spend an eternity together. If you believe in that, of course."

I knew his family did.

He swallowed again.

"Anyone ever talked to you about this? These feelings?"

He shook his head.

"Why not? You never talked to them about it?"

"No."

"You got a therapist?"

"Why? Because I'm a chicken shit so I should have one?"

"You should have one because you want to kill people. I mean, if anyone was a poster child for therapy, you can't deny that it's you."

His jaw clenched. "Why are you here?"

"To stop you, of course. By any means necessary." I flicked the knife toward him. He froze, let out a whimper as it sailed past his throat, by barely a quarter inch. Enough that he'd have a slight graze from its passing as it lodged itself in the door jamb.

As he stared at me, eyes blank with shock, I pulled out another knife and started picking my nails with it.

"Like I said... any means necessary."

"You're going to kill me?" he whispered.

"You said you wanted to die," I pointed out.

"I-I do. I did. I mean, I don't..." His mouth wobbled. "I just want it to stop. I just really need it to stop. I can't take it anymore. I said that if they left me alone on the first day back at school, that was it. I-I'd avoid them too. I wouldn't hurt anyone. It depends on them. It's their fault."

"Ain't their fault," I disregarded. "They don't deserve to die. No kid deserves to die, especially not in school."

"So it's okay for them to torment me? To beat me until I bleed. To steal from me and to humiliate me?"

"Not okay. Doesn't mean you should shoot them. Means you should report them."

"I have. No one listens," he rasped. "No one fucking listens to me." His hands fisted again and he punched the air, hitting down as he snapped, "I'm invisible. Everything I do or say, no one hears or cares. I tell my folks, and Dad says I'm a pussy and Mom tries to help, but when she reports them to the faculty, they don't listen." Tears had started coursing down his cheeks. He swiped at them with his knuckles. "Last time, they even told Brandon who'd reported them, and it made it worse." He sniffled. "I just want to escape. I don't want this anymore. There's no other way. I'm trapped."

"You will be trapped if you take this next step," I said softly. "There's no PS5 in jail, kid." I peered around his room, spotting the myriad home comforts there. "The next decision *you* make won't just affect your life, it'll affect the kids you hurt too. Do you think that's fair?"

"They laugh when he humiliates me. All of them. They laugh. Is that fair?"

"Being complicit doesn't mean they deserve a death sentence."

He closed his eyes. "I want out."

"Knife's in the door, Drew," I informed him, speaking his name aloud for the first time. "There's an exit strategy. It's your choice, on your terms, won't hurt no one else. You go as you came into this world. Alone."

His mouth tightened. "I don't want to be alone. I'm tired of being alone."

"You're not alone. Your dad might be a piece of shit but he's there. Your mom cares. This bedroom has more tech than a lab. They love you; they're with you. It might not be how you need, but trust me, when it's gone, you'll feel the vacuum they leave behind.

"Shit's bad now, and I'm not saying it's not going to get worse, but is this really the solution?"

This time, when his eyes drifted open, I saw the entreaty there.

It had engulfed the fear and the self-righteous anger.

"What do I do?"

"You don't kill innocent people. You don't terrorize them. You go to your mom and you tell her what you were planning. You tell her that you were going to kill yourself."

"She'll—"

"What? She'll punish you? You think jail's a walk in the park? You think having your PS5 taken away is worse than that?"

"N-No, but they'll look at me different—"

"Better for that now than after you've murdered your class, right? You think she'll look at you with love then? Think she'll visit you in jail?"

His cheeks blanched.

"Once you take this step, that's it, Drew. No going back. Ten years of therapy is better than ten years of jail."

"What if they put me in a mental institution?"

"Well, you won't have to deal with Brandon, will you?" I countered flatly.

"N-No," he agreed.

"There's no one-size-fits-all solution, Drew. But the best way forward is not to kill people. Can we both agree on that?"

"You said you killed people," he whispered.

"I have."

"Why?"

"Vengeance. For my mother." My eyes were cold as I explained, "In the end, they weren't even the ones who'd killed my mom. I know what it's like to take lives, and I know that it leaves a mark on you."

"You're a hypocrite!" he cried. "Preaching at me like you're perfect when you don't know what I've been through." He shuddered, revulsion twisting his face into a maw that'd haunt me until the day I died. "You don't know what they've done to me!"

"Never said I was perfect," I told him, as calmly as I could. "I'm the opposite in fact. And I'm not a hypocrite. If anything, I'm perfectly placed to tell you that you're about to land yourself in a world of hurt and there's no turning back." I leaned down and picked up the gun. "I'm going to take this with me because I don't trust you, Drew.

"Unfortunately for you, whichever path you take, I don't trust you to not hurt innocent kids. Brandon might be a piece of shit, but that doesn't mean they all are."

Slowly, he shook his head. "You're saying I should just kill Brandon?"

My lips almost twitched.

I remembered a long time ago, dealing with Nyx. Homicidal and hurting, grief-stricken and enraged. His fury hadn't died. His righteous need to avenge his sister hadn't abated.

Maybe I *was* a hypocrite.

Not only had I killed out of vengeance, I hadn't been punished for it.

But this was different, no?

These were kids, for Christ's sake.

I scraped a hand over my jaw again and slowly articulated, "I think you're the kind of person the world would be better off having in it."

That had him gaping at me. "Me? Why would you say that?"

"Had a nose around your things, Drew. Saw the stuff you're studying. Read a couple of your assignment essays while I waited on you to have dinner. Your critical thinking skills should be better than this, kid. You know that two wrongs don't make a right.

"Here and now, it's the desperation talking. The need to escape. And I get that. I really fucking do. That's why I'm here. Because I needed to escape. I needed to get away, and I'm an adult, so that's okay. I'm not a kid who's tied to this house or school. You can't escape. That's why this whacked reaction seems like your only solution, but if you were sitting in my shoes, talking to a kid like you, what would you say? What would you tell him about this permanent solution to what's, essentially, a very temporary problem?"

His mouth worked again as I felt my words hit home. "I-I don't know," he whispered.

"You do. You just don't want to admit it. You're filled with rage and confusion and sorrow and hurt. You've been humiliated and belittled...

"You're desperate, Drew. You're trying to escape. Well, I'm telling you, this ain't the way forward."

His fists clenched again, but his answer wasn't angry, just lost. "What should I do?"

"Tell your mom. Make her listen. Tell her that your dad calling you a pussy is making this worse. Tell her that you were thinking of buying a gun and taking it to school. That you were going to make them listen *that way*. Tell her that if she doesn't do something, that's what'll happen."

"And what do I do if she doesn't listen?"

I blinked at him, stunned that, in his mind, that might be an option. What kind of fucking mother would ignore a cry for help like that?

"You email me." I dropped a card on his nightstand, one that I'd annotated with an untraceable email address Maverick had told me he'd monitor. "And we'll figure it out."

He frowned. "Why would you do that? Why do you even care?"

"Because we all hit crossroads in this life, kid. Thinking shit, planning shit, it don't make you a bad person. *Doing* it does. You make a decision that ends your life, that's on you. But the minute I heard about you, what you were planning, I wasn't about to let that be on *my* conscience."

"Why would that matter? If you've taken lives—"

"I still know what's right and what's wrong even if I don't lead my life how regular folk do.

"You're sixteen, Drew. You got a bright future ahead of you if you don't fuck things up. If I can help, I will. If I can't, I can't. I tried. You're going to do what you're going to do. I can't report you for a crime you ain't committed. I can slip a note to them, maybe show them footage of you buying a gun which, just FYI, I have—" He blanched. "I can make them see how dangerous you are and, all of a sudden, things have escalated. The authorities will get involved instead of this being dealt with by your family.

"I'm giving you a choice, Drew. That's what it boils down to. *A choice.* You're about to decide what you want to do with the rest of your life, because I can promise you this: you choose the wrong path, I won't let you hurt those kids. I will stop you from doing something stupid.

"But you're not alone anymore, and this warning ain't to say that I won't make your boy Brandon suffer for what he's done to you."

For the first time, an interested gleam appeared in his eyes. The desperation faded somewhat, replaced by a hunger for payback.

"What'll you do?"

"Plant a couple baggies of coke on him." I shrugged. "Enough for a possession charge."

"He's underage."

I smiled. "It'll still get him off your back."

A breath gusted from his lungs. "You'll really do that?"

"Ain't just you who'd get those kids killed," I reasoned.

He swallowed. "No."

"If he left you alone, would school be better?"

"Yes. He's the ringleader. H-He... he has friends. They're bullies, too, but they're idiots. He encourages it."

Nodding, I said, "Consider it done."

"Thank you," he whispered.

"The way to thank me is to make the right choice, Drew. You're messed up, kid, so let's try to fix shit before it's unfixable. I don't want to come back here. I don't want to see you again, and I don't think you want to see me, either, do you?"

His head whipped from side to side, a squeak escaping him as I took a step closer, the threat clear.

"You think Brandon's bad, Drew? You've met someone a thousand times worse."

## TWENTY-TWO

## INDY

I hissed as I took a seat on the hard bench. My butt cheeks burned from last night's spanking, and the ache was real today.

The little voice in my head chanted, 'You will not speak ill of yourself.'

That little voice sounded remarkably like Cruz.

'You will not put yourself down.'

'You will not diminish your worth.'

The mantra had been spanked into me, and my ass felt red raw as a result.

A spanking made an orgasm hit hotter and harder, but damn, the aftermath was nasty.

"Ms. Sisson?"

Blinking at the officer, I rasped, "Sorry, Officer Lewiston, I—" How did I excuse sore ass cheeks? "I fell on my butt yesterday and it's hurting."

A soft smile curved his lips. "Your tailbone? God, that hurts."

"It really does," I said, cringing. It was a lie, but he didn't need to know my pain was further south than that. "Anyway, Officer, how can I help? I told you everything I know about David."

Aside from the fact that in life, he'd been a creepy stalker whom I'd killed in self-defense, and that, in death, he was just as much of a headache.

"I wondered if you could recount the last time you saw him. Maybe it would help us narrow the timeline down so we could figure out when he actually left town."

A knock sounded in the small interrogation room. A short, sharp, *brisk* tap. The person behind the door didn't wait for the officer to call out to open it.

Rachel's stern features made an appearance, and I jerked back in surprise. "Rach? What are you doing here?"

"Ms. Laker?" the officer intoned, his surprise clear too. Well, that and there was some displeasure thrown into the mix.

I almost snorted.

This clearly wasn't the first time he'd had a run-in with Rachel.

No man survived those without coming out with claw marks.

"I don't appreciate you arranging interviews with my clients without allowing time for her counsel to show up."

"She doesn't need a lawyer. This is an informal chat."

"Then why aren't you in her tattoo shop? Why have you invited her into the precinct?"

Officer Lewiston pursed his lips. "For privacy."

"Why is privacy required? This is most irregular. Are you recording this interview? Is there someone behind the glass?" She tapped the mirror before she stepped over to the table and placed her briefcase on it. "I only know Ms. Sisson is here because her partner contacted me."

Cruz had phoned Rachel?

My brow furrowed in confusion but I kept my trap shut.

Clearly, something was happening that Cruz hadn't shared with me.

Pissed, I watched as Rachel ran circles around Lewiston whose cheeks burned brighter than the sun with every sniped comment she made.

"She doesn't need a lawyer," he insisted again. "I just wanted to ask her if she'd remembered any details."

"I think this is turning into harassment," Rachel tossed down. "How many times have you spoken with Officer Lewiston, Indiana?"

"Five times. This is the sixth."

Her face puckered with disapproval. Seriously, it looked like she'd deepthroated a lime. "If the information didn't help those initial times, what did you hope to discover on this occasion?"

"A man's missing, Ms. Laker. Did you forget that?"

"I didn't. But we don't even know if he *is* missing. Did you forget that my client has no knowledge as to where her receptionist has gone? She isn't to blame for him deciding to take off to only God knows where and to not key his family into his travel plans. If anything, she's a man down at her tattoo shop."

"I never said she was to blame," he retorted sullenly.

"Then why harass her?"

"I'm not," he ground out.

"The next time you wish to speak with Ms. Sisson, I will be there to ensure that nothing improper occurs."

"Improper? What the hell are you insinuating?"

"I'm insinuating nothing," Rachel intoned before she grabbed my arm and said, "Come, Indiana."

As she hauled me onto my feet, I winced as my ass protested the scrape of denim against it, but I followed her when she told me to.

Rachel wasn't the kind of woman you said no to.

Especially not in a police station.

As we made it outside, I shot an apologetic wave to Lewiston, who looked as perplexed as I felt, then, when we were beyond the doors to the station, asked, "Cruz sent you?"

"You should have called me," Rachel reprimanded.

"I didn't think I needed to."

"You always need a lawyer there when the cops call you in."

"Doesn't it make me look guilty? That I need you, I mean?"

"That's a ploy of theirs," she scoffed. "To pressure you into speaking without counsel present. Don't do it again."

I took orders off Cruz, but that was consensual. This didn't feel very consensual.

Still, it was free with the MC footing her bill, and I *hadn't* liked how Lewiston waltzed into Indiana Ink asking for a moment of my time. I charged two hundred bucks an hour. My time wasn't free.

"Is there a problem?" I asked softly when I realized Rachel was returning to her car.

"Aside from the fact that David's missing and his family has sent in a private investigator to find out where he is?"

"Yeah, aside from that?"

We shared a look that told me she'd discerned where David really was—in a bottle of Cruz's homemade soup.

"No. You haven't done anything wrong. We just need to make sure the cops remember that."

"There's no trail," I whispered.

"No body, no crime either," she whispered back, but her eyes were cold.

Damn, she was always cold.

I'd forever wondered if she was this frigid in every aspect of her life, but Rain was a good kid, a warm one.

When I hung out with Giulia at Rach's place, I'd heard Rain joking around with her even if I hadn't heard Rachel's responses, so I knew she wasn't always like an iceberg. Just with certain people.

That saddened me.

She wasn't born into the life, but she'd been around long enough that she might as well have been.

We could have been friends, but we weren't. She'd hung around with older kids like my sister even though there'd been a five-year age gap between them.

Reaching up, I tugged on my lip and asked, "Everything okay, Rach?"

"Why wouldn't it be?"

She didn't let me answer, just slipped into her car when her driver opened the door for her, and I watched as he drove her to whatever hellhole she'd been existing in lately.

"Because you look like you haven't slept in a month," I said to no one, uncaring that I was talking to myself.

Huddling into my coat, I watched her taillights disappear then crossed the road to return to my tattoo shop.

The heat blasted me the second I was inside, making my cheeks burn and my hands itch from the temperature difference. I shuddered as I stomped my feet to get rid of some of the snow from my boots.

"How'd it go?"

I peered at Giulia then glanced around, surprised to realize Cruz was nowhere to be found. Behind her, I saw the news drift from a report on a hockey player who'd been kidnapped and onto that piece of shit rapist who was preying on women in Harlem.

"Cruz got called to the clubhouse," Giulia answered before I could ask, switching off the TV with a click of the remote. "And he was wicked pissed about having to go. What happened at the precinct?"

Warmth filled me at the news of Cruz's irritation.

God, I adored how much he loved me.

Dragging my scarf and coat off, I muttered, "Rachel stormed in like Ally McBeal."

Giulia pursed her lips at that. "Do you think she's looking sick?"

"More like tired. She looks like she ain't slept for a month."

"She has killer nightmares." Her gaze welded itself to mine. "I hear her screaming some nights, despite her being at the other end of that massive house."

I scowled "Screaming?"

"Yeah. Like she's being attacked. Asked Nyx about it the other day. He didn't have much to say about it."

I angled my head as I studied her. She'd brought this up for a reason. "Spit it out, Giulia. Whatever you want to ask, just ask."

She shrugged as I hung up my coat. "Not sure what I'm asking. I just... I've never heard anyone really talk about her. Nyx clearly knows something but he's keeping it private. That's not like him. We share everything."

"There's not much to say. She keeps to herself, always has."

"The way she screams, those are night terrors. Something triggered them."

"Doubt we'll ever know what." I reached up and ran my fingers through my hair. "Any news about Rex?"

"No. Nyx is concerned."

"I'll bet. How's he doing?"

I hadn't seen her for a couple days. My nephew was making shit impossible on his mom. Giulia was a hard worker, so when she phoned in sick, I knew she had to be close to dying to make the call.

"Things are rough. He's thriving on the extra pressure from the club though. Swore a Prospect in yesterday."

"I heard about the party."

"Surprised you didn't go."

"Cruz was mad at me. Did you go?"

"Showed my face, then Nyx's spawn decided I had to nap." She studied me. "Nyx said we won't be seeing Inked around any time soon. He made a big speech about not betraying the club." Her gaze turned inward. "Made out like his punishment was exile, but I don't think it was."

Arching a brow at her, I sliced my finger across my throat.

She nodded. "Think so."

Because I hadn't heard any news about Inked from Cruz, or anyone to be fair, I questioned, "Why would they get rid of him?"

"He was on the take from the strip joint."

"Was he a fucking moron?"

She hummed. "I wish I'd been there when they dealt with him, actually."

"To watch him have the shit kicked out of him?"

Her grin was twisted as she patted her belly. "Remember, this is

Nyx's spawn. I'm bloodthirstier than I was before. He had more than the shit kicked outta him, Indy. They're one-percenters, not the fucking Brady Bunch."

"Jesus H. Christ," I grumbled, rolling my eyes.

The grin morphed into a smirk as she queried, "What did you do to piss Cruz off anyways?"

My cheeks turned bright pink. "Someone in a magazine complimented my work on the TV show and I downplayed it."

"He was mad about that?" Giulia scorned. "Jesus, I thought you'd put glitter in his shaving foam or something—"

"Was that why Nyx was sparkly last time I saw him?" I butted in, only, when she smirked at me, I huffed. "I know that smirk. Do I even want to know what he did to deserve that?"

"Probably not."

"How the fuck did you even get the glitter in the foam?" Before she could answer, I raised a hand to stall her. "Never mind. Well, the next time you decide to turn my brother into one of the cast from Twilight—"

Giulia burst out laughing before I could finish my sentence. She hooted, slamming her hand into the desk before crying, "Oh, man, I need to pee now. I need to pee so bad."

The crazy pregnant lady kept coming out with shit like that, shit that made me determined not to have babies.

I crinkled my nose. "Use the bathroom?"

"Well, I'm not gonna go potty on the chair," she mocked around a cackle, sounding breathless.

"What *did* he do?" I asked, curiosity biting me in the ass as she got out of the chair and waddled over to the restroom.

"Told me that three orgasms was plenty."

I snorted. "You're greedy."

She shot me a smirk. "You trying to tell me you ain't? With all that hobbling of your own you do? And hissing every time you sit down?" Her eyes rolled. "Get real."

Because I had no come back, I just flipped her the bird.

Giulia: 1. Indy: 0.

Goddammit.

"Not sure who I feel sorrier for—Nyx or that kid," I muttered wryly to myself as she closed the door to the restroom.

Turning back to the shop, I grimaced. Without her there to distract me, it was too easy to think about what had happened between David and me that night. When I'd defended myself, and when Cruz and Nyx had cleaned up my mess for me.

Seeking comfort, I reached up and rubbed my brand. The act made me feel connected to Cruz.

No matter what, I knew he'd keep me safe.

I had to have faith in *him* if nothing else.

As if he'd heard me, my cell buzzed, his name flashing across the screen.

Relief filtered through me.

And love.

A whole lot of love.

***Unknown Sender:*** Mikhail Korolev
***Nyx:*** Who?
***Unknown Sender:*** Priest. Kiddy diddler. Got proof. Some vermin just need exterminating.
***Nyx:*** Call in a rat catcher.
***Unknown Sender:*** Thought I had?

# TWENTY-THREE

## RACHEL

"Rachel?"

I was exhausted. Beyond exhausted. But the person on the other end of the line had me sitting straighter in my chair as I placed my phone on speaker.

"That time of the year already, Rory?" I asked as I scanned an email from Susanne, my paralegal.

I heard the smirk in her voice as she said, "Just wanting to check on the situation."

"I sent you an update two weeks ago. You know Currau Valentini's case is one of my priorities," I groused.

For an old man who'd been sent up for a crime he hadn't committed, one who'd happily die in prison, I spent a good chunk of every day working on freeing him.

"Actually, that wasn't what I meant. I wanted to let you know I'll be resigning soon."

"You will?" I asked warily.

"Yes."

"Why are you calling from this number?" I questioned, eying the Caller ID.

*New York DA* flashed on it.

Not Rory.

"I didn't think you'd answer if I called you on my personal cell. You've been avoiding me."

"I haven't," I said, but I knew I sounded guilty.

"You have," she countered. "But that's okay. You always avoid me this time of the year."

I winced because she wasn't wrong.

"If I cut the line, will you answer my personal cell?"

I heaved a sigh. "Yes."

She didn't reply, just ended the call. A second later, my phone rang again, and this time, 'Rory' was on the screen.

Pursing my lips, I answered, "You're a pain in my ass, do you know that?"

"Aren't we that for each other?"

I stared out of the window that overlooked a small section of countryside in the distance. Normally, I tried to allow it to calm me down. To bring me peace. In my line of work, I needed peace more than a Buddhist monk. But it didn't work.

Aurora was, *officially*, my enemy.

As New York's DA, she prosecuted the people I defended.

Personally?

She was one of my best friends.

She was also one of the reasons I had horrendous nightmares.

Okay, that wasn't fair. It wasn't her fault her husband was a piece of shit. She'd even been the reason I got out of there in one piece. Well, Hunter was the reason. Hunter, my other best friend...

Jesus, it was complicated.

What wasn't in my life?

Rubbing my temple, I muttered, "Okay, pain in the ass, what's going on? Why are you resigning?"

"There's been a development."

Suspiciously, I asked, "What kind of development? I wasn't notified about any changes in Currau's case."

Rory grunted. "Not where he's concerned. I'm talking on a different front. The *Famiglia* has made an arrangement with the Irish Mob—"

"I don't need to know this," I grated out. "Can't you keep me in the loop without telling me stuff that'll get my head blown up?"

She snorted. "Since when are you in danger of that?"

"I'm not Wonder Woman. I'm pretty sure even her damn skull would cave in from a bullet to the temple."

"The way you're spread thin among Manhattan's criminal elite tells me you have your security locked up nice and tight."

"Dear God, did you just laugh?" I asked, horrified.

"I'm happy."

"You are?"

If I sounded disbelieving, that wasn't because I was a bitch. Although, undoubtedly, most of the people who knew me thought I was one…

"Yes. We're close, Rach. So damn close."

I let that assimilate then asked, "I haven't heard anything."

"The Irish agreed to meet with the Italians… It's time to finally get out." Her voice turned softer as she whispered, "It's happening, Rach. It's happening."

I swallowed. "That's… Well, I don't know what that is, Rory. But if it makes you happy then I'm glad."

Another soft laugh echoed down the line. "There's a sweet irony to the fact that you're a good girl surrounded by bad people, Rachel."

"I'm good at getting bad people out of dicey situations," I grumbled, pinching the bridge of my nose.

"There's no denying that." She sighed. "I didn't speak with you over Christmas. I tried to call but there was no answer."

"It was crazy."

"Why? We haven't caught up in ages."

"No," I said sadly. "It's been a while, hasn't it?"

"Are you coming to the city soon?"

"Tomorrow."

"Feel like meeting up? I found a delicious Zinfandel—"

"Rory? I have to tell you something."

"What?" It was her turn to sound suspicious. "Is it why I haven't spoken to you in ages?"

"No." Awkwardly, I muttered, "You know I prefer rosé."

She paused. "What?"

I grimaced. "I mean... Never mind. I-I only found this out on Christmas Eve. Well, I had it confirmed."

"Are you sick?" She gasped. "Oh, God, you are, aren't you?"

"No, no, nothing like that." I braced myself for the fallout. "I'm pregnant."

Silence fell at that, and I got it.

I really did.

"You still there?" I asked after a couple minutes of quiet. I mean, I knew she *was* there. I could hear her breathing. But I figured it was time to wake her up from whatever was making her sound like I had a heavy breather down the line. "Rory?" I prompted impatiently.

"I thought you weren't going to do that again?"

I felt the sting of tears at the betrayal in her voice. "Why do you think I didn't want to tell you, Rory?"

"Parting with Wynter was one of the hardest things you ever had to do. I watched you mourn her for months, Rachel. You were like the walking dead back then. Why are you putting yourself through that again?"

"I'm not going to give this one up."

"You're not?"

"No. I-I can't do that again."

"King's the father, of course," she said flatly. Not a single lilt in the words to make it a question.

"Of course."

"I bet he's over the moon, isn't he?"

Her bitterness took me aback. "No. He doesn't know yet."

"He doesn't?"

"No. You're the first person I've told." That wasn't a lie. Giulia had found out on her own, and she'd told the council. Not me.

"If you think that gives you brownie points, you'd be right."

My lips twitched.

"Does Hunter know?"

"I just told you you're the first person I've clued in, Rory."

"Was just trying to see if you'd perjure yourself."

"I don't need you keeping me on my toes."

"No. You're the only defense attorney I don't whoop in court." She huffed disgustedly. "Are you going to tell Hunter?"

"I will, yes," I said, carefully. "You've spoken to him recently?"

"No."

The short answer had me rolling my eyes. I was pretty sure Rory needed a good fuck.

And I said that with all the love in my heart.

If Hunter would just get on with it, and stop acting like Rory walked on water, they'd both get over this... this... whatever the hell *this* was.

I grumbled, "I refuse to be caught in the middle."

"Oh, I know," she grumbled back. "You're like Switzerland."

"No, I'm a safe place for both of you to land."

"Like Switzerland," she retorted.

"If you're going to be a dick, I'm hanging up on you."

"Okay, okay. Don't hang up. We can meet tomorrow night?"

"Yes. No Zinfandel though."

"Ice cream?"

I shuddered. "Yes. Plenty of it."

She paused. "Things are that bad?"

"Things are *crazy*. I wasn't lying earlier."

"Are you okay?"

"Not really." The urge to tell her that Rex had gone missing was a strong one, but if I did... I knew Rory too well. She'd involve the cops and Nyx and the rest had made it quite clear that wasn't an option. "I'll tell you tomorrow."

"Fine."

"Rory?"

"Yeah?"

"I'm glad things are working out for you. I-I know this has been the end goal."

"It has. Thanks, Rach," she said softly. "See you tomorrow."

I hummed as we cut the call then reached for my bottle of water when the little light on it flashed, reminding me that I needed to drink.

As I sipped, I thought about those end goals of hers.

It was funny, really. We'd been bitter rivals at the start of college, until later that first year when we'd been paired together for an assignment and we'd realized how alike we actually were.

From there, we'd become roommates after there'd been a fire in my dorm.

Then, in our apartment... her husband.

God.

The only reason I knew about those end goals was because we'd grown closer after covering up his murder to protect Hunter.

Once you did something like that, once something that haunting connected you, you learned the real and true meaning of trust.

I bit my lip at the thought and immediately dialed Hunter's number. It had been way too long since we'd spoken. A lot longer than with Rory, because when I went quiet, Rory pushed, Hunter didn't.

"How's my favorite woman in the world?"

His easy charm settled something inside me. Hunter was my version of antacids. For Rory? He was the reason she had indigestion.

I smiled and told him, "Liar. I'm your second favorite woman."

"I'm too much of a gentleman to confirm or deny that statement."

My smile morphed into a grin.

A part of me had always wondered why things between Hunter

and I couldn't have evolved into something *more*. Things were so easy with him. They always had been.

But I guessed that was the point.

Nothing worth anything was easy in this life.

Painful but true.

"Well, I'll confirm it for you. How are you doing?"

"Ticking along."

"Yeah? *Where* are you?"

"Right now? Vegas. It's interesting here."

I snorted. "That's one way of putting it. Do you have noise canceling earphones in and I can't hear the titty bar music in the background."

Snickering, he said, "No, I'm in my office."

"Your office?" I arched a brow at nothing then absently checked my emails when I saw one had come in.

A part of me hoped Rex would contact me but I hadn't heard from him since Christmas.

Was it bizarre to admit that I was going into withdrawals?

I hadn't been away from him for this long since college. It was only now that he was cutting me out of his days that I realized how he always touched base with me.

Every goddamn day.

Recently, it had been via email. But we always had a call or a text conversation together.

Until now.

I couldn't be angry. Even if I was hurting. I, after all, had hurt *him*.

God, how he'd looked at me...

The pain of it sliced into me whenever I closed my eyes.

Gritting my teeth, I almost didn't hear Hunter asking, "Rach? Rach? You there?"

Quickly clearing my throat, I replied, "Yeah, I'm here. Sorry. Just... my mind wandered. Not your fault. Mine."

He snickered. "I'd ask if it was a personal thing, but I doubt it seeing as you don't have a life outside of work."

"Fuck off," I grumbled.

"Where would I fuck off to? You phoned me," he pointed out.

"I'm pregnant, Hunter," I blurted into dead silence.

He was quiet a second, then he laughed. "Congratulations, Rach! God, you're going to make an awesome mom. They'll all be terrified of you, but when they get into trouble, you'll have the teachers petrified."

Despite myself, I knew I wore a dopy smile. "You know how to give a compliment, Hunter."

He chuckled. "Am I wrong?"

"No," I retorted with a snort.

"How's King feeling about it?"

I blew out a breath, touched that, even though we were out of regular contact, he and Rory knew the only baby daddy I'd ever have would be King.

"King doesn't know yet."

"Why not?"

"His dad just died."

"Oh, shit. I'm so sorry, Rach. I know you loved King's father. Bear, wasn't it?"

"Thanks, Hunter," I said, my tone wobbly. Hunter always remembered the little things. "It's been hard."

"Of course it has. You should have told me," he chided.

"What would you have done? Sent flowers?"

"Well, that or ice cream. I think you'd have preferred that..."

"You still could send ice cream," I pointed out.

"Consider it done. Anyway, you were saying about King? Why you haven't told him about the baby?"

"What with Bear and everything, I didn't want to burden him."

"Maybe it'd cheer him up."

I blinked. "Maybe it would. I-I can't tell him yet though. He..."

"He...?" Hunter prompted when I hesitated.

"I had one of my nightmares."

Hunter knew all about those. *After*, we'd continued sharing the same flat. Sometimes, I'd pitied our neighbors. I wasn't the only one screaming at night. Rory was just as bad as me back then.

Not now though.

A part of me wondered if I was defective or something.

She was over it—why wasn't I?

Rubbing my eyes, I muttered, "I had one of my dreams. I told him to get out, and he took me literally."

"Huh. He's never listened before, has he?"

"No," I whispered miserably, hating that Hunter was right.

This wasn't the first time I'd looked at him as if *he* were Grizzly.

Why did they have to look so much alike?

Why?

Hating genetics, I gnawed on the inside of my cheek as Hunter asked, "What changed?"

"It was the day his dad died."

"Oh. Ouch."

"Yeah." A breath whistled from between my teeth. "I suck."

"Hardly, Rach. You love the man. You can't be with him because of your past. I think that sucks more for both of you. It isn't your fault he looks just like his uncle. Neither is it his fault, in all fairness."

"You don't have to tell me that," I said bitterly.

"You still love him, right?"

"Of course. There's no one else. Never has been."

He sighed. "That's the saddest thing I've ever heard."

I closed my eyes. Rex's wounded expression flashed before them. "Tell me about it. Anyway, I didn't call you to whine."

"You're not whining. But why did you call?"

"I got off the phone with Rory, and she said she hadn't talked to you recently and I realized I hadn't either. I wanted to check in."

"Rory's ignoring me," he said flatly. "She deals with things like you do."

"She doesn't," I scoffed. "She's strong. I'm weak."

He scoffed back, "You're one of the strongest women I know. Definitely one of the smartest. I'd say you were *the* smartest, but you and Rory are too competitive for me to declare one of you ahead of the other.

"You're brilliant, Rachel. Absolutely brilliant. You regularly astound me—"

While his defense touched me, I mumbled, "How can I regularly do anything when we haven't spoken in ages?"

"You think I don't keep tabs on both of you? I actually watched the Long Beach Butcher trial."

"You did?" My eyes widened. "Why didn't you tell me you were there?"

He laughed. "I didn't watch it in a way that would be considered strictly legal."

"Of course not," I said drolly.

"You were a genius in that court. How you twisted the jury around your finger? How you got the DA so tied into knots and pushed so deeply into a corner that he was fucked?" He chuckled. "Sheer poetry of the courtroom kind."

I grinned at nothing. "Thanks, Hunter. You're always good for my ego."

"You gonna ask me to be kiddo's godfather?"

Laughing, I told him, "You really want that?"

"Of course!"

I wondered if Rex would want one of the brothers to be a godfather, and then I thought, 'Fuck it.' Why shouldn't one of my best friends be there for our kid?

Hell, why shouldn't both of them, the people who'd gotten me through school, who'd helped me get out of bed every goddamn day after I gave up Wynter, be the ones who were there for me *now*?

"Okay then. You're sure?"

"Wouldn't have said I was if I wasn't." He barked out another laugh and I could hear his chair squeak in the background. "You better make Rory the godmother too. I have plans this year."

I arched a brow. "What kind of plans?"

"To make her mine, of course."

He said it so pleasantly that I had to smile. "Just like that, huh?"

"Well, it's been long enough, wouldn't you say?"

"Definitely." Still, I pursed my lips. "She's going to be difficult to win over."

"I'm sick of settling for second best, Rach. I want her."

I didn't know what to tell him.

I appreciated his Golden Retriever nature more than anyone could possibly understand, but I, more than anyone, knew this Golden Retriever wasn't afraid to go for the throat.

I didn't want to hurt him, neither did I want to discourage him.

He and Rory had been dancing around each other for far too long.

"You might want her, Hunter, but I don't know if she wants you."

"Like I said, I have a plan."

I smiled. "You do?"

"I do. Will you be my best man, Rach?"

I had to laugh. "How can I be that when I'll be Aurora's maid of honor?"

"You can be both. We're non-traditional."

I thought about Rory's very traditional background and cleared my throat. "I guess if anyone would make waves, it's her."

He hummed. "Exactly. Wish me luck?"

Sighing, I told him, "Always."

And I meant it too.

I wanted my best friends to be happy, and if I could also have some of that, I wouldn't say no.

"Got a question for you."

"Ask away," was my instant reply. "I'll do anything for you, you know that."

"Apart from adjudicate between Rory and me."

My lips curved. "She's more frightening than a serial killer."

He pshawed but questioned, "You heard of a hacker called Lodestar."

Whatever the fuck I'd expected him to ask me, it wasn't that.

Loyalties warring, I queried, "Why?"

"I'll take that as a yes."

I didn't answer.

"It's okay. I mean her no harm." I heard his chair squeaking. "The Valentinis have been sending a lot of work my way recently, and it's starting to clash with my duties here."

"You want to hire her?" I thought about Lodestar, who was already strung out from a heavy workload, and found myself at a loss.

"Well, not me. I was going to recommend her to them. What do you think?"

"Do you know she's working with the Sinners?" I queried, my tone cautious.

"I know all, see all—"

"Shut up," I grumbled, which made him snicker.

Rubbing my temple, I contemplated our conversation.

The Valentinis were on my client list. Luciu Valentini had just ascended to the head of the Italian collective—the *Famiglia*.

If Lodestar worked for them too, I could call on her for information when I needed it... It would be easier than now.

I loved speaking with Hunter, but his work process was a lot more manic than I could handle.

Lodestar was like me—cold as ice, ruthless, analytical, and unafraid to do what needed to be done to achieve whatever result she was seeking.

"Rach?" Hunter prompted.

"Yeah," I said eventually. "I can recommend her."

"You wanna tell Custanzu—"

"He's the one who approaches you?" I queried, curious as to the inner workings of the Sicilians.

Though Luciu would probably have told me, I found it wasn't in my best interests to be overly curious about my clients' working habits.

Hunter hummed. "Stan's on the front, you know that. Luc only gets his hands dirty at the end."

'The end.'

I rolled my eyes.

Luciu had a passion for the dramatic. How he went around slicing up men and women's faces like his knife was a paintbrush was all the more disturbing for his intelligence.

Luciu did nothing without a purpose.

Not unlike some people I knew...

"You tell them. I don't like getting involved."

"I know. I wouldn't have asked, but I didn't want to pass along a name that you wouldn't want to liaise with."

Warmth unfurled inside me. "You're a sweetheart, Hunter."

He laughed. "You keep on telling Rory that."

"I'll put in a good word for you." My lips twitched. "Not sure if it'll be much use. You know what she's like."

A sigh came down the line. "Perfection?"

I snorted. "Yeah, you keep on telling yourself that."

## TWENTY-FOUR

### REX

"The weather today is an unseasonably warm seventy-two degrees—"

Switching off the TV set in my motel room, I tossed the remote onto the nightstand and stared up at the ceiling.

I'd decided to stick around New Mexico. A part of me had thought it might be a good idea to head into Texas, catch up with the Hell's Rebels'—we were allies, not exactly friends—but I was curious about what Drew would do.

School had started two days ago, so I hung around my motel, waiting for Maverick to keep me in the loop while monitoring the news obsessively.

Only Mav knew where I was, and he was the only brother I checked in with.

I didn't need, nor want, to speak to anyone else in the MC.

I needed to get away.

I needed some space from every-fucking-thing.

It was just too much right now. Much too fucking much.

My cell buzzed at that exact moment, but recognizing the tone, I scanned the text.

**Emile:** *Busy couple days.*

*picture sent*

She looked stressed. Dressed in a three-piece skirt suit, her head was bowed over her phone as she walked down some stairs toward her car.

My thumb stroked over the screen.

**Rex:** *Keep me updated.*

**Emile:** *Will do.*

Placing my cell on the nightstand then crossing my feet at the ankle, I closed my eyes, immediately thought of that picture, and decided to get some sleep.

It was only now that I was away from the hospital that I realized how fucking exhausted I was. How I'd been running on fumes and for so goddamn long that it was almost a relief just to sink into this shitty bed and to sleep. Do dick all else, just to rest and recuperate.

Crazy, right? I wasn't sick, hadn't been injured, but I needed R&R too? Whacked.

On the brink of sleep, my cellphone buzzed, and because I'd only allowed incoming calls from Maverick to trigger a notification, I grumbled under my breath and muttered, "What?"

"A Drew McInnen has been registered with Shady Pines."

I blinked. "Shady Pines? Sounds like a nursing home."

He grunted. "It ain't. It's a rehabilitation center."

"Kid didn't need rehab."

"No, he needed hardcore fucking therapy. That's what he's getting." He hummed. "Mom filed for divorce from the dad too."

"Interesting."

"Interesting?"

"He told the kid he was a pussy."

"Why do guys do that?"

"I dunno. I told Drew that pussies take a pounding."

"Is that really what he needed to hear?" Maverick drawled, and despite the goddamn ache in my entire fucking being, I had to laugh.

"It worked, didn't it? No kids were harmed in the making of this new year."

He sniffed. "True."

"I'm glad it worked. He was messed up, but he was hurting."

"Do I wanna know the details?"

"You wouldn't approve of them. Hell, I don't think I approve either, but sometimes, a short, sharp shock is what's needed. Might not be PC, but fuck it. I ain't exactly PC."

"You're more politically correct than most of the Sinners."

"That don't say much about my MC." Snorting at the thought and thinking of the orders I'd sent Mav, I asked, "Speaking of... Harlow. Has he been sworn in as a Prospect yet?"

"Yup. Most of the council didn't like it."

"Was Nyx one of the grumblers?"

"Nah. But he's putting Harlow through his paces."

"Makes sense. Gotta figure out how he works. See if they can get along."

"Yup. You coming home?"

"No."

"Why not?"

'Get. Out.'

My jaw clenched as those words ricocheted around my head like they were stray bullets.

"Not ready to."

"Is it because of the funeral?"

"No."

"Then, why not? Why don't you want to be with family?"

I did. But the one person who could make me feel fucking better didn't want to be with me.

Clearing my throat, I rasped, "I'm going to see Wynter."

"Thought you might while you were down there."

"Fucking know-it-all."

"Don't hate on me. Ain't you glad that I know everything?"

"Suppose." I huffed. "Rachel okay?"

"Wouldn't say so."

I stiffened. "What does that mean?"

"Means she's concerned about you."

Something about his tone had me frowning. "What ain't you saying?"

"Plenty. Like always. You can't bitch at me for keeping quiet when I'm doing the exact same thing for you."

I narrowed my eyes at the ceiling. "Asswipe."

"Fucker."

"Dipshit."

"Jerk off."

I grunted. "I'm going."

"Before you do, we got the licenses through. Did Rachel tell you?"

"She did."

"You want me to start the ball rolling with the contractors? Get quotes in?"

"Can do," I said disinterestedly.

"Ain't like you not to care, Rex."

It was on the tip of my tongue to tell him. To share what I'd done. To admit it. Confess all. But I couldn't. The words were stuck in my throat. Lodged in my chest.

I blew out a breath. "I'll get over it."

"Some pains are easier than others to get over. I'm not asking you to get over this, just checking in. Making sure that you know you ain't alone."

I knew Maverick had been through hell. So much so that my own pain was minimal by comparison. That he could tell me that spoke of his generosity. His kind spirit.

"I just need some time, Mav."

"I'll give you so much rope but I won't let you hang yourself, Rex."

The warning had me rolling my eyes. "Who said I was suicidal?"

"No one. Just a saying. I mean it though. You stay away too long, I'll reel you back in."

Squinting at nothing, I muttered, "Dicksucker."

Maverick laughed. "Thought you were gonna insult me for a second."

My lips curved as I cut the line.

Drew had done as I asked.

I wasn't going to lie—I was relieved.

When he'd gone to school two days ago, when there hadn't appeared to be a change in his routine, I'd been fucking scared he was gonna find a gun and go through with it.

Maybe it had helped that I'd planted enough coke on Brandon fucking Cooper to look like he was dealing...

Shady Pines might sound like a place where old people went to fucking die, but if it got the kid over being traumatized, who was I to complain?

Relieved that some innocent brats were gonna be spared, I didn't need to nap anymore.

I got up, packed my shit together, and shoved it in my saddlebags. I didn't have much, and most of what I'd bought was from a department store, but it all fit nicely in my packs.

Hauling them over my shoulder, I went to check out. With no one at the reception, I dropped my key in the box, signed the register, then headed over to my bike.

As I stared around the area, grateful that I could get the hell out of this place, I toed the kickstand up then threw my leg over the seat. Settling onto it, I hit the engine, and rolled out of fucking town.

In seventeen years, I hadn't met Wynter. Not since the day I gave her up for adoption.

I'd wanted to. I'd really fucking wanted to. But my wants didn't matter. I knew Jeremy and Ally, her adoptive parents, had told her she wasn't theirs biologically, and I knew Wynter even knew *who*

Rach and I were, but I didn't think it was fair to intrude on them when all the parenting fell on their shoulders.

That didn't mean I hadn't taken an interest in her life though.

I'd attended the swimming gala where she won bronze in the state heats, and I'd even flown out to the hospital when she'd had her tonsils removed four years ago.

She was my kid.

My responsibility.

I paid her way and made sure she was doing well.

Not that that was enough.

By going to visit her now, I knew I was being a selfish bastard.

With her birthday being so close to Dad's passing, I needed to… Christ, I didn't know what I needed. It was all a fucking mess, but I just wanted her to know that she mattered.

Maybe that was dumb.

Maybe I was just going to fuck shit up, but my intentions were pure.

I'd lost both parents. As had Rachel.

Wynter had four.

I wished, at that moment, that I had two more waiting in the wings, that was for fucking sure. And that was why I was heading to Burbank, California.

Whether I was welcome or not.

A kid could never have too much love.

## TWENTY-FIVE

## RACHEL

I didn't end up going to meet with Rory in the city the next day. Instead, it was almost a week later after crisis after crisis had befallen the MC.

At least they were administrative issues and not custodial ones.

There was some relief from that.

Parker had to reschedule my meetings in New York and had to restructure the next month's worth of appointments, but I managed to deal with most of the fallout.

"Thank God Rex gave me power of attorney," I muttered under my breath as I rubbed my temple where the ever persistent ache was brewing.

I wasn't sure if it was a situational kind of headache, one that was directly forged from the fact my life was hell right now, my baby daddy was missing, I was pregnant when being pregnant terrified me, Bear had died at said baby daddy's hands, or the fact that the MC was going through a major shuffle which necessitated the entire council to be on hand to see it through....

Well, when I put it like that, why the hell *wouldn't* I have a headache?

The only bright spot this week had been a massive delivery from Hunter—I had more ice cream than an ice cream parlor in my freezer.

"You going to see a doctor?"

Spying Giulia in the doorway, I arched a brow at her. "What are you doing here?"

She shrugged. "I was supposed to be at Indy's place today but I had a backache."

"Wouldn't have thought that'd stop you."

"You'd be right," she grumbled.

"Nyx?" I asked with an amused smile.

"Overprotective jerk." She huffed.

"He's just on edge right now."

"My Old Man's always on edge," she mocked.

"More than usual." I tipped up my chin. "You had no right to tell him I was pregnant."

"We have no secrets," she said demurely.

"Ha. That's a lie if ever I heard one. Remind me if you're in court to teach you how to utter complete bullshit with a straight face."

She sniffed at me. "It wasn't a lie."

"Just a half truth?" I rolled my eyes. "Either way, it wasn't your place to tell him."

"Nyx and I keep *few* secrets between us. I didn't expect the jackass to tell you I figured out you had a bun in the oven. Men," she finished disgustedly. "Anyway, do you know what's wrong with him?"

"In particular or in general?"

She narrowed her eyes at me. "After what we talked about before Christmas, Rachel, don't mess with me."

"I'm not. Rex's absence has..." I rubbed my temple again. "It led to some home truths being confessed."

"By who?" Giulia asked, tone curious.

"Me. Some things I didn't particularly want to share but which triggered Rex's departure, so I had to admit to them."

She fell silent a second, then, as she looked at me, a soft breath whispered from her lips. "Oh, Rachel."

"What is it?"

"The only reason Nyx would be so upset with any 'home truths' you told him is if..." She raised a hand to cover her eyes. "How many of us have gone through this? How many men have taken something from us?"

A bitter laugh scorched my lips. "Too many."

Her nod was slow, *sad*. "I wish..." She stepped deeper into the room. "Is there anything I can do?"

"This is old news, Giulia," I told her calmly. "It happened a long time ago."

"Doesn't mean it isn't affecting you." She nibbled on the inside of her cheek, sucking it in as she planted herself, without invitation, into my visitor's chair. "I still have nightmares about Luke Lancaster, and he barely—"

"Don't," I bit off. "Don't diminish what you went through. If anyone knows the miserable details, it's me. We drafted your statement for the cops together, didn't we?"

Giulia pursed her lips. "I wish I'd killed him."

More laughter bubbled from me. I wasn't sure if it came from a place of panic or if it was disbelief.

"It's no wonder you and Nyx are so perfect for each other."

A smile danced in her eyes, but it didn't manifest anywhere else. "We're bloodthirsty."

Then, a thought occurred to me. "Wait—"

Giulia's eyes met mine. "I didn't kill Luke Lancaster."

My mouth rounded. "What?" My shoulders straightened. "Who were you covering up for? It couldn't have been Nyx. At the time of your attack, he was on a run to Canada."

"I know he was." She swallowed. "Guess it doesn't matter who knows now. Seeing as Bear's gone."

"Bear? Bear killed Lancaster?" I sputtered.

"It isn't much of a secret anymore—"

"Why keep it a secret at all?"

"Didn't trust you at first; plus Bear asked me to keep it quiet."

"Why?"

"Dunno. I got the feeling he wasn't supposed to be in West Orange."

I blinked, taken aback by the remark.

Bear *had* been in West Orange. But I'd only thought it was a quick visit. He'd come to arrange his...

God.

His will.

I didn't react to the realization; it wasn't my place to.

It was difficult though. So difficult.

He'd wanted to arrange the matters of his estate because he knew his death was coming...

He'd known he was diving headfirst into trouble.

Feeling like I'd swallowed my tongue, I attempted to change the subject to one I could handle right now. "Do you think it'd have made much of a difference if you'd killed him rather than Bear?"

Her words indicated that might be the case, but I didn't see how it mattered.

Dead was dead, after all.

"I do. I'd have controlled it. I'd have the satisfaction of knowing he had tried to take me down but I got to him first." Her mouth tautened as she stared at her knees. "It'd give me some comfort, you know?"

I didn't. Not really.

"Anyway, I'm not here for that."

"No, you're here for Nyx—"

"Actually, he isn't why I disturbed you either."

"No?" I arched a disbelieving brow.

"No. Lily is."

Blinking, I asked, "Link's Lily?"

She nodded. "When Maverick was bad, Lily was handling the accounts."

"I remember."

"He's taken some of the workload off her shoulders now that he's better."

"He shouldn't have done that. CTE isn't something you can take lightly."

"Well, either way, he has. I was wondering if..."

"What?"

She blew out her cheeks. "Lily's smart. Hella smart."

"I'm sure she is."

"Maybe she could help?"

"With what?"

Giulia shrugged. "Whatever has you working until eleven at night."

My brow puckered. "I'm a lawyer. She isn't."

"Yeah, but I know you're doing a lot of MC stuff, and that isn't shit you'd ordinarily be doing in your capacity as the MC's lawyer, is it?"

"Some of it is."

"All of it?" she challenged.

"No," I conceded.

She hummed. "Thought so. Anyway, just figured you wouldn't think to look to the Old Ladies, but we're not just cum buckets—"

My mouth rounded at that. "I never thought you were!"

"If you say so. Lily's clever, and she'll only hang around so much before she figures out what she wants to do with herself. I'm concerned..."

"What are you concerned about?" I asked when her words waned.

"That she'll step away from our world, figure out that she doesn't really belong here, and she'll leave Link."

"That's a touch drastic, isn't it?"

She sniffed. "Is it? Stone became a doctor and moved away for years. You're a lawyer; you moved away and barely associate with the club unless it's for business.

"However you look at it, Link doesn't deserve that. He loves Lily, and he'd do anything for her. It'd kill him if she left because she couldn't find a place, and that's just not true. There's plenty of shit to do for the MC, if they'd just let her.

"When Maverick was sick, she had a purpose. She was helping out while he was on the fritz, but now, well, she might have been raised to be a society wife, but we know that's not her."

I considered her. "I agree."

She pursed her lips. "You do?"

"I do."

"Why?"

I snorted. "Did you expect an argument?"

"Yes."

Her simple answer had me shaking my head. "I know how smart Lily is."

"Then why didn't you ask her to help you out?"

"I just..." My mind went blank. "I didn't think to."

"Why not? Because she's a cum bucket?"

I growled, "No, Giulia. Stop saying that. Hell, in another life, I'd have been an Old Lady. I'm certainly not a cum bucket."

"Why another life? Why not this one?"

"Because Rex deserves better than a broken soul."

Giulia scowled at me. "You really believe that?"

"I don't believe it. I know it." I stared her down. "But that isn't something I wish to discuss. I didn't ask her to help out because I never do."

"Never do what?"

"Never ask for help." I swallowed. "It's not in my nature. I just get on with whatever I'm doing and continue until the task is complete."

"Soldier mentality." She tapped her chin. "Or is that martyr complex?"

I glowered at her. "Are you trying to annoy me?"

"Is it working?" She smirked. "Anyway, you'll call Lily? Give her some shit to do? Don't make it really easy stuff or she'll get offended.

"My girl's brilliant. Her talents are wasting away, Rachel. The guys have all learned business on the streets, you know? She's been trained.

"Their instincts are solid, but she's had an Ivy League education that'll only take the MC to an even higher level. Why waste that? It's a fucking shame not to take advantage of all those smarts."

She wasn't wrong.

The business side of the MC wasn't something that had ever intrigued me, which was fortunate as I was only their lawyer. My specialty was criminal law, but I'd done enough corporate courses and had some accreditation that meant I could act on their behalf in a business capacity.

My field of advice was limited.

The MC really *was* missing out by not getting her on board.

How very myopic of me, Rex, and the rest of the council.

"You're right," I said softly. "I'll contact her today."

When I thought about the minefield of this week, I wanted to groan.

I could have done with some help but I genuinely hadn't thought about reaching out.

"Good. You know her ma was a Lindenbourg, don't you?"

Quirking a brow, I shook my head. "I didn't know that."

The Lindenbourgs were American royalty.

Jesus, Link was boning a Lindenbourg?

No wonder Giulia was worried about Lily leaving. I loved Link, but God, the Lindenbourgs were *Lindenbourgs*.

"You do now." She grunted as she got to her feet. "Maybe with some help, you'll get into bed before nine and will see the doctor."

"Are you mothering me?"

She smirked again before she wandered out of the office. "Figured I'd get some practice in before mine comes along."

Giulia was going to be a mother.

How fucking terrifying a prospect was that?

Shaking my head as she departed, I reached for my cellphone and called Link, and when there was no answer, I called Sin instead.

"'Sup, Rach?"

"I need Lily's number."

"You don't have it already?" Sin asked, his tone absentminded.

"No."

"You got a pen handy?"

"Yeah."

As he reeled off her number, I took note of it in my diary then started to transfer it to my computer contacts.

"What's Link done?"

"Nothing as far as I know."

His tone turned suspicious as he questioned, "What do *you* know?"

"Nothing," I retorted sweetly.

"Rach, what's going on—"

Letting him fester, I grinned to myself as I ended the call. He immediately rang back, but the second he cut off, I phoned Lily.

"Hello?"

"Hi, Lily. This is Rachel Laker. You may not know me—"

A laugh sounded down the line. "Of course I know you."

"I didn't know if you would over the phone," I said, a tad sheepishly.

"Well, I do. Is everything okay?"

"Yeah. Everything's fine. I was wondering if you were free to help out with some MC business." The FAST gala was approaching too... Could I dump some of that on her lap?

"MC business?" She sounded wary. "What kind of MC business?"

"The legal side of things, not the illegal," I drawled.

"Oh. Sure, I'd love to help out. You'd be saving me actually. Tiffany's mother is driving me crazy."

I arched a brow. "Is she still living with you?"

Christ, I really was out of the loop.

Guilt and unease went to war inside me at the realization. The MC was the closest thing I had to family, but I hadn't just locked Rex out in my bid for independence as I sought to escape the ties of my past. I'd also shut the door in the MC's face as a whole.

In a sense, it was understandable.

Two of the MC brothers were the reason I was broken, after all.

But two small cogs didn't make up the whole machine.

"Yeah," Lily confirmed grimly. "She's still living with me. Tiff and Sin's place is far too small for a houseguest. And trust me, even my place is too small for a houseguest like her.

"I didn't mind at first because she just used to shop like mad on Amazon. Now, she's—" She huffed. "Sorry, Rachel. This is very unprofessional of me. You didn't call to gossip. You called about business. How can I help?"

A part of me was relieved for the change of subject.

Work was all I had, and personal information was something I tended to avoid at all costs.

But... this was Link's woman.

I cared for him. He loved her.

I swallowed. "No, it's okay. It's clear that she's been annoying you."

"She has. She stuck to her room for the most part, but now she's started eating dinner with us. She's behaving better ever since Link told her he'd throw her out if she kept on with the insults, but she's so damn snide it's wearisome."

"I can imagine." I cleared my throat. "Why don't you find her somewhere else to stay?"

"That would make Tiffany feel guilty."

I didn't know Tiffany well enough to give her an opinion.

God, I didn't know any of the Old Ladies well apart from Stone and Indy, and I didn't even really know who they were aside from the fact they'd been a part of the life longer than I had and had always been around.

From the very start, I'd kept things superficial with the MC. I'd been so certain that when Axel took us in, it wouldn't be for long. The only way to diminish future hurt was to invest very little of myself from the beginning.

How had I only just realized I'd never changed how I interacted with people I genuinely considered kin?

Horror washed through me as I choked out, "Why would she feel guilty?"

"Are you okay?"

"Sorry, frog in my throat. Why would Tiffany feel guilty?"

Lily hesitated. "It doesn't matter. I'm sorry for bringing this up." Her tone changed, brightened. "I'd love to help, Rachel. Anything to get me out of this damned house right now."

"Do you know where I live?"

She snorted. "Yes, Rachel. I do."

It sounded obvious to her, but I didn't know where *she* lived.

More guilt assailing me, I muttered, "The MC is currently working on several projects—"

"Yes. I know. Maverick mostly passed on the basic bookkeeping. But I was aware of which plans were in place."

"Oh. With Rex not here, I could use some help."

"I'll be there in under an hour. Do you want me to bring coffee or snacks?"

"No. That's okay. I have coffee here."

"Great," she chirped. "See you in a short while."

Mouth rounding as she hung up, I stared down at the phone then slowly placed it on the desk.

That was... unexpected.

But not necessarily a bad thing.

I *did* need help. Rex was as much of a workaholic as I was. With him away, I hadn't realized how much there'd be to do, even with

Parker working more hours than usual and Susanne working flat out too, and my intention, my method of apology, was to make it easier on him upon his return.

Keeping his family ticking over in his absence... I didn't think it would be enough, but I had to try.

## TWENTY-SIX

## LILY

I laughed when Link snagged me around the waist and dragged me back into him. As he dipped down and nipped my ass, I snorted.

"I have to go help Rachel!" I chided as I twisted back to rub my butt.

Sometimes, the memories returned to me, but most of them had been overtaken.

Pain caused a long shadow, but happiness and pleasure, from a man who loved you and cared about both, shined a lot of light into the darkness of the past.

"Why did she have to call now?"

His pouting had my grin widening and made those shadows fade even further. "Big baby. You just got off!"

"But I was warming you up again," he said with a huff.

I rolled my eyes as he slipped his fingers between my legs. I'd have slapped his hand if he didn't immediately find my clit.

I was drenched from both of our releases, so that meant when he rubbed the nub, it made fireworks explode before my eyes.

Hands flopping to his shoulders, I stared down at him blindly as I rocked my hips.

"Fuck, that feels good," I whimpered, fingers digging into his traps, the tips of my nails leaving as much of an impression as his teeth did in my ass cheek.

As always, his strength stunned me. One second, I was standing there on shaking legs, the next, he'd lifted me up and had laid me on the bed.

He knew well enough not to let his fingers stop or I'd come back to the moment, but he let his thumb breach my slit while making space for his mouth.

"I haven't showered yet," I said thickly.

"You taste like us, sugar tits. Delicious," he crooned.

I groaned as he went to town on my clit. Open-mouthed kisses and deep sucks had me arching my back, hips shimmying so that I rubbed my whole pussy against his face as I scraped my nails over his scalp how I knew he loved.

The noises he made were bestial, ravenous. They triggered something inside me that was equally as primal.

I'd never have imagined I could experience something with such abandon, but there was no denying that he took me to another place. Allowed me to explore parts of myself that I knew was possible only with someone as generous with himself as Link was.

His tongue fluttered against my clit, small licks that sent shivers up and down my spine. I widened my legs to let him get closer, and that was when he thrust two fingers inside me. I growled as he started to finger fuck me, and like we *were* animals, he growled back like he was telling me to shut up.

The vibrations against my slit made me close my eyes and dig my nails harder into his skull.

Just before I was seconds from release, he pulled back. Panting, I stared blindly up at him. Seeing his chin and mouth and nose slick from my juices, I licked my lips and arched up for a kiss.

Though his eyes darkened in response, he didn't let me get too close. He flipped me on my belly and encouraged me onto my knees and for me to rock my ass up and back.

When his face returned to the scene of the crime—leaving me hanging like that was definitely a punishable offense—he rocked his head from side to side. I almost burst out laughing as he motorboated my pussy, but it felt too fucking good to do anything other than moan.

A final suck on my clit had him backing off, and this time, I snarled, "Get back there! Where the fuck do you think you're going?"

"Thought you had an appointment?" he drawled, but he sounded breathless.

Seeing as he'd been suffocating in my pussy a couple seconds ago, I couldn't blame him.

I twisted around to glower at him, but that was when I saw he'd snagged something from the nightstand.

My eyes blurred at the sight.

Cock ring on, vibe already on high, his head was arched back as he got himself under control. Pissed I'd missed the show of him sliding into that torture device, I saw he had a butt plug in his hand.

Before I could tense, he was dragging it through my juices. Popping the tip into my pussy, he twisted it left and right, drenching it in my natural lubricant, then pulled it back out. When he pressed it to the pucker of my ass, my arms flopped down and I face-planted into the sheets with a guttural groan.

That was nothing to my shriek when he switched it on.

Moaning into the bed, I shuddered when the tip of his cock was nudging my pussy, and the gentle vibrations that rocked through his shaft had my eyes almost crossing.

I was so wet there was little resistance. So as he slid in deep, I shivered as he rubbed his hands down my sides, making all the tiny hairs stand to attention. He did that again as the vibrator pressed down against my clit.

"Link!" I sobbed at the triple whammy he was handing me.

His response?

To drag his short, blunt nails down where he'd just teased.

As he scraped them against my back, I swore my nerve endings short circuited. With a cry, I felt the fullness in my pussy, the heavy weight in my ass. The vibes deep against my G-spot, and the ones against my clit. Throw in the sensory switch, my mind blew a fuse.

A keening wail escaped me as he started to move. Short, blunt thrusts powered into me, making me feel every damn inch he had with each one packing the punch of an atomic bomb.

I was no longer just seeing fireworks. I had my own display going on in my head.

When the orgasm hit, I went blind. The light show disappeared. The buzz of the vibes faded, and even the slap of skin to skin and his groans whispered away.

I screamed, but I didn't even hear it, as the pleasure tore through me. Ripped at my nerves and decimated me like nothing else could.

Like *nobody* else could.

Link took me up to another stratosphere without even exerting himself. To be centered in the search for his own pleasure just amped everything up a notch.

I felt fingers in my mouth, and I sucked down on them hard. That was when I heard him hissing and groaning, hips bucking as he sought his own release.

The vibrations were too much.

I was going to die.

This was it.

Death by orgasm.

And once more, I understood why the French called it *la petite mort*.

He'd made me feel excruciating pleasure before, but this was different. I didn't know why; it just was.

As I cried out again, feeling the waves of bliss starting to take the toll on my already battered senses, I heard him cry out, then I knew when he came because his thrusts became jerky. Barely anything at all as my pussy clamped down around him.

When he fell onto me, his weight blanketing me, I stared blindly into nothing, letting myself come to. I stayed there when he shifted to my side, didn't even move when he cocked his leg up and angled it over the backs of my thighs to pin me in place.

Trying to process what had just happened was impossible when my brain was still foggy, so I didn't even bother. Just lay there, covered by him, his second dose of cum this morning slipping out of my cunt.

When his fingers returned, thrusting into me again, I twisted away and complained, "No more!"

He hushed me, then stunned me further by turning me over, then dropping down and tonguing my slit.

I shuddered, but the licks were gentle this time. Not to incite but to soothe.

As he hummed, sighing with every lapping motion of his tongue, I wriggled until he was done then slid my hand through his hair when he dropped his head onto my stomach, finally sated.

"Thank God you're nearly forty," I rasped.

"Is that supposed to be a compliment?"

"You'd have killed me if you were in your twenties," I said hoarsely.

I barely kept up with him despite the age gap.

"Nah," he disagreed. "You've got honey between your legs. How can I not eat that up every day?"

My very sore and very exhausted pussy clamped down at that.

"I'm going to be walking like I've been riding a horse."

"A horse or a bull?"

Laughter burst from me as I slapped his shoulders. "Both have big dicks. That wasn't a slight against your manhood."

"Good, or I'd have to prove myself—"

"No! No more proving. Twice is enough for any woman first thing."

He rocked his sweaty forehead against my belly. "Good to know."

Something about his tired words had me frowning. I lifted my head to stare at him. All that golden hair and golden skin still got to me like little else could, but I could see the shadows and the strain beneath his eyes from this angle.

Reaching down, I gently traced the crinkles there and murmured, "Everything okay, baby?"

"I'm with you, sugar tits, so of course everything is."

My heart might as well have just flip-flopped in my chest.

"I love you so much," I breathed.

He angled his head so that he could catch a hold of my eyes, and there was something deep inside them that had my frown darkening. "I love you too, Lily." He pressed a kiss to my belly then muttered, "I should let you up."

"You should," I agreed but I didn't move. "What aren't you telling me? Is it about that Harlow kid?"

Harlow was high on the Posse's list of topics of conversation.

Link snorted. "No."

"What is it then?"

He shrugged. "Nothing. Just tired."

"We can go to bed early tonight," I offered softly.

"We can try," he teased, but I tugged on his hand when he made to move off the bed.

"I mean it. We can just be together, Link, sweetheart. Me and you. No one else. We could watch *Blackadder*."

His lips quirked in a grin. "Really?"

I grinned back. "Really." Scrabbling toward the edge of the bed, I quickly parted my legs—which killed like a motherfucker—and hooked them around his so he couldn't move away. I placed my hands at the ridged muscles on his hips, stared up at him, and whispered, "You know I love being with you."

He stroked my hair which had me sighing in delight. "I know you do."

Nerves filled me at his response. "Why don't you sound glad about that?"

"I'm very glad about that. Just..."

"Just what?"

"I'm just scared it won't be enough for you soon."

For *me* soon?

Blinking, I stared up at him. "Why wouldn't it be?"

"You're smart, sugar tits. I'm not."

My eyes narrowed. "You take that back."

He pursed his lips. "I can't even manage the fucking accounts at the shop."

"So? You can fix those bikes like you made them from scratch! I've seen that cage you're building in the garage, Link. Don't you tell me you're not smart."

"Not like you, baby." He dipped down to press a kiss to my temple. "It's all right. You don't have to defend me—"

"I'm not. I'm speaking the truth." I dug my nails into his waist. "Where's this coming from?"

"You've not been happy—"

"No, because we have the houseguest from hell staying with us."

He frowned. "What?"

"That can't come as a surprise? You just heard me complaining about her to Rachel."

"It doesn't but... that's it? That's why you never want to be anywhere but in the bedroom?"

"Well, duh. It's the only place she'll leave us alone!"

His eyes darkened. "I thought you were—"

"What?" I demanded when he didn't finish.

"I thought I wasn't enough for you."

My mouth rounded. "Is that why you're trying to kill me with orgasms?" I shrieked. "Link, if we have any more sex, you're going to break my pussy! Seriously," I whined. "Can we have a sabbatical? I'm so sore and you make me feel so good it's crazy."

He did a double take. "My cock feels like it's going to fall off."

I gaped at him even more. "You—I don't believe this! The next time you think something is going on, come and talk to me about it before I have to hobble around like a cowgirl."

"I'm so tired that I can't even joke about enjoying being your ride," he groused, scrubbing a hand over his face. "But, this place is massive. We don't ever have to see Bitch Face."

"We shouldn't but we always do. I can't deal with her. That doesn't matter. We can hang out in here, but we don't always have to fuck."

"So, you're not bored with me?"

"No." Jesus.

"I'm not too dumb—"

"No!" My hair whipped as I shook my head. "I've been bored with... since Mav took the books back. Being in here all the time, it's been kind of dull when you're at the MC, but that's it—"

"I'm going to kill her."

"Who?"

"The houseguest from hell," he mocked, using the same words I had, and made to stalk off.

Gasping, I grabbed his hand and dragged him back. "No! Just leave her. Everything's okay. Rachel asked me to help out. That'll get me out of the house and keep me busy."

"Lily, this is *your* house. She's the guest! You should toss her out."

My cheeks burned. "I can't. I've known her too long. It'd be like tossing my mom out."

"If she makes you so fucking unhappy, baby, then you should."

"I can't. Not yet, at least." I tugged on his hand. "Please, let's not argue."

"She broke my dick."

"Technically, I did that."

He snickered. "Yeah, you did."

"I didn't know I could come so hard," I admitted gruffly.

"No. Those vibrations... Let me tell you, I don't need a prostate checkup this year."

I chuckled. "Yes, you do. You're not allowed to leave me, do you hear?"

He graced me with a lopsided grin. "My sugar tits wants me around?"

"Yes, she does," I said primly. Groaning as I got to my feet, I whimpered as I straightened up so I could kiss him on the lips. "Ask me next time. Okay?"

"Okay."

"Miscommunication is the death of every relationship," I preached.

"No dying," he concurred, his mouth supping from mine.

As we stood there, naked, aching and sore and dripping from orifices that badly needed a break and access to a shower, I sighed into his embrace.

I loved this man.

Even if he *had* killed me with sex.

**From: Rach3lLadyLiberty@gmail.com**
**To: K1ngS1nn3r1@gmail.com**
**Subject: Please**

I know you're pissed at me, Rex, but please, email me back?

I'm concerned you're lying dead in a ditch somewhere.

Nyx and the rest say I'm overreacting, but they don't understand what happened.

I can't get away from this feeling that I broke something forever between us.

I hit you on the raw, and I'm so sorry for that.

Please, don't hate me.

Rachel

## TWENTY-SEVEN

## REX

Having finally made it to LA after taking a long detour, I took a seat outside a bar, letting some of the heat warm my shoulders which were tense after the ride.

Burbank was Disciples' territory, so a meet-up with their council was necessary if I was going to stick around.

I'd shown my face and flashed my cut around one of their most popular joints, so I knew the message would have been relayed back to them. Now, I just had to wait, and the JD was helping with that nicely.

Back when Wynter was four, there'd been a slight misunderstanding between Ally and Jeremy—Wynter's adoptive parents.

That slight misunderstanding had made them think they could run away with her.

Hide from me.

They'd done so by leaving Fresno and entering another bikers' territory deep in the heart of LA, just northwest of downtown.

They clearly thought they were dealing with fucking amateurs if they didn't realize I could find them. But after I made it known that moving again was a no-no that came with consequences of the bullet variety, and that I had no intention of playing any part in my daughter's life aside from afar, they hadn't given me any trouble since.

Neither had they moved.

Blade, the Disciples' Prez, was supposed to be a decent motherfucker. As decent as anyone in a one-percenter could be, I guessed. I knew he was a veteran like Mav, and that he had mad lab skills. He'd even created this punked out drug that had put the Disciples on the map.

All I knew was that drugs weren't as rife in this part of LA since they stopped producing their white gold, crime was relatively low, and the MC did what MCs tended to do—kept the peace through the threat of violence.

It was why I hadn't 'encouraged' Ally and Jeremy to move.

As I raised my shot of JD to my lips, taking a deep, *deep* sip, I heaved a sigh.

I hated the West Coast.

I always fucking had, always goddamn would.

It was a testament, I figured, to the state of things right now. My head was all over the place, and I really needed a fucking break. I wanted to meet my kid, at last, make an introduction, and maybe build a relationship with her. Nothing heavy, just whatever she'd allow of me.

Maybe it was a sign I was getting fucking old, maybe it was just losing my dad, or maybe it was because shit never changed between Rach and me, but I needed to connect with her.

Selfish, but true.

She could throw me out and I wouldn't make a fuss, but I had to try.

As the alcohol worked its way through my system, I kept my ears pricked for the sound of incoming traffic.

With my back to the exterior wall of the bar, in a corner where I could see anyone who approached from all sides, I was almost relieved when the rumble of hogs made themselves known in the distance.

I paced myself with my drink, taking it slow, and when a couple of bikes appeared in my line of sight, I didn't bother getting up.

From patches alone, I knew I was facing the Prez and the Enforcer.

I was intimately acquainted with everything there was to know about Blade's and Ryder's pasts. Including some beef the Enforcer had had with the Russians a decade or so before which was causing havoc with the MC right now.

Still, that wasn't of any interest to me.

Politeness had brought me to this bar, the rules of the road insisting that I got 'permission' for being in Burbank.

"When Ryder told me a Satan's Sinner was riding through my territory, I told him he was wrong. Seeing is believing," Blade drawled as he nudged the kickstand with his foot, propped his bike up, then started walking through the tables toward me.

I could have gone to a biker bar, but instead, I'd headed for a cosmopolitan little place where I knew my presence would still make waves while trying to look as low-key as possible. Not that that was an easy feat when I stuck out like a sore fucking thumb.

"Seeing *is* believing," I agreed, getting to my feet and holding out my hand.

Ryder tensed at the sight, his own hand disappearing into his cut where, tucked against his chest, he had a gun holstered out of view.

Blade didn't react, other than to grab mine and pump it. "Last time I saw you, you looked like you were losing your mind. Now, here you are again, looking like a fucking wreckage. What happened? Something go down with that girl of yours?"

My nostrils flared, a reaction that had him smirking.

"Don't worry, Rex." He raised his hands. "Only messing with you. As a courtesy from one Prez to another, I made sure to check in on her."

A clamp felt like it had been settled on my lungs. "Does she know you were checking in?"

"Nah. It was only once a year. Had to make sure there was no reason you'd bring your band of hellions down here."

"I guess," I admitted begrudgingly.

The laughter in his eyes told me he knew that, in his shoes, I'd have done the same thing. It was clear that he found it funny I was pissed off.

Was it just me or did the fucker look like Maverick when he was amused?

"As far as I know, she's okay. Had some issues recently with that stepfather of hers. Mostly, she's a good girl. Plays in the school band. That type of kid, you know?"

Stepfather?

"Jeremy Kinnock?" I clarified.

Blade nodded.

"What type of issues?"

"The wife called the cops in three weeks ago. There'd been a domestic. Officers turfed him out and calmed things down, but she never filed charges."

"How do you know that?"

His smug smile deepened. "Ways and means."

I grunted, aware he wouldn't share anything else with me. He was just playing mind games. Wanting to fuck with my head. Genius prick was tangling with the wrong motherfucker.

"I'm here to meet her."

Ryder scoffed, "You ain't met her before now?"

Being honest when in another MC's territory was the best way to go, but I didn't like laying down my family's vulnerabilities to a bunch of outlaws.

And I didn't give a fuck if that made me a hypocrite, either.

"No," I bit off. "I didn't want to mess with her family dynamic."

"Why you messing with it now then?"

Ryder's sneer made my fists itch with the need to collide with that pretty boy face of his.

I grunted, "Because my dad just died."

Blade stilled, but not for the reason I assumed. "I heard about that. I'm sorry, man. Bear was... Well, he was an East Coast legend."

Pride lodged in my throat, and I barely managed to grate out, "Yeah, he was."

"That blast was fucked up. I can't believe those Sparrow asswipes bombed your goddamn compound." He shook his head. "We ain't had too many problems with them around here."

"You have," I said grimly. "You just don't realize it yet."

Blade didn't like that. His scowl told me so as he postured, "I think I'd fucking know."

"The Sparrows had trade routes all over the US."

"Trade routes? What is this? The Silk Road?"

My top lip quirked up into a sneer that rivaled Ryder's. "Nothing so fancy. They sold women. Kids. Shipped them across the seaboard."

Ryder rasped, "I'd have heard about it."

"Some shit's buried deep." I shrugged. "They're not so much my problem anymore. I got my own mess to be handling and the Five Points over in Manhattan are dismantling their operation."

Blade cocked a brow. "The Five Points?"

"Irish Mob," I explained.

"I've heard of them." He rubbed his chin. "They say that Aidan O'Donnelly Sr. is a head case, don't they?"

"He is," I confirmed before I tapped my pointer finger against my temple. "But his boys are all there."

Folding his arms across his chest, Blade rumbled, "I'll be sure to contact them if I come across any news about Sparrows' activity in this area."

I nodded. "I'm sure they'd appreciate that."

"You alone?" Ryder demanded.

"I am."

Blade stared at me. "That wise?"

"Nothing's wise right now." My mouth tightened. "I just wanna see my girl. Stick around if she wants to know me, then go the fuck home. I don't want to cause trouble."

"Sinners never do," Ryder muttered.

"I really don't fucking like you," I snapped.

"I never asked you fucking to," he snarled back.

"Ryder," Blade said smoothly. "Wait for me by the hogs."

The Enforcer's eyes narrowed with displeasure, but he trudged over to the bikes. He could probably hear as much from there as he had from a few steps away, but he was no longer involved in the conversation—that much was clear.

"I'll give you three days before I want to know more about why you're really here," Blade said calmly. "Ryder has a point. Where Sinners go, there's always a mess to clean up." He arched a brow. "You sure there's no pedophile in the area who needs his throat slit?"

"Not that I'm aware of." That wasn't a lie.

He studied me, but I could sense he didn't believe me. He grunted. "Three days. That's it. And I'm being generous because you've got a good girl, and that dad of hers, stepdad..." He rolled his eyes. "Whatever the fuck he is, is a jackass."

"Jeremy?" I tensed. "What's he done?"

Blade shrugged. "He's up to his eyes in debt with the Triads."

"What?" I could feel my shoulders bunching. "How the fuck did he get involved with them? He's a goddamn teacher."

"Likes Mahjong."

"Mahjong?" I repeated blankly.

"Think dominos but with debts that end with being kneecapped."

Jesus Christ.

I swiped a hand over my head as a million worst-case scenarios bombarded me. "Have they threatened the family?"

"No. Not yet. He's managed the payments up until now, but the girl... she moved out about a week ago."

Straightening up, I rasped, "It was her seventeenth birthday last week."

"Seems she wanted out." He studied me. "You didn't know." It wasn't really a question.

"It's been hectic."

Sympathy had him grimacing. "I'm sorry, your dad... Yeah, of course."

"You know where she's living?"

He nodded. "44 Millbank Road. She's in unit 220."

"That came to you pretty quickly," I ground out.

"Got a good memory." Unease filled me as his gaze turned stark with a warning I knew I'd be a fool to ignore. As much as the Sinners had a rep, the Disciples did too. "Remember, Rex. Seventy-two hours, then I want answers."

I didn't argue with him, just nodded. "If I give them to you, and shit works out with her, can I stay?"

He pursed his lips. "We'll see."

Disliking being beholden to anyone, I reached for my JD to sink it back as he twisted around and returned to his hog.

Watching him and his Enforcer ride off into the fucking sunset, I grabbed my cell and keyed in her address.

Finding the route to her place, I wondered how the fuck a seventeen-year-old had managed to get an apartment on her own. If she'd emancipated herself, then I had to reason Maverick would have heard about *that*.

Had Ally left Jeremy?

And if she hadn't, if Ally wasn't there, *how* had Wynter gotten her own place, and would it be easier or harder without her adoptive parents there while I explained our mutual history?

There was no guarantee that Jeremy and Ally would let me into the fucking house, but if they did, then at least they'd be able to explain that I wasn't some deranged lunatic who was also her biological dad.

Grimacing, wishing I could have about ten more JDs, instead, I reached into my jacket, downed a packet of gum, and considered finding a motel to clean up first. But I'd showered this morning, my gear was fresh and clean, and I didn't stink of smoke or booze from the bar, so I knew if I did try to find a motel first, I was just stalling.

Like a goddamn coward.

The menthol explosion in my skull was strong as I tried to chew away the taste of JD, and it plagued me as I drove the short ride to my kid's place.

The neighborhood wasn't the best. So much so that I was grateful the Disciples had their eyes on her.

The apartment building wasn't worthy of a goddamn drug runner. Never mind my kid, that was for fucking sure.

There were bars on every window, and the front door didn't have a proper lock. Something that was only confirmed when I walked over to it after parking my hog and dragging my saddlebag with me, and it swung open with the kick of my foot.

No working intercom, no lock to keep non-residents out—this was a father's idea of hell.

Nervous and pissed off, wondering what the fuck kind of game Jeremy was playing, I figured out that 220 was on the second floor.

Once I made it outside her place, I knocked on the door, half expecting no one to answer because it was early enough that she could have been in school still.

Well, that was unless she'd quit school and I just hadn't known.

The last time Maverick and I had spoken, he hadn't said dick about her moving out. Hadn't said anything about her prick father being in debt up to his eyeballs with the Triads.

Although... in fairness, Mav wouldn't pick up on that unless there were unusual withdrawals being removed from his account.

By the sounds of it, Jeremy made *regular* payments. Might have even done that for years so Mav likely wouldn't have seen a pattern.

That didn't stop me from being furious though.

Not just with Jeremy but with Maverick too.

When no one answered the door, I made to turn away, bitterly angry to realize there wasn't even a peephole.

Then, just as I stepped aside, determining to return later, I heard a soft, "Go away."

My kid.

Christ, so like her fucking mother.

What was it with the women in my life?

Always telling me to back off?

Sucking in a sharp breath, I rasped, "I'm not..."

My mouth worked as words failed me.

What *was* I doing here?

I hadn't even thought about what I'd say to her. In all honesty, I'd figured it would be a fight to meet her. Hadn't expected I could just roll up to her place and speak with her immediately.

I thought Ally would be the one to ease things after we argued for a couple hours about how they didn't want a bad influence like me in her life...

Nothing about this was going how I imagined.

Clearing my throat, I continued, "I'm a friend—" A friend of the family? Was I? Jesus.

"I don't care who you are. Go. Away."

The words bit into me again, as she unknowingly beat an exposed nerve with a ball-peen hammer.

I gritted my teeth. "I came a long way to visit with you. You don't know me, and I don't know you but I'm R—" I heaved a sigh. "My name's King. I went to school with your folks."

Silence.

Not even a whisper.

Fuck, this was more of a disaster than I could have predicted.

"I know you moved out recently, and I figured that money must be tough for you to be staying here."

I dug my hand into my pocket and pulled out some bills. I didn't have much on me. A little over four hundred dollars right now. I dumped my bag on the ground, squatted in front of the door, and shoved the money beneath it.

There was a too-big gap that had warning signs flickering to being in my head, so it was easier than I'd like to pass something under the board.

"I don't want your money."

"It's a gift. I just... You should be staying somewhere with an intercom and a front door that locks. Even better, somewhere with an alarm system." That might have been asking for a lot, but fuck, I needed her safe.

"There's four hundred bucks here!" The soft exclamation had me swallowing. My daughter. *My baby girl.*

"I can get you more. However much you need." Anything to get her out of this shithole.

"I don't know you. I can't take money from a stranger."

The words sank into me like bullets.

I staggered to my feet, pressed a hand to the door. "I'm not a stranger, Wynter. I'm your biological father. But it's okay if you don't believe me. It really is. It's okay if you don't want to meet me. But please, take the money. I can get you more. I know four hundred isn't much to get somewhere decent to rent in this area."

There was a slight rattle from the door, and it opened a scant inch.

A chain.

At least she had a fucking chain.

I sucked in a relieved breath that morphed into a stunned one when a beautiful brown eye peeped at me through the sliver of space.

I wished I could see more. Could see who she was staying with to get an apartment in this dump.

Had she bribed the super?

It looked like the kind of place where blind eyes were turned.

"Your name's King?" The chestnut iris flared as her pupil dilated with her apparent disbelief.

I licked my lips. "I have two names. Maybe you know me by the other. My friends call me Rex."

There was no flicker of recognition.

"Rex is Latin for King."

"Yes, it is."

I knew she'd studied Latin at school.

I'd paid for a private academy, wanting her to have the best education money could buy.

"Is that intentional?"

My lips almost twitched. "It was."

The wad of cash was stuffed into the space. "I don't want your money."

"I'm sure you don't," I agreed, heart sinking. "But this place isn't safe."

She gulped. "You think I don't know that? It's all I could afford until I get paid next week."

I gritted my teeth. "You're working?"

"As a waitress. Three nights a week."

Her answer was rich enough with details that I knew she recognized my name.

At least, I hoped she didn't tell every bastard who came to her door shit like that.

Reaching up, I scratched my jaw and said, "I can't take that money back."

"I don't want it," she said bitterly.

"Maybe you don't, but I want you to have it. I have no need for it."

She frowned. "It's money. How can you have no need for it?"

"Because I'd prefer for you to have it instead."

"That makes no sense."

"You know I'm your biological dad, Wynter." I hitched a shoulder. "What do you expect me to do?"

"Not stick around?"

Christ, this girl could wound.

"I would've if I could've."

Her mockery stung as she said, "That's a real comfort to me now. *Dad*."

"I know it isn't. But I promise you, if I could have raised you as my own, I would have."

Her sniff told me she thought I was talking out of my ass. "Why are you here?"

"You're seventeen." I swallowed. "I-I tried to stay away because I didn't want to make things confusing for you, but I lost my dad on Christmas Day, your grandfather Bear, and he... I..."

"Did he know about me?"

"No." It was one of my darkest regrets.

I didn't know why, out of everything, that was the trigger, but it was. She made to slam the door closed, but I stuck my booted foot in the opening, wedging it there so she couldn't.

"Go away," she snarled.

"Let me explain!"

"Why should I? Why should I listen to you when this is the first time you've bothered to come into my life?"

"I didn't give you up because I was young and foolish. I didn't set you up with Jeremy and Ally because I didn't *want* you."

"Why did you then?"

Jesus. How did I explain this?

"Your biological mother, Rachel, *was* young when she had you. It wasn't planned. Rachel's a genius. She's so fucking smart, Wynter. I've seen your report cards, and I figure you take after her." I shot her a grin that went down like a lead balloon. "She got into Brown for pre-law, and she was going to take on the world. The condom busted, but that didn't matter. You were unexpected, but we loved each other, Wynter. I swear."

"You didn't make her get rid of me?" she asked, her voice suspicious.

"No!" I barked. "I damn well didn't. Your mom was delicate that year." It was hard to settle on that word, but it was the only one that seemed to sit right with me. "Something had happened to her, but she wouldn't tell me what. Someone had hurt her. It made her distant. Things were awkward between us in the run up to her leaving."

"Who hurt her?"

"I-I found out recently that it was my uncle."

Her eye rounded. "Your uncle hurt my mom?"

I figured the possessive pronouns were a step forward.

"Yeah, he did."

"Badly?"

I rubbed my forehead with the back of my hand. "He assaulted her. Sexually."

"I-I'm his?"

"No! No. You're mine. She was fragile before she went to school, but when she was due to give birth, she was worse than ever." I sucked in a breath. "I don't live a life where... My world is dangerous, Wynter. You've watched *Sons of Anarchy*?"

She blinked. "I have."

"Well, think that but worse."

Her eye drifted down my length, fastened itself to the patches on my cut. "You're a biker?"

"I am."

"The Prez. You're the leader?"

"Yeah, but I wasn't back then. I'd have made it work if Rachel could have coped, but she couldn't. She was broken, Wynter. In many ways, she still is."

"Because of your uncle?"

"Yeah. Even now, if I touch her unawares, she flinches. It's like I've hit her with a taser." The truth rattled through me, hurting me as much as it hurt Rachel. "Whatever he did to her, something she still won't talk about, it crushed her. She dove into her studies then, and now, she lives and breathes her work.

"I wanted you, Wynter. I did. And I know, if things had been different, she'd have wanted you too. But things *weren't* different—"

"You're a biker?" she asked again.

"I am."

"Did you hurt your uncle? For touching her?"

"He died a long time ago."

Her eye closed for a split second. Slower than a blink. "Good. I'm glad."

"Me too."

Especially knowing *how* he died.

At the end of Sin's fists as he beat the bastard to a bloody pulp that resulted in his death.

That was the least he deserved.

I swallowed. "I wanted you to have a stable home. A good life. With people who'd already been looking to adopt. I-I figured Jeremy and Ally were safe choices."

The corner of her mouth that I could see, grew taut. "Ally... Mom... she's good people."

But her dad wasn't.

"Did Jeremy hurt you?" I growled, straightening up as outrage filled me.

"No."

Why wasn't I reassured?

"Why did you move out?"

"That's my business. Not yours."

I decided not to push my luck by prodding for more answers.

"Why are you really here?"

"You're grown up. If you wanted, we could be friends."

She studied me for a second, but her distrust was clear in her silence.

"You had seventeen years to find me. Why bother?"

"I didn't have to find you. I knew where you were," I told her carefully, "but I wasn't about to walk into your life—"

"Just thought you'd do that today?" she sneered. "What's changed?"

"I've changed."

A hard laugh barked from her. "Yeah, okay, what do I look? Ten? I might have believed that bullshit before, but not now."

Patience rattled, I told her, "It's not bullshit. My dad just died. It made me realize that having a lot of family is a positive, not a negative."

"Think I'm gonna call you Daddy and we can just make up and get along?"

"No." Her bitterness shouldn't have come as a surprise, but it did. "But having one more friend can't be all bad, can it?"

"Friends are there for each other. As far as I can tell, you've never been there for me."

I had. But she wasn't to know that.

"I can start now, can't I?"

"Don't you think it's too little too late?"

My smile was sad. "It's not too late until we're dead, and I'm not going anywhere."

I wasn't sure why, but that seemed to trigger a response in her.

At first, I just thought she was going to slam the door in my face, my foot be damned, but then, after staring at me for a minute, she told me, "There's a coffee shop around the corner. It's where I work. We can talk there tomorrow before school. Seven AM."

Stepping back, I unwedged my foot. "I'll be there," I said as she closed the door in my face.

I sagged against the wall, unable to believe that she was letting me in, but I knew if she was anything like her mother, the war would be hard won.

Thanks to a lifetime's experience with Rachel, I was battle ready.

## TWENTY-EIGHT

## RACHEL
### ALWAYS - GAVIN JAMES

I tried Rex's phone three times a day. Before I started work, at lunch, and before I went to bed.

He'd ignored each of my calls since he left... until tonight.

When I hadn't expected him to answer.

While I was in Rory's guest bedroom as she snored away three bottles of Zinfandel on her sofa and I was in a semi-sugar-induced coma.

So, *of course,* he answered.

"Rex?" I blurted out when the call connected.

He didn't utter a word.

"Rex?"

Silence.

"King?"

"What do you want, Rachel?"

I shivered at his cold tone which was more frigid than all the ice cream I'd consumed.

I wished I'd had a Zinfandel to make things easier on me, but I didn't. Just a sugar rush and that really didn't pack the same punch.

I knew I'd hurt him, and that gutted me.

"To apologize."

"Why am I not surprised?"

I ground my teeth together at the bitter retort. "I don't know why you would be."

"Because you're always sorry, Rachel. Always. It never changes anything though, does it?"

Feeling like I was choking, I stared blankly at the ceiling above the bed. I didn't have an answer because what else was there to say?

Okay, that was wrong.

There was so much to say. So many things that I'd never mentioned before that were burning a hole in my tongue.

At this moment in time, the only man I had ever loved knew less about me than his MC brothers did.

He didn't know that he was going to be a father again, didn't understand that I'd been assaulted twice in my life, and didn't realize how deeply those attacks had impacted me.

All of those things added to the choking sensation that gripped me, but for all that, the soft susurration of his breath in my ear had me closing my eyes.

I'd been on the brink of tears throughout his absence, but now, they burned as I finally let them fall.

"Why did you answer the phone tonight?"

"Because I met Wynter today, Rachel, and I knew the only person in the world who'd get what I was feeling would be you."

I jerked upright at that, only I didn't realize I was too close to the edge of the bed, because when my hand went down to support my new upright position, it encountered only blank space.

The second I registered *that*, I tumbled over the side with a yelp and narrowly avoided face-planting on the carpet.

It made a hell of a clatter when my ass collided with the floor, though, especially as it jolted the bed, and I heard Rex's bellowed, "*RACHEL?*" from the other end of the phone.

Snatching up my cell, I panted, "Sorry. I just fell off the bed."

"Are you being serious?"

I cleared my throat. "Yeah. Unfortunately."

"Are you drunk?"

I wished.

I hissed under my breath a muttered, "Ouch." Twisting, I rubbed my side and asked, "You met Wynter? Does that mean you're in California?"

He paused. "You know where she lives?"

"I didn't. Until Maverick told me that was where he thought you were going."

"He told you that, did he?"

Confused by his tone, I murmured, "Yeah, a couple days after you left. He said he could be wrong, and that you might have headed to New Mexico. Either way, he was right, wasn't he?"

Rex just grunted.

Silence fell between us.

I didn't know what to say.

What to ask.

My side ached like a bitch, and where my hip had collided with the floor smarted like hell. But that was nothing to the twisted, gnawing pain in my heart. One that felt as though it had corrupted me soul-deep.

"It took you a while to get to California," I pointed out softly.

"I took it slow."

Slow was an understatement. It was the second week of January!

"Aren't you going to ask how she is?"

"I don't know what to ask," I admitted honestly.

"Do you even care?"

My mouth tightened at that. "Of course I care," I snapped. "Just because I don't process things like you, Rex, doesn't mean I don't *feel*. If anything, I feel too damn much. That's always been my problem." I sucked in a breath. "Instead of making me feel badly about not knowing what to ask, why don't you tell me why you answered the phone? You clearly wanted to share something with me."

His hesitation didn't make me feel any better.

"Rex?" I sighed. "King!"

Although, why he wanted me to call him that, I had no idea.

Nyx had been the first to earn his road name, I knew that much. But King had gained his shortly after. Him separating the two, making a differential between them, was unnerving.

I didn't know why, exactly, it just was.

"Today, I only spoke with her. Tomorrow, we're going for coffee before school."

I had to think that the sugar and the lack of sleep and the exhaustion from work was turning my mind into mush because I couldn't compute any of what he'd just said.

"Rachel?"

He had to know I was still there from my breathing alone; he had to know. I probably sounded like I was having an asthma attack which was a feat seeing as I didn't have asthma.

Reaching up, I pinched the bridge of my nose and let the first words that came to mind drip from my tongue:

"What does she look like?"

I surprised myself with the question.

I hadn't known what I was about to say until I said it.

Perhaps he was surprised, too, because he was quiet until he murmured, "Her situation's unusual."

That had me straightening up. "It is? Why?"

He heaved a sigh. "I'm not sure what's going on with her. She's only seventeen but she's moved out of her parents' place and into a building that's less than ideal. She was smart enough to keep the chain on when she opened the door, and she wasn't entirely inclined to speak with me so she never took it off."

My slow brain wasn't *that* slow. "No one would let her rent an apartment. She'd never be able to sign the lease."

He hummed, but the sound was distinctly disapproving. "I know."

"She could have had someone co-sign on it, I guess? There are sublets or she might even have used a fake ID."

"I'll try to find out tomorrow when we meet before school. But, long answer short, I couldn't tell you what she looks like because I didn't see her."

I bit my lip. "One of my charities is for single moms—"

He snorted. "You think I didn't know that already?"

My head bowed. "Yeah, of course, you know about FAST."

"Where there's a paper trail, I know everything about you, Rachel Laker. I just don't know the shit you've kept from me."

"I'm shocked you don't," I choked out.

Although, maybe it'd be easier if he already knew and I wouldn't have to say a word.

"I *could* have learned the truth. Where there's a will, you know? But I realized a long time ago that if I did, if whatever happened to you wasn't something you shared with me, it'd break a link between us."

My brow furrowed. "I don't think anything could break the ties that bind us, Rex."

"No?"

"No," I said softly. "I'm sorry about Christmas Day."

"Which part?" he demanded grimly. "The hospital or after?"

"Both, but this apology is for after. I shouldn't have told you to get out. I just thought you'd..." I sucked in a breath. "I just thought you'd go upstairs or something. I didn't think you'd—"

"Go to California?"

"Yeah."

A short laugh escaped him. "It wasn't intentional."

"No?" A small kernel of hope unfurled inside me.

"No. I needed to ride, needed to clear my head, and then I just took off."

Staring at the fancy lamp on the nightstand, I reached for the glass of water I'd placed there when I'd headed into the guest room and gulped down a couple of sips.

Wishing it were Zinfandel again, I murmured, "You want to get to know Wynter?"

"I do."

"Why now? Because of Bear?"

"Yeah."

"Is that fair to her?" I asked carefully. "Letting your grief push you into a relationship with her? One that didn't exist before?"

"It probably isn't fair, but now that I'm down here, I'm glad that I came. Her building's a dump, Rachel. She can't stay there. I can't imagine what her family's fucking thinking letting her live in a place like that."

"Maybe they don't know. Maybe she ran away." Which, now that I thought about it, didn't make this conversation any more palatable. Grimacing, I mumbled, "Scratch that. I'm glad you're down there too."

"Do you have feelings for her?"

The pain that question triggered stunned me. "Of course I do," I snapped. "Jesus, Rex. I know I come across a certain way, but I'm not made of stone, dammit."

"You never talk about her. Notwithstanding that argument with Scott."

"Neither do you," I hissed, aggravated by the disapproval in his voice.

"Because I can tell it upsets you."

"Why wouldn't it? I gave my daughter away for strangers to raise, Rex. Do you think that was easy for me to do?"

"I don't know. We weren't talking much back then."

I gritted my teeth. "Bullshit."

"Why is it bullshit? We *weren't* talking, and all I knew was that you looked like you were dying. Not just physically, but whenever you held her."

My fingers tightened to the point of pain around my glass as I thought back to that horrible, horrible time. "I felt like I was."

"If you'd been able to, would you have had an abortion?"

"I'm going to hang up the phone now," I whispered, unable to believe he'd asked me that.

"Don't you dare, Rachel," Rex boomed down the line. "I want answers. If we're three thousand miles apart, maybe you'll give them to me."

"Are you just trying to hurt me? I know I hurt you on Christmas Day, but it wasn't intentional."

"It took me a round trip from one coast to the other to clear my head, Rachel. To know that we don't work." A choked gasp gusted from my lips, but before I could say a word, he continued, "But I want us to. You're the only woman I can imagine loving. You're the only woman I want to be with, and yet, if something doesn't change, the next ten years are going to look exactly the same as the last, and I can't handle that anymore.

"Something's gotta give, or we have to step back and away from each other. Make the incision now and try to move on because I can't do this anymore. I just fucking can't, Rachel."

I thought about the baby in my belly, thought about how the next ten years *would* be different from the last, and I knew this was as good a moment as any to tell him I was pregnant, but the words didn't fall from my lips.

Rex was honorable.

He was a good man.

He might be an outlaw, might be the suspect in a hundred crimes that the cops couldn't pin on him, but that didn't take away from the truth of the matter—he was dutiful. When he loved, he loved hard. When he cared about someone, they were the luckiest person on the planet. His sacrifices, first with Wynter, then with Bear, proved that.

And he wasn't wrong.

That was the worst thing of all.

Something *did* have to give. Something that, preferably, wasn't our sanity *or* our hearts.

I couldn't deal with more heartbreak or with the next decade looking like the last—even with a baby to shake things up.

"Answer me this, Rex."

"Anything."

"How long are you intending on staying down in California?"

He was quiet until he bit off, "*That's* what you want to ask me?" His disappointment was clear.

"For now."

"For as long as she'll talk to me. I want to build a relationship with her. That could mean I'll be on the back of my hog tomorrow or it might mean six months from now—"

"Six months?" I cried.

"Whatever it takes," he said softly.

My throat tightened because that sounded like a threat, but I managed to choke out, "I have a proposal."

"What's that?"

"Before I say a word, I want you to know that I love you, Rex." Nothing. No response. "I've loved you since I was a teenager, and I know that I'll love you until the day I die."

"Loving each other isn't our problem, Rach," he said tiredly. "It's *living* with each other that is."

He was right.

So right.

"I know," I agreed shakily. "But that's half the battle, isn't it? I love you. I'm not sure I've told you that—"

"Not in eighteen years, six months, two weeks, and four days."

Eyes flaring wide, I whispered, "You remember?"

"Of course." He scoffed. "I'm a fucking idiot where you're concerned, Rach. Ain't you figured that out yet?"

Shivers rushed through me at his self-deprecating tone. The bitterness hurt, as did the realization that I'd brought this beautiful, strong man to his knees.

It hadn't been out of selfishness, nor out of a desire to tame him. It had been self-preservation. Pure and simple.

Of course, nothing was simple about my past.

Neither was it pure.

"What's your proposal, Rachel?"

"That while you're away, whether it's for six days or six months," I managed to get out, "we talk. Every day. Every single day. Maybe even twice a day. And *not* about work. We haven't done that in—"

"—eighteen years, six months, two weeks, and four days," he drawled.

"We have a lot to discuss," I concurred hoarsely.

"What if I end up riding home tomorrow?"

Well, that wasn't a *no*, was it?

"W-We can still talk every day. You'll just be down the hill and not across the country."

Rex blew out a breath. "What's the end goal?"

"For us to be more than what we are now."

"Not concrete enough," was his grim retort. "I want us to work toward being together or I'm out, Rachel. I'm telling you that I can't do this anymore. In fact, I'm telling you that I *won't*."

The threat inherent in that hiss had me flinching.

This time without him had proven how badly I needed him to be a part of my life. It had also shown me how limited the interactions were between us.

If this didn't work out, there'd be no one else for me. Not even if I saw him cozying up with another woman. Rex was it for me. He always had been. Always would be.

If this didn't work out, then I loved him enough to let him go.

I just prayed that wasn't how our story ended because I had a lifetime ahead of me, and I didn't want that to mimic the recent past.

Baby or no, I had to protect him.

Baby or no, I needed to make sure that if this did work out, it was because we could be together and be happy as a couple first, then be a family second.

"Okay."

"Okay?" he repeated.

Was that relief that made his voice shaky?

I had to hope so.

"Okay," I confirmed.

"How long?"

"How long do I want us to do this for?" His answer was just a hum, so I mumbled, "For as long as it takes?"

He was silent. Considering. "Every time we call, we get to ask each other two questions, and we *have* to answer them. They don't have to be life-changing, but they have to be answered."

"I can do that," I said softly. Deciding to bite the bullet, I continued, "Your dad stipulated in his will that we be together, in person, when you read his last wishes, but over the phone should fulfil that clause. When I'm back home, do you want me to read it to you?"

"If you want to," he replied, his tone disinterested.

Having read through Bear's Will & Testament, however, and knowing where he was, I figured he'd appreciate my suggestion once he realized what Bear wanted of him.

I wasn't unhappy about delaying the reading.

It was a nightmare waiting to happen.

"Where are you if you're not at home?"

"A friend's place in the city."

"A friend?"

"Is that one of the two questions?"

He snorted. "No."

I almost smiled. "Rory. You remember her, right?"

"From college?"

"Yeah." I didn't tell him that Rory was now Aurora. New York's DA. For all I knew, he was well aware of that already.

"Why are you there?"

"We hadn't caught up in a while. I'm currently drunk on sugar."

"Ice cream?"

My lips quirked into a full smile this time. "Yeah." I paused. "I wouldn't have had an abortion, King."

It was weird to call him that, but maybe he was right. Rex was the MC. He was business and he was an outlaw. King was the kid I'd fallen in love with. Wynter's father.

"No?"

"No. S-She was made from our love. I could never have killed that. It's why I had to go through with it all. Even though it was hell."

"Why was it? Why was pregnancy so hard on you?"

My mouth twisted as I whispered, "Are you sure you want to have that conversation tonight?"

I thought he'd be angry at my evasion, but he merely rumbled, "That bad?"

"Oh, it's the worst," I said, my tone bizarrely bright.

He heaved a sigh. "Before I come home, I want answers."

"You'll get them. Just... when I've prepared myself?"

Telling his brothers had already been like getting a knife and dragging it down a long, badly healed scar, tearing it open again without pain meds and then letting it fester without antibiotics.

With him, it would be ten times more brutal.

Something else I wasn't looking forward to, even if he was right—it was time we got it out in the open.

"Okay." He sucked in a breath. "It's late there. You should get some sleep."

It *was* late.

But...

Turning off the lamp, I clambered to my feet and rolled into bed. It was dumb, so dumb, but I placed a hand on my belly, promising that child that I'd do my best to make this work so he or she could have both parents living together, and I whispered, "Rex?"

"Yeah, Rach?" A soft laugh escaped him, so different than any of the other harsh sounds that'd come from him tonight. "I love you. Is that what you needed to hear?"

"It is," I said gently. "I hope tomorrow goes well."

"Do you want me to bring you up?"

I bit my lip. "Selfishly, yes, but I know that that's a bridge I have to build on my own."

"When did shit get so complicated, Rach?"

"I think we were born complicated, Rex. Speak to you tomorrow?" At his hum, I whispered, "Night."

"Night."

The whisper lingered in my ear, and I stared into the darkness, hand still on my belly, well aware that things were more complicated than he even knew.

But as I drifted to sleep, there was hope in my heart which was 'day' to the 'night' that came from the sorrow of knowing I'd pushed Rex away for good.

*From: K1ngS1nn3r1@gmail.com*
*To: Rach3lLadyLiberty@gmail.com*
*Subject: Re. Please*
I could never hate you.
K


*From: Rach3lLadyLiberty@gmail.com*
*To: K1ngS1nn3r1@gmail.com*
*Subject: Re. Please*
Thank you for answering my call last night.
Rach


*From: K1ngS1nn3r1@gmail.com*
*To: Rach3lLadyLiberty@gmail.com*
*Subject: Re. Please*
I should have called you sooner.
K


*From: Rach3lLadyLiberty@gmail.com*
*To: K1ngS1nn3r1@gmail.com*
*Subject: Re. Please*
Why didn't you?
R

*From: K1ngS1nn3r1@gmail.com*
*To: Rach3lLadyLiberty@gmail.com*
*Subject: Re. Please*

*Because I was hurt.*
*Because I was grieving.*
*Because I had shit to do and a head to put on straight.*
*I should be used to you pulling away, but it hit me on the raw.*
*K*


*From: Rach3lLadyLiberty@gmail.com*
*To: K1ngS1nn3r1@gmail.com*
*Subject: Re. Please*

*I wish things were different.*
*I hate that you're 'used to my pulling away.'*
*I wish for so many things for us, King.*
*R*


*From: K1ngS1nn3r1@gmail.com*
*To: Rach3lLadyLiberty@gmail.com*
*Subject: Re. Please*

*If it came down to it, I'd take the reality over wishes that might never be.*
*K*


*From: Rach3lLadyLiberty@gmail.com*

*To: K1ngS1nn3r1@gmail.com*
*Subject: Re. Please*
You don't mean that.
R.


*From: K1ngS1nn3r1@gmail.com*
*To: Rach3llLadyLiberty@gmail.com*
*Subject: Re. Please*
I do.
K

## TWENTY-NINE

### REX

A rerun of a *Dr. Phil* episode had inspired last night's 'intervention.'

Lying flat out in bed, my head tilted down as I flipped through the channels in my hotel room, I'd started watching shows that'd never normally interest me.

Answering Rachel's call yesterday evening had probably been an idea that stemmed from being bored with what I was watching, but reflecting upon that conversation until I fell asleep made me realize I owed Dr. Phil my gratitude.

She'd suggested the daily calls. Not me.

She'd agreed to a daily Q&A.

It was a step forward rather than back.

For years, I'd let her dance farther and farther away from me because I knew just how fragile she was, because I knew work was her therapy and that if I pushed shit, she'd walk away.

If I hadn't told Drew a week ago that pussies were used to being pounded, I'd have called myself one for how I'd let her get away with this half-life relationship we had.

Well, no more.

Dad's death was making me reconsider things. He'd lived his final chapter, but I was halfway through my goddamn story and I didn't want to spend the rest of my fucking days filled with regrets.

It wasn't like Rachel was even living her best fucking life.

That was the worst of it.

She was as miserable as I was, and we were getting nowhere.

That step forward for us was badly needed, and even though the weight of grief was still heavy on my shoulders, when I got up the next morning and took a shower, I felt brighter than I had since I left West Orange.

I was going to speak with my daughter today, and later on, my woman.

Because Rachel was that.

I'd told her that if this didn't work out, we'd move on, but fuck, there was *no* moving on without her.

She was it for me.

My fucking everything.

I just needed her to realize that we were each other's goddamn everything.

As I washed up, I flicked through the clothes I'd bought yesterday. I felt like an asswipe but I wanted to make the best impression with my kid and figured that her limited view yesterday could be an advantage today.

Out of respect for the Disciples, I wasn't going to wear my cut, and that'd be the first time in years that I was without the battered leather vest. That meant I could look semi-respectable when we met up.

Once I was done in the shower, I pulled out the razor I'd bought yesterday too. Before I could get started, my cell rang in the other room.

I'd allowed notifications from her so I knew from the ringtone alone who was calling.

Sucking in a breath, giving myself a quick pep talk that consisted of me telling myself not to fuck this up, I rushed to grab it then hit the answer button and put it on speaker.

"Rex?"

Her voice sounded like I felt—brighter.

I smiled because I wanted every day to start this way—her voice in my ear—and I murmured, "Hey Rach."

"I figured you'd be getting up soon so I thought I'd—"

A chuckle escaped me. "Rach, are you nervous?"

She hissed. "Don't you dare laugh."

Smirking, I unplugged the phone from the charger then retreated to the bathroom. "You forget I'm not scared of you."

"No one's scared of me," she dismissed.

"You'd be surprised," I drawled.

"Like who?"

"Most of the MC."

"You're crazy."

"I'm not," I informed her as I squirted shaving cream into my palm. "If they didn't grow up knowing you, they're all scared of you. You're as cold as ice with them, remember?"

She didn't answer that. "What are you doing?"

"Why?"

"I can hear a weird noise."

"I'm shaving."

"I hope our daughter realizes she's one of the privileged few who's worthy of her father shaving."

I knew she was teasing, but the words spilling from her lips did shit to my insides.

Our daughter.

Her father.

Such simple goddamn labels, but nothing was simple for us. She'd said it herself last night—we were born complicated.

I sheepishly grinned into the mirror and said, "I'd shave for you."

"Since when? I get stubble burn every time we kiss."

"Mostly because we only do quickies. If I planned it, you wouldn't."

A soft sigh came down the line. "I wouldn't?"

"No."

She hummed. "Interesting."

My lips twitched again though it was, technically, a testy subject. After all, sex wasn't something we did regularly. Even if it meant my balls were perennially blue.

"Interesting?" I taunted. "Next time, I'll make sure my cheeks are as smooth as a baby's ass."

Silence.

She gasped. "Then I need you to promise you'll go down on me."

Eyes flaring, inwardly cheering her on because I knew how this kind of talk was hard for her, I continued, "Oh, sweetheart, don't you worry. That's guaran-damn-teed."

Another gulp. "We shouldn't be talking about this."

"*Au contraire.*" I arched a brow at my reflection as I returned to my shaving. "I think we should. We're laying everything on the table, aren't we? Sex is a part of that. In fact, for a long time, it's the only way we've connected on a personal level."

"That's why I wanted to talk to you. I-I know that's something I haven't allowed."

"You haven't allowed much sex, either," I said dryly.

"N-No." She blew out a breath. "I'm sorry."

"You don't have to apologize, Rachel. I wasn't laying blame."

"No, I know, but still—"

As the razor cut through my stubble, I murmured, "Something traumatized you, baby. Something that I need to understand and that I want you to explain. I said it last night: I could have found out myself. But I've been waiting all this time for you to tell me because my knowing doesn't help *you*. I need to know where your head is at as we talk about this."

"Thank you."

"No need to thank me either."

She heaved a sigh. "King?"

"Yeah?"

"Someone..." She hesitated.

"Someone?"

It came out in a rush, which reminded me of the girl she'd once been. All nerves and anxiety. Stuttering starts to conversations and her nose always buried in a book.

Once upon a time, she hadn't been the polished attorney who was capable of wreaking havoc in the courts of the land.

She'd been an awkward girl who'd morphed into an awkward teenager.

I couldn't say she'd been an ugly duckling who'd turned into a swan because she'd always been pretty. She'd just been weird too.

I liked weird. Always had.

"Link said you didn't fuck Peach. That you used to play chess together."

Making a mental note to beat on Link, I merely said, "That's not a question."

Rach swallowed. "Is that true?"

"Would it change anything if it wasn't?"

"I don't know."

"Then why are you asking?"

I scraped away, revealing cheeks that hadn't been smooth in years. There were more lines than the last time I'd done this, and it merely rammed home that I wasn't getting any fucking younger.

"Because I'd like to know?"

"Would you tell me if you'd been fucking anyone else?"

She scoffed, "You know I haven't. If I'd gone on any dates, you're saying you wouldn't have had me followed?"

She had me there.

"You could have dated when you went into the city."

Another scoff. "I've seen my tail and I'm ninety-nine percent sure that Emile spies on me for you."

"It's for your protection."

"Don't doubt that it is, *but* I'm pretty sure they report back too."

I pursed my lips. "I haven't fucked anyone but you since we started dating."

There.

Everything was laid out on the table.

Her gulp was audible again. "Really?"

"Really."

"Why?"

"Because I love you."

"Oh, King," she whispered. "I love you too."

"I know you do."

"I wish I could tell you the same…"

Pain and understanding twisted together and unraveled inside me. "I wish, for your sake, you could too, sweetheart."

After a couple seconds of quiet, she requested, "If she'll let you, would you get a picture together for me?"

"I'll ask."

"Promise?"

I half-smiled. "Promise. I've finished." I raised the camera to the mirror and took a photo then sent it to her.

"Jesus, it's been years since I've seen you like that." A short laugh escaped her, but it sounded soggy too. "You always were beautiful."

Snorting, I groused, "I'm not beautiful."

"You are," she countered. "Men can be beautiful."

I just rolled my eyes.

"What are you wearing?"

"I bought some cargo pants yesterday and a—"

"You?! In cargo pants?" she blustered.

"This is definitely a parallel universe. I just want to make a good first impression."

I might have fucked that up already with our initial meeting, but that didn't mean I had to stop trying.

"By lying to her?" she joked. "Hell, you haven't been in anything other than jeans since the first day we met."

"I've worn surf shorts to go swimming in," I grumbled.

"That doesn't count. You wear jeans whether it's a hundred degrees outside or ten."

"A Prez has to have some standards."

She snickered. "Apparently. You going to meet her looking like a Ken doll is tantamount to a lie."

I sniffed. "She's meeting with a stranger. I'd prefer her not to be terrified of me when I roll up looking like my reputation precedes me."

"You have a point."

"Imagine that," I grouched, deciding that no way in hell was I going to tell her that I'd bought a Polo shirt too.

It was definitely alien territory, but if it gave Wynter a modicum of comfort then it'd be worth it.

"You going to wish me luck?" I asked.

"I don't think you'll need it. She's my daughter after all. She's going to fall head over heels for you."

My lips twitched. "That's Greek-tragedy level weird."

She huffed. "You know what I mean."

I did.

"Just being a jerk."

"Imagine that," she said, throwing my mocking words back at me. "But, if you want it, good luck."

"Thank you, Rach."

"Take care?"

I hummed. "I will. You too. We'll speak later."

"I'll look forward to it," she told me as she quietly ended the call.

A quick glance at the time made me realize I needed to haul ass, but when I headed out to the coffee shop fifteen minutes later, I was already early.

As I sat there, leaning forward, elbows on my knees as I watched the crowd ebb and flow, eyes trying to find someone who looked like a mini-Rach, it boggled my mind to realize that I was nervous. But that was the long and the short of it.

Jigging my foot against the ground, I allayed some of that tension into fidgeting, which made me feel like Link who was someone who acted like he had ants down his pants at all times.

Feeling off balance, I almost called the dickhead just to give him shit about telling Rach that most of the time, Peach and I hung out playing fucking chess together.

That, of course, was when I saw her.

She... Jesus. She was stunning. A mixture of her mom and me. She had the delicacy of Rachel's features, with the rich dark hair that was all mine. She had my jaw, though, and my height. A bit of my stockiness too, but that could have been a sign of good health. It had been a long while since Rachel was a healthy weight, though she hadn't been as skinny at Christmas.

Her hair was pinned back in a braid, and she wore a pair of black tailored pants and a white shirt that I figured were a part of her uniform.

The warmth of the morning combined with how fast she was walking gave her a rosy-cheeked glow that melted my heart.

I jerked to my feet the second I saw her, and as she crossed the street and her gaze collided with mine, the nerves disappeared. Melted away with the power of recognition.

That was the only way I could describe it.

She knew me, as much as I knew her, and it had nothing to do with how we looked.

Wynter, pausing once she'd crossed the street, sucked in a breath before she moved over to me.

Determined to make this as easy on her as I could, I stuck out my hand for her to shake when she approached the table I'd staked out for us.

Gingerly, she accepted it and shook mine before she murmured, "Hi."

"Hi," I greeted back. "Do you want a coffee or some breakfast?"

Her eyes lit up at that, but it immediately dampened. "Just coffee will be fine, thanks."

Wondering what that was about when she was clearly hungry, I asked, "Will you be okay here? While I go and order?"

She scowled at me. "I think I can handle sitting by myself for five minutes."

Shooting her a sheepish glance, I apologized. "What would you like to drink?"

"A latte, please. One shot of espresso."

Nodding my understanding, I retreated to the counter, and I put in an order for our drinks and then grabbed a couple of pastries and ordered some hot food for breakfast too.

If my kid was hungry, she'd eat.

It was a testament, I thought, to my anxiety that my sweet tooth wasn't triggered by all the pastries. I was too fucking nervous to eat.

This was worse than being interviewed by the cops on a murder charge.

When I returned with a tray stacked high with different kinds of food, she jerked upright, mouth rounding as I made it outside.

That she might love sweet treats as much as I did made me hide a smile.

"I didn't know what you'd like to eat," I said awkwardly. "So figured you could graze whatever caught your eye."

I didn't say that I'd have asked her if she'd have told me what she wanted to order.

This was our first meeting, and I intended for there to be more.

"You're going to eat some?"

"Yeah, 'course," I told her, even though I wasn't hungry at all. "There's an omelet coming and a sausage muffin if you're really hungry."

She didn't have to answer—I saw in her eyes she was.

What the fuck was going on with her?

It set my nerves on edge, but I made myself take a seat and lounge back. Every part of me wanted to shake some answers out of her, fix whatever was broken, but I couldn't. I didn't have the right.

Yet.

As she picked up a *pain au chocolat*, moaning when the chocolate hit her tongue, I took a sip of my espresso and monitored her.

She had shadows under her eyes, and some strain around them too.

"What time does school start?"

Wynter peered at me from under her lashes. "An hour."

"How far away is it?"

"It's a ten-minute walk."

I jerked up my chin. "I can take you there if you're not afraid of bikes?"

"You would?"

"I would."

She bit her lip, looking so much like Rachel at that moment I nearly fucking wept.

Before she could say anything, I pulled out my wallet. Flipping through the folds, I retrieved my driver's license. "So you know I am who I say I am."

Hesitantly, she took my license, and her shoulders dropped some. "I thought you were, but thank you for showing me."

"Trust your instincts, but trust proof even more," I said jokingly.

She graced me with a measured glance.

"Here," I said next, passing her a photo.

Her mouth rounded when she saw a much younger me holding a much younger her.

She'd been swaddled in hospital blankets, faded pink that offset just how rosy her cheeks were.

"That's me?"

"It is."

"You carry it with you?" she asked, her finger tracing a dog-eared corner.

"Always."

Her bottom lip got nibbled some more. "Do you have a picture of my birth mom?"

I nodded and handed her another couple photos. "This is her back then."

Wynter blinked as she took in the truly horrendous sight of

Rachel back when she'd given birth. Her fingertips drifted over her mom's face.

"She's almost skeletal."

"She was in bad shape." I sucked in a breath. "I'm sure you have questions but, in all honesty, I don't have the details yet. I'm working on it."

She frowned. "What makes you think she'll tell you now?"

"I gave her an ultimatum."

"About what?"

"Your mom and me..." I sighed. "Your birth mom and me, I mean—"

"I knew what you meant."

My smile was tight. "We're together. But it's a weird relationship. I'm tired of that. I want to move forward but she's buried in the past. We agreed, last night, that we were going to try to make things more normal between us."

"What's normal?"

Well, how the hell did I explain without her wondering what kind of freaks her birth parents were?

I cleared my throat. "We don't currently live together. She lives next door."

"She's your neighbor?"

"We're exclusive, but we don't date. We don't really hang out that much either. Most of the time, we only talk business."

Her mouth rounded. "Wow. That's very dysfunctional."

"It is," I agreed, laughing self-deprecatingly at her statement of surprise. "It's not ideal. I miss her, and I know she misses me."

"What's made the change? Is it like with me? It's to do with your dad?" Her tone, I noted, wasn't as sour as it had been yesterday.

"Yeah, it is."

I wasn't about to tell her that I didn't think I could take another of Rachel's cutting dismissals. She didn't need to know that. Neither did Rach. That would only set things back.

I knew it would take a while to get through Rachel's barriers, and

I didn't doubt there'd be painful times ahead. But with the promise of us working together to resolve things, I could deal with her being an ice queen from time to time.

I just needed progression.

I just needed to know we were both working toward the same end goal.

"Was she sick?"

"When I left?" I asked.

Wynter's lips tightened. "No. When she gave birth to me."

"Oh. Mentally, psychologically, yes. There were a couple of weeks over the summer break where she was institutionalized."

Her eyes widened, and I realized I wasn't exactly painting a nice picture here. Trouble was, this was the truth. It was why I was just meeting her now instead of raising her. There was no sugarcoating this.

"I didn't think... I just thought I wasn't wanted. You know?" Her fingers traced Rachel's gaunt cheekbones again. Even when she was pregnant, Rachel looked like she was anorexic. "Another teen mom who didn't use a condom."

Anger flushed through me, but I dampened it down. "Sometimes life hands you lemons and you can't make lemonade."

Wordlessly, she returned the photo to me then picked up the other. "She's still very thin. Is she... whatever she was institutionalized for, is that still a problem?"

"I don't believe so."

"You don't know?"

I felt her disapproval and squirmed at it. "Your mother's a very private person."

"You love her, right?"

"I do. Very much."

"Then why don't you keep an eye on her?"

I did. In very illegal ways. It wasn't like I could tell Wynter that. "It's not as simple as you think."

"Why isn't it?"

"Because if I get too close, Rachel either pushes me away or runs to the city for work." I rubbed a hand over the hair I'd gelled when I *never* used gel. The crispy pointed edges agitated me. "She's a successful lawyer, so she drowns herself in her caseload. Before..."

"Before what?"

"She has an eighteen-year-old brother who she's the guardian for."

She reared back. "So, she's his caretaker?"

I heard her jealousy and empathized with her.

"Yeah. Only for the last ten or so years. But she looked after him when he was a baby. It was a lot for her. Her mom walked out, leaving the baby—his name's Rain—with Axel, Rachel's stepfather. He worked long hours to put food on the table, and she did everything until she left for college.

"It was... I never meant to put her in a position where she'd have a kid so young. She'd already had too much responsibility, you know?"

She stared at me, unblinking, and I realized I was revealing all her biological parents' secrets over coffee and croissants before she had to spend the rest of the day in school.

Blowing out a breath, cheeks gusting with it, I muttered, "Sorry, this is heavy shit before a day of studying, isn't it?"

Wynter didn't smile. "It is, but you can't sugarcoat the truth."

Hadn't I just thought that?

She was clearly her parents' daughter.

"She moved away for college."

"From where?"

"West Orange. New Jersey."

Her eyes met mine, and I got the feeling I was about to be tested, "Which college?"

"Brown. Like I told you."

Her mouth rounded. "You said that yesterday but I wasn't sure I believed you. My mom really went to Brown?"

Pride filled me on Rach's behalf. "She did. Then she went onto Yale."

"Wow." She stared down at the picture. "She doesn't look happy."

"I don't think she is."

She turned that gimlet stare on me again. "Are you trying to make things better?"

Jesus.

This kid.

I rubbed my thumb along my chin. "I'm trying."

She frowned at her mom's cool expression. "Good."

I studied her. "How did you get an apartment when you're seventeen?"

"My mom helped me. She co-signed."

"Ally knowingly helped you get an apartment in that building?" I sputtered, my disbelief clear.

Her mouth turned down at the edges. "It's all we can afford."

Though I had to play this cool, it was goddamn hard. "You can afford a better place if you let me help you out."

"It's all right. I'm okay where I am."

"I'm a grown man and I'm frightened of that place."

Her lips curved as she dragged her gaze up and down me. "Somehow, I think that's a lie. Even if you do look like a Ken doll today. Where's the leather vest thingy?"

If I hadn't known better, I'd say she and Rachel had conferred about this.

She didn't need to know about the Disciples, so I just told her, "I wanted to make a good first impression so it's back in my hotel room."

I didn't realize, until that admission, that there was a hardness in her eyes that softened. I couldn't explore that though, as a waitress made an appearance with a couple plates of food.

She gaped in surprise as the dishes were stacked on the table. Once the server left, after she and Wynter greeted each other, I told her, "Eat whatever you want."

She didn't mess around.

As I watched her devour, albeit daintily, the omelet and sausage muffin, we slowly started to talk about other topics.

Without dragging it out of her, she told me that she had history class today and that that was her favorite, and that she had band practice later as well—she played the piano.

When she'd finished her breakfast, then looked at the time, I took note of her reluctance to leave, and I'd admit, relief hit me. I didn't want this to end either.

"Shall I drive you over to school?" I asked carefully.

"If you don't mind."

"I don't," was my quick response.

"Then, thank you." She cleared her throat. "Do you mind if I take the rest of these for lunch?"

There were a couple pastries left.

"I'll get a doggy bag for you."

Her cheeks were pink from embarrassment, but I ignored that as I returned to the café, which had calmed down some, and asked for a takeout box. While I was there, I bought her a large bottle of water, a banana, a pre-packed sandwich, and some chips.

When I returned, she'd shrugged on a school blazer, and though she looked mature, that was diminished by the childish relief at the sight of all the food. "You didn't have to do that."

I shrugged but wisely kept my mouth shut as I watched her pack them into her bag.

Together, we walked over to where I'd parked my bike, and I gave her my helmet which was too big but better than nothing, and I made a mental note to buy her one today. Her hands showed her nerves as they cupped my waist after she climbed on, the fingers pinching slightly, but I remained quiet as I set off, taking it slow so I didn't amp up her anxiety.

Having followed her yelled directions, the ride was much too short when we made it to school.

As she climbed off, I noticed she bounced on her toes as she stood at my side, unfastening the helmet.

"That was awesome," she enthused, gracing me with her first *genuine* grin.

"Once it's in the blood, it's in the blood," I teased, accepting the helmet once she gave it to me.

"I'll bet." Her grin started to die as she stared at me. But when her toe turned in, her shoe scuffing the floor, I braced myself as she muttered, "If… I mean, we can hang out again, if you'd like?"

"I'd love to," I told her honestly. "Tonight?"

Nibbling on her bottom lip, she nodded.

It was a pretty long walk from her apartment to school so I offered, "I can pick you up if you want?"

"That'd be nice. Thanks."

She told me a time, and after I said I'd be there, I murmured casually, "We can go out for something to eat before I drop you at home?"

Relief flashed in her eyes. It had nothing to do with meeting me and everything to do with food.

My kid was hungry.

Fuck, how could I have failed her this much?

"That'd be great." She backed off, turning around after a couple steps, before running into the building.

I almost took off, but I waited, hoping…

Before she walked through the main door, she twisted back to look at me.

I raised a hand in farewell, which prompted her to dart inside.

Blowing out a sharp breath, one that was loaded with relief and lingering nerves, I reached for my cellphone and tapped out a text.

**Rex:** *She's her mother's daughter.*

Which, of course, was when I realized I hadn't gotten a picture of us.

Maybe later. Seeing as there would be a later now.

# THIRTY

## RACHEL

**Rex:** *She's her mother's daughter.*

I stroked my thumb across the screen once I'd read his message.

At face value, I thought he was referring to Wynter's adoptive mother.

Then, it registered he was talking about me and that stirred up a whole host of feelings, most of which were unexpected and were a pleasant escape from the terror gnawing at me.

"Rachel Laker?"

I peered up at the receptionist when she called my name and tucked my phone back into my pocket.

Sweating, nauseated (not from morning sickness,) and jumping like I was a cat on a hot tin roof, I suffered through my appointment. It was hard not to bolt, just to endure, but I had to get used to this.

The alternative wasn't an option.

I wanted this baby; that meant I had to see this through.

This would be my first doctor's visit, and I'd been dreading it. Mostly because of the past, partly because I knew what I'd be told.

And I was right.

I was underweight. Overworked. I was borderline anemic and had low blood pressure. All of which were things my doctor expected to be worked on before I visited with her again.

Like I could wave a magic wand and out of nowhere, the desire to slow down as well as to have more iron in my blood could be fixed.

Right.

There was only one positive from the visit—that pain in my side? She suspected it was an ulcer.

Once the appointment was over, thank fuck, and tired of being poked and prodded, it was with no small amount of relief that I left the office.

As I did, and as luck would have it, Rex sent me a text message.

**Rex:** *Can I call?*

I didn't answer, just presented the nurse with the folder my doctor had given me, made another appointment, proceeded to make a note of it in my calendar, and then I left the damn place as my cell buzzed.

**Parker:** *How did it go?*

**Rachel:** *Badly.*

**Parker:** *She tell you to eat more, take iron supplements, and to try meditation for stress?*

**Rachel:** *Why did I bother going through the trauma of visiting her when I could just have seen you?*

**Parker:** *I'd say that I could have saved you the copay but it's not like you pay it anyways.*

**Rachel:** *Lol. I'll pay you the copay next time.*

**Parker:** *Next time... lemme see. I'd have to get up close and personal with your vajayjay. I love you, honey, but I think that's where our relationship ends.*

**Rachel:** *And I thought we were the next Thelma and Louise.*

**Parker:** *We can be. So long as I don't have to see your lady garden.*

**Rachel:** *LOL. I need to graduate you to non-fade-to-black books. Anyway, gtg.*

**Parker:** *You'd better be going for lunch.*

**Rachel:** *I am. MOM.*

Sucking in a couple deep breaths of chilly air, I didn't bother texting Rex a reply, just directly called him once I'd stuck my earbuds in.

He answered almost immediately. "Rach?"

His voice, damn, sounded so good in my ears. Even if I'd heard it this morning, it was nice to hear it now after being scolded by the doctor.

I bet that bitch would have been different if Rex were there.

Almost huffing at the thought, I asked, "Everything okay?"

"Yeah. I finished up with Wynter and I'm back in my room. I figured you'd want to know how it went."

Hearing her name made me press my hand to my belly. It was a stupid thing to do, but talking about my firstborn while I was carrying my to-be-born child had a weird way of twisting the past and the present together.

Gnawing on my bottom lip, I told him, "I got your text."

"Yeah, I saw you'd read it."

"You meant me, right?"

"Of course I did. I don't remember dick about Ally anymore."

Her adoptive mom.

Ally.

What had made him choose Wynter's adoptive parents? Was it like Mav said... Rex knew they were already looking into adoption?

I pursed my lips. "What's she like?"

"She's a detail-oriented, pedantic pain in the butt. She won't let me get away with shit, barely smiles, and is so hungry it hurts but... she's awesome."

I half-laughed at his description, but the depth of the eagerness I felt to know more about our child took me aback.

The notion of getting back in my car and talking to him there didn't fill me with glee, so I headed to a coffee shop down the street.

"If you hear noise, it's just me going into a café."

"Okay. Where are you?"

"Is that one of your questions?" I teased.

"No," he groused, but I heard the smirk.

Sure, it was technically impossible to hear a smirk, but that was how well I knew Rex.

"I'm in New York."

"Still?"

He wasn't to know that my OB/GYN was there because I didn't want the rest of West Orange knowing that I was pregnant.

"Business."

His hum was dark. "Business."

I grinned as I peered at the menu once I'd taken a seat in a corner booth. It was after lunch so the rush had died down about forty minutes ago.

With the doctor's warnings in my ears, I made my selection and pointed to it when the server came and ordered a chai latte too.

When I was done, I said, "It's for a gala."

"A gala?"

I scoffed, "Like you don't know about the FAST galas."

He snickered. "You're not supposed to know that I know."

"Let's just assume that I believe you know everything there is to know about me, whereas I know piteously little about you."

"Piteously little, huh?"

I grunted. "Yes. Much too little. Anyway, the gala is approaching. I mostly leave it to a couple of events organizers, but some things need my attention. I've brought Lily on board too at Giulia's suggestion. She's been a lifesaver."

"Giulia?"

I snorted. "No. Lily."

He chuckled. "When is it?"

"In a few weeks' time."

"What happens at that one?"

It was on the tip of my tongue to invite him, but I just smiled at the server when she dropped off my drink and told him, "There's a charity auction. It's the biggest fundraiser I organize."

"More than the ticket price?"

"Yeah. We get good donations."

"Let me guess, that's where you come in?"

I smirked at my chai. "Knowing the rich and powerful's dirty secrets comes in handy when you want a favor."

"A favor... Is that what you're calling it?"

"Yep."

"What's the main lot this year?"

"A purse."

"A *purse*? How can that be the main lot?"

I grinned to myself at his bewilderment. "It's very rare and very unique."

Not my style, but who was I to argue with what rich people wasted their cash on?

"It'd have to be. What's its value?"

"About forty grand, but I have a feeling it'll go for over a hundred."

"Jesus Christ. Rach, I'm a fucking millionaire, but I wouldn't waste a hundred grand on a purse."

"That's why you're not invited," I teased, which had the added benefit of making him laugh.

"Oh, that's why, huh? Not because it's black tie and I'd show up in my cut?"

"Well, that might have something to do with it."

It didn't. But we were joking around, and I enjoyed it.

Most of our interactions were fractious to say the least.

This was easy.

God, I needed easy right about now after that scolding from the doctor.

"I'll bet," he mocked. "What else are you auctioning off?"

"Everything from stays in private chalets in Switzerland to jewelry. We get a variety of lots."

"Who attends?"

"Do you want the honest answer?"

"Of course."

"Mostly my clients and their associates."

He was quiet a second, then he chuckled. "You and your goddamn loopholes."

From the second contract I'd signed with his company, I quoted, "'You, Rachel Laker, whose firm is retained by Dark & Dirty Sinners LLC as a sole client, do hereby confirm that you will undertake work only for your chosen charities and no one else.'"

"Queen of Loopholes. So, they, what? Pay you through donations?"

"Yep. For the most part, anyway. I get arrangement fees."

"Goddammit." But he was laughing. "I should be pissed."

"Nah. You get perks."

"What kind of perks? Those guys probably pay through their teeth for you."

"They do and it all funnels to my charities."

"More than the four-hundred-K we pay, I'd assume."

"You assume right. Your perk is that you don't *have* to attend my fundraisers. They do."

"I'm surprised you don't make us go. Why don't you?"

"The rote answer is because the MC helped make me who I am and that's donation enough." I took a sip of my chai, bracing myself for his next question.

"What's the real answer?"

Two weeks ago, I'd never have told him, but we had declared an impasse, and that was more important than anything else.

"That I'm terrified you'll end up in jail, so I'll do whatever I have to to make sure that never happens."

More silence boomed down the line, louder than a foghorn. "You look after me in your own way, huh?" he eventually muttered.

"Yes."

"Thank you, Rach."

"You're welcome."

It might not seem like a nurturing move, but the MC got into a *lot* of hot water. It was a good thing that ice flowed through my veins.

"If I find out Maverick knew about your loopholes, I'll beat the shit out of him."

"Exactly what he doesn't need with his CTE," I drawled.

"Fucker," he grumbled. "He probably does know. My fucking friends but they've always been protective as hell about you, even when it bites *me* in the ass."

My lips curved slightly. "I'm sure that's not true."

He sniffed. "Wanna bet? Anyway, who's your biggest client?"

I didn't mind him changing the subject. "Not gonna tell you that," I taunted. "Ever heard of NDAs?"

"I'm curious!"

"Well, tough. If someone asked me if you were a client, I'd throw the same answer back at them." A moment passed, and I demanded, "Are you pouting?!"

"Maybe."

A chortle escaped me. "You're nuts."

"Just for you."

Those three words settled deep in my being, warming me from the inside out.

"I thought our calls today would be awkward."

"The idea is for us to open up to each other," he answered gently. "That won't happen if we shut each other out."

He was right, but I'd still expected him to give me attitude.

"I'm not complaining."

"Good."

The server appeared again, this time with my salad. As I started to eat, I asked, "How did it go with Wynter?"

"What are you eating?"

"It went bad, huh?"

"Nope. But I want to know what you're eating."

"An avocado salad."

"Sounds disgusting."

"I like it. Go on then, tell me what happened."

"She opened up to me after I told her why we had her adopted."

My stomach started churning and I placed the fork down. "She must hate me."

"No. She might have before. Or, well, to be honest, I think hate's too strong a word. I think it was more like she was angry and resentful. When I explained, she looked sad. Like she could understand."

I released a shaky breath. "Does she want to meet with you again?"

"She agreed. I took her to school on my bike and asked if she wanted me to pick her up—she said yes."

His excitement was clear.

I smiled and picked up my fork again. "I'm so glad. What are you going to do?"

"Mostly feed her. I found out that her mom co-signed on the lease for her. But I don't know why, and I don't think she'll tell me. I offered to help out with the rent, but that might be too soon to get her to agree."

"The place she's living in is that bad?"

"It's a shithole."

I bit my lip. "Maybe you could arrange with her to pick her up for breakfast and to drop her off after school?"

"Do you think she'd be okay with that? It's a lot, isn't it?"

"Suggest it gradually. She's hungry?"

"Yeah. She ate an omelet, a breakfast muffin, and two pastries."

My brows lifted. "Is she underweight?"

"No. But I get the feeling this is a recent change."

Unease filled me again. "Were they abusive? Her adoptive parents, I mean?"

"No. But her dad was, apparently, in debt with the Triads."

"What?" I hissed.

"Calm down, Rach," he soothed. "It pissed me off too. He's a gambler. My sources tell me he always pays his debts."

Hand tightening to the point of pain around my fork, I rasped, "They could have hurt her to get to him."

"I'm trying not to think about that."

"You're right. It's all conjecture until we know what's going on."

"*We?*" he asked quietly. "You interested, Rach?"

"Of course I am!"

"Couple months ago, when I raised the subject of Wynter, you started crying, Rach," he soothed. "Then after Scott... I wasn't being judgmental, just trying to assess your limits."

"She's one of my biggest regrets," I whispered miserably. "Not the adoption. Just that I let her down."

"You wish we'd raised her?"

"I wish I'd been able to."

I stared down at my barely-showing belly and prayed to God that I'd be better with this one. That I'd be able to do it this time.

The actual process of being pregnant was terrifying to me.

This situation with Rex had to resolve itself soon because I'd need him to get through it. Yet.... Wynter needed him too. More than I did. She was only a kid, and I was a grown-ass woman.

"Me too," he said on a sigh. "Should I have fought harder, Rach?"

"No. If you had, I'd have shattered into a million pieces. I barely kept it together as it was." I stared down at the puddles of ranch dressing on my plate, trying not to feel nauseated when I knew I had to finish the meal. "I wish things were different, but they're not."

He sighed. "We can be there for her now, can't we?"

"We can." I raised my hand for the server. "Can I get some bottled water, please? With ice?"

She smiled at me then disappeared.

"You doing okay?"

"Been better."

"Understandable."

"What else did you learn?"

"She plays the piano."

The smile that blossomed on my lips warmed my soul. "She does? You know—"

"You always wanted to learn how to play the piano. Yeah, I remember," he teased me gently.

I picked up my fork. "I can't believe she plays."

"She's with the school band too."

My brows lifted as I swallowed some lettuce. "Really?"

"Really."

I couldn't stop myself from snorting. "Mr. Cool Dude King has a kid who's a band geek."

As I chomped on a walnut, he chuckled. "Yeah, it took me by surprise too. But as long as it makes her happy, that's all that matters, right?"

My smile appeared again. "Right."

After five minutes of him telling me my daughter looked like us both, loved history, and that he was going to buy her her own helmet, my plate was empty and I hadn't even realized I'd been eating.

**From: Rach3lLadyLiberty@gmail.com**
**To: K1ngS1nn3r1@gmail.com**
**Subject: Photo**
You owe me a photo.
R


**From: K1ngS1nn3r1@gmail.com**
**To: Rach3lLadyLiberty@gmail.com**
**Subject: Re. Photo**
I didn't forget.
K


**From: Rach3lLadyLiberty@gmail.com**
**To: K1ngS1nn3r1@gmail.com**
**Subject: Re. Photo**
You sure? I think you might have, but I know what you're like—you hate being wrong.
R


**From: K1ngS1nn3r1@gmail.com**
**To: Rach3lLadyLiberty@gmail.com**
**Subject: Re. Photo**
And you don't? Ha! I'm pretty goddamn sure one of the reasons you went into defense rather than prosecution is to prove other people wrong even when they're right.
K

**From: Rach3lLadyLiberty@gmail.com**
**To: K1ngS1nn3r1@gmail.com**
**Subject: Re. Photo**

Well, that's a character assassination right there.
But... you're partially right.
Nyx and Giulia are still staying with me.
Is it strange that I'm not upset about that?
I was kind of looking forward to an empty house again, but instead, they've still staked out the front living room, and I'm listening to Giulia puke because, for some goddamn reason, I can hear everything that goes on in their bathroom.
Yes, everything.
Good, bad, ugly.
I won't tell her though—she'd be mortified.
R

**From: K1ngS1nn3r1@gmail.com**
**To: Rach3lLadyLiberty@gmail.com**
**Subject: Re. Photo**

Why only partially right? Which part was partially wrong?
And yes, that's weird. I've lived with Nyx almost all my life and I can confirm that he's a bear with a sore head, sore paw, and sore every-fucking-thing else most of the damn time.
Why are they still there? The clubhouse is good to go, isn't it?
Lol, thank you for the heads up. I'll be sure to hold that

*over Giulia when she gets too big for her boots at some point in the future.*

K

**From: Rach3lLadyLiberty@gmail.com**
**To: K1ngS1nn3r1@gmail.com**
**Subject: Re. Photo**

*If I answer the part that's partially wrong, that's the answer to one of your daily questions. You okay with that?*
*And if you tell her I told you, I'll deny everything.*
*Nothing's wrong with the compound. They've decided to move out.*

R

**From: K1ngS1nn3r1@gmail.com**
**To: Rach3lLadyLiberty@gmail.com**
**Subject: Re. Photo**

*Jesus, Nyx is growing up! He wants to move out of the clubhouse?!*
*Guess being a dad isn't gonna be too bad for him.*
*About time he made a life for himself elsewhere. Not that I can judge, but my woman doesn't want me living with her so I don't think that's entirely my fault. What the fuck do I want with a house that I'd have to rattle around in on my own?*
*And yeah, consider one question struck off the list.*

K

**From: Rach3llLadyLiberty@gmail.com**
**To: K1ngS1nn3r1@gmail.com**
**Subject: Re. Photo**

*Remember old James Lawson? Your dad's version of me?*

*I used to watch him in town. His kid had respect and she drove a Merc. He drove a BMW, and I know he went to Crosskeys Country Club because I saw him there when I was waiting tables.*

*He knew everyone.*

*Everyone owed him something.*

*I wanted that. Fuck, I wanted that so badly I could taste it.*

*You've no idea what it's like to be powerless, Rex. I'm so grateful for that. Most of what I've done is to keep you in the position you're in!*

*I knew your dad always kept on Lawson's good side. I knew, of all the people in the whole fucking country, the only person Bear listened to was Lawson.*

*I wanted to be him.*

*I wanted it so badly.*

*I wanted people to owe me. I wanted to be rich and have three imported cars. I wanted to have memberships at country clubs and for people to see me and think, "That's Rachel Laker." I wanted my name to mean something—to inspire fear or respect.*

*I never had that when I was growing up. Mom and the way she was and how she led her life meant that I was treated like white trash too.*

*So that's one of the reasons why I wanted to be a lawyer.*

*But I also like making DAs look foolish—they make it so easy.*

*That's part of why I set up my charities. I don't want **ANYONE** to feel like I felt, and if I can stop that, then I will. They're a pain and cause a lot of stress, but they're worth it.*

*AND, it's not that I don't want you to live with me. It's that it's easier if you're on the compound.*

R


**From: K1ngS1nn3r1@gmail.com**
**To: Rach3lLadyLiberty@gmail.com**
**Subject: Re. Photo**

*Trust me, there's nothing easier about my living on the goddamn compound.*

*And I get it. I do.*

*TBH, you're more powerful than Lawson ever was. He didn't bother passing his bar anywhere else. You did. You have more people in your little black book than a high-class madam.*

*Did I ever tell you that I'm proud of you?*

*I always have been and always will be.*

*I love you, Rachel. That won't change if I spend the rest of my life living in the clubhouse. I want you to know that.*

K

# THIRTY-ONE

# LODESTAR

It was the measure of a man, I thought, how he tortured someone.

Now, that definitely wasn't a politically correct method of discerning if a guy was a worthy partner, but as I snagged a bag of Flamin' Hot Cheetos from the counter while Conor O'Donnelly got his hands dirty, I couldn't deny—my heart twanged in my chest.

My heart never twanged. It wasn't a fucking guitar. But Conor had this way about him that got to me. And with this show of strength, he was speaking my love language.

I knew I'd dug myself a few holes in my life. Where, if I didn't do it my fucking self, I couldn't trust another person's handiwork.

That Conor was willing to wade into the fray to get answers made me appreciate him even more than I already did.

And that 'appreciation' was far more than was technically wise.

"Fuck—" An inhalation. "You." Exhalation.

I stared at the living corpse on the board in the warehouse and had to admit—Conor had style.

This was like something from a horror movie with all the wires coming off the guy whom Conor was grilling.

Huh.

Literally.

I almost laughed.

Conor's torture involved electricity—*grilling* was far more fitting than I'd originally thought.

Not that he was as amused as I was.

This wasn't his style. He didn't have the taste for it like I did, but that was the kind of guy he was—he did shit he didn't want to for the people who mattered to him.

"There are five levels to this program," Conor mused, breaking into my thoughts. "You've only experienced the first one."

If the former Five Points' driver—and traitor—didn't hear the warning in that, then Michael Byrne was a moron.

Pain-filled shrieks boomed from the speakers, making me glad no one was in this part of the house as I tore open the bag of Cheetos.

"Wonder how long it will take for him to break?" I queried as I watched the guy's spine bow under the strain of the current.

Conor peered over at me, guileless and all the more dangerous for it as he took in the sight of my snack with a quirk of his lips. "Settling in for the show?"

God, could he be any more perfect?

Acceptance.

Fucking acceptance.

It was a beautiful, beautiful thing.

Not that I made a fool out of myself by saying that; I just nodded. "You'd better be entertaining."

He rolled his eyes. "This isn't Netflix, Star."

"Nope, it's even better." I waggled a Cheeto at him and watched as he got to work.

It was, in a word, brutal.

Surprisingly so.

I'd been trained to not give a fuck about the human body.

Morals and beliefs were weaned out of my nature over the process of my training—read indoctrination—into the CIA, but Conor didn't have that same training. It was clear in every move he made.

The more I watched, the more I saw that he didn't *want* to do this. He didn't *enjoy* it.

He felt he had no alternative means of making Michael talk.

I knew, in this instance, it was love that made him do this.

Strange, no?

How love, the supposedly purest emotion of them all, could trigger this kind of violence?

Somehow, that made me like him even more. I knew it was technically a weakness, but I couldn't fault him for it.

Not when I could think of nothing better than having this man love me enough that he'd do anything and everything to cherish me because of it.

"Dagda will make you bleed for this—"

The shriek was cut off, much as it slashed at my sentimental train of thought, and I arched a brow as the zapping of the electrical current made the guy finally pass out.

Those last words had me peering at the frazzled dude, who was literally steaming under Conor's ministrations, and questioning, "Is he dead?"

"No."

I took note of the sweat beaded on Conor's forehead and asked, "Why didn't you get one of your brothers to do this?"

He cast me a grim look. "Because my mother entrusted this task to me."

The O'Donnellys were a weird fucking bunch. Intriguing, but goddamn weird. More secrets than a soap opera.

"Why?"

"Because she knows I can keep my mouth shut."

"You told me," I pointed out.

His gaze was measured this time as he glanced away from Michael and let it tangle with mine.

No words passed from his lips.

No words needed to.

I swallowed as I stared at him, the Cheetos bag drifting to the table in front of me as we stared at one another.

At that moment, I knew I'd never been as splayed apart as I was with that glance. I'd been tortured, I'd been abused, I'd been treated like an animal—but nothing cut me to the quick like that look.

Fuck.

My voice was hoarse as I whispered, "Conor?"

"Yes," he rumbled.

"Will you let me know what he confesses to?"

He shrugged. "Set a bot on it. Use whatever you record."

The faith inherent in that offer staggered me enough that I jerked upright. "You trust me to do that?"

"You didn't have to ask. You could have just taken. We already spoke about this when you broke into my penthouse to help Savannah Daniels—I'd have opened the door for you if you'd just asked."

"This is my reward for good behavior?" I tried to tease, but somehow, it fell flat.

"Yes." He pursed his lips as he took in the mess on the board beside him. "He stinks."

"That's what happens when you fry meat," I mocked, smiling when I took note of his grimace. "How did you even make this equipment?"

The wires and electrical pads were all his own design.

"It was a byproduct."

"A byproduct of what?"

"Your Christmas gift."

I blinked. "You want to fry me to death?"

His lips twitched. "No. Ever heard of *la petite mort*?"

I narrowed my eyes. "I don't want to steam to death either."

His chuckle set me alight. "You won't. Don't worry. My prototype didn't work out."

"Well, it did, depending on what your intention was," I drawled, staring at the living corpse again. "Do you know who Dagda is?"

"Do you?" he asked.

"Depends."

"What kind of answer is that?"

My lips tightened. "A truthful one. There are rumors about his real ID."

"Have you clashed with him?"

Feeling that I was at the center of his attention, I shot him a look. "No. My mother did though."

"Your mother?" Then his eyes flared wide, and because he was a smart cookie, he put two and two together. "You think Dagda killed her?"

"I know he did."

"How?"

I studied him. "By investigating her death."

That had him rolling his eyes. "Helpful. Why would an Irish Republican want your mother dead?"

"Dagda's an alias for a sniper," I explained slowly, unsure how much he knew. "They say that he fought for the British during the Troubles in Northern Ireland.

"When he was in Belfast, he went AWOL, got himself arrested, escaped, and then he resurfaced as the leader of this Irish nationalist group—the *Éire le chéile go deo*. They say they're like the IRA, but I think they're worse. We call them the ECD because we can't pronounce their fucking name."

When I shot him a look, I knew I wasn't telling him anything he didn't already know.

He didn't stop me though, just arched a brow when I fell silent.

"Anyway, he set up this bomb in London and got sent up for it. They say that they let him out from time to time to complete jobs…"

*That* shocked him.

"They let him out to kill people?"

"It's a rumor."

"You wouldn't tell me if you didn't think it was true."

I conceded that with a grimace as I reached for a bottle of water I'd placed beside my laptop earlier.

"Why are you telling me this, Star?"

"Because..."

I broke off before I could finish.

Before Christmas, when my childhood friend, Savannah Daniels, had found herself needing to break into Conor's apartment, I'd hacked his security system and gotten her inside.

Like he'd said earlier, he'd told me at the time—after he'd shouted at me for breaking his code again—that he'd have opened the door for me if I'd just asked...

But trust, fuck, trust was so goddamn hard for me.

People let you down.

That was the one solid truth I had.

The harsh reality of my life.

But something about Conor made me *want* to trust him. Danger lay in that path, but some shit I couldn't do alone. We'd already agreed to help each other out.

While he slept, I worked on our mutual projects, and while I slept, he did the same. We doubled our output that way and that unity was the reason those Sparrow fuckers were dropping like flies.

I could have done that on my own but it would have taken so much longer.

"Star?" he queried softly. "It's okay."

I swallowed. "Nothing's okay, Conor. Nothing's been okay for a really long time."

His eyes saw too much.

A piercing chestnut brown that could read my fucking soul.

"I know, Star. I know. I'd like to help if you'd let me."

It hurt to take a step forward. Hurt to open myself up to the potential of betrayal.

My country had let me down. What was to stop the hacker son of an insane mob boss from screwing me over?

It was a leap of faith when I wasn't known for taking jumps—

"I'd like to draw him out into the open."

His eyes narrowed. "You want to draw Dagda out?"

"I believe his real ID is a man called Eamonn Keegan. He was freed recently. There's chatter…" I released a sharp exhalation as the hope that burned inside me started to scorch my insides.

"What kind of chatter? What did your mom get mixed up in, Star?"

My smile was tight. "What I know, I found in redacted files."

"Tell me," he urged. "You wouldn't even be bringing this up if you didn't believe it."

He wasn't wrong.

"My mom's the reason Dagda went from being a sniper in the British Army to the leader of one of the worst Irish nationalist factions." My jaw clenched. "She paid for that with her life, and it's time *he* paid for taking her away from me."

***Wynter:*** I realized I've been kinda rude the last few days. I didn't thank you for the helmet.

***Rex:*** You're welcome. Consider it a belated birthday present.

***Wynter:*** You remembered it was my birthday?

***Rex:*** January fourth is the most bittersweet day in the calendar for me.

***Wynter:*** Gee, thanks.

***Rex:*** That sounds bad, but it isn't. It's a day that's filled with regret for me.

***Wynter:*** You didn't have to regret anything. You could have been a part of my life still.

***Rex:*** Your parents, I don't want to say something that might be misconstrued, but when you were four, I tried to visit you for your birthday.

***Wynter:*** They didn't approve?

***Rex:*** They moved from Fresno to Burbank. There's an MC in your town, and I think they believed that would be a way of controlling me.

***Wynter:*** It worked.

***Rex:*** Not really. The Disciples and I aren't unfriendly. I realized that it wasn't fair to them. Probably wasn't fair to you either. Things were complicated enough, and I just wanted you to be happy.

***Wynter:*** I wish you hadn't given up.

***Rex:*** You say that now, but I tried to act in your best interests. You can disagree with me on that, Wynter, and I accept it. Just know that I always tried to do things with you in mind.

***Wynter:*** If you say so.

**Rex:** I do.
**Wynter:** I'll see you tomorrow?
**Rex:** For breakfast? Sure.
**Rex:** Have a great night. :)

**From:** K1ngS1nn3r1@gmail.com
**To:** Rach3lLadyLiberty@gmail.com
**Subject: Question**
Is it sex that gives you nightmares?
K

**From:** Rach3lLadyLiberty@gmail.com
**To:** K1ngS1nn3r1@gmail.com
**Subject: Re. Question**
No. It's stress usually. Anxiety.
Rachel

**From:** K1ngS1nn3r1@gmail.com
**To:** Rach3lLadyLiberty@gmail.com
**Subject: Re. Question**
Most people would think you weren't anxious by nature.
K

**From:** Rach3lLadyLiberty@gmail.com
**To:** K1ngS1nn3r1@gmail.com
**Subject: Re. Question**
Fake it 'til you make it.
Rachel

*From: K1ngS1nn3r1@gmail.com*
*To: Rach3lLadyLiberty@gmail.com*
*Subject: Re. Question*
You don't have to fake it with me.
K

*From: Rach3lLadyLiberty@gmail.com*
*To: K1ngS1nn3r1@gmail.com*
*Subject: Re. Question*
I know I don't.
Rachel

*From: K1ngS1nn3r1@gmail.com*
*To: Rach3lLadyLiberty@gmail.com*
*Subject: Re. Question*
So why do you?
K

*From: Rach3lLadyLiberty@gmail.com*
*To: K1ngS1nn3r1@gmail.com*
*Subject: Re. Question*
Because you're the one person I want to impress, and you're the one person I consistently let down anyway.
Rachel

*From: K1ngS1nn3r1@gmail.com*
*To: Rach3lLadyLiberty@gmail.com*
*Subject: Re. Question*

When I come back, we're going to be together, Rachel. You can't fake it all the time. Will you be able to cope?

K


*From: Rach3lLadyLiberty@gmail.com*
*To: K1ngS1nn3r1@gmail.com*
*Subject: Re. Question*

Probably not. Will be a learning curve. But I'd prefer to learn to live with you than to learn to live without you. I did that already, and I didn't like it. I hated it.

Rachel


*From: K1ngS1nn3r1@gmail.com*
*To: Rach3lLadyLiberty@gmail.com*
*Subject: Re. Question*

You know what it means, don't you?

K


*From: Rach3lLadyLiberty@gmail.com*
*To: K1ngS1nn3r1@gmail.com*
*Subject: Re. Question*

That I'll be your Old Lady?

Rachel

> *From: K1ngS1nn3r1@gmail.com*
> *To: Rach3lLadyLiberty@gmail.com*
> *Subject: Re. Question*
> In time.
> K

> *From: Rach3lLadyLiberty@gmail.com*
> *To: K1ngS1nn3r1@gmail.com*
> *Subject: Re. Question*
> I think I can handle it.
> Rachel

> *From: K1ngS1nn3r1@gmail.com*
> *To: Rach3lLadyLiberty@gmail.com*
> *Subject: Re. Question*
> That isn't the right answer. You can't 'think' you're ready. You have to be ready. We'll revisit this conversation when you *know* you're ready.
> K

> *From: Rach3lLadyLiberty@gmail.com*
> *To: K1ngS1nn3r1@gmail.com*
> *Subject: Re. Question*

*You know how patronizing you sound, don't you?*
*Rachel*

***From: K1ngS1nn3r1@gmail.com***
***To: Rach3lLadyLiberty@gmail.com***
***Subject: Re. Question***
*Consider it a perk of me being a dad. Been stretching my patronizing wings.*

*K*

***From: Rach3lLadyLiberty@gmail.com***
***To: K1ngS1nn3r1@gmail.com***
***Subject: Re. Question***
*Perk? Okay. Now you're the one who's lying to yourself lol.*
*I'm going to sleep.*
*Rachel*

***From: K1ngS1nn3r1@gmail.com***
***To: Rach3lLadyLiberty@gmail.com***
***Subject: Re. Question***
*I hope it's nightmare-free.*
*I love you, Rachel.*
*We'll get there.*
*K*

***From: Rach3lLadyLiberty@gmail.com***
***To: K1ngS1nn3r1@gmail.com***
***Subject: Re. Question***
*I hope so.*
*Love you too.*

<3

# THIRTY-TWO

## RACHEL

"Luciu, what an unexpected surprise," I drawled as the door to the interviewing room slammed to a close behind me.

Luciu Valentini was more trouble than he was worth.

Not just because of his career choices, but because he had a face that was a gift from the devil himself.

The Valentinis were trouble—that was probably why I liked them.

I didn't have to like my clients, didn't even have to believe they were innocent, but the Valentini brothers amused me.

Custanzu and Luciu were troublemakers, but their journey was a different one. They weren't actually born into this life; they chose it. I understood the need for vengeance. It didn't eat into me like it did them, but their motivations made sense to me.

Their father was murdered by the old leaders of the *Famiglia*. How couldn't I understand the need that had driven them to this point?

"The pleasure's all mine, Rachel," Luciu replied, getting to his feet like the gentleman he was.

He acted like he was born in the eighteen hundreds. Sometimes, I half-expected he'd bow or take my hand and kiss it like we were back in the olden days.

"I'll bet." I arched a brow at him as I placed my briefcase on the table. "I expect murder charges, Luciu. I expect intent to distribute or robbery charges. You pay me a fortune to wrangle you out of those situations.

"What I do *not* expect is to hear that you're suspected of desecrating a cemetery, defacing a casket, and committing arson!"

That sinner's mouth smiled at me. "I like to keep you on your toes."

I huffed out a breath as I flipped through the paperwork the cops had given me. "They're clearly trying to Capone you."

He hummed. "Indeed. How long until you get me out?"

"They're trying to throw the book at you," I warned him. "I'd expect to spend the night in jail at least. They're trying to delay the bail hearing."

Rage flashed in his eyes. "Are you being serious?"

"I am."

"That goddamn DA is going much too far this time."

I rolled my eyes. "Whatever sick games you two play with each other are your own affair."

"I grow tired of these games."

"I heard she wants to resign."

He grunted.

When he didn't answer, I merely shook my head and asked, "Where were you on the night in question?"

"With a friend."

"You have a girlfriend?"

He smirked at me. "Jealous, Rachel?"

"Oh, I can't see straight for all the green in my eyes."

His laughter was genuine. "This is why we work well together."

"Why? Because I make you laugh or because I don't fall for your Sicilian charm?"

"Both."

I merely arched a brow as I asked, "Will this *friend* testify to that?"

"I don't want her bothered with this."

"We might have no alternative—"

"Business and pleasure do not mix, Rachel," he ground out. "Understand?"

"I understand, but we might not have an alternative," I repeated, my eyes freezing over just as his fired up.

*This* was why we worked well together.

When he exploded, I froze him out.

"Find an alternative. Set Stan on it."

"That's what I did. He was the one who called me."

He grunted again. "I've been waiting here for hours."

"Have they offered you refreshments? Allowed you to use the bathroom?"

"They gave me coffee, and no."

"Do you need the bathroom?"

He nodded.

"Have you requested to go?"

"Yes. And they refused."

Irritation surged inside me at that. "Can you hold it?"

"*Se.*"

"They wouldn't let me see you immediately. I've been waiting outside. They're holding their cards to their chest on this one. It's a good thing you pay me a fortune to keep your ass out of jail, isn't it?"

His fire disappeared, replaced with more of that charm that was sweeter than honey. Another woman would have melted in the face of it.

I wasn't another woman.

"It truly is, Rachel," he half-crooned.

But... I had to admit, he was different.

The honey was there. Cloying and thick, but it was...

I realized he hadn't called me *cara mia* once. Only Rachel.

That was unusual.

My brow furrowed as I pondered that, but we were both prickly about personal matters so I didn't push it.

As I studied him, I tried to figure out what he wasn't saying.

As his lawyer, it was best if I didn't know the full truth. My clients never told me whether they were innocent or guilty because, in all frankness, it didn't matter. They paid me to defend them whether they'd committed the crime or not, but something wasn't right here.

My mouth pursed as the door burst open and the detectives on his case walked in without warning.

The lack of respect and the number of protocols ignored were adding up.

As the detectives swaggered in, I stared at the first one and declared, "I hope you're aware that you're wasting both the police's time and my client's."

"We'll see about that," he taunted as he twisted a chair around, straddled it, then pulled out a folder.

Retrieving a couple of photos, ones I'd already seen, he shoved them at Luciu while the other detective dealt with setting up the recording.

"Have you ever been to Green-Wood Cemetery?" he demanded once his colleague had completed the necessary steps to begin the interview.

"Has my client been to one of the most popular cemeteries in Brooklyn?" I tilted my head to the side. "Isn't that like asking if he's ever eaten a Big Mac?"

"The answer would be no," Luciu intoned dryly. "Fast food doesn't agree with me."

The detective narrowed his eyes at me. "A vehicle belonging to your client was seen entering Green-Wood—"

"The vehicle was, I was informed, reported as stolen to a local precinct." I reached into my briefcase. "Officers found the burned-out shell in New Jersey."

"Whereabouts were you on the evening in question?"

"You don't have to answer that, Luciu."

He shot the cops a smile, and I settled in for a long, very tedious interrogation where the cops and I pranced around in a verbal chase where Luciu said very little and I repeated myself over and over.

With my eye on the clock, I waited until a full hour had passed before I commented, "Are you aware that giving a suspect refreshment then not allowing them to use the bathroom is tantamount to torture and can and will besmirch any statements that are made and that you come to rely upon in court?"

"What statement?" bit off the younger cop, Delaney. "Your client hasn't said a goddamn thing."

"I think he told you that he doesn't eat junk food."

"I'm okay with that being on the record," Luciu mocked.

The cop's jaw clenched. "Appertaining to the case."

"Appertaining to your case? What case? Your sole reason for arresting my client is that his vehicle, a vehicle that was reported as stolen and subsequently discovered by your colleagues, was spotted in the vicinity of Green-Wood Cemetery."

The older cop, Hennessey, slammed to his feet. "You need the bathroom, Mr. Valentini?"

Luciu straightened which made the cuffs jangle. "Please."

"Is it really necessary to cuff my client to the table like he's a common criminal?"

"I hate to break it to you, lady, but that's exactly what he is."

"Mr. Valentini is a well-respected member of the community—"

"Yeah, yeah, yeah," Hennessey groused as he hauled Luciu out of the interrogation room.

I stared at Delaney. "You haven't got a leg to stand on with this case. Your evidence makes conjecture look circumstantial."

"Unlucky for your client, that's not what the DA says."

Irritated by the cat and mouse games, I stated, "I'll make arrangements for bail in the morning."

As much as I'd negated the little Luciu had stated with my comfort break argument, I was also aware that the time to appeal for bail had passed.

"I'd like to speak with my client before you place him in holding."

Delaney just grunted. "Stay here."

Twenty minutes later, just when I was starting to wonder if the cop had forgotten my request, or if it was being ignored, Luciu returned. I explained the situation, and I empathized with his irritation at being held overnight.

"Do you want me to speak with Custanzu?"

He shook his head. "If bail wasn't made today, and I was charged, I know that a plan is already in play."

Warily, I asked, "What is it?"

"Better if you don't know. But when you get an emergency call, make sure they take me to Bellevue Hospital."

I blinked. "Why? You won't be able to visit—"

"Just do it, Rachel," he interrupted before I could finish my sentence, and with a smirk, he told me, "Bail won't be a problem."

The door opened a scant second later and Luciu was guided out, leaving me wondering what the hell kind of plan was underway and if I even wanted to goddamn know.

*From: K1ngS1nn3r1@gmail.com*
*To: Rach3lLadyLiberty@gmail.com*
*Subject: Busy?*

I tried calling but it went through to voicemail. Everything okay?

K


*From: Rach3lLadyLiberty@gmail.com*
*To: K1ngS1nn3r1@gmail.com*
*Subject: Re. Busy?*

Yeah. One of my clients got arrested. It was a clusterfuck.

I'm rammed solid. Still, he got beaten in jail so New York City is paying for that mess, haha. I love making the government pay through their noses for this shit.

Anyway, one of the licenses I got passed through was rejected so I'm thinking someone Maverick bribed decided to fuck us over. But I know you don't want to hear about that yet, and that's fine.

I might not call, but I'll reply to an email before I crash.

R


*From: Rach3lLadyLiberty@gmail.com*
*To: K1ngS1nn3r1@gmail.com*
*Subject: Re. Busy?*

I should have said this before...

*I love you.*
*R*


**From: K1ngS1nn3r1@gmail.com**
**To: Rach3lLadyLiberty@gmail.com**
**Subject: Re. Busy?**

*As much as I appreciate corrupt councilors, it pisses me off when you can't rely on their corruption. Fuck's sake. But you're right—I want a sabbatical from the Sinners. Fancy talk for a Prez of a bunch of outlaws, but I don't give a flying fuck. I need a break. You do too. If anyone's as overworked as I am, it's you.*

*I love you. Get some rest. Don't worry about emailing back. We'll talk when things have calmed down for you.*

*And re: your client? Go get that DA, babe.*

*Love,*
*K*

*Lodestar:* I have a theory
*Conor:* What kind of a theory?
*Lodestar:* A working one
*Conor:* LOL. Okay. If you say so.
*Lodestar:* Aren't you going to ask what it is?
*Conor:* Do you want me to tease it out of you?
*Lodestar:* Maybe.
*Conor:* Ha.
*Lodestar:* Pfft. Seeing as that's NOT going to happen, do you want to know what it is?
*Conor:* I don't have anything better to do right now, so sure.
*Lodestar:* So welcoming.
*Conor:* I try.
*Lodestar:* Have you heard about the hockey player who's been kidnapped?
*Conor:* Canadian guy?
*Lodestar:* Yeah.
*Conor:* Liam Dougal or something.
*Lodestar:* Donnghal.
*Conor:* Makes sense. From the little I've read on the subject, it seemed to be a professional job. But, whatever... What about him?
*Lodestar:* I think he's not the first.
*Conor:* To be kidnapped?
*Lodestar:* Nope.
*Conor:* What makes you think that?
*Lodestar:* How truthful do you want me to be?
*Conor:* Where were you snooping?
*Lodestar:* Do you really want to know?
*Conor:* If I say yes, would you tell me?
*Lodestar:* Wouldn't waste my time if I didn't.

***Conor:*** Fair point

***Lodestar:*** Plus, you and me, we're, you know...

***Conor:*** What?

***Lodestar:*** You know.

***Conor:*** Do I? I think you should spell it out.

***Lodestar:*** Fuck off.

***Conor:*** Lol. /sarcasm But yeah, I know what you mean.

***Lodestar:*** You do?

***Conor:*** Uhhuh

***Lodestar:*** Good.

***Conor:*** Good.

***Lodestar:*** So. Donnghal... You want to know my source or you okay just knowing that I have my facts straight?

***Conor:*** You'll tell me when you're ready?

***Lodestar:*** I will.

***Conor:*** Okay, so, what about Donegal.

***Lodestar:*** DONNGHAL. Jesus. You don't watch hockey, huh?

***Conor:*** Do you?

***Lodestar:*** Of course.

***Conor:*** I'll watch it with you.

***Lodestar:*** You will?

***Conor:*** Yeah.

***Lodestar:*** Okay, well, that's a date, then.

***Conor:*** Sure.

***Lodestar:*** So I think this is a kidnapping ring.

***Conor:*** Think? You wouldn't approach me if it was just a 'think.' You need to start remembering that it's straight from God's lips to my ears when I'm dealing with you, Star.

***Conor:*** Go on then. What do you KNOW?

*Lodestar:* Maybe I would.

*Conor:* Maybe you would, what?

*Lodestar:* 'Think.' You know, not have concrete facts when I approach you. That a problem?

*Conor:* No. Not at all.

*Lodestar:* Really?

*Conor:* I'd like to be your sounding board more often.

*Lodestar:* Huh. Okay. You want me to be your sounding board?

*Conor:* You usually are.

*Lodestar:* Not always.

*Conor:* No. But only because sometimes I don't want you to get involved.

*Lodestar:* Like with the guy who set up your ma?

*Conor:* Yeah.

*Lodestar:* You know I'd have helped, right? That's not your scene…

*Conor:* You won't like why I didn't tell you.

*Lodestar:* Go on.

*Conor:* I didn't want you to get your hands dirty.

*Lodestar:* My hands are a lot dirtier than that.

*Conor:* Doesn't mean I don't want to stop you from having to do that kind of stuff.

*Lodestar:* Why?

*Conor:* God knows.

*Lodestar:* Bull.

*Conor:* I've been reading Austen.

*Lodestar:* As in Jane?

*Conor:* As in Jane.

*Lodestar:* Why?

*Conor:* Why not?

*Lodestar:* They don't fuck in those books, do they?

**Conor:** Lol. If they did, I missed those scenes.
**Lodestar:** I'll bet you did.
**Conor:** I think they'd have been a lot more popular if Darcy dicked Elizabeth down in Pemberley.
**Lodestar:** I'll bet. Okay, so what does Darcy have to do with you trying to keep me out of wet work?
**Conor:** Does it really matter?
**Lodestar:** Uh, yeah? I'm not Elizabeth Bennet, Conor. I don't need to be looked after.
**Conor:** Neither do I.
**Lodestar:** Okaaaay.
**Conor:** That doesn't mean I wouldn't like it.
**Lodestar:** To be looked after?
**Conor:** Yeah. Wouldn't you like that?
**Lodestar:** I haven't thought about it.
**Conor:** Because you haven't been with someone who'll wrangle that from you.
**Lodestar:** I don't like having control 'wrangled' from me.
**Conor:** It isn't a sexual thing.
**Lodestar:** Isn't it?
**Conor:** No.
**Lodestar:** What is it then?
**Conor:** It's a caring thing.
**Lodestar:** Oh.
**Conor:** Oh?
**Lodestar:** Oh.
**Conor:** Informative. Anyway, go ahead with the theory. I didn't mean to make you uncomfortable.
**Lodestar:** You usually do.
**Conor:** I do? Damn, I'm sorry.
**Lodestar:** Not in a bad way.

*Conor:* Uncomfortable in a good way?

*Lodestar:* Sort of.

*Conor:* I'm glad?

*Lodestar:* Yeah, figured you might be.

*Conor:* There's something you're not telling me about this Doodle guy.

*Lodestar:* I'm a great shot.

*Conor:* Not sure you could hit me from New Jersey, but sure, you keep telling yourself that. You were saying...

*Lodestar:* Maverick's been developing this pretty nifty worm and I might have appropriated it for my own use.

*Conor:* Lol, can I appropriate it too?

*Lodestar:* Once I've tested its limits.

*Conor:* Tease

*Lodestar:* You know it. :P

*Conor:* Okay, so what have you uncovered?

*Lodestar:* This kidnapping ring... it's been going on for years. All around the country. In and out like a shadow, and each and every time, no matter the target, they never get caught by the cops.

*Conor:* Maybe they have gotten caught, but it's by a Sparrow affiliate?

*Lodestar:* You could be right.

*Conor:* Interesting.

*Lodestar:* Not if you've been kidnapped.

*Conor:* Shit. I didn't mean it like that.

*Lodestar:* No, sorry. It's had me on edge.

*Conor:* I understand. I didn't mean to be dismissive.

*Lodestar:* You weren't. I'm just touchy.

***Conor:*** Honestly, it's understandable. How can I help?

***Lodestar:*** I don't know if you can. I just needed to talk with someone who wouldn't judge me.

***Conor:*** I'll never judge you.

***Lodestar:*** I know. Thank you. <3

***Conor:*** You're welcome. <3

***Lodestar:*** It's hard because they take kids too. That's not common with this level of professionalism. Kids are... Well, it's messier than with adults. I don't like it.

***Conor:*** Jesus, they seriously snatch kids?

***Lodestar:*** They have one now.

***Conor:*** Fuckers.

***Lodestar:*** Yeah. I didn't know I was getting into this. It's more than I anticipated.

***Conor:*** What did you anticipate?

***Lodestar:*** A favor owed.

***Conor:*** Lol, the best laid plans oft go awry.

***Lodestar:*** They do where I'm concerned.

***Conor:*** Who'd owe you?

***Lodestar:*** That's what you won't like.

***Conor:*** Who?

***Lodestar:*** Sicilians.

***Conor:*** Nah, they're okay. We're allies. You going to tell them about the kidnapping ring?

***Lodestar:*** Don't have much alternative.

***Conor:*** You sure you don't need help with anything?

***Lodestar:*** I uncovered some information that I don't know what to do with.

***Conor:*** Because of Maverick's worm?

***Lodestar:*** Yeah.

*Conor:* I'm here, Star.

*Lodestar:* Yeah. You are. I should just get on with stuff. Stop wasting time. But you know as well as I do that the truth hurts.

*Conor:* It does. What's hurting in particular?

*Lodestar:* The ringleader had a whole fucking folder on the bastards he hired over the years. I recognize a name.

*Conor:* Shit. Who?

*Lodestar:* You won't know her.

*Conor:* So?

*Lodestar:* Scarlet O'Shea.

*Conor:* I DO know that name.

*Lodestar:* You do?

*Conor:* Yeah. Gimme a minute to remember why.

**Fifty-nine seconds later**

*Lodestar:* You're aware that you don't have to remember, right? I KNOW who she is.

*Conor:* I might know something you don't.

*Lodestar:* True. You had your minute. How do you know her name then?

*Conor:* Declan's boy, Shay, saw her being murdered by the last Don—Benito Fieri.

*Lodestar:* Yeah. I know why too.

*Conor:* Why?

*Lodestar:* They were going to kidnap Lily Lancaster.

*Conor:* Interesting. They didn't succeed?

*Lodestar:* Not as far as I know. It's not like I can ask.

*Conor:* You probably could.

*Lodestar:* I won't. Anyway, Fieri's punishment was

kinda random IMO. Why hit the monkey when the organ grinder's still out there?

**Conor:** Maybe he thought she was the organ grinder?

**Lodestar:** Maybe.

**Conor:** How do you know Scarlet O'Shea? She's been dead for years, after all.

**Lodestar:** She's a Sinners' brat. Sister of Storm. He's the Prez down in the Ohio Chapter.

**Conor:** You going to tell the Sinners?

**Lodestar:** Not sure if it's important enough to share, but I needed to tell someone.

**Conor:** I get it.

**Lodestar:** Everyone's dead now. Not sure we'll ever know what really happened.

**Conor:** Apart from Lily. She's not dead.

**Lodestar:** No shit. Anyway, you know what I mean.

**Conor:** I do. Lily might know something. You should talk with her.

**Lodestar:** She was a kid. She'd have been a nice gravy train for a kidnapping ring as prolific as this one.

**Conor:** Do you want to call?

**Lodestar:** Not really.

**Conor:** Not to talk. Just to, you know, connect? I have shit to do; you have shit to do. We can get that done and carry on with our work.

**Lodestar:** Actually, that sounds really nice.

**Conor:** Two mins and I'll phone.

**Lodestar:** Thank you <3

## THIRTY-THREE

## CONOR

"Thought you might be busy."

I heard her defensiveness. Heard it and sighed over it.

"Never too busy for you."

A choked silence sounded down the line.

"You're too nice to me."

My lips twitched. "Nah. Not really."

"You are," she argued. "I'm a cunt."

"I'm a dick. Trust me, my brothers tell me all the time."

She snickered. "That's what brothers do. I wish I had siblings."

"You don't," I retorted with a laugh. "They're all well and good as adults, but growing up with the pains in the ass ain't worth it."

"You say that but I know you love them."

"I do. But they're still annoying."

"Maybe that's what I'd like."

"You have it, don't you? With the Sinners?" I queried as I eyed my screen where I had code scrambling and unscrambling in front of me.

I didn't trust Da's sudden caped crusader act, but it wasn't like I was gonna argue with him.

Worthy causes were worthy causes.

Even if they *were* a fucking migraine.

"Not really. I can tell they don't trust me."

"Are they wise not to?"

She chuckled. "Yes."

"Well then." I rolled my eyes. "My brothers know I'd die for them, Star. Loyalty's gotta be earned."

"I haven't earned yours."

"You have."

"Haven't."

"Have."

"We gonna keep on arguing like this?"

"Yup. I got all day."

"No, you don't. I know you're busy."

"I am." I always was.

"What are you working on?"

"You changing the subject?"

"Yup."

"I'm extrapolating data."

"From?"

"A bunch of police files."

"Why?"

"Trying to figure out who someone is."

"A murderer?"

"No. A rapist."

"A rapist?" She hummed. "The fucker who's terrorizing Harlem by any chance?"

"Yup."

"Not that I don't approve, but why?"

"Under orders. You know I have to ask how high when Da tells me to jump."

"Why do you always obey?"

"Because it's expensive not to."

She heaved a sigh. "It's not like money's tight."

"No. But I don't really do it for him. I do as I'm told, but I know that my work keeps my dipshit siblings safe."

"Thought they annoyed you," she snarked.

"They can annoy the fuck out of me but I still want to protect them."

That had been bred into me when I was a kid.

For a second, I saw my eldest brother, Aidan, slamming a candlestick into the head of the priest who'd been raping me, and I could literally feel the blood spatter against my skin as if it were yesterday.

It wasn't yesterday.

It was years ago.

I was over it.

Just... some shit stuck with you.

"Why does your da want you to figure out who the Harlem rapist is?"

"Not a clue. Never know why he does the stuff he does. I can't complain if it'll take the fucker off the streets."

"What are you doing to figure out his identity?"

"Finding commonalities—"

"Aren't the cops doing that already?"

"Yeah, but they don't have access to most of the shit we do," I drawled.

"True. You pulling footage from all cameras in the area?"

"Yeah, and running through licenses and registrations of the cars in the vicinity. The bastard always acts after eight-thirty PM so I'm thinking that's when he gets off work."

"Interesting. Need help?"

"Not really. You're busy enough with the kidnapping ring, ain't you?"

"Yeah, I guess. I found where they're stowing their current victims. I don't know what to do."

"Why not?"

"Do I tell the Valentinis or don't I? Do I tell the cops? The Valentinis might barter with the information—"

"It might be good to have an in with the Sicilians," I pointed out carefully.

"You already got an in. You're allies!"

"Yeah, but you'd be on the front line. That's even better."

"Conor," she said, practically purring my name. Fuck, that sound went straight to my dick. "Do you want me to play double agent?"

Eyes almost crossing at the images *that* inspired, I murmured, "I wouldn't want to do anything that made you uncomfortable."

She cackled, "Nothing makes me uncomfortable... where work is concerned."

That rammed her earlier admission home even harder.

*I* made her uncomfortable, and it was *sort of* a good thing.

"Luciu Valentini's boning the best friend of two of my sisters-in-law—"

"Jesus, talk about incestuous. Here was me thinking NYC was a big place."

My lips curved. "Manhattan's an island. Space poor."

"People poor, apparently, as well."

"Jen's got her head screwed on right," I discounted. "I don't think she'd get tangled with the mafia if she didn't think she was safe—"

"What does her safety have to do with anything?"

"I dunno. I just think that means maybe Luciu Valentini is trustworthy."

"No one's trustworthy." She paused. "Apart from you. And Katina."

I grinned. "I'm as trustworthy as a preteen. Got it."

Her laugh made my fucking hands clench into fists. I wanted to taste that goddamn laugh.

"You know it." She paused. "Thank you for telling me about Dagda."

Shrugging, I said, "You deserved to know."

The trouble with love was that it tore your loyalties in half.

Eamonn Keegan, the man known as Dagda, was my sister-in-law's uncle. He was also the head of an Irish Republican faction, and, more importantly, he was Lodestar's mother's murderer.

When I'd uncovered Dagda's ID, had it confirmed, I'd told Lodestar.

I owed my sister-in-law loyalty, but Lodestar... she was it for me.

It.

I.T.

"Star?"

"Yeah?"

"Is Dagda why you got into the CIA?"

"Never fuck with a woman scorned."

My lips twisted. "I'll make a note of that."

She sighed but informed me, "I sent that sound bite out onto the dark web."

I thought about what she'd stitched together; statements that were the truth, and all the more horrendous for it.

> "She was a lying, filthy slag. Betrayed her people!"
> "Is Elizabeth Davidson a part of the ECD?"
> "YES!"

I rubbed my chin. "Any takers?"

"A few."

"You know we just committed treason, don't you?"

She snorted. "You only just figured that out? Anyway, my loyalty doesn't belong to a First Lady who's tied up with a bunch of terrorist scum."

"Some people might think we're terrorists," I pointed out.

"We're hacktivists." She sniffed. "There's a difference."

"If you say so."

"I do." A huff escaped her. "Okay, let me help with the rapist. Harlem's his stomping ground for a reason. These dumbfucks like to shit in their own backyard. If you send me the traffic reports, I'll work through those—"

"What about the kidnapping ring?"

"I'm still thinking about the best course of action."

"The more you think about it, the more those poor bastards are kept away from their families—"

"If I make the wrong decision, they could become pawns for the Sicilian mafia, Conor," she grumbled. "I want them free, but I don't want them to become collateral damage either. When the fuck did everything become so complicated?"

I heaved a sigh. "Longer than we've been alive."

The Sparrows, Irish Mob, Sicilian mafia, and even the goddamn ECD had been around a lot longer than either of us.

She fell silent. "Well, shit. You're right."

I didn't even have it in me to smile.

***Unknown Sender:*** You've got a problem heading your way. Trust starts both ways.

***Nyx:*** Cryptic much?

***Unknown Sender:*** You'll understand when it happens. It's my pleasure to help resolve this for you.

***Nyx:*** Don't do me no favors.

***Unknown Sender:*** You'll be thankful once the job's done.

## THIRTY-FOUR

## RACHEL

"I have a question."

"One of your two-a-day or just a regular, 'What's your favorite color?' kind of question?"

He scoffed, "If I didn't know your favorite color already, you'd have tossed me to the curb years ago."

"What is it then?"

"Your real favorite color or the one you tell everyone is your favorite?"

Grinning down at my desk as I worked on annotating yet another deposition for Luciu Valentini—seriously, the man had better donate an arm *and* a leg at the gala—and with a rerun of *The Kardashians* on the TV, I asked, "Tell me both. I have to check up on you."

"You tell everyone your favorite color is navy blue, but it's actually fuchsia. And trust me, there's no way I'd ever forget that because when I was a kid, I had to look it up to know what fuchsia even is. I thought it was a curse word at first."

Laughing, I said, "Fair play. Sounds like 'fuck.'"

"Sure does." He cleared his throat. "My question was about that."

"About fuchsias?" I arched a brow, but it was wasted on my lap desk. "Or fucking?"

"Fucking."

"I wondered when we'd talk about sex."

"You have?"

"Yes. Since Link told me you don't fuck Peach."

"Fucking Link."

Doodling on my notepad, I demurred, "He did you a favor."

"He did? Aside from emasculating me?"

"Proving you're faithful is emasculating you?"

"It proves that I've been a dipshit."

"Why does it?" I countered. "You're talking to the woman invested in your faithfulness. Anyway, I'd say you were a dipshit if I'd fucked around... but I didn't. Haven't. Don't want to."

His heavy breath rattled down the line. "We have a lot of wasted time to make up for."

"Women in their late thirties/early forties have a bump in their sex drive."

He groaned. "Is that supposed to make me feel better?"

I chuckled. "It's supposed to reassure you. You'll need Viagra."

"I doubt it."

His snort made me grin. "Anyway, what about sex? We're good together, aren't we?"

"We are."

When his voice dropped, everything in me melted into my armchair. I was in my bedroom, staring at a bed we'd never fucked in, wishing that weren't true so I could at least envision us there together.

God, he wasn't wrong about us having a lot of wasted time to make up for.

"Well?"

"Sometimes I'm concerned I'm going to trigger you."

I pondered that, pondered the hesitancy in his voice, and

remarked, "Did I ever come across as the kind of woman who wouldn't be able to tell you what I wanted or didn't want?"

"No." He sighed. "Maybe it's irrational. Maybe it isn't. After the last time, after how it ended, I mean, I'm wondering if I've always known something wasn't right."

"It isn't your fault that my subconscious is a dick."

"I don't want that to happen again."

Thinking about staring at him, telling him to get out, had my voice deepening as I told him, "I can't promise that."

"Is there something we could do—" He sighed again. "I'm asking for the impossible."

"You're not."

"I guess I'm asking if there's something I do during sex that takes you back to that time."

My eyes rounded in horror. "No, Rex. God, no. Nothing about what we do is in any way, shape, or form like what happened to me."

"Even when I'm rough with you?"

"Rex, what we do is consensual. There's a massive difference," I tried to reason. "I want what we do. Everything." *God, did I.* "What happened to me... I didn't want *that*. I pleaded... I—no. No, Rex." I sucked in a breath and decided to shift this conversation. I was so fucking sick of the past. I wanted to deal with the future. That was what mattered. "I'll tell you what I *do* want though."

"What?" he asked quickly, his eagerness telling me he wanted to change the subject too.

"To have... to do—" Jesus. What verb went with oral? "To give you oral."

"I am beyond willing."

Snickering, relieved that he'd decided not to tease me, I told him, "Good to know."

"Seriously. Willing and able and ready to show up."

"I might be bad at it. I haven't done it in years," I warned.

Eighteen to be precise.

History.

That was the past.

This was the present.

"My dick will explode the second you put your lips around it."

"I'll just have to keep on trying until I do it right then, won't I?"

Another groan escaped him. "You make that sound like explosion isn't what I want."

"Premature explosions are good for no one. Especially not if I want to practice."

"Practice makes perfect. I know what a perfectionist you are. Again, I'm beyond ready and willing."

Smirking to myself, I said, "I guess it's only fair seeing as you turn my innards to mush."

"Well, my outards are anything but mush."

"Right now?"

"Yeah. Right now. So we should change the subject."

"Do we have to?" I stared down at the deposition on my lap desk. "I'd prefer that to what I'm currently doing."

"Which is?"

"I'm going through a witness statement."

He hummed. "It's annoying that I can't ask you for details. Like wanting to know what happens in a show but your friend won't give you spoilers."

"Friend... Is that what I am?"

"You'll always be my friend, Rachel. You just happen to be the love of my life too."

I sighed. "Stop being charming."

"I mean, I can't. It's too ingrained."

"Jackass," I said with a laugh.

"I can't be both, can I?"

"It's possible seeing as you're being a jackass and charming all at the same time."

His chuckle did things to me that were probably illegal in some states. "You should get on with your work. I don't want to be a distraction."

"Too late. Plus, I want to be distracted. Work's always waiting."

"It is, but you should get some rest too."

"Now you're being sweet. You're right though, I should. The next few days are going to be chaotic."

"Oh?"

"Remember I told you my client was beaten while in holding?"

"Yeah."

"It's to do with that," was all I said.

I didn't tell him that Luc being beaten had been a 'master plan.'

Humming my disapproval, knowing he'd accept it as my dislike for mass incarceration, I murmured, "Rex?"

"I miss you too, Rachel."

My smile was so big that it made my jaw ache.

"Night?"

"Night, my love. Sleep well."

## THIRTY-FIVE

## REX

### THREE DAYS LATER

"You sound stressed."

Rachel blew out a breath. "It's been a crazy couple of days."

I knew that without her having to say a word. Though we'd been talking every day, the last couple of calls had ended with her yawning and her words slurring as she fell asleep.

Whatever was going on in NYC, she wouldn't tell me. Client confidentiality.

It didn't sit well with me at all.

Staying out of the MC business wasn't helping matters either. It meant I couldn't call on Maverick for information without getting a barrage of bullshit in return.

I wanted a break. Some respite. I needed that. So that meant I was, for all intents and purposes, blocked from any information that was strictly unavailable to the public.

"Is everything under control?"

"Mostly. There'll be a court case soon enough, but it'll be thrown out."

"How do you know?"

"Trumped-up charges. They don't actually make any sense. I've no idea why the DA is going through with them, but she is."

"A bluff?"

"I doubt it. But maybe. I don't know why the hell the DA decides what she decides."

"For whatever reason, there's no denying that she gets results."

New York's District Attorney had made a name for herself by taking a tough stance on mafia activity in the city.

Predominantly Italian activity.

As far as I was aware, the Irish, Russian, and Chinese escaped her ire, whereas the Italians got the full brunt of it.

If the DA was being a hard ass, I guessed I had confirmation of *who* Rachel's client was.

Even though there'd been a change of leadership over Christmas —even I'd heard about that through the grapevine—the *Famiglia,* the Italian mafia, were still being targeted by the DA's office.

"You couldn't get them to drop the charges for your client?" I asked, surprised.

"No."

She didn't sound happy about it. That was the perfectionist in her.

A sharp sound in my ear had me wincing. "What's that in the background?"

"Traffic. I'm on my way to Manhattan."

"Meetings?"

"Always."

"Was your client angry?"

"No."

I arched a brow. "Unusual."

"I agree." She huffed. "He's playing a bigger endgame."

"What kind of endgame? I know you're not supposed to talk about this with me, but maybe I can help?"

She sighed, her exhaustion drifting down the line. "I doubt it. His great-uncle is in prison on trumped-up charges. The man's in the

Bellevue Hospital Prison Ward; he's dying, and my client wants him to experience some freedom before that happens."

Shocked she'd shared that much, I was silent as I processed the information she'd given me.

"I shouldn't have said that—"

"No, it's fine. You know I won't tell anyone."

"I know you won't, but that doesn't mean you won't try to use it for the MC's gain if you figure out who my client is."

I snorted. "You know me better than anyone, so you also know that if you tell me something in confidence I won't say a damn word."

"I repeat—I know you won't. But I know your brain."

Rolling my eyes, I muttered, "What kind of trumped-up charges?"

"Multiple counts of murder one."

"Jesus."

"Yeah, the case was a mess. The prosecution said the great-uncle wanted to take over his family's business," she explained, her tone careful enough that I knew she was whitewashing over some of the minutiae.

"And that didn't happen?"

"My client's spent years liberating his great-uncle, not to mention wasting a fortune on the endeavor. I doubt he'd have done that if he didn't believe the old man was innocent."

"That's not a yes."

She laughed. "No, it isn't. But you know how I work."

"You'll get him out whether he is or isn't guilty because your client asked you to."

"Exactly. I saw him the other day. He looks like hell."

"You went to the hospital?"

"Yes." Then, blandly, she repeated something she'd said earlier, "If you remember, my client was involved in a fight in his holding cell."

My brow furrowed as I read between the lines. "And got transferred to Bellevue Hospital Prison Ward?"

"Yes."

Where his great-uncle was being treated.

I had to smile. "That's seems coincidental."

"Doesn't it?" she drawled. "Anyway, the pressure's on to get the old man out before he dies. Which, because of end-stage kidney failure, is looking goddamn imminent."

"What's your next move?"

"I'm going to put pressure on the Attorney General."

My eyes widened. "Hardcore."

"After all this time, it needs hardcore. I've pulled all the plays I can. There's clear proof that evidence was falsified and that the DA at the time turned a blind eye to the truth. Either way, my appeals get us nowhere. It's bullshit, so now I need to barter with leverage."

"The Attorney General owes you?"

"He does, but not enough for this. I'm afraid my client's the one who'll owe him the favor."

I pursed my lips. "Shouldn't you ask for approval first?"

"I was told to do whatever it took to get the old man out of jail. He can bitch at me later over how I achieve that," she grouched. "Anyway, enough about work, how's your day been? Have you managed to get some downtime?"

"I have. I got some sleep. I didn't realize how tired I was until I came here. I can't say that I feel better for it, but I must have needed it." I scratched my stubbled jaw. "I got a workout in, ate some lunch. You know how it goes."

"How much is it killing you not to work?"

My lips twitched. "It's hard. I keep thinking about it, but then I force myself to switch off. I just need a break from it, you know?"

"I do." She heaved a sigh, one that sounded like she could do with some R&R too, then, before I could suggest she did something crazy like take some time off and maybe come and visit California, she inserted, "Wynter's helping with that?"

"She is, but when she's at school, not so much," I said dryly.

"Your playmate's busy, huh?" she teased.

"She is."

"You're enjoying hanging out with her?"

"I really am. She's a cool kid. Sometimes, she forgets that she likes being around me and she remembers she's a teenager and that she hates the world, but those times are becoming fewer and farther between."

"I'm glad. Did you get her the helmet?"

"Yeah." I grinned to myself. "She was very happy when I gave it to her."

"Biker spawn. No escaping the call of the road," she joked, but I knew she understood the fire in my belly.

"Damn straight. I spoke with Blade, the Disciples' Prez, again."

"Busier day than you just catching some downtime like you said," she mocked, but she knew that, originally, he'd given me a seventy-two-hour deadline to stay on his territory, and Blade had been surprisingly patient this far.

I had a feeling his MC was dealing with a shitstorm of their own, but without Mav to go hunting for information, I had no real proof of that.

Whatever the reason, so long as I kept on checking in, Blade was okay with me staying for the interim.

"Yeah. I guess."

"What did he want? A pound of flesh as payment for staying?"

"No, just said that he'd kill me if I fucked anything in Burbank up. The usual."

"A nice, everyday conversation then?"

I snorted.

"Any updates on the apartment?" she continued.

"Not really. Maybe next week she'll let me talk about it with her. It's still a sore subject."

"She's got a lot of her daddy's pride," Rachel joked. "You'd be the one who'd know how to get around it."

I grunted. "You'd think so. But no dice yet. How are the plans for the gala coming along?"

"Great. With Lily involved, my life is so much easier. She coordinates with the events organizers so I don't have to. Did you know Lily's a Lindenbourg?"

Her hushed voice had me smiling. "I did. I'm glad that's working out."

"Why?"

"I know she wanted to keep on helping with the books, but..." I shrugged. "Plausible deniability doesn't help when you ain't married to your woman."

"That's always been the flaw with Old Ladies."

I grunted. "Why do you think Dad married Mom?"

She just hummed, but I knew she'd have heard the tension in my voice.

"Anyway, you got a dress?" I queried, wanting, hell, *needing* to change the subject.

"This close to the gala and you think I wouldn't have one already?"

"You gonna take a picture of it for me?"

"Do you want me to take a picture for you?" she drawled.

"I'd like to see it." Because she was tricksy, I muttered, "With you in it."

"Thinking like a lawyer. Smart, Rex. Smart."

"That's me," I joked. My smile faded and I told her the truth, "Miss you, Rach. It's better than it was before, but I miss you."

A breath gusted from her lips. "And I miss you." She didn't ask when I was coming back, which I was grateful for, but said instead, "I'm glad we're talking."

"Me too. I didn't think it would flow as easy as this, but it is."

She cleared her throat. "I know you're trying to relax and everything, but I wondered if you'd like to hear Bear's will? That clause of your dad's that we read it together would be satisfied."

"I can think of better ways to spend my time," I mocked, "but yeah, I guess it needs to be done."

The prospect set my nerves on edge, though, so I got to my feet and clambered over to the mini bar.

This conversation called for JD and Coke.

I didn't give a damn if it was a couple hours after breakfast or not.

"The privacy screen is up," she assured me. "Emile can't hear."

"Wouldn't matter if he could. I'm sure I know what's going to where and to whom."

"The main reason I wanted to speak with you when you were still in California is because there are some stipulations in his will."

"What kind of stipulations?"

"Bequests to certain people. Storm's one of them."

"You waiting to tell him when he rides up for the funeral?" I knew that was being delayed while I was AWOL.

"No."

"Why not?"

"I'm not supposed to say."

"Yeah, okay."

She sighed impatiently. "It's on my discretion."

"What is? The bequest?"

"No. You have to remember that this will was updated last year, so Storm and Keira were separated."

"So? They still are, aren't they? Even if she moved to Ohio."

"So, that upset Bear."

"It upset all of us."

She grunted. "Upon his death, I was to wait no more than twelve months to see if they managed to get back together again."

"Why? He couldn't directly control whether they got back together again or not."

"I know," she hedged.

"You might as well just tell me. You know that Storm will eventually."

Another grunt. "I have two letters here. One to send to him if it appears reconciliation will never happen, and one to send if they get back together again."

"What's the difference?"

"I don't know. I haven't read the letters. They're sealed."

"Does he get an inheritance?"

"Yes."

"Good." I scrubbed my chin. "He was like a second son to my parents; I'm glad Dad's recognized that when it counts."

"I'm frustrated with myself."

"Why?"

"For dreading this. I was expecting you to be annoyed about that and… well, I know you'll be mad about the next matter but I was being dumb about Storm's inclusion in the will."

"You thought I'd begrudge Storm getting an inheritance?" I scoffed. "I don't need Dad's money anyway."

"No, I know. Like I said, I was being dumb."

Unusually for me, I didn't argue because it was definitely dumb of her to think I'd begrudge Storm anything.

He'd had a shitty life and had been handed shittier odds. The only semblance of normalcy came from the times when he'd been living with us as a kid, before his bitch of a mom came and took him away from us. *And* during his marriage to Keira, although that had been fucking weird in its own way.

Not that I could judge.

My relationship with Rachel wasn't exactly normal.

What had Wynter called it?

*Dysfunctional.*

I rubbed my brow as I asked, "What's the second thing you were dreading telling me?"

"Kendra…"

As her voice faded, I demanded, "Kendra? The clubwhore?"

"Yeah, her."

Unease filled me. I might not have been so concerned if she

hadn't prefaced our conversation with her dreading talking to me about this.

"Oh, Jesus, please tell me he didn't knock her up and I have a fucking baby brother or sister somewhere."

The sharp breath that escaped her had horror overtaking my unease.

"He did, didn't he?" I choked.

I didn't remember Kendra being pregnant, but it wasn't like I was interested.

Although, surely Link would have told me. Or Steel? They were nosy bastards.

Rubbing my brow, waiting for the guillotine to fall, I held my breath as Rachel said, "No. Bear left a key in my possession. It's to a safety deposit box. His will stipulates that the key is a gift for..."

When she hesitated, I groused, "Who?"

"He gave me her address."

"Her?" I frowned. "Who is it? Who's the beneficiary?"

"She's not a beneficiary. Not legally, anyway. But it's Kendra's mother," she rasped.

"What the fuck was he leaving her a gift in his will for?"

"Kendra's your half-sister, King. The gift is for her mother."

Her use of my real name cemented those heinous words into reality.

"Kendra is my half-sister?"

Was this a joke?

"Yes," she whispered. "I hate Bear for making me be the one to tell you."

I ground my teeth as I leaped onto my feet. One second, I was staring at nothing, the next, my glass of JD and Coke had been hurled across the room at the TV.

As the screen imploded, Rachel shrieked, "King? King, are you okay?"

No, I fucking wasn't.

Kendra was younger than me by a good couple of years, but not that young.

"He cheated on Mom," I whispered, stating it aloud so that I could better process it.

"Yeah." She exhaled. "He did."

"Why didn't you tell me sooner?" I demanded.

"I had no..." She sighed. "I had no words, Rex. I was as stunned as you, but it... I'm sorry."

Her simple apology didn't ease the sting, but I hissed as I scrubbed a hand over my face. Processing this was going to take some time. "Why's it mentioned in his will? Because he was too chicken shit to tell me in person?"

"Because the will stipulates that you're the one who gives her the key."

She said it in such a rush that I knew she was terrified about sharing that with me.

At another time, with different words filling my ears, I'd have laughed at that.

Rachel Laker, Ms. Ball Buster herself, nervous?

Of me?

But she clearly was.

And I didn't even have it in me to calm her down. To calm *things* down.

I ground my teeth as I snarled, "You have to be joking."

"I'm not," she said softly. Miserably. "I wish I were."

My hands balled into fists. "I have to go."

"King!"

Her cry didn't stop me from cutting the call, nor did it stop me from ignoring her when she tried to ring me again.

I almost flung the damn thing against the wall too, but only knowing this was my point of contact with her and Wynter stopped me.

Reaching up, I rubbed my forehead where an ache had bloomed.

Wynter said she'd be calling later when she was ready for me to come and collect her, but that was hours away.

I had two alternatives—get drunk or go for a walk to clear my head.

"She's just starting to trust you, dipshit," I muttered under my breath.

I gathered my shit together then pulled on my jacket. Once I'd locked up, I made my way down to reception.

"There's been an accident in my room," I said flatly. "I understand that you'll need to rescind my security deposit." I handed the woman the key. "I'm going out now. If you could have the TV replaced before I get back, I'd appreciate it."

Not letting her reply or ask me any goddamn questions, I left the reception with her calling out for me and exited the hotel.

Once I was outside, bars and pubs tempted me as I ambled toward Wynter's school, but knowing she was at the end of it kept me from heading into one of them.

Dad had cheated.

Fucking cheated.

Not just that, he'd had a goddamn daughter.

That daughter had been living with us for years. Whoring herself out. He'd fucking let her. And what if I hadn't been repulsed by her? What if I'd fucked her?

God, I needed a drink. I needed a fucking drink so bad.

Gritting my teeth, I shoved my hands into my pockets and slouched down streets I barely recognized.

Somehow, hours later, I found the school even though I didn't have a clue how I'd made it here without accident, but when I looked at my phone, saw there were five more missed calls that I hadn't heard, I also registered that it was far too early to be here.

There was a small rise beyond the school parking lot, so I set my ass there, raised my knees, and plunked my elbows onto them as I stared at nothing. Just tried to process what the fuck was happening.

The twilight zone—that was what I'd entered.

An alternate universe where my dad cheated on my mom and I had a baby sister, one who whored herself out to my brothers, and who was the worst of all the bunnies.

Fuck, she'd almost had her ass kicked out of the club more times than I could count. She was a troublemaker, was the principle reason Storm and Keira had split up, and was universally hated among the Old Ladies.

I rubbed my brow as I admitted to myself that *I* hated her too.

God, I hated her so fucking much.

My sister.

My goddamn sister.

When my phone started ringing again, I barely noticed it, but then I jolted when I saw that a bunch of kids had left the school and were driving off in their cars.

Grabbing my cell, I saw Wynter's name on the Caller ID, and grimaced when I realized she'd been calling for the last ten minutes.

"Hey!" I answered gruffly, aware that I sounded like hell. "I'm outside in the parking lot."

"You are?" I heard her suspicious surprise and cursed it. I got why she was hard on me sometimes, but I really didn't need that now. "Whereabouts?"

"On the hill at the back."

"On your bike?"

"No. I walked here."

"Why?" She didn't let me answer. "Are you okay? You don't sound too good."

I clenched my jaw. "It's... I just learned some bad shit about my dad."

"Oh." She hesitated, and I heard some kids talking in the background as she moved toward me. Then, sounding like she was tasting the words, she asked, "My granddad?"

"Yeah. Bear."

"I can see you. Be there in two."

I peered up and found her over by the back entrance to the

school. She waved at me and I waved back. She tucked her cell into her pocket then walked over to me.

On the way, she didn't really look at anyone, and I figured that was because, from what I could make out, she wasn't all that popular. Wynter, much like her mom, and definitely not like me, kept to herself.

I wondered if Rachel would recognize just how similar they were.

It was crazy really how in nature vs. nurture, the woman who'd had zero impact on her life was such a strong presence in our kid's personality.

I liked it, to be honest. Even as suspicious of my motives as she was, Wynter reminded me of Rach before she was broken.

Wynter was a breath of fresh air, and I knew she'd be the same for her mom if Rach would ever agree to meet with her.

Wynter tilted her head to the side as she approached me, crossing the road then climbing up the rise. I didn't stand up, just watched her plunk her ass down beside me.

"You look..."

"Like shit?"

She blinked. "Yeah. I haven't heard you swear before."

I reached up and rubbed my eyes. "Lot of bad news today, honey."

I almost jumped when I felt her hand pat my knee. That was the first voluntary touch she'd given me.

"Is there anything I can do to help?"

"Not really." I shot her a tight smile and cautiously, like I was approaching a rabid wolf, placed my hand over hers. When she tucked them together, squeezing my fingers, I felt the strength in her.

"You sure? I'm a good listener?"

I didn't know how to make this PC.

I didn't want my kid who'd only just turned seventeen, who had her own problems she wasn't willing to share with me yet, knowing about clubwhores and MC culture.

But I knew I looked like hell, and I didn't want to freak her out either.

"My dad cheated on my mom."

"I'm sorry. I know how that feels."

For a second, I was offended. I hadn't cheated on her mom, *ever*. Then I realized what she was saying.

Jeremy had cheated on Ally.

I gaped at her. "You knew?"

She shrugged. "I knew."

"How?"

"Dad's not the best kind of guy. He gambles a lot and comes home drunk. Sometimes, he'd come back with lipstick on his clothes." Wynter gnawed on the inside of her cheek. "He'd stink of perfume too. The final straw was last month for me."

The oddly adult comment had me twisting to look at her, my own problems shoved aside in the face of hers. "What happened?"

"A couple things." She tucked a stray strand of hair behind her ear. "But the first was that he came home high." Her gaze darted over to mine then flittered away. "Some of the band, after a game, they smoke a few joints." My expression must have darkened because she blurted out, "I don't. Just the smell makes me feel woozy, so I don't want to inhale too much."

Christ, she had no idea how much she sounded like Rachel.

"So you know how people act when they're high?"

Nodding, she muttered, "I don't like it."

"What else happened to make you leave?"

Wynter cleared her throat and tugged her hand free of mine. "It doesn't matter."

It did.

But I didn't want to push my luck.

Not unlike her mother, she needed gentling.

But God, I missed the feel of her hand in mine.

Needing to man up, I told her, "I'm sorry you had to experience that. Home should be a safe space."

"Mom protected me, but I was..." Her smile tightened. "Never mind. You were saying? About your dad?"

The glimpse into her life gave me more questions I needed answering, but I just said, "I found out that when he cheated on her, he had a kid."

Her brows lifted. "That's... bad."

"It is."

"Do you know the kid? Have you ever met them?"

"She lives by me."

"Oh."

"I hate her," I said grimly. "She's a horrible woman."

She clapped a hand to her mouth when she released an amused snort. "I'm so sorry. I didn't mean to laugh."

My lips twitched. "I'm glad I made you laugh."

"It was inappropriate. I really am sorry."

"There's no need to be. It's a ridiculous situation, but it knocked me sideways. I always thought my dad wasn't like that."

"It's never nice to learn that our heroes are humans too."

I stared at her, bewildered by how mature she sounded. "Yeah, you're right." Liking that a barrier seemed to have fallen between us, I confessed, "I did something bad at the hotel."

Her eyes widened. "What?"

"I threw something at the TV. It shattered."

A sharp gasp escaped her. "Oh, no! Do you think you'll get into trouble?"

Amused and warmed by the innocence of her reply, especially after how grown-up she'd been sounding, I said, "It'll cost me a small fortune. Serves me right for losing control like that."

"It wasn't a nice call."

"No. It wasn't," I said grimly. "It couldn't have been much worse."

"You... The call, it was with my mom, wasn't it? She's your lawyer?"

"It was."

"How is she?" Wynter asked shyly.

It wasn't the first time she'd asked after Rach.

"I don't know. Probably scared," I admitted on a sigh.

"Why?"

"I hung the phone up on her and she keeps calling, but I'm not answering."

"Why not?"

"Because I don't want to say the wrong thing. I don't want to upset her."

She queried, "Is that practical?"

"Probably not."

"Do you feel that way when you're talking to me?"

"Sometimes. I don't want to say anything that'll upset the balance. I like this. I want to get to know more of you."

"I do too, but if this isn't all of you, then how can I know the real you?" It didn't sound like she was upset with me. Something she rammed home when she patted my knee again. "We're past the point of first impressions, aren't we? I mean, you've stopped shaving, so I took that to be a good sign."

I almost smiled. "When did you get to be so wise?"

"I don't know. Mom says I've got an old soul."

"She's right."

Wynter hummed. "Do you want to call Rachel now? Maybe say sorry for scaring her?"

"With you here?" I saw the nerves she was trying to hide. "I can call her later if you're not ready for that."

"Does she want to talk to me?"

"She does. I don't think she's expecting it though."

"Do you talk about me?"

"We do. Every day."

"Do you think..." She bit her lip. "Do you think she wants to meet me?"

"I know she does, but she's scared about that too. She's worried you'll hate her."

Wynter's gaze turned pensive. "I looked up her name."

I arched a brow. "You did?"

She nodded. "She represents a lot of bad people, doesn't she?"

Well, hell, how did I answer that one?

What did that say about me that I was a client of her mom's too?

"Yeah, she does."

"I read the court transcript for one case. She defended a man who was clearly guilty."

"Everyone's entitled to a defense."

"I know. I'm not judging her."

"Okay," I said slowly.

"I'm just wondering how she can defend murderers but is scared of you and me."

"You have a point."

She flashed a grin at me. "I know I do."

"I think that's because not much scares your mom but feelings do."

"We make her feel?"

"We do. So she's nervous because that's something she can't control."

"I wish..."

"What do you wish?" I asked when her words waned.

"I wish that I could have known her before, you know, everything."

Her wistfulness killed me, and I knew I sounded choked when I said, "She was awesome. A little quirky, but awesome. I loved being with her."

"Why?"

"She loves books. She's always reading in her spare time. I don't think that's changed, even though we don't talk about that anymore." I smiled to myself but it disappeared as I explained, "My uncle gave me this coin, and he told me it was priceless—"

"Was it?"

"No." Fuck, the urge to strangle Grizzly was real. "But I believed him. I was showing one of my friends and he dropped it. It fell between the floorboards and into the crawl space beneath the house. I didn't want to lose it so I went down there and tried to find it. Rachel was there."

Wynter frowned. "In the crawl space?"

I nodded, laughing at her bewilderment. "Trust me, I was freaked out too. It was like finding a pretty Gollum under the house. She'd strung up these string lights that were battery powered and read by flashlight. It was crazy.

"When I went in, she was super still, like she could hide from me, and I... I was just worried for her."

"I can imagine. It's a weird thing to do, isn't it?"

"Yeah. She's always been unusual, though."

Wynter surprised me by chuckling. "I'm sure she'd love to hear how you're describing her."

I grinned. "Yeah, let's not tell her?"

"I won't say a word." She nudged me. "Keep going."

"I think she was bullied a lot by some of the kids her age, so that's why she used to hide down there. I started talking to her as I tried to find the coin, and she was quiet at first, then I asked her what book she was reading, and she wouldn't shut up." Chuckling to myself, I continued, "I found the coin but the next day, I went back."

"And the day after too?"

I nodded. "For a few years."

"So long?"

"It took me that long to convince her she didn't have to hide out anymore."

"Wow. She's stubborn."

"I know someone just like her," I teased, amused when her cheeks burned bright red.

"Am I?" She peeped up at me. "Just like her?"

"You are in a lot of ways. It's awesome."

"Really?"

"Really. You were saying how you wished you'd met her before everything went...wrong. Talking to you is kind of like that. You're very similar in how you do things. It's fascinating to see."

She swallowed. "Are you going to call her?"

"Do you mind if I text her first? So she can prepare herself? I know she wants to talk to you but I also know she's nervous."

A bubble of laughter escaped her. "She's nervous to talk with me? When she got the Long Beach Butcher off from that murder charge?"

"He doesn't mean anything to her. You do."

Her shoulders hunched, which made me think she'd say no, but she muttered, "You can text her."

Before she could change her mind, I reached for my phone and quickly tapped out:

**Rex:** *Got someone here who'd like to talk with you.*

**Rachel:** *Wynter?*

**Rex:** *Yeah. Can I call?*

**Rachel:** *I'll call. Just coming out of a meeting. I'll be in my car in two minutes.*

**Rex:** *Okay.*

Wynter was peering at my screen. "You were right about her needing to prepare herself."

My lips twisted. "I usually am where she's concerned."

# THIRTY-SIX

## RACHEL

I was going to be sick.

I could feel it.

My stomach was churning and everything south of my throat was bubbling away like I'd swallowed ten laxatives.

Wynter wanted to talk to me.

The afternoon had turned to shit when Rex had cut the call with me then had refused to answer when I tried phoning back.

I'd been dreading that conversation, but I had no idea how long he'd be down there, and I knew it was unlikely that he wouldn't follow Bear's request to the letter no matter how much it hurt him.

I wanted to kill two birds with one stone, but instead, I was terrified that I'd killed off any chance Rex had of wanting to talk with me.

The anxiety that imploded inside me took me back to some darker times, making it resonate with me again how much I needed him. How much I missed him. Our impasse was one thing, but for him to ignore me was just hell.

His text message brought relief, but it was followed up with more terror.

I could literally feel the acid in my stomach eating away at the lining.

*Hello, Ulcer, pleasure to meet you.*

Having managed to buy myself two minutes, I wished like hell I could down a shot of vodka, but that wasn't to be.

Instead, I plunked myself in the back seat of the car and raised the privacy screen with an order to Emile not to disturb me until I lowered it. Even if it meant driving around the block a couple times outside the Attorney General's office where my next meeting was being held.

I sucked in a few deep breaths which almost made me more nauseated than earlier, and before I could talk myself out of it, I hit the 'connect' button.

When he answered, I quickly tapped the 'mute' button and let out a sob of relief.

"Rach?" he asked. When I didn't answer, he grumbled, "Rach? You there?"

I allowed myself a single sniffle, untapped the 'mute' button, and murmured, "Hi, Rex. Sorry, the line must be bad."

I sounded like I'd been strangled.

"I have someone here who wants to say hello."

There was silence, then the softest voice came down the line. "Hi, Rachel. This is Wynter."

My mouth worked, and I whispered, "Hello, Wynter. Pleasure to meet you."

I had no idea what to say.

Not a single clue.

I was supposed to fill in the gaps—*I* was the adult here.

Was this supposed to be so fucking hard?

Like always, fear shadowed me.

That I'd be like my mom.

That I was just as crappy at parenting as she was.

She'd have let the silence continue too.

She'd have made me do all the work because she didn't care.

She never cared—

"Rex tells me you play the piano," I blurted out, refusing to listen to that stupid inner voice for much longer.

I didn't have to be like Mom.

I was me.

I was Rachel.

"I do," Wynter murmured.

Nerves still taut, I rasped, "I always wanted to play the piano."

"You did?"

"I did. Classes were too expensive though."

"You could learn now."

"I'm too busy—" My brow furrowed as a thought occurred to me. "I guess you make time for things that matter though, don't you?"

"Work's your mother's priority."

Rex's voice was flat enough that it made my cheeks flush then blanch. I wasn't sure if he'd meant to sound so critical, but it came out that way. Which, to be frank, was bullshit. Many people could judge me for being a workaholic but the pot calling kettle black was appropriate here.

"It's something we both lean on," was my only retort, and I tried to keep my own voice as toneless as possible.

"I think that's normal. In my history class, the teacher was talking about how societal evolution means that we're not fighting for survival anymore but our instincts are still there, so we push ourselves into work because that's another, more modern, means of surviving."

Her history teacher needed to stick to the curriculum.

Not that I said that.

Those were two or three sentences she'd uttered that I hadn't had to pry out of her.

After I cleared my throat, I said, "Survival comes in many shapes and sizes. I-I actually just hired someone to help me out with some things so maybe I could take classes?"

I didn't know why I'd voiced that as a question.

I sure as hell wasn't asking permission from Rex.

"That'd be good if you could take some time for yourself," he rumbled.

Closing my eyes at the sound of his voice, the relief hitting me that he was talking and not just being a jackass, that he might forgive the messenger and not keep on shooting at me, I murmured, "Yeah. Lily's a godsend so I might be able to start soon." I didn't know if it was something I was saying to fill in the gaps or if I meant it. I'd figure it out later.

This was worse than the oral exam in French class.

"Who's Lily?" Wynter asked.

"The girlfriend of one of your father's friends." A gasp escaped me. "I'm so sorry. I didn't mean to call him that—"

"It's okay, Rachel," Wynter said calmly.

It wasn't okay.

"To me, he *is* your dad," I whispered miserably. "I wasn't thinking. Truly, Wynter, I apologize."

"Honestly, it's fine. I understand."

How could she?

"Calm down, Rachel," Rex said gruffly. "It's a learning curve."

That meant he found it hard too.

Relieved again, I decided to change the subject back to the one I'd derailed. "Link's one of Rex's closest friends. He and a bunch of other guys here grew up together and now, they help him with his businesses."

"Businesses? Do you own a porn studio like they do in *Sons of Anarchy*?"

My eyes flared wide as Rex started choking as he coughed.

Seeing as he was going to be no help, I blurted out, "No! They don't own a porn studio. Aren't you too young to be watching *Sons of Anarchy*?"

"I'm seventeen." Wynter snorted. "Plus, who's going to stop me?"

It could have sounded bitter, but it wasn't.

It was... playful.

She was amused at our shock.

Because Rex was still spluttering like an idiot, I tried to streamline things again. "They have a bar and a garage, a club—" No way was I telling her it was a titty bar. "—and then there's the diner. They just bought a motel too and are in the process of developing a microbrewery."

"Really?" I heard Wynter's surprise. "That's a lot of businesses, Rex."

"Yeah, it's a lot of responsibility."

"Shouldn't you be there?"

Rex's answer was instantaneous. "I'm where I need to be."

"Oh."

I didn't need to look at Wynter to know she was blushing.

"Lily is," I continued into the silence, "very smart, and Giulia reminded me of that so I brought her in to help me with some of the licensing and some of the more political maneuvering that's needed here in town."

That had probably gone over Wynter's head, but Rex asked, "You talking about the mayor's election?"

"I am. Do you know what NGOs are, Wynter?"

"Like charities, right?"

"Yes. I manage some of those, and though she's only been here a week or so, Lily has already proven herself to be invaluable in helping me out with them. I-I think you know that I'm a defense attorney?"

"I do."

"Well, unfortunately, a lot of the crowd I know are criminals, whereas Lily is a Lindenbourg so she knows the Manhattan socialites.

"I have a gala coming up soon and I wish Lily had been around when I was planning it. It would have been twice the size with all the people she'd have invited."

"Can't you get a bigger venue?" Wynter asked, her curiosity clear.

"The hotel upgraded us to a different suite, but it's too late for anything bigger sadly. But there's always next year, isn't there?" I asked brightly.

"There is," Wynter agreed.

"We've been upgraded to another room, but it's still smaller than it should be."

"I have to admit that I'm surprised. Do you work with charities because you feel bad about helping criminals when they're guilty?"

My throat felt thick, and as I stared at the privacy screen in front of me, my eyes blurred.

A shaken breath spilled from my lips as shame and mortification went to war deep inside me.

I didn't think she'd meant to cut into me, but she had.

She really fucking had.

And Rex wasn't saying a word.

"Rachel?"

Again with the curiosity.

It made me realize she wasn't trying to be cruel. Her words weren't intentionally barbed.

That didn't make them hurt less.

"A lot of bad things have happened to me in my life," I said, voice wobbling. "If I can stop them from happening to someone else, or if I can make things better for other people, at least I'll have accomplished something."

"So it isn't to do with the people you take as clients? Because surely their victims are the ones who need help?"

"N-No," I muttered. "Everyone has the basic right to a defense."

"Do you have to be so good at it?"

"Everything in this life should be done to the best of one's ability." I swallowed. "Look, I-I have to go. It's been great speaking with you, Wynter. I'd love to do it again sometime—"

"How about tomorrow?" Rex inserted before I could finish. "I can call you when we're having breakfast."

I gulped.

He wasn't going to let me get out of this.

"F-Fine," I stuttered. "I'll eat my second breakfast with you."
*If I didn't puke out the first one.*
Rex chortled, "You and *The* goddamn *Hobbit*."
"You like *The Lord of the Rings?*"
"She'd fan girl Tolkien if she could," Rex grumbled.
"We could do a video call," Wynter suggested eagerly.

She didn't sound like she understood how badly her remarks had cut and the Tolkien thing seemed to have smoothed over troubled waters... right?

"O-Okay," I whispered, even if the prospect of her seeing my expression was terrifying.

I guessed I'd be able to see her too though.

Seventeen years ago, I'd never imagined I'd reconnect with my daughter via video call.

"I'll speak with you later, Rachel," Rex said coolly.

I didn't answer him, just said, "It was lovely hearing your voice, Wynter."

Before she could reply, I ended the call and, like a fool, burst into tears.

My cell buzzed after a while.

**Rex:** *I'm sorry I hung up on you earlier. I'm sorry for acting like a dick. This isn't your fault. I shot the messenger, and this is on Dad, not you. Can I call you later?*

Blindly, I looked out onto the road, staring at the traffic, knowing that I had to somehow get through the next meeting without breaking down.

God, the anxiety... it was almost a tangible entity. It might as well have taken a seat beside me in the car.

My cell flashed again.

**Rex:** *I'm sorry I fucked up.*

## THIRTY-SEVEN

## REX

"Are you going to her gala?"

My mind was torn in three different directions—Dad's will, then the fact that Kendra was my fucking half-sister, and Rachel and that conversation where she'd sounded so fucking young that it reminded me of being in the clubhouse's crawl space back in the day.

When Wynter asked me that as we walked toward the coffee shop where she worked, I turned to look at her. "No."

"Why not?"

"You have to be invited to these things," I said with a laugh.

"No, you don't." Her brow puckered. "You have to pay for a seat, don't you? At least, that's what happened in *House of Cards*."

"You watch political series?"

She shrugged. "It was enjoyable."

"Not factual," I pointed out, knowing how she felt about that.

Yesterday, I'd had a diatribe/lecture about a kid in her ethics class who'd rewritten the whys and hows of the US invasion in Iraq and how he'd gotten an A grade from the teacher.

Wynter liked facts.

It amused me because it was one way in which she was very different from her parents.

Rachel and I *blurred* facts for a living. I broke laws and she bent them to protect my liberty.

"Still fun," she disregarded. "Why aren't you going? It sounds like this charity is important to her."

"Once upon a time, my business used to be her sole client."

She frowned. "What does that have to do with anything?"

"She figured out a workaround. I couldn't argue with her doing charity work, so she started the foundations. Then, because your mom is canny as hell, she figured out how to get extra clients."

"Does she need the money?"

"No, she likes the challenge."

Understanding blossomed in her eyes. "I can understand that."

"Plus, she's always working. She never stops."

"She sounded tired."

She *had*, hadn't she?

"You were kinda mean to her."

I started to argue, "I didn't say much—"

"You didn't have to. Words aren't the only means of hurting people out there. Tone is one thing, actions another."

Another lecture.

I didn't usually mind, but this time, I felt bad.

I'd hung up the fucking phone on her. I'd literally shot the goddamn messenger, when she hadn't done anything to hurt me. Not intentionally anyway.

With a guilty sigh, I reached for my phone and typed out:

**Rex:** *I'm sorry I hung up on you. I'm sorry for acting like a dick. This isn't your fault. I shot the messenger, and this is on Dad, not you. Can I call you later?*

Wynter, as nosy as her mom, peered over and read the message. I saw her satisfied smile and had to shake my head over it.

We both saw the two ticks turn blue, but when Rachel didn't reply, I grimaced.

"You must have *really* hurt her feelings." Wynter emphasized the 'really.'

I heaved a sigh.

We carried on walking in silence for a few minutes, then she battered me again by asking shyly, "Do you think she liked me?"

We didn't really touch, but I raised my arm and cautiously curved it around her shoulder. She didn't back off and only peeped those chestnut eyes of hers up at me, her nerves clear.

"I know she did," I told her.

Her grin made me feel as if the sun had come out from behind the clouds after a month of darkness.

Something that I could only liken to giddiness overcame her as she bubbled and effused about the short conversation with her birth mother.

It took me aback because I knew Rachel. Stressed, calm, drunk, unhappy, happy, pissed, grief-stricken. I knew her.

That had been anxious Rachel.

She'd been taut and nervous, fumbling over her words where she was usually as sharp as a scalpel, capable of slicing up a person's bullshit better than a butcher could carve up a side of beef.

Wynter didn't know her mom though.

She clearly wanted to.

When we made it to the coffee shop, Wynter repeating and rehashing most of that awkward conversation, I just smiled and kept the ball rolling so she had someone to bounce it off of.

I took a seat as she shuffled inside to put on the apron she wore, and a few minutes later, she brought out my regular order of a triple-shot espresso.

Rachel, in that time, had yet to message me back.

As Wynter placed my drink on the side, I asked, "Did you get yourself a sandwich?"

Her cheeks burned. "Thanks, Rex."

I didn't look at her, just typed out:

**Rex:** *I'm sorry I fucked up.*

"You don't have to thank me for food. Thought we agreed on that." I cast her a look and saw her nod.

"I-I'm not hungry yet—"

I arched a disbelieving brow at her.

"No. Really. I had a big lunch." This kid, I swore, I had no idea where she packed it all. "But, later, when it's my break, I'll come and eat with you, okay?"

"Sounds like a plan."

She peeped a smile at me then wandered over to a table in need of serving.

As she left, Rachel finally replied.

**Rachel:** *You didn't fuck up. It was a conversation I knew you wouldn't take well. I steeled myself for it.*

**Rex:** *I shouldn't have taken it out on you.*

**Rachel:** *No, you shouldn't have, but we take these things out on the ones we love, don't we?*

A shocked breath escaped me at her words.

We didn't talk like this.

We never fucking talked like this.

Was this goddamn proof that the calls, even though they'd only been happening for a short while, were working?

Heart pounding and blood rushing in my ears, hope fucking filled me.

Goddamn hope.

I was a murderer. I'd stolen. I'd maimed. I'd broken so many laws I deserved to be locked up—I knew that.

There was no way I should be reacting like a zit-pocked teenager because of her throwaway comment.

But playing it cool with Rachel had never been a possibility.

**Rex:** *We do. Call you later?*

**Rachel:** *Yeah. Around six your time?*

**Rex:** *Fine with me.*

When she didn't reply, I raised the espresso cup to my lips and took a sip of the strong brew. Flipping the cell in my hand, I contemplated my next move.

I rarely acted without forethought. Trying to predict what circumstances would arise from whatever path I took, but in this, it was too difficult to say.

There were so many goddamn variables where Rachel was concerned that this could blow up in my face, and I was tired of that.

I liked the feeling of us moving forward.

Of us stepping toward something better and brighter than before.

The prospect of me fucking that up and taking us back a couple steps was something I didn't think I could bear.

Wynter walked past, her tray full, and I kept my gaze locked on her as I calculated the odds and made the call to Lily.

"Lily Lancaster speaking."

"Hey Lily, it's Rex."

"Rex! Oh, my God! It's so good to hear from you. Do you want Link? I know he's desperate to speak with you."

"Yeah, no. I want to speak with you."

"Me? What? Why?"

Indecisiveness wasn't something that plagued me often. When it did, it was always with Rachel.

Why?

Because Rachel was strong. Powerful. A ball buster.

She defended criminals for fun and got them out on loopholes because she could.

She was take charge and domineering and a shark that everyone in legal circles knew to avoid.

That was the Rachel the world saw.

I knew the side of her that cried when she watched black and white movies from the forties, that ate up reality TV shows like they were going out of production. I'd watched her down more hot chocolate than I'd ever seen her drink wine, but when she did, it was always a glass of rosé she chose. Ice cream was her crack, and hot fudge was her amber nectar. She was nostalgic and caring and a fiercely loyal friend.

Her vulnerabilities were many, and that was why I was lucky—because she let me see them.

The rest of the world weren't so lucky.

They just saw the attorney.

I saw the woman.

Flaws and all.

The two distinctly warring sides of her nature were why I was indecisive.

I never knew which side of her I'd catch on any given day.

"Rex? Are you there?"

"Yeah. Sorry. My mind wandered." I grimaced at just how damn long I'd been sitting there vacillating over a simple fucking decision. Pissed at myself, I drawled, "Rachel tells me you've been helping her out with the gala?"

"I have, yes," she said warily. "Is that a problem?"

"Not at all. I'm grateful. I wish she'd had your help from the start."

Lily's nervousness abated. "My mom used to hold these kinds of events all the time. This is... well, I'm in my element."

"Regardless, I'm grateful that you're helping her." Something occurred to me. "Is she paying you or the club?"

"No, she's paying me."

I hummed. "I'll speak with Maverick and have your salary shifted onto the MC's books."

"Oh! Well, shouldn't you ask Rachel about that first?"

"She knows I pay for her staff."

"Clearly not if she decided to pay me herself," Lily retorted, her unease clear.

"Mistakes happen," was all I said. "Anyway, that isn't why I called you."

"Oh? It isn't?"

"No. I want to buy a ticket to the FAST gala."

Her surprise was revealed by her sharp exhalation. "*You?* You want to go to a gala?"

My lips curved at her shock. "Yeah. I do. But I want to keep it a surprise. Can you help me out?"

"I, well, oh, I mean, yes, I don't see why not."

We discussed the particulars of the ticket purchase for a short while, then she mumbled, "You know it's black tie, don't you?"

"I didn't think I could show up in my cut," I joked, lifting my cup to drain the last few drops of espresso.

She snorted. "Just wanted to make sure you knew what you were signing up for."

"I do. Thanks for this, Lily. And... if you could keep this conversation between me and you, I'd appreciate it."

"You mean don't tell Link?"

"I mean, don't tell the rest of the MC. If, need be, you have to tell him, I'd never do anything to come between you and him."

The sound of a soft breath rushed down the line. "That's very thoughtful of you, Rex."

"I'm capable of it sometimes. But, if it's not urgent, I'd appreciate your discretion."

"I understand."

"Okay, send me the details and I'll make payment later on tonight. Bye, Lily."

I didn't wait for her to reply, just cut the call.

Wynter was there, a fresh espresso on her tray, and as I smiled at her in thanks, I told her, "I'm going to that gala of your..." Shit. Rach wasn't the only one who found the labels hard. "Rachel's."

Triumph leaked into her expression. "You listened to me?"

"You were right. It's important to her and I've never gone."

"That's really shitty of you," she concurred, but she bowed down and pressed a quick, unexpected kiss to my cheek. "Thank you for listening."

As I shot her a sheepish grin when she turned bright red, clearly surprised by the impromptu action, a guy called out, "Wynter! My God! What on earth do you think... He's old enough to be my age!"

Wynter stiffened, but the dread in her eyes was as solid as a brick wall. She turned woodenly to face the man standing in front of my table and whispered, "It's not what you think, Dad."

My brows puckered at her complete about-face, and it made me realize how much she'd opened up to me over the last week.

This was like the first day we'd met—she was cool, standoffish. Awkward, even.

I straightened up and intoned, "Jeremy."

I knew I'd changed since the last time we'd spoken, but he didn't recognize me until he heard my voice.

Time hadn't been kind to him. He'd gained at least fifty pounds, and his face was pudgy and set in the lines of a man who was perennially dissatisfied.

The handsome QB who'd had all the girls drooling was no more.

At my words, Jeremy reared back in surprise, then his features twisted into a sneer. "Are you being serious? What the hell are you doing here, King?"

"I came to visit with Wynter. She's nearly of age, so I thought now would be a good time to introduce myself."

"What? After Ally and I were the ones who made all the sacrifices? You thought you could just waltz in and steal her from us?"

My hands balled into fists at my side. "I'm not stealing her from you."

"Then why the fuck has she left home? Why the fuck did I have to bribe one of her friends to find out where she was working?"

"Dad, you're embarrassing me!" Wynter hissed, her cheeks bright red, her mortification clear.

Jeremy's expression turned bitter, and the glint in his eyes put me on edge. "I'm embarrassing you? I had to bribe Chelsea, Wynter. I'm your goddamn father and you're treating me like I'm a criminal."

Wynter whispered, "You are."

Surprise filtered through me, but Jeremy bit out, "And he isn't?"

One of the managers came out and called her name. Wynter swallowed. "I-I'd like you to go, please, before I get into trouble."

Jeremy's sneer made a reappearance, but before he could get another word out, I leaped forward, grabbed his arm, and dragged him off the terrace.

Turning back to Wynter, I shot her a calm look and told her, "I'll be back later to walk you home."

She gave me a shaky nod, and there was a cocktail of misery, anxiety, and gratitude in her eyes.

I never wanted to see that combination again.

Jeremy made to speak, but my grip on him tightened to the point where he yelped.

"You say another word to embarrass her, Kinnock, I'll break your fucking arm the second we're out of sight."

"You son of a bitch," he rasped, but he kept his voice low.

"That's me."

In this instance, Mom would have been prepared to own that label.

The second we were around the corner, I let go of him but I shoved at him so that he was standing a couple steps away.

"Firstly, I came here after she left home. I found her in a shit heap of a building when I've been paying three grand a month for her maintenance," I snarled. "What have you been doing? Pissing that away down at the mahjong clubs?"

His first attempt at conversation was with his fists.

He thrust them forward and tried to smack me. I grabbed one of his hands, twisted it behind his back and up until he was crying out in pain.

Kicking his legs out from under him, I watched him settle to the floor with a bang that had him yelping from the force of the contact.

With him on his knees, I rumbled, "If you hit me again, I'll start breaking bones. I'm trying to keep this pleasant for Wynter's sake, but don't mistake that for me not being willing to show you what a fucking shit father you've been to the girl I entrusted to you and Ally, you piece of crap.

"What's this I've been hearing about you cheating on Ally? About all the goddamn gambling debts? The cops coming around on domestic violence calls?"

"Like you've never cheated on your women. Maybe you can't even cheat on those whores!"

I kicked my leg out, my foot landing square in his trunk, sending him hurtling to the sidewalk. He didn't have a chance to save himself and he cried out when his face collided with the concrete.

"Watch your fucking words."

"My nose!" he sobbed. "My goddamn nose. You broke it!"

I scoffed. "I don't break my promises, unlike you. What the fuck is with you? Going to the place where she works and embarrassing her in front of the patrons and her bosses?"

"She just left! I was ready to call the cops but Ally told me what had happened." His voice was nasal as he cupped his broken nose. "I-I had to talk to her. She can't just move out the way she did."

"She didn't feel safe—"

"And you, a dirty fucking biker, make her feel *safe* and her own family doesn't?"

"No. I'm telling you I came here after she left home. I have nothing to do with this. You fucked it up yourself." I shot him a disgusted scowl. "If I hear of you threatening her at school or at work when I'm not around, I'll make your life a fucking misery, Kinnock.

"I'm pretty sure I know people who have favors owed to them by the Triads. I have no problem in getting them to call in your debt."

His face blanched.

Because that was the reaction I needed, I retreated and started the short walk back to the coffee shop.

Of course, that was when the dipshit tried to jump me.

Seeing as I'd been prepared for it, his attack didn't come as a surprise. Well, not for me. I grabbed his fist in my hand, twisted it until I heard it pop, then jabbed him in the throat before I spun him around and shoved him face-first into the wall.

Spitting the words into his ear, I growled, "You never did know when to back the fuck down, Kinnock. The only reason I let you adopt Wynter was because of Ally. Because she was a good kid, and she should never have ended up with a fucking moron like you.

"Don't you fucking dare show your face around Wynter until you're ready to speak to her with respect. If you don't, then I'll make you."

As I snarled the words into his ear, I made sure to place pressure on the back of his head. Only when he yowled as his broken nose smashed into the wall did I relinquish my hold on him. Only then did I walk away.

This time, there were no surprise attacks.

*From: Rach3lLadyLiberty@gmail.com*
*To: K1ngS1nn3r1@gmail.com*
*Subject: Thank you*

*Thank you for giving me that heads up. It really helped. I can't believe I got to talk with her. Also, thank you for making her not hate me. I deserve nothing less than her hatred because I let her down, but I know that you paved the way for me.*
*I'll never be able to thank you enough for that.*
*I love you.*
*And I forgive you for being a dick earlier. Messengers always get shot—I knew that. It was why I was dreading telling you.*
*R*


*From: K1ngS1nn3r1@gmail.com*
*To: Rach3lLadyLiberty@gmail.com*
*Subject: Re. Thank you*

*You didn't deserve her hatred. You didn't deserve to be the messenger who got shot.*
*You're not the world's dumping ground.*
*I hurt you. I love you and I hurt you. I'm a schmuck, and thank you for your forgiveness. I'll try to make sure that that never happens again. I let you fucking down.*
*K*


*From: Rach3lLadyLiberty@gmail.com*
*To: K1ngS1nn3r1@gmail.com*

**Subject: Re. Thank you**

*You didn't let me down. Emotions are running high right now. Even you, the King of the Sinners has them.*

*Speak later <3*

## THIRTY-EIGHT

## RACHEL

"Attorney General, thank you for speaking with me on such short notice."

"Never could resist locking horns with you, Rachel," David Foundry crooned, his eyes doing more wandering than a bunch of Girl Scouts trying to sell cookies.

The guy was a grade-A creep but he liked me.

Parts of me, anyway.

I could shower later.

"Well, you'll like locking horns with me today, David. I want to offer you a favor."

"This sounds interesting. Far more interesting than my original four o'clock call." He beamed a smile at me. "I'm glad I canceled that for our meeting. What kind of favor?"

"It depends."

"On?"

"Whatever you need to make something happen."

Rubbing the bridge of his nose, his enthusiasm waning, he grumbled, "Is this about Currau Valentini?"

"Yes."

"I already told you if I wade into this, it'll trigger a shitstorm—"

"I know that you're concerned about it kickstarting old cases, however, this time I'm not asking you to act out of the kindness of your heart." Because everyone in the tristate area knew the slimy bastard didn't have one—but I'd had to try. "I'm asking with something different in mind."

"What?"

"Luciu Valentini will owe you a favor."

I'd burned so many bridges trying to get Currau Valentini out, but whoever had made the moves to get him locked away until the day of his death had made it nigh on impossible for me to free him.

If it weren't such a gargantuan task, I'd be impressed.

"Is it true what they're saying about Valentini?" he mused.

"In what sense? There's always chatter, David. Especially about a man like Luciu."

His look was pointed. "You and I both know what we're talking about, Rachel. The Fieris have faded out and a certain family appears to have overtaken the power vacuum within the *Famiglia*."

I parroted, "Luciu Valentini is a successful nightclub owner—"

"Yes, yes, yes," David groused. "But has he had a... *promotion* in recent weeks?"

"Perhaps." That was about as indelicate as I could be.

David hummed. "Interesting."

Allowing the silence to hang heavy between us, I held his gaze, willing him to accede to my wishes, wanting the damn clock to tick down even more.

Four hours and fifty-five minutes.

That was when I told Rex he could call me.

I released a soft breath that had him looking at my tits.

"I'll think about it."

"When will I have an answer?"

"As soon as I've thought about it," he drawled with a playful smirk. "As always, it's been a pleasure meeting with you. The next time you want to visit, make it earlier and we can do lunch."

"I'll look forward to it," I lied. "Give my love to Mariel."

His nose crinkled at the reminder of, ya know, *his wife*. "She's pregnant again."

I arched a brow. "Congratulations are in order."

"I suppose." He got to his feet from behind an antique partner's desk, his arm outstretched. "Don't be a stranger, Rachel."

There was no fear of that when he was the only one who could help me with Currau's case.

"Never," I vowed, but a smile danced on my lips as we shook hands.

He clung a moment too long, but that smile of mine never wavered. He squeezed my palm with his thumb, a gentle pulsing motion, before it lingered and he finally let go.

Throughout, I maintained his gaze, not commenting on the overly long hold.

"I'll be in touch," was all he said.

"Looking forward to hearing from you, David. Trust me, Luciu is a man you want in your corner."

His eyes narrowed and a soft smirk appeared on his lips.

On red alert because that look told me he already knew what he wanted, I began to back off as he said, "Good to know."

There was no point warning Luc, not when he'd told me he wanted his *prozio*, his great-uncle, free at any cost. Still, I prepared myself for that eventual battle.

Not even when I was outside his office saying farewell to his receptionist did I let my relief at being out of there show.

I had no problem dealing with the big guns, but David could get handsy, and my tolerance levels were low. If he'd gotten handsy while I needed a favor from him, that could have been awkward.

"How did it go?" Parker asked me the second our call connected.

"He didn't try to feel me up this time," I grumbled as I finally took a seat in my car, and Emile set off.

She snickered. "I'm sure he's into FemDom. The way he likes it if you slap him down when he gets too touchy-feely."

"If he is, we should know about it. Get one of the Sinners onto it."

"Will do. Nothing like that today?"

"No. He's probably reeling from the last time I slapped his hand." That had been part of the reason I'd waited a tad too long to play this card. "Still, he'll bite."

"He will?"

"He will."

"So sure?"

"He already knows what he wants from Luciu."

"Interesting."

My gaze turned inward, away from the Manhattan traffic ahead of me. "Very."

"It works to our benefit that he's corrupt, but I live in hope that one day, you won't deal with an elected official who'd sell his grandmother for another connection."

"And pigs might fly," I scoffed. "Anyway, I wasted enough time on Foundry. I need to get on. Has the situation with Whitlock changed?"

"No, but I emailed you a brief—"

We spent the rest of my journey home adjusting that before I let her go for the rest of the day because I knew I'd be wasting more time than I could afford thinking about tonight's call with Rex.

When I got home, I dismissed Emile for the day as well. I had no intention of going out again, and sure as hell not to the city.

Unfortunately for me, the moment I changed into a less formal suit and went downstairs to my office, Lily bustled in with a bunch of paperwork to sign for the FAST gala.

I didn't even hear her enter the office. But her hand went to my shoulder and I reacted like she'd prodded me with a hot poker.

We both shrieked as I jolted in my seat, rolling back in my chair with enough force that I collided into the wall behind me. Lily jumped—literally jumped—a good couple of inches off the floor.

If I wasn't so taken aback, I'd have laughed.

"I'm so sorry!" I gasped. "I didn't mean to startle you."

"Neither did I," Lily muttered wryly. She reached up and cupped her throat. "I'm sorry, Rachel. I didn't mean to startle you either. I was just concerned. Is everything all right?"

"It's been a hell of a day."

"Do you want to talk about it?"

Her offer appeared genuine, but I didn't want to discuss any of this with anyone.

Genuine or not.

"Thank you for offering, but it's all right. Can I help with something?"

From her perusal, I knew she wasn't going to push it.

Thank God.

I could also tell that she wanted to.

"I have these to sign, but Link told me the architect sent over plans for the motel's redevelopment. He wanted me to tell you that Maverick says the architect's wrong—"

I rolled my eyes. "Of course he did. What does he want? To fire the guy?"

She nodded.

"Why does he need me for that?"

"Apparently, he's already fired the guy but the architect wants to keep the retainer. Maverick's arguing that the architect hasn't done his job."

Reaching up to rub my temple, I mumbled, "Let me see the plans."

This was the last thing I wanted to be doing, but Rex was right—I did prioritize work.

Not because I was a slave to the industrial machine, and not because I was addicted to the rat race, but because I was damn good at it.

"Rachel? Are you okay?" she asked warily as I prodded a key so hard that my keyboard went flying.

My lips pursed. "Not particularly but I'm not about to let that hold me back."

Lily blinked. "I know how that feels."

I didn't know her, but that didn't mean I didn't know her story. Knew that her father had abused her for years. Knew that she'd been hurt day after day, week after week. For years and years and years.

Goddamn hormones had me wanting to cry.

Suddenly, my mind was in a whirlpool.

Down.

Down.

Down, I went.

It ping-ponged from the various clusterfucks of the day, each one settling on my chest like a lead weight.

Was it getting harder to breathe?

*It was!*

"Can I get you some water?"

I shook my head then jerked in surprise when she crouched down beside me and placed her hand on the one I'd flopped on my lap. "Rachel, would you follow my breath for a moment?"

As my brow puckered, she made a show of inhaling to a count of two, then exhaling to a count of four. I didn't pull back because my lungs *were* burning, and I followed her as she upped the count to a factor of two several times over the next five minutes.

My eyes burned from the contact, but she never let go, and there was never anything but kindness in hers as we stared at one another.

"There," she said softly. "How do you feel?"

"Better." I swallowed. "I'm sorry for that. You shouldn't have to see that."

She tipped her head to the side. "Why not? You did nothing wrong," she pointed out. "Just had an anxiety attack. Do they happen often?"

"They used to," I admitted quietly, because Lily was calm. Kind. Non-threatening. She felt *safe*. "But not for a long time. Bear's death,

Rex's leaving..." My mouth wobbled. "It's affected me more than I'd like. More than I have time for, in all honesty."

Her nose crinkled. "Emotions don't care about schedules and routines."

"That's true," I said with a grimace as I reached up and rubbed my brow. Desperately needing to change the subject, I asked, "Any news on the gala?"

As a Lindenbourg, her name had a lot of clout. Somehow, the event at the Victoria had gone from the so-called 'Princess hall' to the main ballroom—'the Queen's suite.' That had nothing to do with me and everything, I assumed, to do with my new liaison.

"It's all in hand," she assured me. "Do you speak with anyone, Rachel?"

My brow furrowed, discomfort at the question filling me.

"I know that's a very private thing to discuss, but you..." She winced. "You didn't look so good for a second there."

I had to assume that was her being kind.

After the day I'd had, I probably looked like shit. It was no wonder she was asking when she was used to seeing me dressed to impress and not like a bag of laundry.

"I used to see a shrink, but I stopped that years ago."

"Why?"

"Because..." My mouth twisted as I thought about how to answer that without sounding like a lunatic.

Some days, I sure as hell felt like one.

After nights with no sleep and nightmares that were on a loop.

After days of craving Rex only to see his face and be flashed back to those moments when his bastard uncle was writhing on top of me, his body entering mine as Dog held me down, pinching my nose—

A choking sound escaped me, and then Lily was there again. Her hand was on mine, squeezing gently, taking us back to the breathing exercise.

I'd done a million breathing exercises in my time, but it was the way her pretty eyes looked into mine that helped calm me.

*Someone who understood what it was like to have your choices taken from you.*

Who understood the trauma of not being able to escape a memory.

When I'd calmed down, I choked out, "I was suicidal for a long time at the end of my teen years. I had a shrink then. I was always scared they'd hospitalize me again."

Her eyes flickered at the 'again,' but before I could feel any shame, she rasped, "Maybe you should talk with Tiffany? She almost graduated in her field, and while that's not... I know you can afford the best psychiatrists in New York, but if you don't trust them to—" She swallowed. "Tiff helps me. She really does."

I stared into those kind eyes and asked, "Is that why you let her mother live there?"

Her smile was sheepish. "To a certain extent. I've known her all my life, and she really was like a second mother to me. It's only since Richard died that she's turned into such a bitch. If the situation were reversed, I know Tiff would care for my mom."

Her mom who'd been murdered by her dad.

God.

"I haven't been this out of control for years," I admitted.

A part of me knew the pregnancy was the reason for it—excess hormones and I didn't go well together—but I didn't want to tell her that.

I hadn't told anyone in our inner circle.

Giulia had figured it out then told Nyx, who'd informed the goddamn council, but I hadn't said it out loud to anyone close to us.

That was for Rex.

I wouldn't let him down again, and I'd tell him soon. When things were better between us. When...

I didn't know when, but I would.

He'd undoubtedly get pissed at me over delaying, but that was next week's problem. I had enough to handle *this* week.

"Grief shakes everything up," Lily agreed. "It helped that I didn't care about my father at all. I was glad he was dead, glad to take a part in that. Otherwise that would have been very hard to cope with."

Nodding, I said, "Makes sense."

"It also helped that I had Link," Lily said softly. "He never rushed me. Not even after he branded me." She turned her wrist face up and I looked at the geometric lines of her fox tattoo.

"You mean..."

She nodded. "We didn't have penetrative sex for months. He never pushed me. We always went at my pace. It made everything easier, you know? He accepted me for who I am and loved me regardless."

I knew my eyes were massive as I looked at her. "Link—"

Her grin was sheepish but she knew where I was coming from. "I know he was a manwhore."

Understatement.

I didn't say that, just reasoned, "I knew he loved you, but that's definitely unexpected."

"I like to think that that's Link. Always illuminating."

Her smile was multifaceted. It spoke of her love for him, his for her. It spoke of the feelings he imbued in her. But more than anything, it spoke of how lucky she felt.

I was glad for her.

She deserved a man like Link who cared for her the way he did.

I tightened my fingers around hers. "I'm sorry that you had to deal with this. I'm being ridiculous."

She shook her head. "Whatever happened to you, Rachel, you don't have to be sorry for it."

Something flickered in her gaze, and while her tone wasn't hesitant, there was something about it that reminded me of when I was questioning a witness on the stand and was trying to get them to admit to things they wanted to hide from the jury.

Preferring to call her bluff, I asked, "What is it?"

"We didn't ask for these things to happen to us. They were done to us. I know that sounds obvious but sometimes, it's easy to forget and it's easy for that truth to blur."

Throat thick with emotions, I nodded. "I-If it happened and you could erase it, that would be one thing. But it never goes, does it? It's not just something that happened; it's something that *happens*. It keeps happening over and over—"

As I paused to suck in a sharp breath, she nodded. "Would you... tomorrow..."

When she broke off, I swiped a hand over my cheeks, unsurprised to find them drenched, and asked, "What about tomorrow?"

"Thursdays, Tiff has this little group meeting at my house. Would you like to come?"

"What kind of meeting?"

"Indy, me, Amara, Alessa, and Giulia... Stone too if she's not on shift. We all get together and talk."

"About what you've been through?"

"Sometimes it's that. Sometimes it's just, you know, us hanging out. It'd be really great if you could come. Talking about it with someone is better than bottling it up and not expressing it."

I knew she was right.

Worrying my lip with my teeth, I whispered, "What time and can I have your address again?"

## THIRTY-NINE

## RACHEL

Once Lily left, the countdown to nine sped by. There was always so much to do and this evening was no different.

When Rex rang me at nine on the dot, I'd barely had the chance to shower before my phone buzzed with his incoming call.

Exhausted from the day's maneuverings, I found myself relieved that he was trying to be conciliatory. His tone confirmed that he was truly sorry for blaming the messenger and, in all honesty, I couldn't lay any guilt at his door.

When I'd read through Bear's will, I'd been equally as devastated and he wasn't even my dad!

Mostly Rex was pissed about Wynter's adoptive father showing up and causing a scene at her place of work.

As he continued to rage about Jeremy Kinnock's behavior that afternoon, I murmured, "I hope you didn't resolve the situation with your fists?"

His lack of a reply was statement enough.

"Goddammit, Rex," I grated out. "What the hell kind of example is that going to show Wynter?"

"He started it."

"What are you? Six?"

"He attacked me. Twice."

"What are his injuries?"

"Broken nose and fist." He cleared his throat. "Bruising."

"Did anyone see?"

"Don't think so."

My mouth tightened. "I really don't feel like flying over there and sorting things out for you, Rex. It's busy enough over here without you adding to my workload."

He was damn fortunate I could even do that.

After college, after *everything,* in the early days, I'd passed my bar in California first. Then, later, when I'd been able to bear returning to New Jersey, I'd passed it there as well.

Next had come New York.

Aurora and I used to have a personal competition running over how many bar certificates we could collect before we retired.

Sadly, she was winning.

He huffed. "You should come over anyway. Wynter would love to meet you."

Anxiety stirred in the form of a battalion of butterflies that came to life in my stomach. "She would?"

"Yeah. You should have heard her talking about you after the call. She was excited."

"She was? I felt like such a fool," I half-whined.

"I could tell you were anxious as hell, but she didn't know. How could she?"

"I'd have preferred our first conversation not to have taken place while I was sweating like a pig and my blood pressure was close to giving me a stroke."

Rex snorted. "Drama queen."

Rather than be pissed, my lips twitched. "Better than ice queen?"

"Only sometimes." His chuckle was low. Low enough that it did crazy things to my insides. "Rach?"

"Yes?"

"I really am sorry about today."

"I know you are," I told him, my tone as earnest as his, because I needed him to know that I empathized. "And you don't have to apologize again."

Silent for a couple moments, he eventually said, "It's just not... When I think of him, I know the shit he did wrong, but I know he was a good leader, a great dad, and a—"

"He was still a decent husband, Rex," I tried to soothe. "Your mom wouldn't have taken him back if she hadn't forgiven him."

"What if he never told her?"

"I don't think that's likely."

"Why not?"

"Well... the timing."

Having looked Kendra up, I knew her birthday correlated with the time when Rene and Bear had almost separated.

I said 'almost' because it hadn't exactly been that cut and dry.

Rene had miscarried a child and, afterward, had withdrawn from the world.

Her depression had been so intense that, to this day, I could remember how she'd wandered around the compound as if she were in a daze.

"I think you should have faith in the man you knew. He wasn't perfect and never claimed to be. I'm sure Bear, more than anyone, would—"

"How did he let Kendra do it?"

"Do what?"

"Whore herself out," he seethed.

"There's a letter to you about it," I said uncomfortably. "I just know what the will says."

"Did he leave any bequests to Kendra?"

"No. Only her mother."

"That's unusual."

"Maybe he didn't like her?"

"What's to like?" he questioned snidely. "Would you mind reading me the letter?"

"Rex?"

"Yeah?"

"I really would prefer not to." Aware that my voice was small, I wondered if he heard how much he'd hurt me today even if I was fine with forgiving him.

He swallowed. "Sure, Rach. Sure. I'm sorry I asked."

"You don't have to be, I'm just... It's been one of those raw days, you know?"

"I do. Same here. Lots of unexpected shit going down, I get it."

Licking my lips as he spoke, I mumbled, "I-I would like to tell you something."

"What?" he queried warily. "About my dad?"

"No. About me."

"Oh. Oh!"

There was relief and concern in those two ululations.

Ignoring both, I muttered, "Lily suggested that I speak with Tiffany about my—" I heaved a sigh as I got stuck on the words.

He helped me. Like usual. "Nightmares?"

"Yes."

The words 'as well as everything else' went unspoken.

The anxiety, the attacks, the exhaustion, the workaholism, the inability to create connections...

Tiredly, I rubbed my eyes before I looked out onto the garden.

For the first time in a long while, it was nine o'clock and I wasn't in my office. I'd taken the time to shower and change and though I couldn't enjoy a nice Pinot Noir rosé, I could partake in a hot chocolate. I had the patio heater on, a blanket tucked around my legs, and one around my shoulders.

I knew I was crazy for sitting outside but I couldn't stand being cooped up after a day of being stuck in the car and in meetings.

"You okay, sweetheart?"

I loved it when he called me that. Not as much as 'my girl' but almost. Any endearments were a blessing I'd run from, but with the baby in my belly, I was having to accept that all roads led me back to Rex.

I'd been running for so damn long, but here I was, in the same position as I'd been in back when I was on the cusp of turning nineteen.

Releasing a shaky breath, I opened my mouth to start, but I jolted when the door opened.

Blinking back my surprise, I commented, "Harlow, is everything okay?"

His hands were balled into fists, and he jerked like he hadn't anticipated my voice.

When he twisted around to look at me, I saw the raging pain etched into his expression and sensed his hurt.

But when I made to speak, he backed off, heading outside in a swift jog.

He didn't have a bike yet, irony of ironies, so I assumed he'd run either to the town itself or to the clubhouse.

I wasn't about to stop him.

As the gravel on the driveway crunched beneath his feet, Rex demanded, "Harlow's there?"

"He was. He took off," I said pensively. "I think the hazing is bad at the compound. He was staying there, but I've let him bed down here for a couple days."

"Why?"

"Rain found him camping out in the backyard." I didn't tack on the word *again*.

"Camping?"

"Uh huh. On subzero nights. I couldn't let him stay outside."

"No, no. Thanks, Rach."

"No worries. I didn't do it for you," I retorted dryly.

His laughter was gruff. "Guess you didn't."

"He's a Prospect."

"I heard from Maverick."

"A Prospect without a hog," I teased. "A first time for everything."

"He doesn't have a ride?" He grunted. "Jesus. This is a disaster just waiting to happen."

I thought about Harlow's expression for the scant second when he'd looked right at me, and I murmured, "I think it would have been more of a disaster if you didn't give him that option."

Rex seemed to contemplate that. "Ticking time bomb?"

"Yeah. At least with Nyx around, maybe he'll feel like he's got someone on his side?"

"Maybe. Anyway, it felt like you were going to say something important before he interrupted."

I could tell he was irate about that, and amusement had my lips twisting but it soon died.

Where did I start? How did I end? What could I possibly—

It came to me.

Our deal.

"Ask me a question, Rex."

More silence.

"Any question?"

"Yes."

My hands shook as I reached for my hot chocolate. The heat from the mug seeped into my fingers, but it didn't offset the ice that felt as if it were taking over my being.

"Is the reason we can't be together because I look like Grizzly?"

God, of all the things I'd thought he'd ask, that wasn't one of them.

"You know about Grizzly?" I half-squeaked.

Had Maverick told him about the church meeting when I confessed to the council everything that had happened to me?

"Before... when I left... you spoke in your dreams. In all these years, it's the first time you've ever said his name. I realized he was..." His voice broke off. "I realized he was the one who'd raped you."

Rex was one of the smartest men I knew, which was saying something because I worked with a bunch of criminal goddamn masterminds who regularly brought the NYPD to its knees.

I knew he *knew* what had happened to me, but that didn't mean everything about this conversation wasn't going to come as a shock.

"Dog did as well," I told him softly.

A sharp breath escaped him, but the silence made another reappearance, and it was goddamn deafening.

"Do you know how they died?"

"I know Lodestar handled Dog."

"I think you were in Cali when Sin beat Grizzly to death."

I blinked. "I didn't know that was how he died."

"I'd have turned them into Cruz soup while they were still alive if I had my way."

My stomach turned.

"Did you know he has this solution and you can put meat into it, any meat, and it evaporates? Just disintegrates into nothing. It's a new solution. The other used to turn bodies into a kind of mulch. We fed it to the pigs at a local farm. Remember Lever?"

This conversation had not gone where I'd anticipated.

"Barely."

"His dad runs it."

"Oh."

I heard the distinct sound of knuckles being cracked. "Still wouldn't be enough. Them watching themselves die. Feeling the acid eat into their flesh and bone." His tone was musing, conversational.

Had I expected more?

Had I imagined he'd be like Nyx?

It was only then that I realized how much I'd appreciated Nyx's response.

His violence.

But Rex wasn't Nyx.

Rex could be violent, but he was cerebral too.

It was one of the reasons why we worked so well together.

Why we *could* work together, I guessed was more appropriate.

"I look like him, Rach. That's why you always freak the fuck out when I'm there, isn't it? And you wake up? After a nightmare?"

My eyes clenched close. I wished I could say otherwise, but while he wasn't wholly right, neither was he totally wrong. In this instance, neither was great.

"Yes," I whispered miserably.

He let loose a sharp breath at my confirmation.

"It's not as facile as that, though. My rational mind knows you didn't do it."

"But you're *not* rational seconds after you've just woken up from a nightmare where you've been raped again."

I sucked my cheek into my mouth and bit down. Hard. "No, I'm not."

"I always hated Grizzly. I didn't realize he was a rapist though. Dad always let him get away with shit and he shouldn't have. He was nothing special as a councilor."

Still with that same, musing, watchful tone.

This was starting to feel odd again.

Was he angry or upset?

"You saw me without a beard or stubble the other day, Rach."

"Yeah. I did."

The pause was loaded, heavy. With what, I didn't know, until he ground out, "Did I look like Grizzly then?"

My throat suddenly felt tight. Thick. Hope, hot and heavy, settled in my heart. "No."

He released a breath. "You've never slept with anyone..." A hiss sounded down the line. "I know something happened at college. I... I'm not... did—"

For the first time in his life, Rex was clearly lost for words.

Helping him out because it was too painful not to, I muttered, "I never slept with anyone by choice."

"God help me," he breathed. "Do you know how much I fucking love you? Do you know what the fuck I'd do to keep you safe? And I didn't. It wasn't enough. My own goddamn blood hurt you, and then that bastard—"

Though I heard his pain, felt it now, *finally*, his words rammed their way home.

I'd misunderstood.

He hadn't been asking if I'd had consensual sex with anyone.

He'd been saying that he knew I'd been attacked in college.

My throat closed again, but before I could choke, he rasped, "The second Gunner got in touch with me and told me what had happened, I nearly fucking killed myself riding over to your apartment."

Gunner had been there?

Watching over me?

I thought about Hunter, covered in blood. I thought about Aurora, screaming. My mind turned blank. *Black.*

Dizziness hit me.

He'd known all along?

I'd imagined he'd picked together the pieces, but not the outright facts.

"What did you do?" I whispered.

"Got rid of the body."

His voice was flat again.

"I was too late to protect you though. I'm always too fucking late."

"Rex?"

"What, sweetheart?"

"I-I think I'm going to be sick."

I heard him yelp my name but I threw my cell down onto the chair and darted inside. Almost skidding as I made it to the bathroom, my knees ached as they collided with the tiled floor.

Heaving, I puked up what I'd eaten, and that was when I felt some hands in my hair and a soft humming noise.

I smelled a fruity perfume and a bump nudged me in the back.

"It's okay," Giulia said softly, her fingers still in my hair as she held it away from my face. "It's okay, Rachel. Get it out."

My stomach ached from the purge, and I twisted to look at her, eyes wet as I demanded, "What are you doing in here?"

"Rex called Nyx. He wanted me to check on you."

My bottom lip wobbled. "He knew."

"About the baby?"

I shook my head. "He knew about the guy who hurt me in college."

"Does that come as that much of a surprise?" she asked kindly. "Isn't Rex like the MC's God? Sees all, hears all, knows all?" Her words were too much like Hunter's mockery from weeks before. *Goddamn men knowing everything but not reacting how I thought they'd react.* Giulia, unaware of my thoughts, pursed her lips. "Well, apart from where the Sparrows are concerned. His omnipotence is on the fritz with them."

I stared blearily at her.

"Sorry," she mumbled. "Didn't mean to get philosophical on you. Are you okay?"

"H-He said he got rid of the body."

"Isn't that what they do? Clean up after us?"

"I didn't kill him," I whispered.

"Who did?"

"One of my best friends."

"So, he was protecting him?"

"I-I guess."

"And was there a police investigation?"

"N-No. It was more of a missing persons case."

The parallel between the murder of Aurora's husband and David, Indy's receptionist, was uncannily similar.

Uneasily, I tilted my head down again, aware that the urge to puke hadn't abated.

"Never spent as much time in a bathroom with another woman before," Giulia mused. "Gotta say, I wish we chose one of your living rooms. It'd be a lot more comfortable than this."

I spat out the last remainder of vomit in my mouth. "You can go, Giulia. I'm okay."

"Nah, if you looked at yourself in the mirror, you'd realize what utter bullshit that is." She sniffed. "Anyway, you're coming to our meeting tomorrow, aren't you?"

"I'm supposed to."

"You *should* come. You're as fucked up as we are," Giulia said cheerfully. "Might do you some good. You might stop being so repressed."

"I'm not repressed."

Giulia snickered. "Yeah, okay, you tell yourself that. If you're not *re*pressed, then you're *de*pressed. Either way, for a shrink who ain't a shrink yet, Tiff's pretty good at getting us all to open up and talk about shit nobody wants to say out loud."

Resting my arms on the toilet seat, I pressed my head to my bicep and whispered, "I don't know if I belong there."

"Why not?"

"Lily, Alessa, Amara, and Indy... God, they've been through so much."

"And you haven't?"

"Not like them."

"There a limit on trauma and grief?" She arched a brow, but her bottom lip wobbled before she contained it to say, "By that logic, I shouldn't be there either. Luke Lancaster only shoved a finger in me. Does that mean I wasn't assaulted?"

"N-No. Of course not."

"So, if you think I deserve to be there, why wouldn't you deserve to be there too?"

Her logic was sound. I'd have thrown that reasoning at her too. But I was different, wasn't I?

When I licked my lips, the taste of vomit had my nose crinkling. With a grunt, Giulia clambered up into a standing position after I helped support her, guilt hitting me when I realized I'd made the heavily pregnant woman kneel on the floor.

She peered in the vanity cabinet and passed me a bottle of mouthwash. "Here."

"Thank you."

"My pleasure. You're going to come tomorrow, aren't you? No more 'supposed to?'"

After I swigged some of the mouthwash around my teeth and spat it into the bowl, feeling the disgusting taste disperse as I did so, I closed the toilet lid and flushed it.

"I'll be there if you think I'll fit in."

She snorted. "Unfortunately for our guys, they've all picked women who've been fucked over by men. Really, they're lucky that we don't go to bed at night with knives and when they touch us, we don't threaten their dicks."

"Amara does."

Giulia frowned. "She'd better not lop off my brother's dick. Well, unless he deserves it."

I almost laughed. "What would make him almost deserve it?"

"Dunno yet. I don't know if Nyx's dick could even be cut off. It's half metal after all."

My lips twisted. "He's family, Giulia."

"Everyone knows he has a cyborg dick," she dismissed.

"You're right, you know?"

"I usually am," she said with a chuckle.

"No, I mean, about the Old Ladies. They're all victims."

"In one way or another," she agreed. "Stone wasn't fucked over by a man, but she nearly lost her life to someone. Tiffany didn't, thank God, but she got kidnapped." Giulia grimaced. "Honestly, it's a wonder we're all not locked up in an asylum, rocking back and forth in our straitjackets."

"Trust me, been there, done that, bought the T-shirt."

Her eyes widened. "You were institutionalized?"

I turned my gaze away. "I was. I didn't... I mean, the straitjacket thing didn't happen, but I was in a hospital."

"Why?"

"A-After... my best friend, Hunter, he killed—"

"Your rapist," Giulia supplied helpfully.

Well, I figured she assumed she was being helpful.

Mostly, I just felt like I'd been sucker punched.

I didn't talk about this stuff. Not even to Rory. I'd discussed it with Scott and Craig, but that had been a lifetime ago.

"Yes. Him. I-I lost it."

"Why?"

My mouth wobbled. "He said that he loved my curves and my belly."

Giulia's nose crinkled. "That's disgusting. He raped you because you were pregnant? Eww. I'm glad he's dead. That's just gross. You don't covet another dude's baby momma. That's wrong on so many levels."

I swallowed. "Y-Yes. It is." Feeling nauseated again, I whispered, "Every day I got bigger, every day it was like my own body was a threat. I-I stopped eating..."

"You're lucky your kid wasn't premature."

"She nearly was. But Rex got me... He put me in the hospital before that could happen."

"No one at the MC knew?"

"No. I worked that summer and was in the hospital for Christmas."

Giulia studied me. "Rex ain't never said a word of this to anyone, has he?"

"I doubt it. He's a very private man. We both are."

"What? Private men?" Giulia tapped my arm with a smirk. "You definitely belong in our Posse, Rach."

"Posse?" I frowned. "What?"

"Posse. It's my gang of Old Ladies."

"I'm not an Old Lady."

She smirked at me. "You will be. Second he finds out you're baking another bun in that oven, you'll be branded. Mark my words. That's when you'll get the official invite to the Posse."

She said that like it was a royal decree.

Rolling my eyes, I grumbled, "I don't know if I want to be his Old Lady—not for that reason."

Giulia's snort was both kind and dismissive. Which was a lot to pack into a snort, but it helped that her eyes were gentle, and her hand on my arm was affectionate. "You've been pining away for him for years."

"How do you know that?" I demanded crossly. "I've got a very successful—"

"Yada, yada, yada," Giulia interrupted before I could finish. "What you have is no life. You work all hours God sends, you don't do anything aside from sit at your desk and help criminals escape justice—which I'm not complaining about, mind you.

"You don't even eat that much, and I think you used to drink because that's a pretty hefty wine collection, but you can't do that now you're preggers." She sniffed. "Now, I'm a full believer that a woman don't need a man if she don't want one. But you do. You've been wanting this one for years. It's clear to anyone with eyes when you look at him."

"That's not true."

"You should look in the mirror when he's around. Trust me. This whole ice block chic thing you got going on starts to melt when he's there."

"No, that's—"

"The truth," she said firmly. "And Rachel, you know what? That's okay. Love makes the fucking world go around. The cynic in me wants to say it's money and pasta, but nah, love is what puts fire in your belly. It's what makes getting out of bed worthwhile. When you got *the* man at your side, why wouldn't you want to see what life has to throw at you?"

My mouth wobbled again. "I'm weak."

"Nah," she scoffed. "You're hella strong. Rach, I cried. You saw me cry. I don't do tears. If a baby can do that to me, why shouldn't it fuck with *you*? Not even hard as stone bitches can escape estrogen."

It wasn't even just that.

It was what being pregnant meant. It was how Bear had died. It was knowing that Rex was building a relationship with our daughter while I was hiding away in New Jersey.

So many things had gone wrong over the years, and it was like it was all coming to a head at the same time.

Sucking in a breath, I rasped, "He figured out today why I can't sleep with him."

"Sleep as in sleep or fuck?"

"Sleep."

She tipped her head to the side. "What reason's that?"

I stared at her, the daughter of one of my rapists, and I wondered if she could handle the truth. The full truth.

"One of my attackers was his uncle. He looks like him."

Giulia hissed. "Jesus, that fucking sucks." Her brow puckered. "Can't he, I dunno, dye his hair green or something?"

How the hell she made me laugh at that moment, I didn't have a clue.

But it escaped me, bubbling past my lips as if I didn't have any control over it. I slapped a hand over my mouth to contain it, but though she'd smirked at me at first, I saw the concern in her eyes.

"M-Maybe I'll suggest that to him."

"Do. I'd like to see him with green hair." She angled her head to the side. "You said attackers. You mean… on that night?"

"No. The guy who was killed was another night."

"You've been attacked twice? Honey, what the hell is going on with your head that you don't think you deserve help?" Unable to look at her, I just stared down at my arm. She sighed. "Who was the other attacker?"

I swallowed. "Your dad."

# FORTY

## GIULIA

For a second, I just blinked at her.
I just fucking blinked.
Dog.
So called because he was a hound around women.
My sperm donor.
I knew he was a bastard. Had watched him beat my mom, but Lizzie Fontaine always fought back. Punch for punch.
Domestic violence was one shitty thing.
Rape was another.
I stared at her, saw the guilt in her eyes and the shame, and it lit something up inside of me.
Why was it always the survivor who felt bad?
Who had to justify what had happened to them?
Who had to deal with the shame and the misery?
*It* didn't just happen once.
It happened every fucking night in our dreams.
It was why Nyx couldn't move too quickly behind me because if he did, my stupid goddamn mind remembered being back at *Daytona*

and Luke fucking Lancaster coming up behind me and grabbing a hold of me.

It was why tomorrow, we'd sit in a group and we'd discuss the miseries that our attackers had caused us because it *wasn't* just a *one*-time occurrence.

It was raped *into* us.

Into our veins and arteries

The seams of our muscles.

Our very fucking bones.

It was a veil that was torn from us; the reality that our choice didn't matter.

That it could be stolen from us.

I couldn't catch my breath. All I could think was that I shared DNA with that monster, and that was when he rasped, "Giulia."

Low.

Deep.

Husky.

It shivered through me.

I was his.

He was mine.

Sometimes, I thought he was my sanity.

I turned my head to look at him, and our eyes tangled. I inhaled. Exhaled.

"Did you hear?"

Slowly, Nyx nodded. "I did."

"I want his body out of the Sinners' graveyard," I intoned grimly.

Because he was my man, because he was who he was, he granted me a simple, "It'll be done."

That wasn't enough.

"When?"

"You don't have to do that. There are laws to exhumation," Rachel attempted to interrupt.

Eyes flashing, I stared her down, demanding, "You want him sharing space with your family? I know I fucking don't."

She gnawed on her lip. "I shouldn't have said anything."

"You damn well should have. You're going to be Posse. That comes with hard truths."

"Rachel's going to be Posse?" Nyx snorted. "Jesus H. Christ."

I squinted at him. "Do I tell you who to add to your council?"

His lips curved. "No."

"Did you listen when I said you should make room for Cruz?"

"It's not like I can make up goddamn positions for him," he argued.

I hitched a shoulder. "Dude can make bodies disappear like he's making coffee. That's the kind of guy you want at church." I sniffed. "If you're too shortsighted to see that, then it's not on me."

He rolled his eyes. "Let me know if he becomes Posse too, and we'll reconvene on the subject, but for now, we should get you to bed."

"Do I look tired?"

"No. You look fucking beautiful, all riled up and snarky." His grin was lopsided. "But you need to sleep."

"Your spawn is a pain in my ass."

"I know, baby." He stepped into the small bathroom and cozied up to me. "But he'll make it up to you."

"When?"

"You want specifics?"

"'Course I fucking do."

His grin deepened. "Maybe he'll cure cancer."

"That doesn't help me now, does it? When my back's goddamn aching and I want to go and dig up my sperm donor's body from his fucking grave—"

"Giulia! You can't do that!"

My gaze found Rach's again. "Cruz will get rid of him."

She swallowed. "You should leave him where he is. It won't serve any purpose."

"Won't serve any fucking purpose? The bastard's a rapist. Grizzly's a fucking rapist." I turned to Nyx. "Neither of them should be in that graveyard."

"I said I'll handle it."

"You'd better, Nyx, or I will," I snapped.

I tried not to be pissed when I felt his cock stir against my hip.

One of the reasons we worked was because his fire didn't scare me and my fire turned him on and didn't burn him.

"I know you will. I promise—I'll sort it out."

I gritted my teeth. "Good."

My throat felt choked with emotions, and I wasn't used to that. These goddamn hormones were going to be the death of me.

I felt the tremors running down my limbs as the purest, bitterest rage coursed through me.

I was so fucking sick of *us* being the victims.

So goddamn sick of it.

Shakily, I reached up and rubbed my temple.

"Sit down, Giulia," Rachel ordered, grabbing my hand, prompting me to realize that she'd moved.

I plunked my ass down on the toilet seat, but before she could let go of me, I held on tight to her fingers and whispered, "I'm so sorry, Rachel. I'm so sorry for what he did to you."

Her smile was soft, but the pain in her eyes was something I'd live with until the day I died. "It wasn't your fault, Giulia. You have nothing to apologize for."

Nyx cleared his throat. "Rachel, are you okay? Do you think you should go and get some rest?"

Nodding, she mumbled, "It's been a crazy day." She released a soft yawn that seemed to surprise her. "I think I will."

Like a wraith, she drifted away after muttering a 'good night' to us both. I watched her go, then my gaze redirected to Nyx who squatted down in front of me.

Wearing nothing more than a pair of jeans, he'd always have snagged my complete attention, but at that moment, I didn't notice the pecs or the thick length that ran down his inner thigh. I didn't see the ink on his throat, or the biceps that could lug me around as if I weighed nothing.

I saw only his eyes.

I saw the pain I knew was mirrored in mine because *this* was love.

Feeling their pain as if it were your own.

"I feel sick," I whispered. "H-He hurt her, and he got away with it."

"He paid for his shitty treatment of women with his life, Giulia. Lodestar killed him—"

"It's not enough," I said simply.

"What would be?"

"I don't know." I gulped. "Is this how you feel? Like someone set a firework off and it's exploding through your veins?"

That had him blinking. "I wouldn't put it like that but yeah. Like your skin's too tight and you can't sit still, all while your mind's racing."

I grasped his hand. "When you killed Kevin, was it enough?"

He stilled, his entire body freezing in place. For a moment, I thought he wasn't going to answer, then he murmured, "No."

My fingers tightened around his. "That's why you went hunting, right? Because it's never enough?"

Swallowing, he granted me a slow nod.

"So there's no escaping this feeling?" I whispered miserably.

"No. Just... you delay it."

"How can we ever find peace, Nyx?"

He sucked in a breath. "I wish I knew, baby. I wish I knew."

**From: K1ngS1nn3r1@gmail.com**
**To: Rach3lLadyLiberty@gmail.com**
**Subject: Love you**

I know you've seen my texts and aren't answering, so I figure things are crazy over there.

I'm so sorry, baby. So fucking sorry.

I love you. More than my life. I would fucking kill to take this from you, but I can't. Instead, the only thing I've ever been able to do is to be there. Even when you didn't want me.

I didn't run from you when I went to LA. I need you to know that.

I dealt with business, and then, when I was getting gas, something happened and it made me realize I had shit I needed to do on the other side of the country.

I needed a break—that's no lie. I needed to get away.

From everything.

From life.

But *not* you.

I've done some stuff over the years, but I never imagined having to do what I did... That broke me. After... the shattered pieces of my fucking soul were just incapable of holding up under what went down.

I will always be your shelter in a storm.

Get some rest, baby, knowing that I love you.

K

## FORTY-ONE

## RACHEL
### GIRL - DESTINY'S CHILD

Rex texted a few times before I fell asleep, but I didn't have the energy to handle that, not after Giulia went nuclear.

Not at me, but in general.

She and Nyx were exhausting. They seemed to consume all the oxygen in a given space, and that bathroom was far too small for the three of us.

When her eyes lit up like they were on fire, and her hair looked as if it were standing on edge, I knew I was staring at the exact reason why she and Nyx worked—he was the Joker to her Harley Quinn.

Without the breakup.

The next morning, after I cried myself to sleep, I read Rex's email. Too tired to call him, I just replied, telling him that I was okay and that I'd call him sometime later. I also asked to reschedule the video call with Wynter.

After showering and changing, I found myself driving over to Lily's, grateful for the reprieve.

Parker and Susanne were quiet because they had a caseload that told me I needed to hire some more staff, and while I knew I should take advantage of the ride to her place, I'd given Emile the day off because I needed him not to see the wreckage after this initial group meeting.

The house was beautiful. A mansion set amid a blanket of snow. The ornate driveway was twenty-feet long and was dusted with more snow, but it looked like powdered sugar. Some drifted to the ground after I pulled up at the intercom to declare my name, and the gates opened inward. As I drove down the driveway, I found myself impressed by the grandeur.

When I pulled up outside the house, I noticed Lodestar was standing in the doorway.

As I studied her, I thought about how odd a woman she was.

The kind you didn't know whether you liked or not.

I couldn't deny that she was a hard worker, solid and dependable in a sense, especially when it came down to securing the Sinners, but there was also something untrustworthy about her.

I figured it was because I knew she had her own agenda for being here, and right now, it suited her to help the Sinners out.

That wasn't how loyalty worked.

Rex had once told me that her own people had sold her out, that was how she'd gotten involved with the Sparrows. She'd been inducted into their sex trade as a punishment.

A part of me wanted to believe the US was incapable of treating their citizens like that, but I knew better.

Was it any wonder loyalty for her wasn't an olive branch but a potential minefield she had to cross?

When I climbed out of the car, she didn't move, just waited on me to approach her.

I was early, but not that early, and I didn't want to talk about whatever had her looking so grim.

Not that I had a say in that.

As I walked over to her, she dipped her chin and strode out of the doorway so I could step inside too. Following her, I moved into the kitchen and watched as she settled herself behind the kitchen table.

A screech from upstairs had me jerking in surprise and peering up at the ceiling.

"It's Kat," she answered, her gaze on the computer.

"Shouldn't you check if she's okay?" I asked warily.

"She's always screeching."

Okaaay.

"What do you need, Lodestar?"

She pursed her lips. "Got some information today about a body that washed up in Edgewater."

My brow furrowed. "Bodies are out of my wheelhouse."

"They aren't while Rex ain't answering his phone."

I grunted. "Whose body is it?"

"Officially, they're saying it's a missing person."

"Unofficially?"

And who the hell were the 'officials' in question?

I didn't ask that because knowing Lodestar, I'd be wishing I'd kept my mouth shut.

"Prelim DNA suggests it's Kevin Sisson."

The name hit me like a ton of bricks.

Staggering forward, I dragged out one of the stools by the table and sank down heavily onto it.

"When it rains, it pours," I whispered, reaching up to rub my brow.

Lodestar hummed. "It's quite by chance that I learned this, but I like to think that chance *does* favor those with their fingers in all the pies."

Weary from last night, exhausted from my own problems, this was just the final nail in my coffin.

Slumping back against the seat, I rasped, "Was there... what..." My brain clearly wasn't working.

Lodestar's disapproving frown told me she expected more from me.

"Do you have coffee?"

I was trying to cut down on my caffeine intake, but if this wasn't a moment deserving of coffee, I didn't know what was.

Silently, she moved over to the counter and poured me some from a carafe. I hated filtered, but I was so far beyond caring that I'd take what I could get.

I didn't doctor it, just when she handed it to me, took a deep gulp.

The caffeine hit was nice. Beyond nice. Orgasmically nice.

"Okay, what are our options?" I inquired.

"As of right now, offensive. Head to the morgue in Edgewater, swipe the body out from under their noses, and dispose of it ourselves."

I grimaced.

Why was it that everyone was messing around with dead bodies? What with Luciu Valentini, Giulia last night, and now Lodestar?

"Prelim DNA was sent out before an autopsy was completed—"

"That's unusual, isn't it?"

She shrugged. "A fifth wheel detached itself from the cab of a semi. There were people hidden in the back of it who died. That kept the morgue busy—"

"The Sparrows were behind the people smuggling?"

"No. It was from Mexico." She rubbed her nose. "The body's decomposing as we speak, so it's a priority, but everything's slowed down with the fridges full. That means I've no way of knowing if there are clear signs of murder."

I scoffed, "The signs will be there. Nyx doctored Kevin's shotgun. It backfired into his face."

Grunting, Lodestar grumbled, "Destructive, isn't he?"

"Yes," I said dryly.

"Who disposed of the body?"

"Bear." I thought back to the day of Carly's wake and shivered. "I was friends with his sister."

"Carly?"

"You know her name?"

"He's got it inked on his neck," she said with a shrug. "Wasn't she older than you?"

"Five years older," I agreed. "But I always got along better with people older than me. Before my mom met Axel—Rain's father—my nana raised me. Carly was... She didn't deserve what happened to her."

"Does anyone?"

"No. True." I sucked in a breath. "He deserved what happened to him."

"You won't hear me disagreeing, but I'm not a jury."

"Bear promised he'd sort Kevin out, but that didn't stop Nyx. He got there first. I can't imagine Bear won't have been thorough in making sure there's nothing that ties Nyx to Kevin's body."

"Do we really want to risk it?"

The words settled heavily on my heart.

"Why are you asking me? Why aren't you telling the council?"

"Because Rex is their brains."

"That's not fair to the rest of them," I argued hotly.

"Not saying they're dumb, just saying they're not Rex."

That had me conceding with a grimace.

"Rex is one of a kind," I mumbled.

She snorted. "You'd know, not me. What do you want to do? Are you talking to Rex? I assume he isn't cutting you off?"

My jaw worked at the prospect of being the bearer of yet more bad news. Angering Rex didn't scare me, but the prospect of losing him did. I thought about how we'd come to our deal, and with that in mind, I muttered, "Lodestar, could you do me a favor?"

She arched a brow. "More than discovering the corpse from our resident pedo-hunter's earliest case?"

"Yeah."

Clearly curious, she asked, "What?"

"Rex and I... we're trying to get better at communicating."

"Right," she drawled, extending the 'i.'

"Yesterday, I told him something and he kind of blamed me and it's been a tough... *rough* couple days. Would you mind speaking with him if I call him?"

She shrugged. "Sure."

Relieved I wouldn't get blamed for this set of bad news, I withdrew my cell from my purse, hit Rex's number, put it on speaker, then shoved it across the table.

I moved over to the kitchen door and closed it, then turned back to watch it unfold.

"Rach?"

"Nah, it's Lodestar, Rex. Rachel wants me to key you into some shit."

"Dammit," he grunted under his breath.

"Now, now. Don't be blaming her. This ain't in her job description. It comes firmly under yours."

"What is it?"

"Kevin Sisson's body's been found washed up over in Edgewater."

"What?" he hissed.

"You really need me to repeat myself?"

"Jesus Christ," he snarled. "Have the police called around for questioning?"

"No. Not yet. To be honest, Edgewater's having a problem with bodies right now. Fresh ones."

"Dad dealt with him."

"Rachel told me."

"He won't have left any trace behind."

"Doesn't mean they won't come sniffing around here once they can spare a pathologist to run an autopsy on him." She cleared her throat. "Rachel indicated that there'd be clear signs of murder."

"Yeah. Unless Dad separated his head from his body, which I doubt, they'll see he was murdered. Fuck."

"What do you want me to do? I can coordinate with the council and get them to infiltrate the morgue—"

"No. That'll just look even more suspicious. As it stands, we've always stated that Kevin went on a hunting trip, something he did frequently, and he just never came back."

"You've got too many floating bodies, Rex," Lodestar warned.

"This ain't like with David," he dismissed. David was Indy's ex-receptionist. "Kevin used to go hunting over in Wanaque."

"So? He was an associate of the MC."

"No, he was related by blood, but he wasn't an associate."

"You're splitting hairs."

"That's what I do best." He grunted. "Leave it—"

"Seriously?"

"Seriously. We go in, it makes it look like there's something to hide."

"No body, no crime," Lodestar grumbled.

"I've got..." He sucked in a breath. "I have every confidence in my dad."

I knew that had to hurt.

After yesterday.

"He'd never do anything to jeopardize Nyx," he said a few seconds later, his tone staunch, but it was more like he was telling himself that rather than Lodestar.

A part of me wanted to dive into this conversation. The ball buster of old wanted to tear into his reasoning to make sure that he was making the safest and wisest decision, but I just...

I didn't feel like the ball buster of old right now.

I felt bruised by life. Overwhelmed by it.

So I stayed quiet as Lodestar told him, "Okay, well, if you say so."

"I do. Keep an eye out, though?"

"I will."

"How did you even find out about this?"

"That's for me to know and for you not to find out."

He grunted and cut the call.

"Your man's such a charmer."

The fizz that appeared in my veins at her throwaway comment had me sucking in a breath.

"He has his moments," was all I said, not arguing that he was 'my man' before I jumped as the door behind me was shoved open.

"Wait!" I called out, stepping aside so that I wasn't barreled over.

"Why you stand behind door?" Amara groused, glowering at me, accent thicker than oatmeal that had been left to stand.

"She wanted away from the fallout," Lodestar drawled, and I crinkled my nose because she wasn't exactly wrong.

The amused glint in her eyes told me she knew I wasn't going to argue with her.

Amara just huffed. "You have news, Lodestar?"

"Yeah, I'm the Tooth Fairy today. Instead of money, though, I hand out information."

"You speak too much," Amara declared. "What news? Stop with bullshit."

My lips curved at her frank, very Baltic command.

"Found Liliana."

The younger woman released an unholy whoop as she rushed forward, her eagerness clear. "Where?"

"Rhode Island. Providence, to be more specific."

The other woman's glee was apparent.

"Who's Liliana?" I asked, not wanting to be out of the loop.

"She is, what you call, madam?" Amara said thickly. "I hate her. I want her dead."

Heaving a sigh, I muttered, "Amara, you can't go around killing people—"

"I can. Rex told me I can." She sniffed. "You are not Rex. I do not need to listen to you."

Annoyed, I grumbled, "You do if you get caught and I have to defend you."

"I will go to jail to make sure she dies a horrendous death."

"I think there's something in the water." And I wasn't talking about Kevin's body either. Although, technically, his corpse was in the morgue now, wasn't it?

Lodestar frowned. "What?"

"I think there's something in the water," I said again, but I didn't clarify.

I'd been around more death threats this past month than I had in my whole life.

I grunted when I realized the conversation with Rex had made me perspire. Reaching for a tissue I had tucked in my pocket, I raised my ponytail and patted my nape.

Feeling somewhat better, I moved over to the fridge. "Do you think Lily will mind if I get a water?"

Lodestar snorted. "Yeah, she charges by the fluid ounce."

I squinted at her. "You have an attitude problem."

"You only just figured this out?"

"Talk less, explain more," Amara growled. "Where is Liliana?"

"I'm not gonna tell you where she is yet," Lodestar countered. "We've got enough heat right now, and we don't need you to go all Nurse Ratched on us just yet."

"Who is this nurse?" was Amara's suspicious retort.

"Never mind." Lodestar huffed. "Those guys of yours need to work on your cultural references. Don't you watch Netflix together?"

Amara hitched a shoulder. "Yes, but I watch with subtitles otherwise is no fun."

Having retrieved a glass from one of several cupboards I'd opened —neither woman had clued me into the location of Lily's glassware— I retreated to the refrigerator and collected some ice and water that I raised to my forehead.

I wasn't sure why I was so hot, but I really goddamn was.

"Anyone else feel like we're standing in a sauna?" I muttered, but neither were listening. Lodestar and Amara were in the throes of an argument that—

Lodestar spoke Ukrainian?

I blinked at the realization then decided to leave them to it so I could get some fresh air. Neither stopped me from making my departure, and I took the moment to peer around the downstairs' space which was, admittedly, massive.

I'd never seen as much marble in my entire life, and I'd gone to Athens and Rome after senior year in college, for Christ's sake.

Everything was opulent, to a ridiculous degree, and it was really hard to imagine Link living here.

Link who existed in jeans and Henleys, who washed his hands ten thousand times a day because he hated getting engine oil on his fingers but there was always some still remaining in the cracks of his nails. Link who wore boots and rarely shaved and whose cut probably had more pussy juice on it than cologne.

"It's horrendous, isn't it?"

Hearing Lily's sheepish voice, but not seeing her, I twisted around until I found her standing on the upper mezzanine floor, her elbows on the mahogany railing.

"I wouldn't say it's horrendous," I argued uncomfortably. "More like ostentatious?"

She grinned. "You're too kind."

"Sorry. I didn't mean to be rude."

"You're not. I've said worse about the place, but I never seem to change it."

As she moved down the staircase, I watched her graceful form in a sunshine yellow tailored dress come closer.

She walked with a poise that spoke of finishing school. I recognized it from college where a lot of my fellow female students were aiming more for a marriage license than a major.

Her graceful walk, how she tucked her hair behind her ears, the neat way she placed each foot on the step... all of it spoke of class. Expensive class. Sometimes, *that* could be purchased.

When Link made an appearance, storming down the stairs, I jerked in surprise but that was nothing to Lily who yelped when he hauled her by the waist, loaded her over his shoulder, and carried her down the rest of the steps in a fireman's hold.

"Link! You jackass! Put me down!" Lily yowled, but she was giggling as she cried it.

Link grinned at me, his joy clear as he patted Lily's tush, simultaneously keeping her skirt covering her thighs.

When he planted his feet on the hallway steps, I muttered, "You know how dangerous that was, don't you?"

Link shrugged. "Lily's always safe with me." He shot me an incorrigible wink as he swung her around. "Which room today, my lady?"

"Now is not the time to pretend to be my chauffeur."

I arched a brow. "I think I'm too young for this conversation."

"Trust me, you are," Tiffany said with a soft laugh that had me twisting around to face her.

Goddamn, where was she hiding? This place was far too big.

A sniff sounded from overhead, one that wasn't from Lily, but the woman's voice was loaded with disdain. "Disgusting behavior. Have you no decency?"

"Mother!" Tiffany snapped, clueing me in to who'd made the snide comment.

Taking a drink of my water, I found the older woman peering over the bannister much as Lily had been, but her sneer set my teeth on edge.

Link was a good man. He didn't deserve that kind of disdain.

"Leave it, Tiff," Link said good-naturedly. "Your mother can't help that she needs something shoved up her ass."

A shocked gasp escaped the woman who immediately stormed off.

"God, I'm so sorry, Link," Tiff said, her tone miserable.

"You can't control your parents," I said, knowing that more than anyone.

Link pulled a face. "God, your mother was a real piece of work, Rach. Remember that time she smacked Rene at Carly's wake and then pretended to be pregnant afterward?"

"How could I forget?"

"And she walked around with a pillow under her shirt? And kept fainting whenever anyone mentioned Rene kicking her out?"

"Trust me, Link," I groaned. "I remember."

"I'm surprised Axel didn't throw her out."

"He was a fool in love," was my grim reply. "Piece of work—that was definitely my mom. I used to wish Axel *would* throw her out, but if he had then I wouldn't have Rain. He's worth ten of her."

Tiffany stepped out from wherever she'd been standing, and her hand came to my arm. "Rachel, that's a lovely thing to say."

"I only speak the truth."

I stared down into the earnest expression of a woman I didn't know very well, as I peered at Lily and a couple other faces I knew but also not well.

It shamed me, to be honest.

I'd always kept some distance from the Sinners, mostly because I couldn't handle being close to Rex, couldn't deal with the dichotomy of my personality when I was with him.

My focus always remained on the old me and how different this newer version was.

How much worse *she* was by comparison.

But the men were all my family, and I'd made no effort to know their women. Had had no real interest in knowing them.

My selfishness knew no bounds.

With a self-deprecating smile, I murmured, "Thank you for letting me be a part of this."

She blinked at me, her curls bouncing as she laughed. "You'll be cursing me later. This is pretty much how it always starts and ends—chaos."

"That makes sense. Giulia called these meetings Posse? Or something like that?"

Her nose crinkled. "We're her Posse. Are you joining?" she asked, her interest clear.

"Is it like a sorority? Will I have to pledge?"

Something lit up in her eyes at my teasing. I didn't want to think that it was relief because that meant my rep had preceded me—

Oh, who the hell was I kidding?

Of course it had preceded me.

"I mean, you can if you want, but I won't be sending you on wild goose chases and making you switch that glass of water for vodka," Giulia drawled.

Her voice was close, and it took me a second to find her in the doorway. She looked like hell. The air around her was charged, as if she had the power to start her own hurricane and to tether it to her.

I'd seen her in various rages over the course of her stay at my place, so her bad mood wasn't difficult for me to spot.

"I hated pledging," Lily grumbled as Link finally put her down when she complained all the blood was rushing to her head.

He supported her as she got her bearings, asking curiously, "Was it like in *Legally Blonde*?"

I snorted, but Tiff arched a brow. "You've watched *Legally Blonde*, Link?"

Lily grinned. "What do you think? We can't always watch *Chopped*."

That was clearly some kind of inside-joke because warmth filtered into Link's expression and he bowed down, whispered something in her ear, then pressed a kiss to her lips.

"On that note," he intoned, "I'd better be going." His gaze caught mine and he smiled. "Good to know you'll be keeping these reprobates out of jail, Rach."

Amused by how different his reaction was to Nyx's, I shot him a smile in return as he wandered away, taking a different exit to the one I'd come through.

"He'll be going to see Maverick," Lily explained as she walked over to me. Her hand came to my arm and she squeezed gently. "There's a drink station set up in the living room where we're going to be sitting if you need a refill. Want to come with me?"

I nodded, surprised by her gentle tone.

"It's okay, Lily. You don't have to be watchful around me. I won't run off."

She squeezed. "I know, but it can be intimidating. These women are..." She shrugged, and while her smile was impish, it was also loaded with a genuine caring. "They're strong and forceful. I don't doubt you'll fit in, but it could be nerve-wracking to wade into the fray."

"I appreciate the thought."

And I did.

I smiled at her as she murmured, "We're sitting in this room."

"Not the glass room?" Giulia complained. "I like the sofa."

"Not today," Lily countered. "The pink room's in a loose circle. I figured it might ease Rachel in better."

"You don't have to make any changes for me," I argued, feeling the flush of heat burn a path along the crest of my cheekbones.

"No, it's a smart move for your first time."

Amara grumbled, "Why was my first time not smart?"

"Because you're dangerous," Giulia sniped. "You need comfort not structure."

Amara pondered that. "I see this."

"She's a loaded gun," Lily drawled with a soft laugh as she tugged me toward the 'pink room.' "But she means us no harm."

I had to snort at that.

"But the rest of the world isn't so safe?"

Shooting me a smirk, Lily agreed, "Exactly."

The pink room lived up to its name.

Magenta armchairs, stylized with hard edges and lines to give them a cubic shape, gleamed under the glow of a large golden chandelier. They were spaced in a loose circle with a kind of extended glass table between them. It was lower to the ground than a regular dining table, made for the armchairs, I guessed.

Hell, it was pretty much an upper-class version of the new clubhouse bar.

"It's a weird room, isn't it?" Lily confided. "But I couldn't change it."

"Why not?"

"I like the chairs too much."

She guided me to one and I took a seat, understanding why when the chair seemed to suck me in.

Placing my glass on the table, I watched as the others drifted into the room too.

Amara stormed in, Giulia pretty much surged in on that wind of hers she seemed to be generating on her own. Alessa, living up to her old nickname, Ghost, seemed to float in, Tiffany like she was a catwalk model, Indy stomping in in her Doc Martens and Stone rushing in, a hectic color on her cheeks.

No one seemed surprised to see me, but I was surprised to see them.

Indy and Stone had been friends since they were younger, and I knew Tiffany and Lily were the same. Alessa and Amara had been through similar trials by fire but I could see they weren't close.

Giulia and I weren't the odd ducks, no one was, even though connections had been made years earlier and friendships forged before these women had become Old Ladies.

It was a surprisingly poignant sight.

We came from so many different walks of life yet we all knew what it was like to survive something heinous.

Of course, that wasn't our only connection.

A gathering of women who were strong enough to tame the Sinners' councilors, a rowdy bunch of bastards who'd been wild and free until they'd all been snagged up by their Old Ladies.

Okay, who was I kidding?

The Sinners would never be tamed.

I knew that from seeing Nyx with Giulia.

She dampened down the wildness in him, but it still raged on—she just never got burned by it.

As everyone took a seat, Tiffany made to close the door, but Lodestar sneaked in before it snickered to a close.

Giulia arched a brow at her. "What are you doing in here?"

"Might not be an Old Lady but I'm an honorary Sinner," Lodestar groused.

Giulia didn't argue, so her presence wasn't a problem, but it made me wonder if Lodestar had never attended one of these group meetings despite her past.

Either way, Tiffany moved a chair from beside an expensive vanity table that had an even more expensive bronze looming over it which sat pretty beside a drink tray with glasses and an ice bucket for anyone needing refreshment. She passed the seat to Lodestar who sat down with a sigh.

Her injuries from the clubhouse blast had been extensive, and I knew she'd only been released from her casts and the wheelchair recently. Her stiffness indicated that she wasn't back to normal just yet.

As everyone settled in, a weird bundle of nerves unfurled inside me.

I didn't belong here.

This wasn't right.

I had no place here—

"Okay, Posse, new faces are with us today so I think we all need to agree that we'll keep that in mind and won't scare them away."

Amara grinned. "Scaring is what I do best."

Giulia, who was seated to her left, shoved her in the side. "Shut up, you."

It wasn't bitchy, more amused.

Jesus.

Amara and Giulia—*kindred spirits?*

The other woman had been living at my place too, so I knew what she was like. Knew that her caustic tongue had only been exacerbated since Hawk and Quin had become her Old Men.

"You don't have to temper yourselves for me," I stated calmly. "I deal with your men on the regular."

Tiffany just smiled. "You might do that, but this is different. This isn't 'business Rachel,' this is the 'real Rachel' we're going to be talking to."

"I guess," I said uneasily, not appreciating the comparison.

Who the hell was the 'real Rachel?'

Sometimes, I spoke business like it was its own language.

*I don't belong here—*

Tiffany hummed as she took a seat. "I'm not going to make you talk, Rachel. If anything, you don't have to say a word. You can listen. But if you have questions, feel free to ask them. Just raise your hand, okay?" She beamed a smile at me, one that was supposed to put me at ease but made me more nervous. How could someone expect so little yet it made me feel like she was asking for the world? "Anyone got anything on their minds?"

Giulia shot me a glance. "Is it okay if I tell them?"

I darted her a look then stared fixedly at the table. "Yeah. It's fine."

Maybe it'd be easier—her saying what had happened without me having to actually tell the story.

"I found out yesterday that my dad was a rapist."

Her words settled amid the women like fallout from a nuclear bomb.

Lodestar grunted and cracked her knuckles. Fitting seeing as she'd been the one to 'recycle' Dog.

The act came without apology, as if Giulia had merely confirmed that she'd been right to handle Dog.

"That's a lot to process," Tiffany said softly.

"Damn straight it is," Giulia snarled, slamming her hand against the glass. Amara jumped at the sound, so did Alessa, but no one else appeared shocked by Giulia's outburst. Not even myself, and I didn't really know her that well, just knew she was volatile. "I-I can't get it out of my head."

"You found out yesterday?" Indy asked, and her voice housed a quiver that made me cement my gaze to the table.

She'd known Dog all her life.

Grizzly too.

They were familiar faces; Grizzly had even held a position of power on the council.

The terror was as real now as it ever was.

Would they believe me?

But... why would they?

My mom was a whore. Why shouldn't I be one too?

"Yeah. Last night," Giulia breathed.

"Well, it's still fresh. That's why it's in your head—"

"No, Indy. It's not that. Did he rape my mom too? She was a cunt, don't get me wrong, and if he hit her, she hit him back, but this is different. They wouldn't always have been like that."

I thought back to my childhood. Axel had brought us to West Orange when I was nine, and there was an eleven-year age gap between Giulia and me. I'd babysat her, Hawk, and North, so I'd been around to see their rocky relationship a lot more than she had.

"Lizzie changed," I said slowly, gaze fixed on my glass now where a bead of condensation dripped down the side of it.

Stone nodded. "She did."

"In what way?" Tiffany questioned.

"She wasn't always like that—so quick to fight back," I muttered, reaching for my water now.

Giulia swallowed. "Do you think he—"

"I don't know. How *could* I know?" I sucked in a breath. "They were high, Giulia. Both of them stank of weed. To this day, I can't—" I choked on the words. "That smell. God, I hate it. I hate it so much." My spare hand tightened into a fist and I pressed my knuckles into the table. "But they were stoned. I'm not even sure if they remember what happened."

"Who was your other attacker?" Tiffany queried gently.

"Grizzly," I said grimly, eyes on my knuckles which were a bright white.

"Sin's dad?" she demanded, her tone sharp.

Shoulders hunching, I nodded. "Yeah."

"He's Bear's brother?" Alessa rasped, her damaged voice soft and low.

"Yes, he was. He's dead now."

"Sin beat him to death," Tiffany remarked, her focus on me. "Weed doesn't trigger memory loss."

"Maybe they were on something else—"

"Would it be easier on you if they'd forgotten what they did?"

I had no idea why the question hit me on the raw. "Does it matter?"

"Yeah, it matters," Indy concurred. "I mean, they didn't leave, did they? They stuck around. Their lives weren't impacted. It'd be easier to think that they didn't remember, because how could they act as if nothing happened if they did? But they were dicks. Grizzly more than most.

"I remember when he died, thinking, 'Well, thank God that prick's gonna be maggot food soon.' He was a troublemaker and always starting shit that got everyone into trouble. I'm pretty sure he's the reason why Two Knives' dad is still in prison."

"Whereas, if they did know, the fact they could waltz around the clubhouse like nothing had happened is a thousand times worse, isn't it?" Stone queried, but her tone was kind.

I gave her a jerky nod, surprised by how quickly we'd dived into these kinds of details.

"Waltzing?" Amara laughed, but it was dark. Bitter. "These bastards. I'd make them waltz. I'd string them up—"

"Yes, yes, yes," Tiffany grumbled. "We know, Amara, but torture isn't always the answer. That's not going to help Rachel, is it?"

She sniffed. "Maybe it would. They would hurt like they made her hurt. Justice is sweet."

"Justice isn't possible when both men are dead," Lily said sharply, reiterating, "That's not going to help, Amara."

The other woman clucked her tongue but shot me a look. Her expression was... unusual. I was pretty certain that everyone here knew Amara was batshit, but for all that her regular craziness shone through loud and clear; her expression was also softer.

Piteous.

No. *Kind.*

We were all victims here.

Pity held no place when we'd all experienced a mutual horror.

Giulia was right—we knew what it was to be at the mercy of other people.

This was a safe space.

Their understanding and acceptance didn't stop the nausea from plaguing me; it was a heavy weight in my stomach as Tiffany asked, "Have you ever talked about what happened that night? Was it the one time or did it happen again?"

"I made sure it *couldn't* happen again," I said bitterly. "And no. Not really. Talking about it—" I swallowed. "I never wanted to."

"Does Rex know?" Indy demanded.

"Not until recently."

Stone frowned. "Rex knows everything."

"He knew I'd been attacked. But he never pushed me to talk about it."

"Why not?" Giulia growled, sitting up straighter, her affront on my behalf touching.

I plucked at my lower lip. "Rex is..." How did I explain this? "Rex treats me like an equal. He always has. He expects me to come to him with things, and while he'll amend his behavior, he won't push me."

"Do you want to be pushed?"

"No, Tiffany, I don't." The answer was resolute. "He knows me too well," I said sheepishly.

"How does he amend his behavior?"

My cheeks turned pink before they blanched. "I never do oral." I reached up and rubbed my nape, nerves hitting me when I thought about the conversation with Rex where we'd discussed this. "Grizzly, he... he made me. Dog, too. I can't handle that." *Not yet.*

"You have sex?"

"Only with Rex," I admitted. "And only on my terms."

Tiffany nodded. "You like to be in control?"

"Not like a Domme or anything." I shot her a sheepish glance. "I don't dress up like Catwoman."

"Shame, you have the ass for it," Giulia retorted.

I had no idea why that broke my tension but it did. I saw she was grinning so I grinned back at her.

"Who is this Catwoman?"

Lily answered Amara, "A character from *Batman.*"

"Why is this funny?" Amara asked.

"I'll explain it later," Lily promised.

"*Tak.*"

"Do you wish Rex punished them on your behalf?" Tiffany prompted me.

"No!" I bit off, and it was the first time my voice had sharpened, gotten louder, and it made a couple of them jump. "If he knew, he'd have killed them, and if he had killed them, he'd be in jail. I couldn't stand that. I need him," I rasped, then repeated, "I need him. I just can't always deal with that need."

Tiffany studied me but I didn't feel like a bug on a slide so that was something. All my other shrinks had made me feel like I was subhuman.

"So, at the time, you must have hidden it? Didn't he figure it out? We all know how smart Rex is, Rachel."

Having to explain it was hard, but I could sense they were disappointed in Rex, and there was no need to be. It wasn't his fault I was a damn good actress when I chose to be.

"I think, at the time, he knew *something* had happened, but I don't think he knew what. I-I was always busy. I stopped hanging out with him.

"He approached me afterward, about two months later, two months of my avoiding him, and ducking and diving out of his way, to ask if I wanted to break up with him." My mouth wobbled at the memory. "I said yes."

"Did he expect that?"

"No. I think he thought he was bringing things to a head. H-He's... I know he loves me. I've always loved him." I swallowed. "It hurts not being with him, but it hurts being with him too."

"How did you avoid him for two months?" Indy asked, her voice soft. Empathetic.

"I worked three jobs, and then Mom had Rain to stop Axel from breaking up with her, and she never looked after him so I had him to watch as well." I rubbed my brow, thinking back to those times. "I had school and everything, and he knew I wanted to go to college. I-I think he thought letting me go was the best thing to do."

"Knowing Rex, though, he didn't let you go entirely?" Stone asked.

"I'm not sure." I shrugged. "I know when I left for college, he had a brother watching over me."

"Sounds like him," Indy said with a nod.

"I left for Brown a year late because of Rain, and that was when Axel really stepped up. My mom devastated him when she left, so everything fell to me. I think Rex had a word with him because suddenly, the start of the next year, I was in college."

That was how Wynter had been born.

When I realized what he'd done for me, the arrangements he'd made on my behalf, I'd thanked him.

It had been heaven.

And hell.

"Shouldn't Rex have asked you?" Alessa queried. "Shouldn't he have—" She shook her head. "I do not mean to judge, but Maverick would not let me not answer."

"Cruz wouldn't either," Indy agreed.

"Steel neither."

"Nyx definitely wouldn't have."

Lodestar grunted and for the first time spoke, "Look, we get it. You all have boss ass men who'd die and kill for you. But that's not the point, is it? Sometimes we don't need men to fight our fucking battles for us. We need them to have our backs, *but* we want them to stand at our sides and let us make our own decisions."

"Doesn't seem like he did that. Just seems as if he maneuvered shit around to facilitate her—"

"And what's wrong with that, Stone? You're all fired up because he didn't demand to know what was going on with her, but maybe he knew that'd fucking break her. Maybe he knew that he had to have her back, had to make shit happen. Had to make things right for her so she could move on.

"That sounds like a fucking hero to me. Someone who knows his woman was hurt but also knows that placing her on a pedestal wouldn't do dick. His woman wasn't a victim. She was a fucking survivor, and he made sure that happened and all of that with no expectations on his side.

"Men need patting on the head for doing the fucking dishes and Rex made sure she got to college *after* they split up.

"He cared for her, just in a different way. He fixed things just like your men do for you, but how he did it was tailored to Rachel." She sat back. "You can't judge a man for protecting his woman as an equal. I'd want *my* man to do that. I don't want him to go to war *for* me. I want him to go to war *with* me."

Her shrug was nonchalant, but she'd somehow managed to sum up exactly how I felt.

Silence fell, settling into the cracks until Tiffany asked, "Is that how you feel, Rachel? You don't want Rex to 'save' you?"

When all eyes turned on me, I could feel the heat crawling over my skin as if it were bugs.

"For someone who had no interest in being a mom, mine taught me a lot of lessons. You can depend on no one but yourself. W-When Dog and Grizzly, when—"

"When they raped you," Tiffany said calmly. "There's no shame here, Rachel. And any shame belongs on them, not you."

Nodding, I reasoned, "I determined that I'd do everything in my power to never feel so *power*less again. I wanted to be in a position of strength. I knew if they did tell anyone, they'd let the MC know that I was a whore. That I'd come onto them. That I was like my mom and that I wanted to be dicked down so I'd get myself an Old Man." A shudder wracked me. "I *knew* I'd be painted in a bad light. I knew it.

"So I determined that I'd never, *ever* be put in that position again."

"You didn't become a lawyer to protect other people?" Alessa asked kindly.

"I know that's the polite answer, but no. I-It made me selfish, I guess. I know that's horrible of me, but—"

"Self-preservation isn't horrible," Giulia denied.

Grateful, I nodded. "I wanted big cases. I wanted money. I wanted to make a name for myself. Anything to never be in that position again." Revulsion whispered through me. "Grizzly always used to give me shit for hanging around Rex. Saying that I was only with him because he was Bear's son. I knew to avoid him like the plague, but I couldn't avoid him that night."

"It's interesting that you defend the scum of the earth," Lodestar mused as she reached for a bottle of Coke, but I could tell she *was* interested. She didn't judge me, merely found my actions confusing.

"They pay the most." I hitched a shoulder. "Rex pays me a fortune to be on retainer for the Sinners, and then there are my other clients. No one can touch me unless I want them to now. No one could ever say that I was the daughter of a whore and that I asked for it." My mouth tightened. "I pay it back in other ways."

"How?" Tiffany asked.

"I'm sure Lily's told you," I replied impatiently.

"No. She hasn't," was Tiffany's reply. "Confidentiality is important to us."

"I wouldn't jeopardize my position by talking about things that you might not want discussed," Lily answered with a soft smile. "I like my new position. I don't want to find myself out of it."

"It's not a secret that I have charities I-I founded. That's where I make changes happen." I sucked in a breath. "I went to war, on my own terms, and Rex helped me.

"Lodestar, you're right. He stood by me even when I told him I didn't want to see him anymore. But..." This time, my exhalation was shakier than the subsequent inhalation. "I wonder if I did us both a disservice. I thought, with time, this would get better. Easier to manage. Instead, there's no real difference between back then and now."

"Probably because you've bottled it up, babe," Giulia remarked. "It happened nearly twenty years ago and you still find it hard to say you were raped. Plus, last night, you were all, 'What I've gone through isn't as bad as what some of the others here have gone through.'"

Tiffany's nose crinkled. "Comparing yourself, your trauma, to another person doesn't serve anyone. Did you know PTSD can be triggered in some people by simply watching a TV documentary of wars? It can be that simple and still complex.

"We're so desensitized to violence and extreme behavior now that we forget to recognize the devastating effects of such things on our minds. You comparing yourself to another woman merely locks your trauma away. It diminishes it.

"At the time, you were hurt. At the time, your choice was denied to you. At the time, they made you feel lesser than. At the time, you knew you had no recourse, no way to stop them from doing it again. You do *yourself* a disservice by comparing what you went through to another woman." She cast a look around the table. "And I say this to all of you. You know we've talked about this so many times. You invalidate your own pain when you do this, and it merely makes it harder on you to accept what happened as fact.

"They had no right to do what they did." She shot me an apologetic look. "This might sound trite, but I'd like you all to repeat that."

Giulia cleared her throat. "*He* had no right to do what he did."

She was the first to say it, and then, almost in tandem, the rest of the group, including myself, whispered, "They had no right to do what they did." Even Lodestar joined in.

I couldn't say that the utterance of those words made it easier for me to breathe. That it lowered the burden on me. That it diminished what had happened. But something about us all going through that, about us all being together, chanting it like it was a mantra—it wormed its way inside me.

We spent another forty minutes talking in that circle, and then, we drifted apart. Lodestar returned to her computer, Stone had to rush off for her shift, but Indy and Giulia trudged into another room to go and watch TV, and Lily and Tiff stayed at the table and had some coffee. Amara and Alessa started chatting in Ukrainian, and while I could have joined in with any of them, for some bewildering reason, I found myself heading toward Lodestar in the kitchen.

She peered over her screen at me. "What do you want?"

I shrugged. "Nothing." Her gaze was suspicious, but I ignored it to tell her, "Thank you for what you said in there."

"Nothing to thank me for," she dismissed, fingers clacking as she worked. "It's how I feel, and I've seen you in a courtroom. I've also taken note of the cases you cherry pick.

"Murders are fine, especially if it's mafia or gang-related. If a woman's been butchered, you'll have nothing to do with it. No rapists or anything like that. You want money and you'll abandon some of your principles, but you have standards. I can empathize."

Studying her a second, I murmured, "I'd have liked to have met you before the world hurt you, Lodestar."

She blinked at me. "Same, Rachel. Same."

*From: Rach3lLadyLiberty@gmail.com*
*To: K1ngS1nn3r1@gmail.com*
*Subject: Re. Meeting*

I spoke about what happened to me today.
It was hard.
If I don't answer the phone, that's why, okay? There's nothing wrong; it was just intense.
R

*From: K1ngS1nn3r1@gmail.com*
*To: Rach3lLadyLiberty@gmail.com*
*Subject: Re. Meeting*

What did you tell them?
You know, when we were younger, I used to dream about the day you'd tell me what happened. Well, it was more of a nightmare. But, you know what I mean.
I used to hope there'd come a day where you'd open up, only you never did.
I know it was a defense mechanism. I know you were protecting yourself. I'm proud of you for that.
K

*From: Rach3lLadyLiberty@gmail.com*
*To: K1ngS1nn3r1@gmail.com*
*Subject: Re. Meeting*

I've started this email a couple times. I wasn't going to reply, but I couldn't stop myself. That doesn't mean this is the original email. I've written it a few times, but it's difficult to express the words. Even harder to express them to you.
In the end, it was Giulia who started the discussion.

*I'm grateful for that even if it's proof I still find it impossible to talk about it.*
*After, Tiffany asked me how you reacted to what happened to me.*
*I said I'd never told you.*
*The others were up in arms, saying their guys would have made them talk, but Lodestar stood up for you.*
*She verbalized something I don't think I ever could—you backed me.*
*It was just in your own way.*
*You always do that though. You fix and you support and you believe in boundaries.*
*After everything happened, I needed that.*
*I just don't know if I do now.*
*I've changed. Before you say anything—some things haven't changed. I can't tell you how badly I regret waking up and demanding that you get away from me.*
*Thinking of you riding off how you did will haunt me until the day I goddamn die.*
*Did I tell you I puked after you left?*
*A part of that was because of the nightmare, but thinking I'd pushed you away was even worse.*
*There's some stuff going on, and I think that's helped me change too. It's a slow process, but I don't think I need you to fix and to support and to believe in boundaries now.*
*I think I need you to push.*
*I just don't know what form that takes.*
*Sorry that's not more help.*
*I love you. Thank you for being there for me.*
*Rachel*

**From: K1ngS1nn3r1@gmail.com**
**To: Rach3llLadyLiberty@gmail.com**
**Subject: Re. Meeting**

*We're adults.*

*Those are the words you were looking for.*

*That's the major source of the changes in you. You're not a scared kid anymore, but a strong, independent woman who knows her worth.*

*And you never have to thank me for being there for you, Rachel. You're my fucking life. Don't you know that by now?*

*Every day spent apart from you is a wasted goddamn day. The only worthwhile time away from you has been here, now. Our kid needs me. She might not want to admit it, but she does.*

*I think, God help me, when I look at her, I see you.*

*Rough around the edges and battered by life —**already**.*

*That's why I'm still here.*

*If she'd been happily tucked away in suburbia, content in her twelve-grand-a-semester high school, I might have been able to come home.*

*But she isn't, Rach.*

*She's not supposed to be battered by life at her fucking age. I paid to make sure that didn't happen, goddammit. I wanted her to have the best, and somehow, even though I fucking tried, I messed that up as well.*

*There's an irony to the fact that you're thanking me for not pushing, for fixing, back when you were seventeen.*

*Do you know how impossible that was for me?*

*I swear, you made me into the man standing here today.*

*I didn't just want to fix. I wanted to solve. I wanted to make everything better for you. I wanted to whitewash over the problems and to make them go away. I only didn't because Mom stepped in.*

*You know what she was like: always aware of everything that was happening in the clubhouse. Did you go to her afterward? Did she help you?*

*I hope she did.*

*I hope you had her love in the aftermath when you wouldn't accept mine.*

*She was the one who told me to stand by your side, but to let you forge your own path.*

*It was so fucking hard to listen, especially when you pulled away. Then shit seemed to get better. You got into college, and you came to me and... Well, you know. That's why Wynter's here. I thought maybe, with time, you'd come around, but then that fucker died and everything derailed.*

*I've been coasting ever since; did you know that?*

*Stuck in fucking neutral.*

*I can't even tell you how badly I wanna be in first fucking gear.*

*Love you,*

*K*

**From: Rach3lLadyLiberty@gmail.com**
**To: K1ngS1nn3r1@gmail.com**
**Subject: Re. Meeting**

*Hell, I didn't even go to Axel, never mind your mom. Looking back, I probably should have. If there was*

*anyone who'd have told me I wasn't like my mother, who'd have fought for me and who'd have listened, it was her.*
*I was a dumbass not to go to her.*
*She'd have gotten Grizzly kicked out of the MC; I know she would have.*
*Damn, I'm so mad at myself.*
*So many things would have been different if I'd done that.*
*Your email made me realize how crazy it was that I didn't draw a parallel between both of you before.*
*Your dad acted first, regretted his actions later.*
*Your mom thought first, acted, and every move she made was as precise as the strike of a surgeon's scalpel.*
*That wasn't to say your dad was thoughtless. Just not as strategic, I guess.*
*You've been herding me for years, haven't you? Waiting for the day I'd come around...*
*I guess I should be pissed about that.*
*R*

**From: K1ngS1nn3r1@gmail.com**
**To: Rach3lLadyLiberty@gmail.com**
**Subject: Re. Meeting**
*Nothing to be pissed about.*
*Anyone with eyes could see that I was paving the way forward. This will be the first time that I admit I had no idea what path I was paving. Forward was my only destination. Because forward was the future and each day put distance between then and now.*

*Mom would have gotten Grizzly kicked out. It was dumb of me to think you'd gone to her because there were no consequences for that fucker, were there?*

*She'd have made sure he paid. I wish you had gone to her too but there's no use in regretting what happened. We can only try to make tomorrow brighter than yesterday.*

*You know what Sin did to him, don't you?*

*I hope you do.*

*I'll tell you when we next meet.*

*There will always be a next time for us, Rachel.*

*That's a truth I live by.*

*K*

## PART 3

"MANY THAT LIVE DESERVE DEATH. AND SOME THAT DIE DESERVE LIFE. CAN YOU GIVE IT TO THEM? THEN DO NOT BE TOO EAGER TO DEAL OUT DEATH IN JUDGEMENT. FOR EVEN THE VERY WISE CANNOT SEE ALL ENDS."

- J. R. R. TOLKIEN

# FORTY-TWO

## NYX

The scent of dog shit was heavy in the air.

The last time I'd seen this done, I'd laughed.

It was a classic act of hazing.

Shove some dog shit in a bag, dump it on the front stoop, then set fire to the fucker, leaving a poor unsuspecting Prospect to stomp it out and have dog shit exploding everywhere.

Hi-fucking-larious.

Using shit in pranks was high on the brothers' limited repertoire.

When Hawk had been hit with a similar prank—shit under a pile of leaves that smeared everywhere when he swept it away—I'd thought he deserved it.

He'd been a miserable fucker most of the time; barely twitched his lips into a grimace, never mind a smile.

Things had changed since then. He'd proven himself to be a dependable guy, one of Sin's most trustworthy men. He still didn't smile all that much, even if I knew he was happy. Technically, we were brothers-in-law, but that didn't mean I had to cut him any slack.

Unlike Hawk, however, Harlow was being put through his paces but I didn't approve of their methods.

And that was saying fucking something.

I knew he'd been spending the last couple days at Rachel's, despite the fact that he had a bed here, and figured that was because of stunts like this.

I watched as he tried his best to pick up as much of the crap on the floor with a wad of toilet paper he kept shoving into a sandwich bag from the kitchen, and annoyed, I strode into the bar.

The place had long since stopped being pink. Bikers trawling ten tons of shit in with them had the tendency to make a place look grody real fast, and I'd never been more grateful for grody.

*Note to self: the Posse's idea of revenge was far worse than the fun of fucking with them.*

Still, aside from the lingering remnants of pink, everything was fucking normal in here.

Could no one else smell the crap?

Pissed, I hollered, "Who the fuck put dog shit on our brand new stoop?"

The bar was half full of snickering dipshits who froze at my yell.

Gunner blinked at me and cautiously asked, "You mind, Nyx?"

"Bet your fucking ass I mind. That stench ain't gonna be leaving the hall any time soon." My eyes narrowed on him. "You the one behind it?"

He raised his hands. "Not me, VP, nope."

I grunted. "Whoever the fuck did it, don't do it again. In fact, stop with the fucking hazing, yeah? You're not fifteen and we got bigger things on our plate than you making Harlow's life hell. I figure it's plenty hell enough."

The cluster of brothers to my left hunched their shoulders in agreement. To the right, Kendra was sucking off Lever and he shot me a defiant glare as he sniped, "Since when did the council dictate our right to prove if a Prospect's worthy of being a brother?"

"You think having dog shit explode over our front door does that?" I growled back, my eyes flashing with temper.

All around me, silence fluttered, and Kendra even stopped sucking on his cock. When he burrowed his hand in her hair, forcing her back down, I sneered at him. "You want me to slice off your dick, Lever? You're going about it the right way."

He swallowed hard, but being an asswipe gave him enough confidence to mutter, "We've all been through this kind of shit. It's a rite of passage. Why shouldn't Harlow?"

"Because Harlow ain't gonna be like you, motherfuckers."

"What's he gonna be then?" Lever snarled.

"My protege." I tipped up my chin. "If you've got a fucking problem with that, then you can come and talk to me in private, where I'll make sure that all my knives are sharpened because you visiting me about this bullshit is a declaration of fucking war.

"This is *not* a democracy. This is an MC. We got shit to do, and you playing high school pranks on Prospects gets us nowhere. Make him do your fucking jobs for the day. Get him to balance your goddamn checkbook or have him haul all the firewood inside.

"If I hear of any dipshit moves you pull, I'll make you pay, do you hear me?"

I received a lot of bobbing shoulders for my pains, and only Gunner had the balls to ask, "Nyx? We still on for the run this week?"

I eyed him. "Link send a message to any of you saying that it's canceled?"

Gunner cleared his throat. "No."

"Well, then, it's fucking on."

Grousing under my breath, I turned on my heel, well aware they were glowering at me, but I dismissed them as my phone chimed.

Harlow, still on his knees, muttered, "You didn't have to do that. It's just a rite of passage."

"It's a waste of fucking time, and this place is brand new. I don't want it covered in dog shit because they're hazing you."

He peered up at me with those eyes of his that reminded me of the ones I looked at in the mirror every goddamn day. "You mean that about my becoming your protege?"

"That's why you're here, ain't it?" I retorted, tone bland.

"Yeah, but I didn't think—"

"You know what thinking did, don't you?" I countered. "Don't think. Just do. I'll let you know when I trust you enough to take you out with me on the road."

If the eyes were the windows to the soul, I was looking at broken glass, but my words had hope gleaming in them. It was plenty clear that he didn't want to be here. That this wasn't his world. But I knew about the sacrifices a man made for those he'd failed. Who better to understand the torture that was his life?

Every fucking day was a torment.

Every fucking day was a reminder of all the shit he'd failed to do...

No, Harlow didn't need the extra pressure. Just breathing was misery enough.

"Where did they even get dog shit from anyway?" I grumbled, staring down at the brown smears that had me hoping Giulia wouldn't come to the clubhouse today.

The last thing I fucking needed was the Posse moaning in my ear about hygiene.

We were a goddamn 1%-er MC. Hygiene didn't matter. DNA, sure. Not fucking germs.

"There's a bunch outside."

My brow furrowed at Harlow's answer. "Where?"

"Outside."

Of course. Fucking Quin.

My brother was staying in one of the bunkhouses, and because he had some weird Dr. Doolittle mojo where every animal in the fucking country wanted to be near him, that meant we were getting daily visitors—of the furball variety.

Dismissing him, I left him to the carnage that came with a

burning bag of dog shit, and I headed into the yard, crossing over to the bunkhouse.

It wasn't like Quin could help that he was the Pied Piper of everything in the animal kingdom, but he could damn well clear up the shit if he was going to turn us into a sanctuary.

On my way, my cell buzzed again. Seeing the *Unknown* on the screen had my mouth tightening, but before the desire to hurl my cell at the ground hit me, I heard a yip, followed by a snarl, followed by a booming goddamn bark that had me twisting around to see what the fuck was going on.

The yip and the snarl came from a pocket chihuahua. It was clearly a she because the little bitch wore what had once been a bright pink collar that came complete with diamantes—the stones had long since disappeared, but the settings were still there.

She snarled at me before she darted at my boots and clung to the cuff of my jeans, right above the ankle.

"What the fuck did I do to deserve this?" I muttered to myself as I lifted my leg—the pain in the ass hung on tighter, dangling in midair for a second, refusing to let go.

Another booming bark sounded, and as tiny as this ankle-biter was, the other one was about the size of a fucking dire wolf.

Newfoundlander.

All black fur and drool.

"Bet you're the one behind that massive pile of shit on the stoop," I groused as it ambled toward me.

I was Quin's brother—that meant I was used to animals, even if I didn't want to be. The big bear of a dog padded toward me, barking and growling, and I figured it was trying to protect the chihuahua.

Connecting my gaze with it, I lowered my leg. The fucker didn't let go but the Newfoundlander brushed close to me, enough to make me fear for my junk, before it picked up the fun-size dog in its massive jaw.

The chihuahua bared her fangs at me, hissing and spitting, bug eyes glowering at me with a disdain for all humans that life had taught it.

A weird feeling centered itself in my soul.

Humans were scum.

No dog was born scared of us—it was learned.

I fucking hated people.

"Your spirit animals, *tak?*"

Finding Amara watching me, her hands shoved into her pockets as she walked toward me, I demanded, "What the hell are you talking about?"

"Nyx means black."

"It means darkness," I corrected.

She smirked. "Big dog dark, you. Little dog nasty, biter, Giulia."

Despite myself, my lips curled. "If you think all I do is drool and pick up after her—"

"You do," she said with a laugh. "At home. On the road, I think it is very different, but at home, you're the one who stops Giulia from being stomped on by the world."

The words resonated more than I'd like.

"She needs a protector," I said defensively.

Something blazed in Amara's eyes. "*Tak.*"

She drifted away as silently as she'd appeared—fucking creepy—and my cell buzzed one more goddamn time.

*Unknown.*

Attention well and truly snagged, I growled under my breath, not spotting how the Newfoundlander ambled out of the compound gates, the tiny chihuahua still clamped between its teeth.

Nerve flicking at my temple, and well aware they'd keep on calling until I picked up, I answered the second time as I retreated to the clubhouse, my argument with Quin forgotten, and slid into Rex's new office.

"What?" I snapped.

A soft chuckle sounded in my ear. "You're the only man with the balls to talk to me like that."

I sneered at nothing. "That's what happens when you ain't afraid of no one."

"I think that used to be the case," came the harsh voice down the line. "But it always changes when you get a woman, when they have a kid. Families make you vulnerable. They'll be your biggest weakness. You weren't afraid of anyone before, but that's changing, isn't it?"

He was right.

The bastard.

"What do you want?"

Another laugh rang in my ear, but he didn't ram it home. "I want to meet."

"Like you said," I sneered. "I got myself a woman. I don't date random bastards who call me even though I've told them to fuck off a dozen times."

"And here I was thinking that you were starting to trust me."

My jaw clenched. "I didn't ask you to get rid of that body."

"You didn't have to ask me. That's how favors work."

"I don't owe you anything."

"I never said you did. But I wasn't about to let you go down for your uncle's murder. Not when that was a righteous death."

"What did you do with him?"

"You don't need to worry about that."

"I'm not worried," I said, and I meant it. "The body was clean."

"There was a gun found with the corpse. Did you know that?"

I grunted. "No. But I don't care. I have nothing to worry about."

"Whatever. I dealt with that problem not because I wanted you to owe me. I did it because I want you to trust me. If I were a pig, would I really have gotten rid of it for you?"

He had a point.

"What do you want?"

"To talk with you."

"We're talking now."

"In person."

"What's the difference? You wanna see my pretty face?" I mocked.

"I'm an old-fashioned man, Nyx. I like to do things in a certain way."

I stared at Rex's desk. "What do you want from me?" I asked, repeating the same question I'd been asking over and fucking over again.

How the hell *Unknown* knew about the body that'd washed up on the shore in Edgewater, I didn't have a goddamn clue.

It was an inconvenience, but I wasn't worried.

Nothing on that body would implicate me.

Bear would have seen to that.

A heavy sigh whistled in my ear, but I found myself surprised when the stranger answered, "I'm on a crusade of my own. I know what it's like to have someone in the family who was hurt how your sister was hurt. Sometimes, the good Lord doesn't act swiftly enough in sending those sick bastards to perdition."

I straightened up at his words.

They were earnest.

Pained.

No, *agonized*.

We suffered with the same disease—*regret*.

Temptation trickled into me. Sweet. Cloying. Desperate. A cure.

I needed a cure.

Like a junkie needing a fix, my hand clenched at my side as I rasped, "Tell me more."

# FORTY-THREE

## STONE

It was quite by chance that I saw Rachel in a coffee shop in Manhattan.

It wasn't like I visited the island all that much anymore, and I was only here this time because I'd wanted to catch up with some friends who were still residents at High Lidren Hospital.

When I saw her picking at a salad, though, I figured it was a great chance to speak with her.

I'd been wanting to ever since the Posse meeting, to be honest.

Plunking my ass down on the bench opposite her, I watched her blink slowly at me. She was either scanning me or trying to remember who I was. I genuinely didn't know which.

"I'll call you back later, Parker."

I frowned then realized she was talking to someone on the phone.

These damn earbuds—in my job, it was more likely that someone was talking to themselves than into their 'ears.'

"Sorry, I didn't realize you were on a call."

"It doesn't matter. It was just work. It's not like it won't be there after we stop talking."

"I used to be like that."

"Not anymore?"

I shook my head, absentmindedly tapped my side where my brand was, and muttered, "With an Old Man like Steel, he keeps you on your toes."

"Must be hard seeing as you're still recuperating."

"I'm tired of recuperating," I grumbled as I raised a hand for a server to approach me. When she eyed my raised arm in surprise, I arched a brow at her. "I wanted to talk to you."

"I can see. What about?"

"Should you be drinking coffee?"

"It's decaffeinated."

I hummed. "I wanted to talk about us."

"What about us?"

"That it's strange we're not closer."

"Why is it strange?"

"We're family. We're practically the same age. We should be closer than what we are. You were too busy hiding in the crawl spaces as a kid to let me become friendly with you."

Her cheeks colored. "I understood the unspoken lines that were drawn around me."

"What unspoken lines?"

"I knew I wasn't popular."

"You spent your time under the clubhouse, Rachel. We thought you were weird. To be fair, I still think it's weird. What the fuck did you do under there anyway?"

"I read. It wasn't like I was collecting mice corpses."

"There were mice down there?" I grimaced. "Fucking mice."

"No, there weren't actually. It was clean." Her head bowed. "I found out a couple years ago that Bear used to have it cleaned for me."

"Bear was like that." We shared a smile, but it was sorrowful. "I miss him."

"Me too."

"Any news on when Rex is coming back so we can have his funeral?"

"No."

"Doesn't tell you much?"

"He tells me plenty, just nothing concrete about dates."

"Why not?"

She heaved a sigh. "Is this you trying to bully your way into a friendship with me?"

"Bully you? Hell no. I'm no bully. I just never tried before because, well, the matter of the crawl space, and then Rex being so fucking protective—" When the server showed up, I requested, "What cookies are you serving?" As she rattled off a list, I ordered, "I'll have the white chocolate and raspberry, please, with a latte. One shot." I didn't need the caffeine either. Turning back to Rachel, I continued, "Then there was Carly. You used to hang out with her on the rare occasions I saw you in the clubhouse."

"I didn't think you'd want to talk to me. You were always with Steel and Co."

"Usually. But I made time for Indy," I pointed out. "I just... I guess I don't understand why we didn't get friendlier, you know? After what you shared at Lily's—" I ignored her tension. "—I realized that you dealt with that on your own. No one knew, and I mean *no one*, because if they had, Grizzly and Dog would have died a lot earlier than they did. Which means you went through all that on your own. That makes me sad."

"I'm not good with sharing these things."

"Is anyone?" I countered. "Doesn't take away from the fact that I'd have liked to be a safe space for you to land."

"Not even Rex was that."

Wondering if she realized how bitter she sounded, I asked, "I know how it feels to not have the MC at my back."

"The guys always supported you," she disagreed.

"No. They took Steel's side. Just like Rex did, but you know when I came back, one thing I realized was how they were massive dipshits."

Her lips twitched. "You forgot they were that?"

I grinned. "No, I didn't forget, but I was reminded of it."

"Why? What did they do?"

"To them, even though I felt excluded by how they defended Steel over me, I was still family. They were actually pissed at me for not realizing that."

She huffed. "I've had a similar argument with them recently."

"I know. Steel told me. He's a—"

"Dipshit."

Smirking when she finished my sentence for me, I nodded. "He is. They're all so fucking blind to how women work, it's a miracle they branded anyone."

"They're getting better."

"Are they?" I shrugged. "They're still men."

"There's no cure for that," she drawled.

I snickered. "Yeah, cure for plenty, but not that yet." The server appeared again, dropping off my coffee and cookie. "I guess I wanted to make sure that you knew you weren't an outsider. Even if you felt like you were. Or *feel* like you *are*, I guess. Whichever it is, I just wanted you to know that you're not alone."

As she entangled her fork in what looked like a cold pasta salad, I wasn't sure if she was even going to reply.

Rachel had always been an odd duck.

It wasn't even that she was cold or stoic. With our background, and with our chosen professions, we couldn't just be business-like—we had to be hard asses. People thought we were lesser for our ties to the MC, and we had to work twice as much to prove otherwise.

Now, looking back to the past and to that group meeting, I realized how intrinsically private she was and how that kept her locked up tight.

"I want a tattoo."

Whatever the hell I'd thought she was going to say, it wasn't that.

"You're pregnant."

"Goddamn Giulia," she hissed under her breath. Then, she snapped at me, "So?"

My lips twitched. "You can't have ink until after you've given birth."

Her nose crinkled. "Fuck."

"That eager, huh?"

"I've put my ass on the line for the Sinners," she mumbled. "I've gone above and beyond for years—I want to belong."

"Ink doesn't do that. Whether it's a brand or a Sinners' logo on your butt, ink won't make you belong. You have to feel like you do."

"What's your brand?" she asked quietly.

"My cat." I smiled. "With a little robin on her shoulder." Robin was Steel's real name.

"That's cute." Her return smile was genuine.

"There are a bunch of mandalas too. I'd whip them out but no one needs to see all the scars on my stomach."

She huffed. "Don't say that."

I winked at her. "It's okay. Steel deals with any self-esteem issues I have."

"How?"

"Fucks me until I admit I'm beautiful. As a method, it's surprisingly effective."

A snicker escaped her, but it softened as, wistfully, she asked, "How does the brand make you feel?"

I knew what she was talking about.

"I can't make you feel like you belong, but I can tell you that we all know you're family. It's just down to you to embrace those fuckwits as kin but I think you did that a long while ago and didn't realize it yet." Seeing that resonate, I murmured, "At least we're not Giulia."

"What do you mean?"

"I mean she had no backup. Not at the start. It's no wonder she's feral."

We shared a grin.

Clearly still amused, Rachel picked up her fork and took a large bite of her lunch. I sampled some of my coffee, and I stayed with her as she finished up her meal.

It was a first step.

Maybe not toward friendship, but what the Sinners were went beyond that. And she and I *were* Sinners. We'd been raised in the club. We knew how hard it was to mark out a path for ourselves, one that didn't allow the MC to swallow us up and spit us out whole.

Just like Steel called those morons brothers, we were sisters.

Afterward, when she offered me a ride back in her chauffeured car, I thought she saw that too because after I refused, telling her Steel was picking me up, she hugged me for real in farewell.

"You're looking thoughtful," Steel told me a couple minutes later after I sent him my live location and he'd kissed me in greeting.

"Just thinking that Rachel's got no idea what she's given up for this club and that your council doesn't either."

He blinked at me. "Huh?"

I rolled my eyes. "Never mind."

## FORTY-FOUR

## REX
### MIRRORS - JUSTIN TIMBERLAKE

It took me four days to get Wynter to open up to me after the incident with Jeremy.

I walked her from work to school or picked her up and took her home. We ate together, and she even did some of her homework in front of me at the coffee shop where we staked a place for ourselves, but she didn't talk.

I didn't like that she was cowed.

I hated that she was scared of Kinnock.

Much as Rachel had told me in one of our email conversations, I was a fixer. For those I loved, I wanted to make everything as copacetic as was physically possible.

It killed something inside me not to make this better, to make it right, but I couldn't do anything if she wouldn't let me in.

I'd asked her what had happened afterward, I'd asked her to talk to me, but one of the waitresses who worked with her had called in sick with a stomach bug and Wynter had picked up those extra shifts, so it wasn't as easy to find time to talk with her about important things.

The same couldn't be said for her mother.

Rachel didn't avoid me, which came as a surprise. Especially as I knew she was pissed at me for beating Kinnock up. But something had changed between us and I was glad for it.

"I'd like to talk to Rachel today."

I shot Wynter a glance. "You would? You talking again?"

Her cheeks flushed. "I didn't stop talking."

"You did. You froze me out." My gaze was candid. I could handle her freezing me out—I'd had plenty of practice over the years with Rachel—I just couldn't deal with her lying about it.

She grimaced. "I-I was processing."

"Did he hurt you once you were on your own?"

"No. He doesn't hurt me," she said uncomfortably.

"But he hurts your mom?"

Her gaze darted away.

I had my answer.

"Why did you pick them?"

"For your adoptive parents?"

She nodded.

"You won't like my answer," I warned.

"I'd still like to know."

"I never liked your father," I said easily. "He was the school quarterback, and he was a jackass. *But* he wasn't a bully. The linebacker and his cronies were, but your dad always hung around Ally and she tempered the douche in him. Or, I guess, I thought she did.

"I had no inkling that he was a wife beater because if I had, there was no way in hell I'd have approached them about adopting you."

The more I spoke, the rounder her eyes grew, but she blurted out, "He wasn't always like this."

"What changed?"

"Tenure."

"Tenure?"

"He didn't get it. There was a spot that opened up in his department, and it went to a guy ten years younger than him."

"So? That doesn't excuse what he did."

"Not saying it does, but that was the trigger."

"Vain prick. That was always his flaw." I grunted. "Anyway, Ally was kind. She always was. I liked her. I'd have probably dated her if your mom didn't have her hooks dug into me."

Something peeped into her eyes. "When did you know you loved her?"

"When I was thirteen." I shot her a grin. "I didn't realize that was what it was back then, of course. She came to the clubhouse and she was so fucking small, and I just wanted to protect her." My nose crinkled. "Irony being your mom doesn't want to be protected."

"Doesn't everyone want to be protected?"

"No. Not always. Some people like to fight their own battles." I cleared my throat before I pointedly asked, "Remind you of someone?"

She flushed. "I'm not—"

"Aren't you? I'm here, I'll gladly pay for better accommodation, and whatever your dad does or says, I'll sort it out for you. But for four days, you've been drifting around like a ghost."

Wynter gnawed on her lip. "Dad said something to me. I don't think he meant to. But... is it true you pay maintenance?"

"Of course."

"Of course?" Her brow puckered. "I don't understand. That's not how adoption works."

"It's how adoption works for *me*. I wanted you to have the best, and I was well aware that life as a professor and a homemaker doesn't always permit those luxuries."

"You pay for my school?"

"I do." Annoyed, I demanded, "What did he tell you that for?"

"You didn't want me to know?"

"I didn't."

"Why not?"

"Because it's irrelevant."

"It isn't. It's... you cared. You didn't stop caring. It matters." She fiddled with the handle on her mug. "Does Rachel know?"

"No."

"Why not?"

"Because I'd imagine she doesn't need to know to be aware that I'm a control freak where the people I love are concerned."

"Meaning?"

"She'd have expected me to be financially involved in your life. If I asked her, she'd be surprised. But if she thought about it for a minute, she wouldn't be."

"You do things your own way, don't you?"

I nodded. "Always have. Your mom, I mean, Rachel, she's the same. It just manifests differently."

"You're leaving for New Jersey soon, aren't you?"

The change of topic was abrupt. "Yes. But I'm coming back. I'll fly out, then return. For however long you'd like me to hang out."

"What if I said forever?"

I heard her rebellious tone and understood it.

"Then we might have to make some adjustments."

She studied me. "You have to ride your bike back home, don't you?"

"I do. I also have to arrange my father's funeral."

"Your life is on the East Coast."

"Yours is on the West."

"Do you think Rachel would come visit? Maybe she'd fly back with you?"

"I could ask her," I said carefully, not wanting to get her hopes up.

It wasn't that I didn't think Rachel would come, but I liked to manage expectations.

"Would you ask her now?"

Again with the spurt of defiance.

I shrugged. "Can I give her a warning again?"

"Yes."

Quickly, I sent Rachel a message.

**Rex:** *Wynter wants to talk.*

**Rachel:** *Just a minute. On the phone. I'll call after I'm done.*

**Rex:** *Fine.*

I tipped the screen to her so she could see the exchange, well aware what her game was—she wanted Rachel's raw reaction to the request.

To be frank, I understood. I was curious too.

With a satisfied nod, she murmured, "Thank you."

"Testing Rachel won't work out well for you," I told her calmly.

"Why not?"

"Because she's always going to surprise you." I tapped my chin. "Wouldn't you prefer to know if she'll make the decision herself?"

"You mean, after you go and then fly back, she might decide to visit too?"

"Isn't it the logical move?"

"What's logical here?" she queried. "I mean, I get why she put me up for adoption, I do, and I understand she had issues and that she didn't just want to throw me away—"

"Rachel *is not* like that," I inserted forcefully, my temper surging. "Rachel, when she was a kid, wanted nothing more than her own family. She wanted a place where she belonged, and she wanted her kids to have that sense of belonging too.

"Her mom was a joke. I'm pretty damn sure if you asked Rachel, she'd tell you she wished she'd been put up for adoption instead of being traipsed around the country how she was, neglected and forgotten about for most of the time.

"When everything went wrong, that was what scared her the most. She wanted better for you than she had."

Wynter eyed me with a calm expression. "You're very protective of her, aren't you?"

"Aren't I of you?"

Her lips twitched at my aggressive retort. I half expected her to bring up Kinnock's injuries, but she didn't. She'd yet to mention them—thank Christ. "Yes," was all she said.

Huffing, I shot her a nod. "I understand that you have reasons to question every decision we made, but you need to recognize that when you're a parent, and you don't have the best examples, fear of being as shitty as the one you had is a big motivator."

"You loved your mom and dad, didn't you?"

"I did. They were great examples. The best. That's why I knew Rachel would be a fantastic parent. I saw in her what I saw in my mom. Patience and kindness. A fierce strength and streak of protectiveness that would see her through every stress and strain.

"I just didn't think those traits would make her be brave enough to let you go so that you'd have the best childhood you could have. Something she didn't believe she could give to you."

Wynter rested a calm glance on me, and I let her study me in silence, didn't say another word as she processed all I'd had to say.

When Rachel called ten minutes later than promised, I heard how rattled she was and so did Wynter.

Was I surprised when Wynter listened to me?

When they just talked about their days? When Wynter asked about the gala and how the organization of it was going? When they spoke about what they'd be having for dinner of all things?

No, I wasn't totally shocked.

Sometimes, you just had to see how the cards fell.

Sometimes the only way to know something was to let a situation unroll on its own.

I was pretty proud that my kid, at seventeen years old, was as capable of that as her almost forty-year-old dad.

The week rolled around until the day of my flight hit us.

I'd had an awesome time hanging out with her, getting to know my kid, her getting to know me. Integrating myself into her schedule to facilitate that process, all as I was being totally irresponsible and not doing a damn thing for my MC.

I knew Nyx would be able to manage, and we had a solid council in place to make everything happen. Now that Lily was working with Rachel, I felt better too because I knew any overflow that the council couldn't deal with on their own, they could approach her with.

For that short while, I guessed I enjoyed my first vacation in years.

When Mom had died, I'd been shoved into the position of Prez years ahead of schedule. In my grief and in his, Dad had wanted freedom, and that was what I needed right now. A reminder of what mattered. That family was all.

I was more like him than I realized.

I just wasn't a fucking cheater.

That bitterness hadn't eased, and I knew I'd have to fulfill his bequest at some point, and I was gradually getting to be okay with that.

If Wynter could forgive me, if she could open up to Rachel and forgive what she perceived as abandonment, then I knew I had to grow the fuck up and be as mature as my teenaged daughter.

Still, the morning of my red-eye, Wynter was oddly quiet when we walked to work together.

I didn't mind, in all honesty.

She was a pensive, thoughtful kid, much as her old man was, but I knew today was different.

A small thrill whipped its way inside me—I knew she didn't want me to go.

It felt good to be needed by her. I didn't want her to feel the pain of missing me, even as I wanted her to miss me. It was strange.

In all this time, I'd yet to meet any of her friends. I'd almost thought she didn't have any, but I knew Kinnock had said he'd approached a kid called Chelsea to find out where Wynter was holing up.

I didn't think she was ashamed of me, more that she was isolated, so I didn't like the prospect of leaving her either.

Logically, I knew I didn't own all her waking hours. I'd yet to even see Ally, so I knew she was keeping some stuff from me, but I didn't like that she was so alone, especially in that fucking apartment building of hers.

It set me on edge.

"You'll call me, won't you?" she blurted out halfway to the coffee shop.

I snorted. "You just try and stop me."

She shot me a grin.

"You'll answer, won't you?"

"Of course," she said gruffly, her gaze on her feet. Bottom lip firmly tucked between her teeth, she murmured, "You'll take photos?"

"Of the gala? Or of your mo—Rachel—and I together?"

With every day that had passed, we'd talked on the phone, and it was obnoxiously difficult not to think of Rachel as her mom.

I was grateful she never made a fuss about the Freudian slip.

"Both?" She peeped at me. "I want to see her dress and..." Her grin broadened. "You in a tux."

I grimaced. "Only for your mom would I wear a penguin suit."

Her gaze turned inward. "I think you should have a haircut."

"You do, do you? What other fashion tips do you have for me?" I drawled.

When she giggled, it lit up my fucking soul. "I think we need to clean you up."

"Why?"

"So that you don't look like your uncle anymore." She looked at me from the corner of her eye. "Now you know who you remind her of, don't you think it'd be smart to have a makeover?"

"I refuse to be Queer Eyed; I'd never hear the goddamn end of it."

Wynter snickered. "Shuddup."

I grinned but confirmed, "I was going to have a haircut and a shave before I met her. I promise."

"You were?" Her brow was arched, and I could tell she was unconvinced.

"Yeah, once I'd charmed you I didn't need to impress you anymore." I winked at her. "Hence the ragtag look."

"I wondered what had happened to the Ken doll."

I chuckled.

"Y-You do know that if it works and she stops associating you with him, you'd have to do it forever, don't you?"

"If a shot at *forever* is even doable if I have a haircut and a shave, Wynter, I'll start my own barbershop and have a daily appointment with them."

"You love her that much?"

I blinked at her. "What do you think of when you see the future?"

Her brow furrowed, but I shot her a patient look, silently telling her that I was going somewhere with this.

"It's changed."

"Your future?"

She nodded, and her smile was shy as she looked at me. Warmth hit my heart like it was hammering nails into it, and I choked at the sight—she liked me.

Logically, I knew she did.

I wasn't a fucking moron.

Why the hell else would she want to hang out with me?

Sure, there was free food and I offered to pay for any and everything she might need, but she was a prideful little thing—had to be. Both her parents were stubborn and proud.

Still, to see it, to *hear* it, it was almost too fucking much.

"I used to think I'd go to Berkeley, but now I'm thinking about NYU or something like that."

My eyes widened. "Really?"

She tucked her chin down. "Really. There's more to the US than the West Coast."

"You don't have to worry about tuition, Wynter," I told her gruffly, mostly just fucking proud that my daughter was taking after her mom and not me. "I'll pay for everything."

"You don't have to do that! I wasn't saying this for that."

"I know you weren't, but I'd have paid anyway. I want you to know that."

Gnawing on her bottom lip, she peered at me and said, "I'm very lucky."

"I'm the lucky one," I told her.

She cleared her throat. "I-I see my future being different than the one I always envisioned. I-I wanted to become a professional so my mom could move out, so that she could live with me. She's still young, really, but she acts like she's ancient." She gave a deep sigh. "Whenever I suggest getting a job, you know, so she can move out, she always acts like she can't use a computer. I'm not sure if she's lazy or just scared."

"Maybe it's a mixture of both," I drawled, amused by her irritation.

Wynter wasn't the kind of girl who let much hold her back.

Fuck, it was terrifying how powerful nature vs. nurture could be.

"Maybe," she agreed grumpily. "She's been a homemaker for so long that I think she doesn't know how to change. So, I wanted to be that for her."

That wasn't the girl I remembered. But twenty years of marriage to that fucker, Kinnock, had clearly undermined Ally's confidence.

"I get it," I told her, "but you should also remember that kids aren't put on this planet for that. It's not your job to make sure she gets her life in order.

"I mean, you can make that choice when you're older. But seventeen is when you should be thinking about parties and boys or girls—" I choked on the latter, but out of fairness, I had to see it from her point of view. Not that I cared who she fell in love with, just... Christ, dating in general was a nightmare prospect for me.

She noticed too—her grin turned wicked at my discomfort. "How very forward-thinking of you, Rex," she said primly.

"Yeah, isn't it?" I asked. "But you know what I mean, don't you?"

"I do. I'm not the party type, but I get where you're coming from."

"College is a whole other ball game. Things change when you're there. You're an adult, and you'll be taught and treated as if you're one." I thought about Rachel, about the positive changes that had happened while she was away at college. Before all the shit had started. "Your mom was like a different person when she was there. It was good for her. I think it'll be good for you too.

"Plus, you'll be in New York! I mean, that's gotta be cool, right? You'll have the safety net of knowing we're close by and that you can call on us if you're in a pinch. Just try not to get arrested, huh?" I joked, gently nudging her with my elbow.

"I'll try my best," she informed me with a grin.

"So, you see how your future changed? Because I came into it?"

That had her tilting her head at me. "I see that."

"Well, that happened to me when I was thirteen."

Understanding struck. "When you met Rachel."

Not a question. A statement.

I nodded. "Everything shifted. I didn't realize it back then, but it did. I had no legitimate reason to want to hang around a little girl," I mocked. "So I just used to watch over her. She got picked on a lot, so that made it easy for me to protect her from afar, but she grew more and more isolated as a result."

"Why?"

"I think I frightened everyone away. Not just the bullies, but the potential friends."

She should have had a relationship with Indy and Stone, but she hadn't.

Somehow, she'd grown close with Carly.

To this day, I still didn't understand what happened there.

"She had *no* friends?"

"In school, yeah. Two gay kids."

"Is she friends with them now?"

"Not exactly. They were, but they had a falling out. Anyway, back then, Scott and Craig were ostracized too. Outsiders. They got along great with each other."

"Why were they outsiders? Because they were gay?"

"That and because they got caught having sex in the locker room."

A snort escaped her. "See, people would have filmed that now and put it on the Internet. They'd have been popular, not exiled."

"Different times." I shrugged then decided to get the subject back on track. "The truth is, Wynter, my future is tied to your mom's. It has been for years, and that's not going to change."

"You told me once that you gave her an ultimatum..."

"I called her bluff. There wasn't a snowball in hell's chance that I was going anywhere."

"You really love her, don't you?"

"She's it for me. Simple."

"That isn't simple," my kid argued. "If anything, that's super complicated."

I tucked my arm around her shoulder. "That's love for you."

Though she huffed, she slipped her arm around my waist and hugged me closer. "I'm going to miss you, Rex."

"I'm gonna miss you too, kiddo."

Wynter peered up at me. "What makeover are you going to have?"

"I'll take a picture once it happens," I promised, amused. "You trying to matchmake?"

"Maybe. I-I just... Rachel always sounds so weird on the phone. I'm not sure if that's because of me and because she's nervous because I know she is, even if she pushes past it." She shook her head, and I knew that was because she couldn't assimilate how Rachel could deal with murderers but couldn't cope with her. "Or if it's to do with her life. She never sounds happy until you tease her into laughing."

"I don't tease her!"

"You do!" She gave me the side eye. "You don't realize you're doing it, do you?"

"Doing what?"

"Softening her up. It'd be borderline manipulative if you weren't coming from a good place."

"Gee, thanks for the character assassination."

"You're welcome," she told me tongue-in-cheek, eyes gleaming. "I'd like her to be happy."

"Not me?" I asked, cocking a brow at her.

"I think it'd take very little for you to be happy, and most of that revolves around her not just being your lawyer and being your actual girlfriend where you can eat dinner together and maybe go to sleep at night together." Her cheeks flushed as she said that, and I appreciated that thinking about her bio parents maybe 'doing it' wasn't something she wanted on her mind.

"You'd be right," I admitted, surprised and oddly impressed by her insight.

She just hummed. "So, makeover. Let's see if that's a step forward, hmm?"

Wynter sounded so oddly adult that I'd have laughed if I didn't think it'd have hurt her feelings.

"Agreed."

"You promise you'll come back to see me?"

I dragged my cut from the bag I'd been carrying, handed it to her and asked, "Know what this means?"

"Of course."

"*Sons of Anarchy* really isn't your Wikipedia for all the things I do..." I pointed out.

She just smirked but continued staring down at the worn leather.

"Keep that safe for me until I come back?"

Wynter's mouth rounded. "You really mean that?"

Teasing aside, she knew what I was leaving behind.

"I do. I ain't coming back for the cut, but for you, but that's your insurance." I winked at her. "It's worth a lot of ransom money."

She grinned and held it to her chest for the rest of the walk.

I was gonna miss her, and the best part? From a relationship that had been non-existent at the start, I knew she'd miss me too.

***Unknown Sender:*** I'll meet you on W 125th St and Adam Clayton Powell Jr Blvd at 9pm.
***Nyx:*** See you there.
***Unknown Sender:*** Don't be late.

# FORTY-FIVE

## HAWK

### THE FOLLOWING EVENING

"I like your sister."

It was an innocent enough statement, but I knew my little bird too well to fall for that.

Studying her warily, I asked, "Who'd she hurt?"

Amara's eyes twinkled as she pranced over to me. When she did a complete pirouette, I cocked an ear and listened out for a fucking ambulance.

My woman was a melancholic. Understandable considering her past, but happiness came in different guises. When she was with me, for example, Quin, both of us, eating, watching *The Mentalist*, or when someone she didn't like was being hurt.

If that made her sound sadistic, well, she was.

Being kidnapped and sold into the sex trade did that to a person.

I thought we were fucking blessed that she was as high functioning as she was.

Finally plunking herself beside me on the sofa, she pressed her hand to my chest then shifted her leg so that she was straddling me. Her slight behind, getting curvier now that we'd discovered she adored Mexican food—she was costing us a fortune in avocados—settled on my thighs as she peeped a smile up at me.

"Kendra told Giulia that Nyx was fucking her." She snorted. "Giulia was not very smart to believe her—"

"Not like Giulia to be anxious about these things," I pointed out with a frown as I placed my hands on her hips, sliding my thumbs into the loops of her denim skirt. "Kendra's a cunt—"

"*Tak,* that she is. She says Giulia is too fat. That Nyx likes them thin." Amara sniffed. "Kendra does not have eyes."

"She does." I smirked. "Two of them to be precise."

She clicked her fingers. "You know what I mean. She does not *use* them. If she did, she would see Nyx is..." A hum sounded from her lips. "What is the word?"

"Whipped?" I drawled with a grin.

She tutted. "*Nii,* Hawk. She is all he sees. Much like with me you," she mangled.

"'Much like I am with you,'" I corrected.

People didn't get our relationship, and I was okay with that. They thought that I was shoved in a corner of Quin and Amara's, served sloppy seconds... Even with mangled English, Amara disproved that.

"Much like I am with you," she confirmed. "I see you—"

"And I see you."

"*Tak.*" She clicked her fingers again. "Soul friends."

I grinned. "You've been watching TV in Ukrainian again when we're out."

Her nose crinkled. "Is much easier than English."

"And how will you learn if you keep on watching in Ukrainian?"

"Maybe you should learn Ukrainian," she grumbled.

"I will if you teach me."

She squinted at me. "This bullshit?"

"No. God's honest truth."

"What does God have to do with it?"

I snickered. "Nothing. Or a lot. Depending on your religion."

She pondered my expression. "You mean this?"

"I do." And because I wasn't above throwing Quin under a bus too, I told her, "I bet Quin will want to learn as well."

Amara tapped her finger against her chin. "I would make good incentives for you learning."

"You would?" I arched a brow. "What kind of incentives?"

"I don't know yet. But they would be good."

Snorting, I told her, "I'm sure."

She patted my chest. "Is wise you know this."

"I'm a wise man," I drawled. "Anyway, what did Giulia do?"

"She held a knife to Kendra's throat and told her she'd cut off a tit if she went near her man." She gave a stout nod. "Your sister is wise too."

My lips twitched. "Can you cut off a breast?"

"Why not?" She hitched a shoulder. "I think I will do this to Liliana when Lodestar tells me where she hides—"

I rolled my eyes. "Note to self, we need a *Dexter* chop-shop room."

"Dexter—I like him too."

"I know."

"I watch him in Ukrainian. Much darker." She smacked her lips. "Better."

"Little whack job," I told her fondly, reaching up to give those lips of hers a kiss.

Before I could, she shimmied back and said, "I did not tell you best part yet."

"Better than an artisanal mastectomy?" I didn't think there was a technical term for what my sister had threatened. But who the fuck knew?

"Artisanile what?"

I cleared my throat. "Artisanal means 'homemade.' A mastectomy is breast tissue removal."

"Oh! *Tak*." She beamed. "She—how you say—vomeeteed."

"Vomited," I corrected automatically, blinking at her as I translated. "She vomited on her?"

"*Tak.*" Amara beamed at me again. "She has style."

I didn't bother correcting her butchery of the word 'style,' just peered at her. "Is she okay?"

Amara waved a hand. "She is pregnant. Lots of liquids in pregnancy."

"Liquids?"

"In all holes."

I shook my head in confusion. "What the hell are you talking about?"

She huffed. "You know. They pee a lot, vomeet a lot—"

Grimacing, I reached for my phone as Amara told me about how Kendra had started sobbing while the rest of the clubwhores clucked around her. She spoke with a lot of satisfied relish about the other woman's misery—Amara had a distinct loathing for the club bunnies—as I texted my baby sister.

I figured I was being punished for some transgression in a past life that both my sister and woman were as bloodthirsty as they were.

**Hawk:** *Amara just told me you were sick? You okay, sis?*
**Giulia:** *I'm fine.*
**Hawk:** *Sounds like it. Threatening to cut off a woman's tit?*
**Giulia:** *A new high in the club.*
**Hawk:** *You sure you're okay?*
**Giulia:** *I'm fine.*
**Hawk:** *Why were you sick?*
**Giulia:** *I'm pregnant.*
**Hawk:** *Did you learn how to puke on command?*
**Giulia:** *Maybe.*

If anyone was capable of it, Giulia was.

**Hawk:** *You know Kendra was talking bullshit, don't you?*
**Giulia:** *Do I?*
**Hawk:** *Nyx ain't got eyes for anyone but you, Giulia.*

**Giulia:** *I know that.*
**Hawk:** *Then why did you get so mad?*
**Giulia:** *Why are men the only ones allowed to stake a claim?*
**Hawk:** *So, this is you being a feminist?*
**Giulia:** *Exactly.*
**Hawk:** *Where's Nyx?*
**Giulia:** *He had to go out.*
**Hawk:** *Need me to come around?*
**Giulia:** *What am I? Ten?*
**Hawk:** *Fine. Call me if you need me.*
**Giulia:** *I won't need to. But thanks, Hawk. Xo*

Knowing she really was okay, I rolled my eyes and shoved my phone away.

"She's as insane as ever," I grumbled, squeezing Amara's butt who immediately rocked into me.

Because I was as whipped for her as Nyx was for my sister, my dick hardened almost instantly.

"I like her," Amara chided as she pressed her lips to mine.

"Can we not talk about my sister?"

She laughed, and that fucking laugh gave my brain a boner.

It was wicked and pure and filled with delight and love and all kinds of shit that I never thought I'd have.

Amara might be... special.

But she was fucking mine.

All of her.

I nipped her bottom lip and shoved us both into a standing position so that I could walk us into the bedroom.

When she crossed her legs around my hips and tightened her ankles about my ass, I squeezed that perky butt and murmured, "You doing okay, little bird?"

"I am with you, no?"

I smirked. "You are."

She pushed her forehead against mine. "I am lucky woman."

"I'm lucky man," I half-teased. Not because I didn't mean the words, but because her broken English was infectious.

"You are, *tak*, but when Giulia threatened Kendra, I saw that I would be like her—" Jesus fuck. "I would spit fire at her and like Nyx, you would not stop me."

My dick got uncomfortably hard.

Her smile told me she felt it too.

"I know you like it when I'm crazy even if you say you don't."

"It's not that I like it—"

She rocked her hips.

I hissed under my breath.

"A part of you does."

"Yes, well, that part has no brain."

A cackle escaped her. "It does, it does. Smart part of body. I like your penis."

I liked how she said peenus.

So did my cock.

Her watching Ukrainian shows and enjoying US shows with Ukrainian audio meant her accent was getting thicker.

Much like her butt.

Delicious.

Grumbling, I told her, "I prefer you not to get jealous because it isn't necessary."

"Is necessary—"

"Isn't." I grunted. "*It* isn't. I'm not interested in another woman."

I had enough to handle with her, and Quin shared the fucking load.

Amara, for one so slight, was a hell of a lot of woman.

It took both of us to keep her balanced.

Some men might consider that a chore; some men, however, were morons.

Quin and I knew we were the lucky ones.

She might be a fry short of a Happy Meal, but her heart was big.

After what she'd endured, we were fortunate that it wasn't a shriveled husk. Instead, we had a woman who'd kill for us, and who would love us until the day we died.

Quin also had a woman who'd put up with all the goddamn animals.

Saying that, he had douchebag over here who'd deal with them too. I was a fucking idiot for both of them.

When she nuzzled her face in my throat, nipping me there slightly, I tried not to groan but she knew all my hot spots now.

"Is good that you're not interested in other women," she growled, pressing a kiss to the place she'd nipped.

I tilted my face to the side and slid my tongue along the line of her jaw. When she shivered, I said, "It works both ways—"

"Of course," was her stout reply, which she ruined by moaning breathily when I sucked on the join between neck and shoulder.

I twisted us around once I made it to the bedroom and carefully fell back onto the bed. She shrieked out a laugh but shoved some space between us as she loomed over me, her eyes gleaming with good humor.

"I love you, little bird," I whispered, reaching up to trace the sinews in her throat. "You're it for me."

"I love you, my Hawk." She bopped a kiss on the end of my nose. "I am lucky to have your love—"

"I consider myself the lucky one," I rumbled as I let my hands move to her waist. "Now, you gonna kiss me or just torment me? That sweet pussy of yours is too far away from my cock."

Something flickered in her eyes—Quin and I had agreed to limit our use of American profanity because it could trigger her all while trying to expose her to the words in a safe space—but she rocked her hips.

"I love your cock," she said softly, slowly. Like she was tasting the word and wasn't hating it.

"It loves your pussy," I retorted with a laugh, adoring the random shit she came out with.

I let my hands slide up the length of her thighs, skimming the hem of her skirt higher up as I went. She rounded her spine and settled her elbows on either side of my ears, looming over me in a way that surrounded me in her scent.

Allspice.

Cinnamon.

God, she smelled like snickerdoodles, and I wanted to fucking glut on her.

I reached up and nipped her chin, testing the pad with my teeth before I let go.

In her eyes, a tempest brewed, and I inwardly groaned at the sight as she rasped, "Mine."

I smirked. "Prove it."

As she kissed me, she growled—her tongue immediately thrusting against mine as she took my declaration of war and deployed troops into the battle.

Letting one hand rub her thigh, the other went up to her hair and I tipped her head so that she could get even nearer to me.

She fought a good game, but I was the one who won when she fucked my mouth, when her body started to ripple against mine, dragging her core against my cock, making me wish I was deep inside her.

That fucking tongue of hers was a menace—it sought mine out and demanded I surrender. Only, my mom hadn't raised no pussy. With my hold on her hair, I surged upward so that I had better access to her.

Dropping one hand to her waist, I dragged her shirt up then slipped my fingers beneath the fabric so I could cup one of her tits. The silken flesh felt goddamn awesome against my callused palms. She groaned when I found one of her nipples, and I groaned back when I realized she wasn't wearing a bra.

Both of us retreated, the war at a stalemate for the moment, as we pushed our foreheads into the other, our breaths gusting onto each other's mouths.

Panting, she delved between us and unzipped my fly to free my cock. One hand slipped between the tines, coming to hold the thick length that was already wet with pre-cum.

As she jacked me off, she whispered words in Ukrainian that I didn't have a hope in hell of translating, but I could sense her pleasure.

Her need.

That she could feel those things, after what she'd gone through, always honored me.

It wasn't just that she wanted me, *us*; it meant more than that. It meant that she felt safe, loved. It meant that she was confident enough in herself and in us to know her boundaries and to know that she was okay with slipping past them.

Every day she granted me was a fucking gift.

With a groan, my head fell back as she thumbed the slit of my dick, rubbing the pre-cum into the glans. I felt like I could explode already and I knew that was because she'd gone all psycho on my ass.

I wasn't sure who was the fucking weirdo in this relationship—her for being crazy, or me for loving it when she was at her most possessive.

For a man who'd never wanted anything like that with a woman before, it sure as hell took me by surprise.

Head still angled back, I nearly shuddered when she made her next move.

All of a sudden, I could feel the branding heat of her cunt, and I groaned. Deep and long and low. The crotch of her panties dug into me from the side where she'd shoved it, but I didn't give a damn. This was fucking heaven.

Slick, slick, *slick* flesh. So fucking wet and juicy that my mouth watered. I wanted her on my fucking tongue, wanted to drown in her, but she was in charge today.

Tonight, I'd get my way.

There was, I realized, give and take in a relationship.

I hissed when she rubbed her clit with my glans, and it morphed into a groan as she slipped the tip into her.

As we both began to moan, she pressed her lips to mine, and this time, I was so far gone that I let her take control of the kiss.

Those tight, tight, *tight* walls clamped down around me, making me and gravity fight hard for every claimed inch, but it was more than worth the struggle.

"Fuck," I groaned, my hands finding her ass, kneading the cheeks as I encouraged her to ride me.

"This dick is mine," she said thickly.

"It goddamn is," I agreed with a sigh as I decided to enjoy the show and fell back against the sheets.

Watching her, I enjoyed it even more when her hands went to the hem of her shirt and she dragged it over her head.

Once her tits were bared to my gaze, I reached up and cupped one of them, tweaking her nipple as my other hand slipped between us so I could rub her clit.

As I did, her cunt fluttered around my cock, and we shared a look as, again, we released a dual moan.

"God," I grunted.

"*Korva,*" she keened.

When she reached for my hands, bridging our fingers together and pinning them on either side of my head again, I let her. I wasn't about to mess with her when she got that look—hunger.

For me.

Fuck.

"I love you," she whispered, her lips not even moving.

The words filtered through me, resonating along every nerve ending in my being.

"And I love you," I rasped back, content to watch that hungry look morph into the wildfire that was this woman.

My woman.

Mine.

## FORTY-SIX

## RACHEL

### TONIGHT, TONIGHT - SMASHING PUMPKINS

THAT SAME EVENING

"Holy shit, Rachel!"

Lily's exclamation had me hiding a grin. "Do I dress up well?"

"Damn straight you do." She blinked. "Rex doesn't know what he's missing."

"I don't think he's the designer sort," I mocked as I slipped into my heels and put on my earrings.

It was a deceptively simple dress. Sweetheart neckline, fishtail skirt, but it had a kind of bustle at the back with a bow that was made for sin—a couple of tugs on that bow and the back gaped and it'd be beyond easy to slip out of.

Funny how I was dressed for sex but the only guy I wanted was on the other side of the country.

"I figured you'd be wearing a black turtleneck or something."

I snorted. "It's a black-tie event."

"I said *black* turtleneck. I've never seen you in anything other than workwear."

"That's most of my wardrobe, but I always dress up for the

fundraisers." I cast her a glance as I patted my hair down. "You look gorgeous too. No Link to drool over you?"

Her smile was smug as she patted the neat LBD that hugged her slim curves. "He drooled earlier, but nah. Not only is this *not* his scene, there was a..." Her lips firmed, but her eyes gleamed with amusement. "...shall we say *altercation* at the clubhouse, so he's there."

"What kind of altercation?" I groused. "I'd better not get a call halfway through the goddamn event, Lily!"

"Nothing like that. Kendra pissed Giulia off, and Giulia was cooking, so—"

"She was armed?"

Lily snickered. "Yeah. Went at her with a cleaver, or so Steel told Tiff. Then, and this is the best part—she puked all over her!"

My nose crinkled, but I was fighting a smile too. "I'm sure Kendra deserved it."

We shared a look, and Lily nodded. "I'm sure she did."

With that news perking me up, I asked, "Everything set?"

"It is. Management here actually offered to donate a weekend break in their Presidential suite too. I just got an email from them—"

My brows rose. "Your doing?"

She shot me a sheepish look. "Maybe."

"You're good at this," I told her softly. "I wish you'd been around when I was starting up."

Hope lit up her eyes, but excitement made her cheeks flush. "Donavan—" *Her father.* The piece of shit. "—wanted me to major in husband, but I decided that I could make use of school too. I minored in accounting and event management. With what Mom taught me as well, it's exciting to get things happening. To make change."

"I hate this side of things," I admitted. "It's a weight off that you don't and that you're good at it."

Casually, I looked at her in the mirror as I slipped on the tennis bracelet I was wearing tonight.

"Need some help with that?" she offered.

"Thanks."

As she reached out, from beneath her own diamond-studded tennis bracelet, I saw her 'Property of Link' brand.

It wasn't the first time I'd seen it, but an odd feeling settled in my being. Much as it had when Stone and I had talked about the MC and belonging.

A craving had stirred inside me.

A need.

But it was also a reminder of her loyalty to the MC. She was an Old Lady. One who needed more than just to be Link's woman.

I understood that duality, however. The need to belong, as well as the need to forge one's own path.

As she slotted the bracelet's clasp into place for me, I asked, "Would you like to be more involved in the next event?"

"I'd love that," she breathed shakily, her glee clear and more befitting a lottery win than the offer that she'd be shouldering months' worth of headaches on my behalf. "You mean that?"

"Wouldn't say it if I didn't. The last couple weeks ran ten times more smoothly than the previous twelve, and trust me, things are supposed to get more chaotic, not less. I can't even thank you enough for all you've done." I turned to her and reached out to grab her hand so I could squeeze her fingers. "You've been a lifesaver. I genuinely don't know what I'd have done without you."

Her gaze turned knowing. "How's the morning sickness?"

"You're not supposed to know."

"Giulia asked me to watch out for you," was her unapologetic reply. "How is it?"

"Worse than before."

"Giulia said there's nothing you can do."

My lips curved. "I know. I don't want the antiemetics the doctor suggested. Mostly she told me to calm down, which doesn't exactly make a person calm down, does it?"

"Not really, no," she said with a laugh.

"That's why I'm grateful too. I can't imagine how hard it would have been if I didn't have your help. So, if you're amenable, I'd like to take this from a part-time thing to a full-time operation—"

"You're not serious?!" Lily squeaked, her eyes flaring wide.

"I am. Deadly," I teased. "I arrange three to four of these a year, but I've always been constrained, timewise, to keep the events localized.

"If you could make them bigger, get more of a push out there, liaise with whomever to get these fundraisers more known—"

"I have ideas," she enthused, her voice high and squeaky. "*So* many ideas. I was going to talk to you about them, see if you thought they were achievable.

"I own the Landis Scraper on the Upper East Side—"

My eyes bugged. "You do?"

"Yeah," she admitted sheepishly. "So I can pretty much guarantee that we'd have a venue tailored to our needs."

I beamed a smile at her. "That's brilliant. Next week, we'll pencil down some time to sort through your ideas—"

She snagged both my hands and squeezed my fingers. "Thank you, Rachel. Thank you so damn much. I've been trying to get things off the ground with a foundation in my mom's name, but what with everything, it's just not been doable. To be a part of the good work you're already doing is more than I could have hoped for."

"You're welcome," I said, both amused and touched by her enthusiasm as I slipped my cell phones into my clutch purse and tucked it under my arm.

Giulia, it seemed, was right.

Lily *had* been struggling to find her place, and for Link's sake, I was glad to have given her somewhere to land.

This might not work out; Lily could hate working for me or might not want to carry on, but we all needed to feel as if we had roots.

It made sense that someone with her past, from her family, who'd dived into the MC lifestyle, would flounder.

Before I could head out the door, Parker texted me.

**Parker:** *You haven't sent me a picture yet.*

**Rachel:** *Damn. I barely finished getting dressed! Bossy!*

**Parker:** *Just making sure you don't forget.*

*\*picture sent\**

**Rachel:** *Happy now?*

**Parker:** *You look beautiful. Rex doesn't know what he's missing out on.*

**Rachel:** *Lol. Lily just said that.*

**Parker:** *Everything okay there?*

**Rachel:** *Yeah, she's got it all in hand.*

**Parker:** *Break a leg.*

**Rachel:** *I'll try to break two. <3*

**Parker:** <3

The next twenty minutes were spent confirming the schedule and that there were no changes to any of the auction lots.

There'd be a meal, dancing, an auction, some speeches, followed by more dancing.

Personally, I'd be glad when the damn thing was over.

I hated dancing with clients and making small talk, but it was all for a good cause.

Reminding them of the favors that indebted them to me always made for better auction prices.

Mostly, what I loathed was the behind-the-scenes stress.

If I could put those jobs on Lily's shoulders too, I knew I'd dread these things much less. She was far more fitting as the face of FAST than the MC brat of a whore, anyway. Self-made criminals loved rubbing shoulders with American royalty like the Lindenbourgs.

You had to love the US. She might be the daughter of a criminal sex trafficker, but being associated with the Lindenbourgs stopped her from being a total social pariah.

Time squirreled away from us as we headed downstairs and made sure that everything was running smoothly.

I greeted some of the new arrivals, watched as most people found their seats without any problem, smiled when I saw a bunch of these so-called hardened criminals dancing with their women like they were on *Dancing with the Stars*.

The Victoria was a five-star hotel deep in the heart of Manhattan, and I'd always used their event halls because they gave a touch of much-needed class to my foundations.

Maybe Lily and her help had brought it to my attention, but I realized I had a chip on my shoulder. A massive one.

Nobody here made me feel like I didn't belong—how could they? Most of them had worse reps than I did! But that limited my charities' endeavors. It meant that we weren't receiving as many donations as we should be getting.

Lily would rectify that, and FAST and my other foundations would benefit from it.

FAST, more than the others, was particularly close to my heart.

Amid the Art Deco glamor of a ballroom that twinkled with lights from massive chandeliers with beautiful parquet flooring that only added to that touch of class, I swirled among the crowd, wearing diamonds I'd bought myself, a ten-thousand-dollar gown that I'd comfortably purchased for this event, and with a set of heels that made my inner teenager swoon.

I'd done this.

That was the thought that rammed its way home as I circulated.

Me.

I'd done this.

I'd bought and paid for everything. My foundation existed because it was my brainchild.

It was only now that I realized what I'd achieved, what I'd accomplished, and while I knew I *had* let Wynter down, this was something I could be proud of.

The next time she asked me about my job and my clients, this was what I'd talk about—not the murderers I defended because they paid exorbitant fees for me to get them off capital punishments, not the mafioso who had me on retainer because I was better with loopholes than a knitter. *This.*

*This* was my legacy.

Flushed with success, I did the unthinkable—after listening to the speeches of some of the charity workers, the heads of the homes my charities funded, the coordinators, I took to the stage.

I'd never done that before, but I felt on top of the world for once.

Most of the attendees had been listening to the other speeches with half an ear, their interest waning. They weren't here for the cause, just to curry favor with me, so when I stood before the podium, I drew the room's gaze.

With no speech planned, I decided just to verbalize what I was feeling. How proud I was of FAST. How proud I was of what I'd achieved.

Funny how that pride was something I felt because Wynter had made me realize how ashamed I was of my career.

Dirty money.

Blood money.

But, through both, my charities existed so it couldn't be all bad.

"I see very few strangers amid the crowd and know most of you all intimately." It didn't hurt to remind them of those favors they owed me again. "Your repeated support of FAST means more than you could possibly know, and to be fair, more than a lot of you even care to know.

"I'm aware that your support is tied to your work with me, and I don't begrudge that." I shot the crowd a rueful smile and it drew some titters of amusement from around the room before I declared, "You're here, and that's all that matters.

"This year, things are a little different on a personal front. I lost a man who was like a second father to me, and my own personal circumstances are changing. It reminds me of a time when I was eighteen, just about to turn nineteen, and I was pregnant... I was terrified. Absolutely petrified. I had no idea where to go, what to do, who to turn to. A foundation like this one would have meant the world to me."

I never shared private information, and I knew from the shock on the faces of those in the front row, that they hadn't anticipated my revealing something so personal.

But it was okay.

Two group meetings with Giulia's Posse, and I was realizing that Tiffany was right—I wasn't the one who'd done anything wrong.

I was the victim.

I was the survivor.

Shame wasn't something I should be feeling when I thought about my attacks.

That was on *them*.

Tiffany hadn't wrought miracles, but being around people whom Rex's brothers loved, women who were all like me, there was no denying that it helped.

A lot.

And that it gave me hope.

A lot.

Still, the hardened cynic in me had me pursing my lips as I said, "Life being what it is, things didn't work out for me but I'd like to think that some women out there get to have their child and an education at the same time."

That didn't cut through to the heart of my personal circumstances, but that would definitely have been oversharing.

I let my words settle and cast my gaze around the room once more.

That, of course, was when I saw him.

It was only years of maintaining and developing my poker face in the courtroom that enabled me to carry on talking.

"That's why FAST exists," I continued, even though the sight of him had my heart pounding.

Had he had a haircut? It wasn't like he was unrecognizable, but in the tuxedo, he couldn't have looked any more different.

Throat thick, a strange ache in my chest appearing as I watched him raise his glass to me, I managed to choke out, "To make sure that women have options." I blinked. "They *can* have both. This isn't the

Dark Ages. It doesn't have to be either/or. So, that's why I'm grateful to you all. Because you help make that happen." I knew my smile turned strained, it probably even wobbled as my eyes turned to Rex again. "Thank you for being here."

Though the applause I received was boisterous, the confidence and flushed joy I'd had before dissipated some, even as a slow burn heat started to grow inside me.

As supportive as I knew Link was, even he hadn't attended tonight's gala.

Not only because of Giulia and Kendra's fight, but because of the tux too.

Yet, here Rex was... sitting at a table, hobnobbing with Manhattan's elite like he belonged in these environs.

And to be frank, in that get-up, he did.

I licked my lips as I stepped away from the podium.

When the auction began, I always helped the assistants with the lots, so it wasn't like I could go to him.

Wasn't like I could do much more than stare at him as he stared at me.

It helped that I wasn't on the stage, but at the side, so I could watch as he raised his flute of champagne again and took another sip all while his gaze was locked on mine, and the act of drinking became an extended affair.

I had never known anything like it.

As I watched him, I was sure time slowed. All I knew was the heat of his gaze, the warmth of that regard, the need that unfurled throughout my limbs. That craving, again, lodging deep inside my being.

I'd always been his. Always. That brand Lily wore, I should have one, but I didn't deserve one.

I'd pushed him away, always pushing, never drawing him to me. But the love I felt for him was real. So real. It was an ache in my being, one that had my heart crying out for him.

I'd denied us both.

Wasted so much time.

But it wasn't my fault.

It wasn't.

The Posse had taught me that.

Those bastards were to blame.

That didn't mean I had to let them keep on stealing more precious moments from me.

Change was coming; a thought that was rammed home as he watched me watch him.

I didn't even hear the gasps as a lot heated up, not until one of the assistants elbowed me in the side.

"Eighty thousand on the Hermés bag!" she half-gasped in my ear.

Torn from the moment, I turned to watch the crowd and saw Luciu Valentini was engaged in a bidding war for the questionable bag that had been donated by a husband who was sick of the sight of it.

"Ninety."

My lips quirked as, aware attention was *not* on me, I called out, "One hundred!"

There was dead silence, then Luciu tossed down, "One-twenty."

My eyes bugged at the price, but the woman at his side squealed with delight.

I studied her, certain I'd seen her before...

Then it hit me.

She'd been at Bellevue Hospital when I'd gone to collect Luciu from there with a police escort.

His arm had been broken in the holding cell after his arrest and, like he'd asked, I'd had him taken to Bellevue where I'd met up with him after he'd visited with his sick great-uncle who was in the prison hospital there.

Mind whirring as I watched the woman throw her arms around Luciu, I collected the bag once the auction was over.

I wanted nothing more than to go to Rex, but with a single donation of a hundred and twenty thousand dollars, Luciu deserved to have the damn monstrosity delivered to him by hand.

"For you, I assume?"

The woman with him squealed again which made Luciu laugh as she cradled the purse I handed to her.

Curiosity struck as to who the woman was, but smiling, I drawled, "You beat me to it."

It took a second for him to register my meaning.

"You were the one who raised the bid?" He shook his head. "That should be illegal."

Smile widening, I shrugged. "You can afford it. Thank you for the donation."

"You're welcome."

I dipped my chin. "I should have news regarding your great-uncle soon."

"Pleased to hear it."

"Enjoy the rest of your evening, Luciu and... *guest*."

When he didn't introduce her, I faded into the crowd now my duties were done. He was a reminder of my responsibilities, one that I didn't need.

You couldn't get blood out of a stone, but Luciu had been fighting for years to free his great-uncle from prison.

After being jailed for a crime Luciu believed the older man hadn't committed, Currau's days in prison were numbered.

I'd yet to hear from David Foundry, the Attorney General, and I was tempted to call him to see if he'd made a decision.

Still, that was tomorrow's problem.

Instead of socializing with the auction winners as I usually did, thanking them for their generosity, I decided to be selfish, decided that thoughts about work could wait, and that the event could be left in Lily's hands, with any problems arising being hers to handle, not mine.

I also decided that I wanted to see Rex.

There was only one problem—when I headed to his table, I couldn't actually see him.

He'd moved.

Dammit.

My gaze darted here and there as I drifted through the crowd, greeting people who complimented me on yet another successful fundraiser. I had a hundred air kisses bestowed upon my cheeks and had my hand shaken a few dozen times before I found him at long last.

He was leaning against the bar.

It was so bizarre to see him standing there in a tux, looking dapper and handsome, that I froze, taking a moment to absorb the sight of him.

He was majestic.

His hair was neat and slicked back at the sides, his jaw was smooth and like silk—I knew there'd be no prickle against my cheeks when he kissed me. He wore the tux like he was born to it, but I'd often reasoned that Rex was.

His father had aptly named him—King.

He should have been a politician. Should have ruled over a state or even the country. Should have been the one to bring order back to this mess of a nation that had been corrupted from the inside out by Sparrows and to right the wrongs that had been sown here.

Instead, he reigned over a band of outlaws.

It wasn't, and never had been, what I wanted for him.

But I knew he was happy with his place, and it *was* his life. His happiness wasn't my happiness, even if we *were* intrinsically bound.

He stood with his elbow leaning against the gleaming countertop, a tumbler of Jack Daniel's nonchalantly clasped in his hand, the amber liquid tilted from the position. One leg supported him, the other he had kicked out in front of him, propped up on his leather Oxford-clad toes.

As much as I studied him, he studied me.

I could feel the weight of his look like his fingers were tracing up and down my arms, sliding over my shoulders and down my back.

The connection between us throbbed, twanging into place when he straightened up, leaving his glass on the bar the second that I started to move toward him.

We collided.

Like atoms and stars.

Merging like the cells in my womb formed the life we'd created.

It was beautiful. It was powerful. It was *everything*.

His hands came around me, sliding about my waist, hauling me into him. His hands cupped me and shaped me as his mouth found mine.

Finally.

Lips parting, I absorbed his kiss, accepting the claiming. Needing it.

The pressure of his fingers increased as he maneuvered me into him, tongue and teeth tasting and nipping as one hand slid up higher into the sleek locks of my hair. He tilted me this way and that, making sure that he could get as close to me as possible.

His dick was hot and thick against my belly, and I swore to God that he could have pinned me against the bar right then and there.

Sex and I... we were complicated.

I knew it could be painful. I knew it could be terrifying.

Yet, where Rex was concerned, nothing was.

So the dichotomy of those two warring beliefs were always a battle that ended up a stalemate.

I knew it could hurt but I wanted him anyway.

Tonight, however, there was no denying that I'd missed him. After thinking that I'd lost him, after him throwing down an ultimatum, after weeks of phone calls and emails and texts, of relearning each other, I was all in.

As hungry as he was, as needy, as desperate for his touch and his kisses and his love.

God, I wanted *that* more than anything.

His lips broke away from mine, leaving us both panting.

Tongue tracing the line of my jaw, with no prickle from his stubble against my cheek, he reached my ear and whispered, "I got us a suite."

The rumble of his voice settled inside me.

I peered up at him with dazed eyes and whispered back, "I missed you."

His gaze darkened in turn. "I missed you."

Nails digging into his arms, my mouth wobbled. "Don't leave me again."

"If you don't leave me, I won't leave you. How's that for a compromise?"

His hand, calloused and rough from the work he did on his bike, made the hairs at my nape stand to attention as the sensation rushed through me.

Angling my chin into his hold, I thought about Lily's brand and rasped, "I want your brand."

His pupils bloated like he was glutting on delight, and he snarled, "Don't say shit like that if you don't mean it, Rachel."

I swallowed, hearing his anger and finding myself shocked by it. "I do mean it."

"You can't. We're not even together that way yet—"

"We are. It's just an atypical romance."

"Well, I don't *want* atypical anymore. I want to go to bed with you. I want to eat breakfast and lunch and fucking dinner with you. I want to watch movies with you and to read in bed with you.

"I want to fuck you on the kitchen table and eat you out in the living room. I want everything with you, Rachel, so don't tell me you want my brand unless you're ready for what that means."

Before I could tell him that I knew, that I wanted all that, he pressed his mouth to mine.

This time, the kiss was hungrier. Desperate. Seeking.

He nipped and bit at my lips, thrusting his tongue against mine like he was thinking about fucking me; his hands even grew harder in their possessive hold.

But I wasn't afraid.

I knew what it meant.

He wanted my brand on him.

More than I did, and that was saying something.

I sighed, sinking into him, my bones turning lax as I leaned on him for support.

As his mouth tore into mine, I knew he was angry with me. Angry for making him hope, and I understood.

A couple weeks away and I was asking for his brand?

A few meetings with Giulia's Posse and suddenly all was right with the world?

The short answer was no.

Of course all the broken parts of me weren't fixed.

Tiffany hadn't wrought a miracle and Rex's time away hadn't turned me off our usual status quo and made me want a 'regular' relationship.

But I'd missed him.

I'd realized what I was doing without.

I needed more, but I needed to figure out the landscape of what 'more' looked like.

I couldn't do that without him.

"Come upstairs with me?" he growled against my lips.

I nodded and pressed a softer peck on his mouth. "Of course. I'm still needed down here, but later...?"

As my words trailed off, he nodded.

Reaching up, I let my fingers trace his jaw and whispered, "I like this."

"It was Wynter's suggestion."

I smiled at him. "It was?"

"She seemed to think it might help you."

He'd...

God, he'd told her *that*?

Nervously, I asked, "You explained...?"

"I did. I think she wants us to be together." Something flickered in his eyes. "She isn't the only one."

A shaky breath escaped me. "I want that too."

"How do we make it happen?"

"You don't look like Grizzly now," I whispered, unaware that my heart was in my eyes.

He gritted his teeth. "I wish I'd known that before."

"How... What—" I paused. "I couldn't tell you."

"Why not?"

"You'd have killed him."

"I should have. You denied me that."

"I kept you safe, and he'd have lied, Rex. He'd have told you I asked for it." My mouth trembled. "I-I couldn't have taken you believing him and not me. I-I think that would have broken me more than what they did. Them telling me I was like my mom, that I was just a whore..." I shuddered. "No. It was for the best."

His face flushed with his temper, but he didn't argue. Just looked at me with gleaming eyes that burned like hot coals. "I'd have known the truth."

"How could you?"

"You're mine, Rachel. You always have been, and you always will be."

"You never branded me."

His brow furrowed but those goddamn eyes of his set me alight. "You were too young, and after, you broke up with me. Ever since, it's not like we've been going steady, is it?"

It wasn't like I could argue with him, even if a part of me wanted to.

"No," I conceded with a grimace.

"Brand or no, you've had a 'hands off' sign to anyone who knows us both. I won't mark you until you know for goddamn sure that you're all in, Rachel, and you can't tell me that you are now. I won't believe you."

It hurt, but I got it.

There was a ball of emotions in my chest that I couldn't seem to unravel, and I stared at him, feeling lost and afraid yet somehow found and safe because I was with him.

"What is it, Rach?" he rasped. "Where's this coming from?"

"It's coming from the fact that I want your brand."

"Don't say shit like that unless you mean it," he reiterated, tiredly this time. "It isn't fair, Rachel. It isn't fucking fair."

His anger burned away by that point, instead, turning to hurt.

Hurt.

I'd hurt him.

I hadn't even meant to.

"Why are you looking at me like that?"

"Because you're fucking breaking me, Rach. You've spent the last twenty years wrecking me, destroying everything I know about myself. Making me change and alter how I do shit to accommodate you.

"Every day, I wanted to kill whoever hurt you. Every fucking day. But I couldn't. Because you didn't tell me. You didn't share with me. I had to wait. I knew that I did. It wouldn't mean the same if I forced you to tell me, because that was just me, being another fucking bastard who owned a dick imposing my will on you.

"I was not about to be a man who took something from you like that. I was not going to be like them. But it hurt me, Rach. It hurt me not to fix shit. Not to make it better, not to make the world right for you again." He pressed his fist to his heart. "It killed me to take Wynter away, to give her to someone else to raise, but I did it because having her near was killing *you*.

"I was stuck between a rock and a hard place, so I did what I thought was right—I gave her to Ally. She had more maternal instinct than Carol Brady—"

I knew the words burst free from jealousy. "How do you even know her?"

His gaze was measured upon mine. "She dated Link for a while. You have no reason to be jealous."

Gritting my teeth, I turned away from him. "Things should have been different."

"Damn straight they should have been," he snapped. "In no way am I comparing this with what you went through, but Grizzly stole our future from us both; that didn't just happen to you.

"You're the love of my fucking life. You're my soul mate, Rach, and I can't touch you sometimes without thinking you're about to leap out of your skin. I want to make him hurt like he made you hurt. I want him to suffer how you have. Because, baby, if I feel like hell, if I feel like my life is on hiatus because of him, how the fuck do you feel?

"Fixing is what I do for the people I love. I make shit right, but there's no making this shit right. I can only do that by being there for you, to be whatever you need me to be for you, but I don't even know if that's enough. This has been our reality for almost two fucking decades, Rach—"

Staring into his tortured eyes, I reached up and pressed a finger to his lips to still his words. "You're right. They stole from us both." I sucked in a breath. "I'm tired of that being our reality, Rex. I'm tired of my life being stolen from me."

I pressed my forehead against his shoulder, and as I did, the solid presence of the pooch on my belly made itself known to me. It was too small for him, but not for me to recognize.

The ability to raise Wynter had been hijacked from me.

The chance of living a full and happy life with this man had been robbed from me too.

And I'd let it happen.

I'd let them win.

His hands slid around my waist and he held me against him.

It felt so fucking good.

So right.

Our babies were the only people who should ever come between us.

No one else.

Nerves hit me, but his anger wasn't what scared me. It never had been.

"Dance with me?"

I blinked in surprise at his request, my words blown from me as he snatched the wind from my sails. "Can you dance?" I blurted out.

His grin was sheepish. "Yeah. I can dance. Mom taught me."

"Oh, to be a fly on the wall for *that* lesson."

"I hated every minute of it," he groused, "but she was right about one thing."

He twisted us so that I no longer leaned against him as he guided us over to the edge of the dance floor so we weren't making a nuisance of ourselves to the wait staff.

"What's that?" I asked as I found myself back in his arms.

"There'd come a day when I'd want to dance with my woman and I'd thank her then."

Heat filled me when I reached up and settled my arms on his shoulders just as his hands went to my waist, and slowly, we started to move against the other.

I'd never thought Rex would breach this half of my life, but seeing him here, dressed in a tux, socializing with Manhattan's underbelly—I never imagined he'd fit in.

Never imagined he'd try to.

Yet another way he was a perfect partner for me.

A thought occurred to me, and I asked, "Did you drive up?"

"Nah, I flew."

"*You?*" My brows lifted. "Where did you store your bike?"

"A secured parking lot."

Despite myself, I had to grin. "I'm just trying to imagine you on a shuttle bus to LAX."

He grunted. "Only for you would I rideshare and park my bike."

His lips were light, as were mine, but I knew he meant it. It was a throwaway comment, but he meant it.

*Only for me...*

I tilted my head forward as the band moved into a tune I didn't recognize. It was slow and moody. I could almost imagine it was a blues song with how it whispered along my sorrow and agitated the edges.

"I need to tell you something," I whispered.

"I'm listening."

The words were on my lips—*I love you.*

*I've never stopped loving you.*

*I've only ever wanted you.*

*You're the reason I woke up some mornings.*

*I wish things had been different.*

*I want to go to sleep beside you and not dream of your uncle.*

So many things that needed to be said.

Instead, I rasped, "I'm pregnant."

His tension wasn't immediate.

He didn't stop the slow and steady sway of us as we danced to the sultry sounds echoing around the ballroom dance floor.

If anything, his hands moved, one coming to the bottom of my back. The heat soothing something inside me that I didn't know was a torn and ragged mess.

It took away my nerves. It took away my anxiety.

This was Rex.

In times of trouble, he didn't fall by the wayside.

I just had to have faith.

So I didn't prod him for an answer.

I didn't challenge him for a response.

I waited.

And I waited.

Then, he put me out of my misery: "I want to see."

## FORTY-SEVEN

## NYX

### DARKSIDE - OSHINS, HAEL

"What's wrong?"

"Why do you think anything's wrong?" I hedged.

Lodestar didn't immediately answer, but I frowned as she pulled out a pack and started rearranging it.

I considered it a rucksack—not a bag—for a reason. While the metallic barrels and the bullets would have triggered questions in anyone else, they didn't with me.

Not when she'd proven her loyalty to the club several times over.

Secrets—I knew how to keep them.

Still, I needed to make sure she wasn't heading into a fight without backup.

"You going to war and not telling me?"

Her eyes glanced off mine as she shrugged. "Always good to be prepared."

"That's all this is?"

"Sure is," she replied as she ran her fingers along the tips of some bullets that weren't for a revolver or a handgun.

The gauge alone was questionable.

"If you say so," I muttered, rubbing the back of my neck.

"You heard about your uncle?"

I frowned at her. "What about him?"

"That his body went missing from the morgue?"

I knew that bastard's remains had washed up on the Hudson's shore, and I was also aware that his corpse had gone missing.

Not that I told her that.

Secrets—I knew how to keep them.

I just said, "Someone else clearly had a grudge against the piece of shit. Not surprising. Maybe he molested someone else's kids too."

Her hum was disbelieving as she studied me, making me think she'd ask more questions, interrogate me some, but she didn't, just grumbled, "Why are you here, Nyx? It ain't to keep me company, is it? Trust me, I have more than enough of that in this household."

"Maverick told me you're rich."

"I am."

"So why do you stay here if it's so fucking noisy?"

A high-pitched giggle echoed down the hall in answer, and a soft light, one that was pretty much creepy where Lodestar was concerned, appeared in her eyes.

"Oh."

She smiled. "Yeah, oh. Her family's here. I don't want to break them up, and I don't want to leave without her. Even though those fucking brats at the local school definitely need to be taught a lesson—"

"Let's not set the villagers on us," I warned. "I don't need the normals driving up to the compound with pitchforks."

Lodestar pursed her lips as she completely ignored what I'd just said—I could see the cogs churning as she dismissed my warning. "You here for parenting advice then? Because you really don't want to be asking me. I'm pretty sure some social worker somewhere is trying to find Kat—"

Who the hell would go to her for parenting advice?

I pinched the bridge of my nose. "No, that's not why I'm here. Does Rex know about you stealing Kat?"

"I think so. I think Maverick might have mentioned it to him at some point."

"I should fucking hope he did. Which state?"

"Which state did I steal her from?"

"Yeah."

"Colorado." She smirked. "Or maybe it was Ohio. I forget."

"You're a fucking pain in my ass."

"I won't apologize for it either. We've all heard how you won't let Giulia play with it—"

Anger flashed in my eyes, but she didn't back down. "Fucking women. Never know when to keep your goddamn mouths shut."

The smirk faded and morphed into a smug grin. "Why are you here, Nyx? If it isn't for parental advice or a 'how to' on pegging, what could you possibly want from me?"

"Fuck knows," I groused, storming away from the kitchen table and heading away from the exasperating bitch.

Before I left, she called out, "I know you made Kevin suffer, Nyx. I'm glad you did."

Sliding a hand over my hair, I just grunted as I escaped Lily's place and retreated to my bike.

Fucking Kevin.

Some nights, when I couldn't sleep, I thought about the backfiring shotgun shredding his face.

Some nights, it was the only thing that let me get any rest at all.

I hit the road, needing the peace from the journey to calm me down.

Something about Lodestar managed to piss me off more than anyone fucking else, and considering my brothers were all douchebags, that was saying something.

"Stupid to ask her for advice anyway," I muttered under my breath, but with the wind blasting me, no one could hear.

Despite the chill of the evening, I was hot beneath my winter gear. My palms were even sweating, and there was an uncomfortable amount of perspiration dotting my back.

"I'm not doing anything wrong," I told myself.

And I wasn't.

This was just a meeting.

A meeting that might help facilitate the capture of more sick fuckers who needed their cocks sliced and diced...

A meeting that would help me give training wheels to Harlow...

That was what I told myself.

What I believed.

But why I hadn't told anyone about the phone calls and texts I'd been getting, the outside help in regard to Kevin's missing corpse, I really didn't know.

Lights flickered on behind me, catching my attention in my side mirrors, and I saw one of the beat-up trucks Link kept going out of sheer muleheadedness. Most of our cages were three to four years old max, but that one was at least twenty. Link said he maintained it out of spite, but I knew he was being a smug asshole about his skills in the garage every time he got the clunker running again.

For once, I was grateful because it stuck out like a sore thumb to me on the road to Manhattan.

As I veered in and out of traffic, switching lanes and dropping back so I could determine who was behind the wheel, I wasn't sure if I was relieved or disappointed to find Harlow staring blankly at the gridlocked traffic ahead.

He was too eager for the kill, and it'd fuck things up for him if he didn't contain it. But it wasn't like I could judge. Wasn't like I could give him another coping mechanism. If I had one, then I wouldn't be here, potentially walking into a fucking trap just so I could take another pedophile out.

It was too soon.

He was still only a Prospect.

But I didn't try to lose him. Neither did I let him know I'd figured out that he was tailing me.

I had no idea what was waiting for me in Manhattan. Could be allies or Sparrows for all I fucking knew, but if it was a legit operation to clean up muddied waters, then Harlow could listen in.

I wouldn't be breaking my promise to Indy.

Neither would I be breaking the vows I'd made to Giulia and our kid.

That didn't mean I wouldn't test the limits.

I allotted more than enough time to get onto the island and be punctual for my meeting, but because of an accident somewhere on the way—no change there—I was running late.

I sped through the Lincoln Tunnel and rushed down the center of Manhattan to reach Harlem. I didn't even look to see if Harlow was still tailing me; I needed to get to W 125th St. and fast.

With the GPS guiding me to the meeting point, I pulled up just as a great big fucking boom sounded. At first, I thought there was a bomb, but I realized the charge had run out on my headphones and the church bells had started tolling.

Once I'd parked, I stared around at the dark streets. In my side mirrors, I saw Harlow settling into a space about thirty feet away, and I made no move to draw him over to me.

I just peered around, trying to figure out who I was meeting with. Wondering if this was a trap or if it was a solid connection.

Slotting the earphones back in the charging case then tucking it into my pocket, I straightened off my bike and stretched. It was a move designed to make anyone watching me think I was relaxed, but I was on red alert.

Only trouble was, there was no reason for the red alert.

Not that I could see.

I was standing on a street that could be any street in the city. There were streetlights that didn't illuminate the area well enough. Puddles of amber light that gleamed on the slick sidewalks and glittered in puddles when cars drove past and unsettled them.

Vehicles lined both sides, and twenty yards away, a crosswalk blinked and beeped even though no one was standing anywhere near it.

After five minutes passed of nothingness, I started to wonder if Lodestar *could* figure out who'd contacted me. I'd tried to broach the topic with Maverick, but his CTE was fucking with him and he had a heavy workload because of Rex's absence.

Just as I went to reach for my phone, on the brink of conceding defeat and calling Lodestar for some input, I heard it.

A soft cry.

Cut off.

Sharp and loaded with fear.

Every instinct in my body leaped to attention at that sound.

I knew what fear looked like, sounded like, and fucking felt like.

Head whipping to the side as I started to hunt down who'd made that sound, I got a visual on a potential alleyway a short way up the street.

Leaving my bike, I headed for it, unsure if it *was* a passageway or just a cluster of shadows, but the nearer I got, the more sounds I heard.

Bile choked me. Suffocated me.

It sounded like Carly.

I nearly froze at the realization.

Dazed and terrified, soft whimpers and panicked mumbles of pleas were cut off by a hand held against someone's mouth.

The wrenching of fabric—stitches torn and material shredded.

A gasp of pain.

A grunt. Different this time. Not pain-soaked but loaded with pleasure.

That was when I moved.

I didn't need to *know* what was happening to *know* what was fucking happening.

I stormed down that alleyway, ignoring the pitch dark that made it easier for the bastard to hide, making my footsteps as silent as I possibly could while cursing my night-blind state from the streetlights.

A further cry, this time of pain, had me shoving stealth aside and I ran down the narrow alley. A gleam of silver caught my attention, a flash of red hair, a flash of blond—the guy's watch had lit up as he moved his arm.

I saw cavernous shadows on a craggy face, eyes filled with rage and lust, a mouth curved in a sneer but a hunger tore at him that was undeniable. *Recognizable.*

I felt that hunger—but mine wasn't for the innocent.

Mine was appeased by the spilling of blood of bastards like this one.

He watched me watch him for a split second, and that was when we both reacted.

I had over two dozen kills to my name—I was the faster draw.

My knife slipped out of its holster on my forearm like it was made of butter on a hot day, and as if it were magnetized and his throat was full of iron filings, I found my way there.

He was inside her.

I was too fucking late.

I was always too fucking late.

My fist glanced off his temple.

It was a righteous blow because he staggered, his knees starting to fold out from under him.

I took full advantage; grabbing a hold of his hair, I pulled his head back and dragged him off her. As she screamed, I sliced the blade across his throat, and she shrieked when his lifeblood arced and caught her in the spray.

A slash to the jugular wasn't enough, not when the girl's whimpers and desperate sobbing filled my ears.

I thrust it in his stomach the second he was choking on his own blood, and I made sure to twist that fucking knife.

Clockwise.

Counterclockwise.

As he cried out, I realized the sound of my heart pumping in my ears and the tunnel vision that came from a situation where it was either kill or be killed had shielded me from what was actually happening.

*The sirens.*

"Nyx! Quick! We have to get out of here!"

*Harlow?*

Red and blue lights suddenly flashed, bouncing off the narrow walls in the alley, while the heavy thudding of boots made themselves known to me at the same time as someone yelled, "Drop the weapon and put your hands in the air!"

## FORTY-EIGHT

## REX
### TAKE ME HOME - JESS GLYNNE

"I'm pregnant."

The words rattled around my ears as if she were saying them on repeat, only she wasn't.

She wasn't saying anything. I wasn't either.

We'd left the ballroom, were heading to the suite I'd reserved for us, and her hand was tucked in mine, our fingers latched together as we stood in the elevator.

Neither of us spoke with a couple chatting softly behind us, but our reflections were as discordant as the buzz in my brain.

*She's pregnant.*

That was all I could think.

Did she look pregnant?

Though she'd been curvier than I remembered back before I'd left for New Mexico, Rachel was perennially slender. Still, there was a soft roundness to her face, and she had some color in her cheeks that I knew didn't come from makeup. There was a pinched edge to her mouth, as if she were pursing her lips out of nervousness, but aside from that, her expression was blank.

Wearing a gown that was sin itself, that clung to her curves while shielding her belly from the world, I knew I should be thinking about dragging that skirt up and finding a way to get into her panties.

Instead, all I could think of was seeing *and* doing things I'd been denied with Wynter.

My thoughts were broken off when the doors opened and, glancing at the illuminated screen overhead, I knew this was our floor.

The soft carpet cushioned our footsteps as I led us to the suite where I'd gotten changed, and only when I'd closed the door behind us and guided her inside did I break the silence I'd allowed to fall between us.

"Did you not tell me sooner because you were thinking of having an abortion?"

Her head whipped around to the side at that, and the shock in her expression appeased me some.

"No!" she bit off.

Her anger was all the answer I needed.

She wasn't lying.

Before she could defend herself, I murmured, "My mom once told me something. She said that if we were on a ship, and it had capsized—"

"What the hell does this have to do with anything? We're not on a goddamn ship—"

I steamrolled over her interruption like she hadn't said a word. "And she could only save my dad or me, she said she'd save me. Every time. My dad laughed at that anecdote because he said, and I quote, 'Sorry, son, but we're all going down because I won't choose.'"

She blinked, and the color in her cheeks faded as she understood what I was saying.

"I won't make you choose again," she vowed, her voice shaky.

"You can't promise that," I retorted, "and I don't expect you to. I'm just making a point.

"I know you don't want kids, Rach, but I can't let you—" I reached up and rubbed the back of my neck. "I won't give this kid up. Not again. I did it last time because I knew having Wynter around would lead you to doing something insane, and it wasn't worth the risk—"

"You say that like I was a danger to her!" she sniped.

I hitched a shoulder nonchalantly, when nothing about this conversation was that. "Your doctor told me you *could* be a danger to her."

Her mouth rounded. "I'd never have hurt her!"

"I didn't know that at the time, and I wasn't willing to take a chance on that. Not on you hurting her or yourself and then either ending up in a coffin or locked up for thirty years for killing our child.

"You were different..." I frowned, tried to verbalize how she'd been back then, but I didn't think she'd believe me. "You were like a completely different woman, Rachel. Understandably, but I couldn't predict what you were going to do so I took her out of the equation. I can't do that again."

"I'm not asking you to," she whispered, her grief in her eyes. "You think I could do that again? I'm not a monster, Rex. Jesus—"

"I'm not saying that you are, Rachel. Honey, I understand what happened before. You'd gone through hell. Had endured things that no woman should have to experience. I was on your side. I'm on your side now. But I can't just be Rex here. The guy who wants to be your man—"

"You are my man," she whispered miserably.

"I'm the father of your kids, Rachel. That's what I have to be here, *now*. Do you get that?"

She swallowed. "I love you for that."

I shook my head but rasped, "I want to see."

Biting her lip, she nodded, dropped her clutch to the bed, and slowly pulled on a couple of buttons that I hadn't even noticed. Suddenly, the side of her dress was folding inward and a seam had appeared. She stepped out of it, revealing a slip that got my dick harder than that sexy dress had.

Without the clever tucks, the silken fabric clung to every curve and I could see the bump like I hadn't before.

Unable to stop myself, needing to see even more than that, to see her body ripening with the curves that came from the life we'd made together, I strode forward.

At that moment, the past fell away; the present faded into nothing because I was faced with the future.

A future I wanted so fucking badly I could almost taste it.

I wanted her.

I wanted my ring on her finger.

I wanted my brand on her.

I wanted to be the father of her kids.

I wanted Wynter at college in the city, this one growing up like a hellion who made me lose all my damn hair by fifty because he ran us ragged.

I wanted more.

I wanted fucking everything with her.

Only her.

My hands slipped around the solid bump of her stomach, and I slowly started to raise the hem of the négligée.

My eyes flickered to hers, waiting for her to protest, but she didn't.

She stared at me, her bottom lip wobbling with trepidation, but before I could *feel* our kid, my cell buzzed, vibrating against my chest from where I'd stored it in the inside pocket of my jacket.

I jolted in surprise but ignored it.

Only, the goddamn thing wouldn't stop ringing.

And that wasn't all.

A soft chirp sounded from her clutch. It repeated itself a couple times.

We stared at each other, reality intruding into our private bubble, and I almost hurled something at the fucking wall when I saw that shield of ice overtake her expression.

Goddammit to hell.

But that chirp of an incoming message from what I recognized was her personal cell was drowned out by her business phone ringing.

Three notifications—all at once.

"Fuck, the clubhouse better not have been bombed again," I growled as I reached down and snagged her clutch then handed it to her.

As she fiddled with the clasp, I grabbed my phone, watching as she opened the message on her personal cell first.

As a picture flashed up on the screen, my brow furrowed.

A gift bag.

Pink and black balloons tied to the handle.

*Sucks to be you* printed on the side.

Dead To Me had a new client.

"Who sent you that photo?"

Her frown was confused, and it told me she didn't understand what she was looking at. "Hunter. My old college roommate."

The guy who'd murdered her rapist.

The guy who acted like a Golden fucking Retriever but was as lethal as an abused pitbull.

Before I could comment, her business phone buzzed again and, somewhat dazedly, she answered, "Rachel Laker."

Her eyes grew rounder and rounder as she rasped, "I'll be there ASAP, Nyx. Don't say a fucking word to them, do you hear me? I'll come and get you both out on bail."

Nyx had been arrested?

Before I could demand answers, my own phone rang.

Wynter.

Shit!

She knew tonight was the gala, so I was tempted to delay the call because I figured she'd want to hear the details, but it'd take a second to tell her that I'd ring her later.

As I connected the call, I didn't have a chance to utter a damn word.

My baby girl whimpered, "D-Dad, I need help. T-There are Triads here and they won't leave until they've spoken with you."

## FORTY-NINE

## LODESTAR

### JE TE LAISSERAI DES MOTS - PATRICK WATSON

I didn't like to admit it, but my back was killing me. So were my hips.

The last time I'd been in this position, I'd been on top of the old Sinners' clubhouse and a fucking bomb had me soaring through the air like I was Tinkerbell without the wings.

I wasn't keen on a repeat, not after all those goddamn months in casts.

Despite the ache and my position, there were many things that weren't the same as that last occasion when I'd had my hands on a sniper rifle.

One: the location.

Not only was I not in New Jersey, but NYC; I was also on top of a skyscraper.

The wind chill up here wasn't making the aches in my bones any better, either.

Two: my nerves.

Last time, I'd been invested in making sure that the Sinners weren't hurt.

Now, I was, in a word, shitting myself.

Nerves made my palms slick, and when you were handling this much firepower, that didn't bode well.

I wasn't perfect. I knew my flaws, and it was one of the reasons why I never tied myself to a man—I didn't expect anyone to have to deal with me. I hated making mistakes, but that didn't mean they didn't happen.

Usually, when they did, they were fucking doozies.

Sucking in a breath as I thought about how my plans had gone awry, I peered through my sights and scoped out the area.

In the near distance, Yankee Stadium was slumbering because baseball wasn't in season, but that didn't mean the rest of the city was asleep.

I hated this fucking place.

New York could bite my ass and I wouldn't mind.

Perched atop a skyscraper how I was, my hatred for the city was only growing.

One thing the CIA didn't erase from my personality—a distaste for heights.

I wasn't just high right now. My feet were so far from the ground even birds would start getting queasy.

"Just don't look down," I whispered under my breath. "Across. Not down."

Forcing myself to calm, telling myself to woman up, I waited.

And I waited.

And I goddamn waited.

Time ticked slowly as I scoped the area, making sweeps as I scanned the buildings around me, finding it bizarrely easy to fall back into the habit of not feeling the cold, of controlling my heart rate.

After one such sweep, that was when I saw him.

And that was when I placed my finger on the trigger.

Floppy black hair that looked soft to the touch. Smile lines at the sides of his eyes. A hard jaw that spoke of his obstinate nature. And damn, aCooooig was packing. Beneath his shirt, I could see the abs that peeped through the fabric.

Like he could sense my gaze on him, he turned away from the kitchen where he was talking to his brother's wife and stared out of the window.

My heart surged into my throat.

He stood there, his torso the perfect target.

Not moving.

I could do this.

At this height and distance, I had no markers, so I was going in blind.

I glanced around the area, trying to find any signs that would key me in on wind speed, but I knew, as with all these things, you had to go with your gut.

I found my target once again.

God, *time*—I was running out of it.

Milliseconds slipped through my fingers, heartbeats passed. I squinted against the sights and set the crosshairs in place.

I pulled the trigger.

Are you ready for RACHEL?
www.books2read.com/RachelSerenaAkeroyd

## AUTHOR NOTE

Remember I said, 'don't hate me?'

Rachel's story is coming in a month!!

I know it feels like a long time, but it feels hella short for me. LOL.

BTW, if you want to know what the Sinners did to deserve a pink bar in the clubhouse, lol, check out the exclusive content in the newly released boxset: www.books2read.com/SinnersBoxset1to8

You've met some people along the journey that is Rex and Rachel's story, and yes, they do have books, be they published or on their way.

Published stories outside of the Sinners' series include:

Luciu & Jen - THE DON - www.books2read.com/ValentiniOne

Declan & Aela - FILTHY DARK - www.books2read.com/FilthyDark

Savannah & Aidan Jr. - FILTHY HOT - www.books2read.com/FilthyHot

To-be-published stories:

Conor & Lodestar - FILTHY FECK - www.books2read.com/FilthyFeck

Hunter & Rory - The Revelation Duet (Title TBA) - www.books2read.com/ValentiniThree

Savannah & Aidan Jr. - FILTHY KING - www.books2read.com/FilthyKing

MaryCat & Digger - FILTHY SINNER - www.books2read.com/FilthySinnerSerenaAkeroyd

AND!!

You met The Disciples!!

I'm so pleased to announce that I'll be co-authoring a project with Cassandra A. Robbins!! A character from her Disciples will be falling for a Fecker!!

You can preorder here: www.books2read.com/FilthyDisciple

:O

I hope you're as excited about that as I am!

For all the lowdown, feel free to join my newsletter: www.serenaakeroyd.com/newsletter

But more importantly, be sure to join my Diva reader group. There'll be massive giveaways going on during release week AND it's where I drop news and updates that aren't really revealed elsewhere! www.facebook.com/groups/SerenaAkeroydsDivas

Flick over a page for the reading order for the universe. <3

Much love to you all, and hope you're excited for Rachel!

Serena

xoxo

# THE CROSSOVER READING ORDER WITH THE SINNERS & VALENTINIS

FILTHY
NYX
LINK
FILTHY RICH
SIN
STEEL
FILTHY DARK
CRUZ
MAVERICK
FILTHY SEX
HAWK
FILTHY HOT
STORM
THE DON
THE LADY
FILTHY SECRET
REX <— YOU ARE HERE
RACHEL

FILTHY KING
REVELATION BOOK ONE
REVELATION BOOK TWO
FILTHY FECK - Conor's story

# FREE BOOK!

Don't forget to grab your free e-Book!
Secrets & Lies is now free!

Meg's love life was missing a spark until she discovered her need to be dominated. When her fiancé shared the same kink, she thought all her birthdays had come at once, and then she came to learn their relationship was one big fat lie.

Gabe has loved Meg for years, watching her from afar, and always wishing he'd been the one to date her first and not his brother. When he has the chance to have Meg in his bed—even better, tied to it—it's an opportunity he can't refuse.

*With disastrous consequences.*

Can Gabe make Meg realize she's the one woman he's always wanted? But once secrets and lies have wormed their way into a relationship, is it impossible to establish the firm base of trust needed between lovers, and more importantly, between sub and Sir…?

This story features orgasm control in a BDSM setting. Secrets & Lies is now free!

## CONNECT WITH SERENA

For the latest updates, be sure to check out my website! But if you'd like to hang out with me and get to know me better, then I'd love to see you in my Diva reader's group where you can find out all the gossip on new releases as and when they happen. You can join here: www.facebook.com/groups/SerenaAkeroydsDivas. Or you can always PM or email me. I love to hear from you guys: serenaakeroyd@gmail.com.

## ABOUT THE AUTHOR

I'm a romance novelaholic and I won't touch a book unless I know there's a happy ending. This addiction is what made me craft stories that suit my voracious need for raunchy romance. I love twists and unexpected turns, and my novels all contain sexy guys, dark humor, and hot AF love scenes.

I write MF, menage, and reverse harem (also known as why choose romance,) in both contemporary and paranormal. Some of my stories are darker than others, but I can promise you one thing, you will always get the happy ending your heart needs!

Printed in Great Britain
by Amazon

84169798R00328